THE BATTLE OF PNEUMATIKA

IN THE BEGINNING...

BRIAN NEWBERRY

SIGNALMAN PUBLISHING

The Battle of Pneumatika
by Brian Newberry

Signalman Publishing
www.signalmanpublishing.com
email: info@signalmanpublishing.com
Kissimmee, Florida

Cover design by: Kate Danailov

ISBN: 978-1-940145-12-9 (paperback)
978-1-940145-13-6 (ebook)

Library of Congress Control Number: 2013954826

Signalman
Publishing

This book is dedicated to my awesome wife, Maria "Susie" Newberry. Without her loving support, this work would not have been possible. All of the late nights she has endured while I was researching and writing, and taking care of the bulk of household responsibilities while I have been overwhelmed with work and deadlines has earned my deepest respect and love, and surely she reflects the grace of God. If I could, I would add a chapter 32 to Proverbs to describe her beautiful character!

Table of Contents

1

THE FLIGHT OF CHRISTIAN SAGE

The turbulence of the 747 awakened Dr. Christian Sage from his sleep. He had been dreaming vividly about his wife Rachel, who had passed away over five years ago in an automobile accident involving a drunk driver. The dreams had decreased over the years, which made it easier to continue with life under the reality of being a widower—although he would do anything for one more day with his beloved Rachel and to be able to say good-bye to her before she left. The suddenness of her death made it all the more painful.

As a professor and the Head of the Department of Religious Studies at Lakewood University in Salem, Oregon, Dr. Sage's faith in Jesus Christ did not waver at the death of his wife. He knew that in a fallen world tragedies do occur, all the while God is still sovereign. For reasons unknown to humanity, God allows tragedies to happen to his children to test them and to strengthen them. Dr. Sage's devotional meditations on the book of Job really helped him during the most difficult times of mourning his wife. His children, on the other hand, had much more difficulty reconciling the

Christian worldview with the fact that their mother had been taken during the prime of their teen years. Dr. Sage prayed for his children intensely on a daily basis, and he understood their internal struggles, and he was hoping for the day that they would both understand who God really is.

When Dr. Sage had awakened, he felt the urgent need to urinate—but, of course, he had been stuck in the middle seat of the plane between two large men who were both sound asleep! The man on his left was snoring softly with his head tilted toward his window. The man in the aisle seat was stirring about softly as if dreaming. Christian did not want to disturb his sleeping neighbors so he would have to wait a little while longer. He did not understand why he was sitting next to total strangers while most of the other university professors were sitting together not far from him. In years past, the university would have had them fly first class, but a reduced budget now had them sitting coach.

When the flight attendant passed by, Dr. Sage asked her, "Ma'am, how much longer until we land?"

"We'll be starting our descent in about a half-hour, sir," she replied.

"Thank you."

The University of Lakewood, along with most other schools with distinguished history and religious studies departments, were all on their way to Mount Ararat in Turkey for a potentially awesome discovery. Although the University of Lakewood was probably one of the smallest of representative schools that would be going, Dr. Sage was quite the renowned expert in his field, having a B.A. in Ancient History, an M.A. in Old Testament Studies, a Th.M., and a Ph.D. in the Philosophy of Religion and Ethics. He turned down the opportunity to work at much larger and prestigious schools because he loved living in Oregon and working in a much smaller classroom environment where he could personally interact with his students. That being said, he did travel throughout the U.S. and around the world giving speeches, teaching at seminars, and going to archaeological dig sites for his research, while publishing his findings.

This new discovery was mind-blowing to the modern world, although Dr. Sage was not particularly surprised. A large 7.4 earthquake in Turkey had caused an avalanche and a major rockslide in the Ararat Mountains, partially revealing a large wooden structure that was previously buried in ice and sedimentary rock. The photos of this structure made it difficult to discern, so archaeologists from around the world were on their way to try to dig the large wooden artifact out from the rock. Many believed that this structure was none other than Noah's Ark, although just as many, if not more, were skeptical. If this were Noah's Ark, what would that mean for the Jewish, Christian, and Muslim people of the world? And would that cause skeptics to reconsider taking the Bible seriously, particularly the first eleven chapters of the book of Genesis? These thoughts raced through Christian's mind, but he also knew that evidence does not usually *produce* faith, rather it *confirms* faith that already exists. He could only hope that the discovery was indeed Noah's Ark and that it would produce and confirm the faith of many.

2

A GIANT CRASH LANDING

Lieutenant Alex Sage was flying in formation in his F-15 Strike Eagle. He had been technically stationed in Germany for the past year, but it seemed that he had been traveling all across Europe most of the time. He had arrived in Iceland two days earlier, and now he and his unit were doing field exercises over the Arctic Circle. Alex was wondering when his father would be leaving for Turkey. He had just spoken to him the week before when his father had found out the exciting news about being sponsored to the newfound archaeological dig site, and the possibility of discovering the legendary Noah's Ark. They usually did speak once per week, and every phone conversation ended in prayer. After the passing of his mother five years earlier, Alex was no longer sure about God—did he even exist? And if he did, how can he be a loving God and allow such a devout Christian family to suffer as such, with the loss of his mother?

Alex grew up in the Free Methodist Church, and knew all of the Bible stories and the basics of Christian theology. But now that his mother was gone, nothing really made sense anymore. It seemed that all of the educated people scoffed at most Christian beliefs, and there was so much turmoil in the world, fighting, suffering, corruption—how can a loving God allow this? His father had tried many times to explain to him that God also allows people to have free will, and that having free will comes with the responsibility to make wise choices, while also having the potential for people to make evil choices. These evil choices come with the corresponding evil consequences. *How could human free will co-exist with God's sovereignty?* Alex thought. All of these thoughts gave Alex a headache, and even though he had already begun his ROTC training while in high school before his mother had died, he could not wait to escape his household to join the U.S. Air Force. He truly loved his father—and he was indeed a great father—but his 25 year-old mind could not integrate biblical theology with the world that he experienced. Now, he was on his own, and only his superior officers could tell him what to do. He was free at last, so he thought, and he could blaze his own trails and begin his own legacy and prove to his father that there was more than one way to live the good life!

Alex's co-pilot, Kyle Sanchez, had just received word about an approaching low pressure snow storm moving in on their flight path. This storm had previously been anticipated to move west, but now a shift in wind was moving it eastward toward them. The other four jets communicated this news to one another, and now they had to radio this back to base and wait for further instructions. Alex was flying on the outward left flank of the formation. Before they could get word back from "Talk-One" at base, the storm was suddenly upon them! Particles of ice, the size of marbles, pelted the aircraft as they continued on their mission. Suddenly, Alex witnessed a bright flash which he thought to be lightning. He momentarily lost his vision.

"Sanchez, did you see that?"

"Affirmative, Sage. I can't see!"

"Me either," exclaimed Alex.

Sanchez radioed the other pilots, "Fox-One, do you copy?"

No answer.

"Echo-One, do you read me?"

Silence.

"Delta-One, are you still with us?" cried Sanchez, but he heard nothing but radio static.

Sanchez spoke again to Sage, "They're gone! They're all gone! We're alone out here!"

"Calm down, Sanchez," Alex said. "Radio back to Talk-One."

"Talk-One, this is Golf-One, over."

There was no answer. Lt. Sanchez tried twice more, and still, there was nothing but silence. Now Alex began to worry. "What the Fahrvergnugen?!" thought Alex to himself.

"Okay, Sanchez, we're turning back," said Alex.

"Fine by me," replied Kyle.

The mysterious, icy-snow storm was now gone and the skies were clear and both men had regained their vision that they momentarily lost. As Alex began turning the jet to his left, something shocking caught his eye. In the distance, between two ice-capped mountains, he saw what looked to be a bright green valley!

"Sanchez, what is our location?" said Alex.

"Our navigation systems are down," answered Sanchez. "In fact, all of our systems are down! The lightning must've fried them. It looks like we'll have to find our own way home."

"Look to your two o'clock. What are those mountains? And what is that green valley? I thought we were over the Arctic Circle—what in the world is going on?" cried Alex.

Sanchez replied, "Well, we have plenty of fuel. Fly over and check it out."

"Roger that," said Alex.

As they drew nearer to the first mountain range, both Alex and Kyle felt nauseated and what felt like sinus headaches began to set in.

"I feel sick," said Sanchez.

"Me too," answered Sage. "Hey, what's that Kyle?"

"What?"

"That over there, 11 o'clock. Are those people?"

Both of their jaws dropped as they saw a line of people pushing large carts of goods down into a chasm in the ground. It was difficult to tell from where they were flying, but the people looked very large in relation to the surrounding trees, rocks, and other landmarks. It also looked as if all of the people had long, blonde hair. Neither Alex nor Kyle said a word to one another for at least two minutes, as they flew in circles high above the valley, trying to figure out what they were seeing. Just then, all of the blonde people simultaneously looked up toward the sky where Alex was flying. It looked like they began speaking to each other.

"I think they see us," said Sanchez.

"Yea, I think so too," replied Sage.

Suddenly, something flew out of the chasm with lightning speed, straight into the sky right in front of Alex's jet, and then up into the air above them. Shortly after, Alex lost all control of his jet.

"We're going down!" cried Alex. "We're heading straight for those mountains! Eject, eject!"

"Roger that, Sage," exclaimed Sanchez.

The two Air Force pilots ejected from their jet about 450 feet above the peak of the mountain range. The blast of their exploding aircraft, as it crashed into the mountains, blew their parachutes eastward, away from the valley and the chasm. Kyle's parachute landed first, in an open area between sets of trees in the mountain forest. His landing was almost ideal, and his training allowed him to escape his landing with only a few scrapes and bruises. Alex was not so lucky. His chute got stuck in the tree branches, not too far from Kyle. Alex could see Kyle's chute in the clearing, about 200 feet from him.

"Kyle, Kyle! Are you okay?" screamed Alex.

"Yeah, I'm okay. Where are you?" asked Kyle.

Alex answered, "I'm stuck in these trees. Come and help me."

"Here I come," said Kyle, walking toward Alex as he was cutting himself loose from his parachute with his pocket knife. As Kyle approached the trees where Alex was stuck, he heard a loud crackling sound. The branches that were holding up Alex broke, as he fell about 40 feet down, with other branches breaking his fall on the way down. He fell somewhat awkwardly, but other than a few abrasions and a sprained ankle, Alex was okay.

"Are you okay, man?" asked Kyle.

"Yeah, I think so," answered Alex, as he stood up and brushed himself off. "I think I might've sprained my ankle, but other than that I'll survive."

Just as Kyle helped Alex cut himself loose from his chute, they heard people coming.

"Someone's coming," said Alex. "We have to hide."

"Where?" asked Kyle.

"Over there, in that cave."

The both of them quietly hurried out of the line of trees and into the cave. Unfortunately, neither one of them had their sidearm with them because it was not necessary for the exercise their unit was performing. They were armed with nothing but Kyle's pocket knife, and had nothing but a set of mini-binoculars, their dog tags, and their flight jackets. The two of them were hiding in a cave, in a place where they did not know, surrounded by a clan of large people with long, blonde hair, whom may or may not be friendly. They would soon find out.

3

PERUVIAN ALICIA

Alicia Sage was awakened from her nap by the stopping of the bus. Ever since she could remember, the soft, humming vibrations of bus rides put her to sleep. Even the loud conversations of her fellow classmates from the anthropology and history departments of Pepperdine University were no match for the hypnotic vibrations of the bus. She exited the bus right behind her best friend Amanda, who was among the loudest of her classmates. The students were greeted by their Peruvian tour guide, Luis, "Welcome to the city of Cusco," he said, in perfect English. As a history major, Alicia followed in the footsteps of her father much more than her brother Alex did. Her fellow prospective historians were on a field trip to visit the ancient Incan ruins of Machu Picchu, which are often referred to as the "Lost City of the Incas."

Alicia knew that her father was very proud of her. She only had wished her mother was around to see how she was excelling in her academics. While her faith was not quite as shaken as her brother Alex's, she still had many questions about how God could allow such a tragedy to whom she considered a very faithful Christian family. And even though her father seemed to have all of the right theological explanations for such terrible, heart-wrenching events, she was not psychologically satisfied—at least from her own point of view—with his answers. His answers were logical, objective, and intellectually satisfying, but she still hurt inside— even after five years of prayer and counseling from her church. Even so, Alicia still had faith in Christ, although she had not been following him quite as fervently as before.

Their tour guide, Luis, had brought them to the hotel that they would be staying at, and it was at a very scenic location. They would be staying on a high plateau overlooking the distant Machu Picchu, where they would be hiking down to early the next morning. They could also hear the rushing of the Urubamba River in the distance. The elevation of almost 11,000 feet had left Alicia nearly out of breath and her ears had not yet adjusted to the altitude. She could barely hear what Luis had to say. Finally, after being shown the café, where local coffee beans were ground every hour, and being shown the restaurant and recreation area, they arrived at their rooms. After a long flight, with a two hour layover in Mexico City, Alicia was exhausted. It was almost 7:00 pm and she had been up since nearly 3:00 am. After both her and Amanda, her roommate, emptied their bags, hung up their clothes, and showered, both of them were in a deep sleep by 8:30. They had to be at the restaurant for breakfast no later than 6:00 am so that they could get on another bus which left at 7:00 so that they could hike down to Machu Picchu to do their studies.

4

TURKISH SAGE

D r. Sage did indeed make it to the restroom right before the descent into the city of Igdir, which was in Eastern Anatolia, Turkey. As Christian returned to his seat, he smirked at his colleagues, including Professor Richard Mockens, who would be Dr. Sage's roommate and hiking partner. There were a total of six professors from Lakewood University that would be observing the newfound discovery, which was in and of itself six days old now. Professor Mockens had previously taught at the University of Seattle, but he had transferred over to Lakewood University three months ago. Christian looked forward to getting to know Richard on a personal level, since he had only brief, cordial discussions at that point. All six professors had to be in decent physical condition in order to reach to discovery zone, which was on the lower end of Greater Ararat, somewhere about 13,000 feet in elevation. Christian was the oldest of the bunch, at age 46, be he had kept himself in excellent physical condition, even competing in local triathlons.

As the professors regrouped after exiting the plane, they were met by a Turkish liaison, who took them into two taxis, and then to their hotel in Igdir. They were all greeted honorably by the hotel personnel when they checked in. Dr. Goldberg, who taught Jewish and other Semitic Studies, was rooming with Dr. Norton, who was the head of the English Literature department. Dr. Saal, who taught Middle Eastern Culture and History, was rooming with Professor Cooper, who taught Geology. Professor Cooper had a personal interest in this story that went beyond his own field. And Dr. Sage was roomed with Professor Richard Mockens, who taught Ancient History, and was closing in on his doctorate degree. Out of the six, only Dr. Sage and Professor Cooper were professing Christians. Dr. Saal was a Muslim, but thoroughly Americanized. Dr. Norton and Dr. Goldberg were agnostics, although Dr. Goldberg was a cultural and ceremonial Jew. Nobody knew too much about Professor Mockens yet, but Dr. Sage was about to find out. Originally, they had all planned to eat dinner together at a local restaurant. But now, they were all exhausted, and were willing to settle for the free room service dinner. It was already 8:30 pm, and they had to be up by 6:30 in the morning to begin their long day on Mount Ararat.

5

SAGE VS. MOCKENS

Both Dr. Christian Sage and Professor Richard Mockens were wary about how foreign foods could sometimes be unsettling in the stomachs of newly arrived guests, so they both decided to allow their bodies to gradually become acclimated by ordering American dishes with Turkish seasoning: Christian ordered a salmon filet with a vegetable medley, and Richard ordered barbequed chicken, scalloped potatoes, and macaroni and cheese. They were both so hungry that neither spoke a word until they were both nearly finished eating in their hotel room. The conversation began with cordial small-talk that led to quite an interesting discussion that went as follows:

Sage: I remember the last time we spoke you had mentioned that you grew up in Florida. So what made you want to move to the opposite corner of the country?

Mockens: Well, my folks split up when I was a junior in high school. And to be honest, it was a devastating experience for me. I joined the U.S. Army only a few weeks after I graduated. My last duty station was at Fort Lewis in Washington and I loved it there, so I stayed. And you, you grew up in San Jose, right? What brought you to Oregon?

Sage: This job. I've done a lot of traveling, and I even went to Oxford for my doctorate. But I prefer the smaller, more community oriented atmosphere that is provided at Lakewood.

Mockens: I know that you are the head of the Religious Studies department, but I forgot what your PhD and your dissertation was about...

Sage: The Philosophy of Religion and Ethics. And I did my dissertation on the social impact of modernism and post-modernism in light of the Judeo-Christian ethics, which preceded those eras.

Mockens: Oh yes, I've heard about you. You are one of the few heads of Religious Studies in non-Christian schools who actually believe what the Bible has to say about God. I'm sure you could've taught at any Christian University in the country, maybe even the world. Why would you settle for a secular school?

Sage: Well, growing up in the very liberal Bay Area, I actually feel more at home with non-believers than a church full of like-minded individuals—or at least people who are *supposed* to be like-minded. And besides, it is not those who are well who need a doctor, but those who are sick. [Smirking].

Mockens: It sounds like you are conceding the fact that Christians can't even get along with themselves, much less be the lights of the world that they claim to be. And yet, you are implying that the vast majority of the rest of us who believe different than you guys do, are sick, or even worse, headed for hell. Nothing personal against you—I'm sure you're a good person and are sincere about your beliefs, but it's this kind of general hypocrisy that caused me to become skeptical in the first place. You see, I was raised in a Southern Baptist household, and we went to church twice a week for most of my life. But yet, my father ended up having an affair with a woman *in the very church that we went to!* That's why my mother divorced him, and that's one of the reasons I had to get the hell out of that house as soon as I possibly could. And even worse, my parents both still preach to me about forgiveness, and Jesus dying for my sins, and they are both very concerned that I'm on my way to hell if I don't repent from being an agnostic.

Sage: First, your complaint is a legitimate one, and I'm sorry that you had to experience that. But the actions of sinful human beings, even Christians, do not make the teachings of Jesus or any other Biblical event, not true. If anything, it confirms what the Bible teaches. Sinful behavior has negative consequences that are unavoidable, and you are correct in saying that Christians ought to set the example for the world, being ambassadors for Christ. And I know that as an historian, you are fully aware of all of the wars in Europe concerning what was thought to be "Christianity" between Catholics and Protestants, and between nations. But let me assure you that neither side acted very Christ-like at all, I mean they totally ignored his teachings. But again, this in no way negates the Bible at all.

Mockens: Yes, I fully agree with what you're saying. But my main point is that the teachings of the Bible are not real to people in a way that truly impacts their everyday life. They go to church on Sunday, then they go to work on Monday with a "Holier-than-thou" mentality and try to preach to their co-workers, and when their message isn't accepted they get frustrated and discouraged. By Thursday, they're cussing, lusting, and then lying to cover up whatever they get caught doing. If the Bible is truly God's word, then it should have a greater impact on a greater number of people than what I've witnessed in my life.

Sage: Aha! The last line of what you just said is at the heart of your criticism. You said, "What *you* have witnessed." Your skepticism is primarily subjective, based on your negative experiences. There are plenty of solid Christians who walk-the-walk, but unfortunately, bad press gets more exposure and makes the headlines.

Mockens: Again, I agree with you that what I've said so far is subjective, but it's not like I can't give you intellectual reasons why I don't believe the Bible. In fact, the more educated I become, the more reasons I have to be a skeptical agnostic. In fact, I'm surprised that with all of your education that you're still as faithful as you are. But I've studied sociology, so I know how a person's upbringing has an effect on a person throughout their life.

Sage: [chuckling] First off, I'd like to tell you that there is nothing glamorous about being identified as an agnostic. The word literally means, "Without knowledge." In fact, the Latin equivalent of agnostic is *ignoramus*! Second, I grew up as a Roman Catholic, and while I had *knowledge* about God, the Bible, and Jesus Christ, I did not have a personal relationship with him. I did not come to Christ personally until age 20 when I began to read the Bible for myself a couple of years earlier. I never knew my biological father, so growing up with a single-mother was very difficult.

By reading the Bible, there were apparent discrepancies from my Catholic upbringing, so I kept asking questions, and I kept getting answers, and then everything suddenly made sense. At age 20, I was on fire for the Lord—full of zeal but without wisdom and sufficient knowledge. I would try to share Christ with people and they would say things like, "That's good for you, but you're not educated. Once you get some education, then you won't believe that stuff anymore." That drove me into the depths of education. Now that I'm educated and I try to share Christ, people say things like, "You educated people think you're better than everyone else." Or even worse, "Yeah, you're educated, but you're biased!" So I can give all of the evidence, positive proofs, and excellent logic of the Bible as God's Word, but that in and of itself does not produce faith. In much the same way, the miracles of Jesus did not produce faith either. Evidence and miracles *confirm* faith, they do not *produce* faith. That being said, I am willing to provide you with sufficient evidence and reasoning if you are willing and humble enough to consider such things.

Mockens: Well, we'll have two full weeks together, so I'll allow you to entertain me with your proofs and your reasoning. I will admit that some of my initial presuppositions have been wrong—things like the Bible being corrupted, and other collusion-slash-conspiracy theories that the social elites used religion to keep their slaves and serfs from rebelling. I was amazed when I learned that the earliest manuscripts of the New Testament and the quotes of early Christian leaders from the Bible are remarkably accurate as pertaining to the Bible that we have today. So I can no longer say that the Bible was corrupted by Medieval Catholic monks and scribes. And I know that Dan Brown's *Da Vinci Code* allegations are a bunch of bunk too—controversy sells. But even if the New Testament has remained unchanged, the Old Testament has no such evidence, except that which was found at Qumran, the Dead Sea Scrolls. But that's only a couple of centuries before Christ. And even if the Bible has remained unchanged, it doesn't make it true or accurate as pertaining to the events and people it describes.

Sage: Well, Richard, you are a well-versed historian! And perhaps even still a little curious about God, as I can see you have kept up with some of the latest theological discussions. Now I can give you excellent reasons to believe in the God of the Bible. I can use inductive reasoning, or deductive reasoning, the latter being a short-cut. I know that since you grew up in the church that you pretty much know about the Bible stories and much of its historical outline, but what are some of the intellectual hurdles that keep you from honestly, and objectively considering Jesus Christ as Lord and Savior?

Mockens: The Bible talks about people hearing directly from God, even that God told them to invade foreign territories and to slaughter its inhabitants. Today, the only people that claim to hear from God are schizophrenics and other crazy people who drown their children in their bathtubs. So either those Bible characters were just as crazy as these modern loons, including Jesus, or that God suddenly stopped speaking to people when other people were watching. If God spoke to Noah, Moses, and Jesus, why doesn't he speak to us the same way today?

Sage: If you want to hear God speak, read the Bible out loud. Ha! But seriously though, I know that by reading the Bible it seems like God regularly spoke to people. In actuality though, God only spoke to a select few people and only in ways that were specific to his plans and purposes for humanity. So it's not like in the old days that God spoke to every person audibly and there were times of detailed conversations where people could ask God about all the secrets of the universe, or ask him to grant them three wishes like a genie. Whenever God did speak to someone, it was God who controlled the conversation and the subject matter, and it was only related to what God was going to do concerning the person with whom he spoke. Additionally, back then almost nobody had any written Scriptures to refer to, and as you know, in antiquity most cultures spread knowledge and traditions orally. Today, we have the full cannon of Scripture in which we can hear from God practically anytime we want to—especially in the Western world with all of the freedom that we have. But instead, we have taken our freedom for granted and use it to pursue our own sinful desires. So why *would* God feel obligated to speak audibly to such people?

Mockens: Well, that's just it. For one, you have the preconceived notion that everybody's personal pursuits are, by default, sinful. Two, you readily accept the cannon of Scripture, which was decided after three centuries of Christianity, after much debate, when there could be books that are less than inspired, or even books that are missing.

Sage: You may have a *small* point with regard to the cannon. But if God is sovereign, and his word is the authority of his people, then I trust that he presided over the Council of Nicaea, and afterward when the 66-book cannon was decided once and for all. Now, if it turns out that there are books that were lost, then God allowed it, and perhaps they are irrelevant for today's believers. And even, perchance, that some minor book of less relevance, such as Obadiah, Jude, or Esther were to be found discredited, it wouldn't bother my faith at all, and it wouldn't negate what Jesus Christ did for us on the cross two thousand years ago.

Concerning sinful humanity, just take a look around: it's obvious that the world is falling apart and that people are self-centered, self-serving, and have inclinations toward evil. It doesn't take an advanced theologian, or historian, to observe that humans can be quite cruel and evil towards one another. They lust for power, they lust for possessions, they wish to gratify their own desires at almost any cost that they think they can get away with. And look at what these things have caused, historically. And just when the intellectual elites thought that people have finally evolved to the point where warfare was no longer necessary and where rational thinking and science could *solve* the problems of humanity, here comes Nazi Germany, Soviet Russia, and atomic weapons! Surely, any notion that people are *evolving* to a higher state of being, becoming more sophisticated, or on the verge of creating a utopian society is contrary to the evidence. If anything, we are *DE-volving*, following the prior historic civilizations that occasionally rise to a certain point, and then diminish and fall apart.

Mockens: Well, you are actually proving my point. If the God of the Bible actually exists, being a God of love, compassion, forgiveness, or even judgment—how can he allow all of these things to happen and not intervene? How could God allow so many people to live on the brink of starvation? How could he allow children to get raped, women to be sold into sex-slavery, and entire nations to fall under dictatorial regimes that deprive humanity of its dignity?

Sage: Far from proving your point, God is demonstrating that without him and his dominion, it is impossible for humanity to thrive and to live in peace. I'm with you as far as human suffering is concerned—something needs to be done about it, and when the time is right, God will intervene. But the flaw of your thinking is your point of view: you are looking through the lens of humanism, with the dignity of man being of prime importance. That is actually the original sin in the Garden of Eden. The Serpent deceived Eve by telling her that God was keeping something good from her, and that if she ate of the forbidden fruit, she would become god-like—something that is sought after even today, although under different terminology. Ultimately, people desire to be the masters of their own destiny, and to create their own identity and self-autonomy apart from God—that's the ultimate root of sin.

The answer to what you consider a riddle is this: God gave people free will, or perhaps to put it better, the ability to make choices. Having free will and the like comes with responsibility, and it also comes with the potential for people to make wrong choices, which results in evil. This means that God is not responsible for evil in the world, he merely gave people a choice, and they must live with those choices. It would not be virtuous for God to decide personal matters *for* people, or *force* them to acknowledge and worship him—it would not be genuine. Furthermore, if *one* sinful decision got Adam and Eve kicked out of paradise, resulting in the fall of humanity and its evil consequences, how much more would billions of sinful decisions by billions of people over thousands of years result in the world that we observe today with all of its evils? God is just allowing for perversion to take its natural course, and when the time is right, he will judge individuals and nations, just as he has done in the past. But we must be careful when we demand divine justice—God might judge us along with everyone else. Rather, we should desire his grace and mercy even more.

Mockens: What you are saying follows logically, except that there is not a hint of evidence for Adam, Eve, or the Garden of Eden. That account is not much different than the contemporary myths of other ancient civilizations.

Sage: There might not be any forensic or scientific evidence for the Garden of Eden, Adam, or Eve, but there is indirect evidence: the Lord Jesus quoted from the early chapters of Genesis as actual history, as did Paul the apostle. And if you don't believe the things that Jesus said, you have bigger problems than trying to discover scientific evidence for Adam and Eve. Besides, I don't need that kind of evidence when it is obvious that human nature hasn't changed since then. When we are caught doing wrong, we hide, we try to cover ourselves up, and then we blame others for our deeds when confronted by authority. Sometimes, modern scientific techniques make us lazy in our thinking, and overly dependent on it as the ultimate source or proof of any given truth.

Mockens: Your rhetoric is amusing, and I can't argue with the human nature argument either. And yes, science has its limitations, but it cannot be underemphasized because scientific knowledge has been a major contributor to the advancement of Western Civilization.

Sage: But not of human morality, though.

Mockens: True, but that's assuming that there is an ultimate, objective moral code—and a direct revelation from a transcendent creator would be necessary for that to be the case.

Sage: Now you're talking!

Mockens: I was being partially facetious. If a transcendent creator does exist, and I believe that one does exist, based on the complexity of nature and all living things, then he either has revealed himself in some way, or he hasn't. And if God exists and he hasn't revealed himself to his creation, then he doesn't care, and if that's the case, why should *I* care?

Sage: Well, which do you believe?

Mockens: I'm basically a modernist-deist. I believe that someone or some ones outside of time, space, and matter had to create our universe. Once he or they did that, the natural laws of the universe were established. And after that, the universe was left alone to abide by those laws. So I'm basically saying that the only rules that are ultimate or objectively true, are the physical laws of nature. Moral ethics are relative to culture, and for the most part, all cultures share similarities in their social laws. Things like murder, adultery, theft, and property rights, are almost universal.

Sage: Ah ha! *Almost!* The fact that some cultures do accept certain types of murder, adultery, theft, and the confiscation of property—and even things we in the West consider abhorrent, like pedophilia—proves that our inherent consciences and emotions cannot be trusted for universal ethics. In fact, how the Bible describes all humanity to be infected—*sick* even—with the curse of sin, which we inherit from our father, Adam, more accurately describes reality than your point of view of moral relativism.

And as far as your other point is concerned, if a Creator God does exist, it would be illogical for him not to attempt to communicate, love, and have relationships with his people. Since we, as humans, love *our* offspring and desire to communicate and form relationships with them, it would be illogical for God to create humans—as the pinnacle of creation—and *not* love them, communicate with them, and to pursue relationships with them in a tangible, objective way that is available for *all* people. If humans have these traits—which I assume you would agree to be *good* traits—and God did not have them, that would make humans to be more virtuous, and thus, greater than God! That itself is a contradiction in terms! Only Biblical theology reveals such a God—a God who loves the world so much that he sent his one and only Son, Jesus Christ, to die the death that we deserve, to die in our place for our sins, and that whoever believes this with all of their soul is granted the free gift of eternal life and is forgiven of all of their sins! Surely, this message resonates deep down in your heart.

Mockens: I agree that it *sounds* good, but if something sounds too good to be true, then it usually is. Churches form, they take peoples' money, and then you see the Reverend driving a fancy car, wearing an expensive suit, and so on.

Sage: That's the sinfulness in you speaking, using human fallibility as an excuse again, as you did to begin our conversation.

Mockens: Yeah, but that's reality—at least as I see it. If God were to show me a sign...

Sage: People saw the signs that Jesus performed, but yet many of those same people were yelling, "Crucify him, Crucify him!" only a few days later.

Mockens: That's assuming those texts are historically accurate, and there are numerous New Testament scholars who disagree about the historical accuracy of the Gospels.

Sage: While that may be true, it depends on the assumptions and presuppositions of each scholar. If the Biblical assumption of human sinfulness is correct—for which the evidence is obvious—then even if a scholar wishes to justify his or her lifestyle and deny his or her sinfulness, or try to excuse him or herself, then he or she will use those presuppositions and be biased as to his or her conclusions regarding the New Testament and the teachings of Jesus.

Mockens: Yeah, but that argument works both ways. Scholars who believe the Bible can use *their* presuppositions to ignore or find ways to dismiss some of the obvious problems-slash-contradictions in the Bible, and come to their own conclusions of its accuracy.

Sage: You are correct in saying that they *can* be dishonest about their research and prognosis. But what would be their motive? Why proclaim a movement that preaches honesty but be dishonest with their scholarship? Why believe a worldview that teaches about the limitations and weakness of humanity while trying to promote *themselves* as the exceptions or anomalies? The skeptics assume a humanistic, self-glorifying, and usually a Darwinist "survival-of-the-fittest" mentality, to which they are attempting to be the "fittest" with their scholarship. Which of the two camps would be most consistent with their worldview?

Mockens: While you're right about the importance of assumptions leading to corresponding conclusions, it's just more complicated than that. I need God to show me something in Biblical proportions, for me, during my lifetime. Send me an angel, give me a dream, a vision—something that's real to me—not just stories or philosophy in a book written by mortals.

Sage: Now you're really opening up a large can of worms! It's like the person who says, "I will believe in God if he were to appear to me." Well, God *did* appear to people, about two thousand years ago in the person of Jesus Christ! And the people saw his miracles, they heard his amazing teaching, but yet the most prestigious of men didn't like what he had to say, so they tried to kill him!

Mockens: And they were successful, by the way.

Sage: No, Jesus *willingly* laid his life down to save humanity. Then he was raised from the dead three days later! I can give you great evidence for that event, and that event basically proves the entire Bible because Jesus quoted from the Old Testament as the authoritative word of God and also predicted that his disciples would write the New Testament in the near future. Thus, the resurrection of Jesus Christ more-or-less proves the Bible to be God's infallible word.

Mockens: *This*, I would like to hear! I've seen plenty of documentaries on the subject, and again, the scholars cannot agree. But look, it's almost midnight and we have to be up early tomorrow. We can continue after breakfast tomorrow.

Sage: Agreed. Good-night, Richard.

Mockens: Good-night, Christian.

6

A BLONDE MOMENT

Alex and Kyle stood about as still as people could possibly do while still breathing. Their feelings of nausea and their headaches completely escaped their minds for the time being, as fear nearly paralyzed their bodies. Much like a military marching formation, the blonde men walked in four straight lines between the trees of the forest. Each one was armed with what looked like a sci-fi version of a technologically advanced crossbow. One of the squad leaders picked up Sanchez's parachute remains while the blonde troops marched toward Sage's parachute. Kyle and Alex crouched down low behind a large rock which partially blocked the entrance to the cave. The warm breeze cooled the sweat from Alex's brow. Even though they were supposedly in the Arctic Circle region, the weather seemed subtropical—somewhere in the high 70's with a significant amount of humidity.

Alex and Kyle looked over to their right at the investigation of the blonde troops. It appeared that each one had a distinct type of body armor, which was fashioned from reptilian scales. Some of their armor looked brown, other pieces of armor were various shades of green and gray. Each one also was armed with what looked to be a short sword, with which the steel was so polished that it appeared to glow! As the blondes began to be more visible, and as they drew closer, their body armor appeared to be part of their actual bodies. There was no distinction between their clothing and their bodies—the armor was indeed, part of their bodies! Each one had a beard as well, although they were not uniform in length. And the most dreadful feature of this clan was that each one had to have been at least nine feet tall! Additionally, each one was built with a slender, muscular physique—like a prototypical basketball player.

Alex and Kyle began to inch back further into the cave as the blondes crept closer to their vicinity. Alex gave Kyle a look as if he were to say, "What do we do if they come toward the cave?" Just then, a small aircraft landed in the clearing of the trees where Sanchez had landed. Alex had never seen an aircraft maneuver like this one did! The aircraft was disc-shaped, with two small wings on each side. Actually, the aircraft did not touch the ground, but it hovered, making a soft humming sound. "This must've been the aircraft that flew up from the chasm and caused our jet to crash," thought Alex. Two blondes exited the aircraft and two more blondes arrived on what looked like portable air-chariots that flew low to the ground. These craft had tri-pod wheels that came from the vehicle. Most of the blondes huddled around these four newcomers and they appeared to be having a meeting.

Kyle was afraid to even whisper, fearing that the blondes might detect their location. They each took turns with the binoculars, trying to figure out who these people were—assuming that they were people. They *looked* human, and they were somewhat fair skinned, although they did each have somewhat of a golden tan. Their mannerisms and body movements were consistent with humans. One difference was their clothing, assuming that it was clothing, and their technology was advanced, even unprecedented from much of what Alex or Kyle had ever witnessed. Even more strange than this clan of people, was the geography and terrain that surrounded them. They were supposed to be in the Arctic Circle—not some northern forest with a subtropical climate. "Was this a dream?" Alex wondered.

While the thoughts continued to race through the heads of Alex and Kyle, the blonde meeting ended with loud shouts—similar to what would be expected by a college football team when first running onto the field from the locker room. At first, they all walked in different directions. They seemed enthusiastic about something, and their conversations became audible. Alex had expected men of such an appearance to speak maybe Dutch, German, or Russian—but these men spoke a language that was similar to a Middle Eastern dialect. Alex had remembered his dad speaking Hebrew very often, and sometimes Arabic—the little that he knew. The dialect of the blondes was very similar to those, although the voices of these men were much deeper than the average Semite. None of the blondes were directly approaching the cave, but they were getting closer in proximity, with their scattered formations. "Why didn't they come back from the direction they came from?" thought Alex. It became obvious they were being searched for.

The anxiety of Alex and Kyle steadily increased as the blondes grew closer. They both gave each other that look that said to move deeper into the cave. At the worst time one could possibly imagine, Alex felt the urge to sneeze! He tried to hold it back, but to no avail. He covered his sneeze with his arm, but the sneeze echoed in the cave. Immediately, they both heard what sounded like a deep trumpet, similar to thunder, but definitely a war trumpet. This was followed by loud shouts and then the unison of running footsteps. "Oh my God!" exclaimed Kyle, "They're coming for us!"

As the pilots ran quickly into the cave, their vision became dimmer and dimmer, as the darkness of the cave increased. Just as well, the sound of the blondes' footsteps drew closer. They couldn't have been more than 100 yards away now! As Alex and Kyle quickly moved deeper into the cave, they had to use their hands along the wall to feel their way through. The cave then turned sharply to their left, followed by a slight decline. Both pilots tried to remain calm and control their breathing, but at this point it was almost impossible. Panic had set in. This became especially true when it seemed like they had reached the end of the cave. "We're trapped," said Kyle. "Get down low. Try to hide," said Alex. "Let's hope they won't find us."

By this time, the first of the blondes to enter the cave let his presence be known, as he was apparently yelling for Alex and Kyle. While Kyle was stretched out on the ground, his foot rubbed against something sticking out of the ground. As he quietly turned his body around, he grabbed the object and pulled upward on it. It was a trap door. By then there were at least six blondes in the cave now and they were approaching quickly. Kyle pulled the door open and used his hands to feel around beneath the door. "It feels like some sort of pipe," whispered Sanchez. Alex replied, "Well, they'll find us in less than a minute, and they don't sound friendly. We have no choice but to go down the pipe." Kyle agreed. He crawled down into the pipe for about seven feet, and then suddenly he slid downward, almost vertically. "Whoa, Whoa!" yelled Kyle. When Alex heard Kyle's voice diminishing downward, he decided to go into the pipe feet first. He had no idea were this secret slide went to, but it couldn't have been worse than a confrontation with the blondes, so he thought.

7

THE TRAIL TO NOWHERE

Alicia and Amanda arrived with the group of students in front of Alfredo's Family Restaurant about ten minutes before 6 a.m. Every one of the students were still sleepy-eyed and fairly quiet. As soon as the doors opened for business, all of the students rushed towards the complimentary coffee. Alicia was not as impressed as most of the other students about the quality of the coffee. Most of the students chose to eat Peruvian-style omelets, but Alicia and Amanda both went with a morning stew with lamb, corn, beans, potatoes, and an assortment of vegetables. By the end of the meal, the students were all wide awake and ready for action.

The bus ride down the mountain was very bumpy and close to frightening. An assortment of wildlife ran across the road in front of the bus as if it were a daily exercise. When the bus came to its final stop, the students dismounted, taking their backpacks and cameras with them. Virgil, the group leader, announced, "Okay ladies and gentlemen, we're getting ready for our hike down to Machu Picchu. It's about a two-and-a-half mile hike over some fairly rough terrain. The hike should take about an hour and a half. Make sure you all have water in your canteens and remember to stay with your partners. Are there any questions? Okay, then we're ready to rock-and-roll!"

The initial descent from the bus stop was fairly steep and the trail wound around rocks and the trees of the jungle-like forest. Some of the students stopped to take a rock or a leaf from a plant as a souvenir. Amanda was her usual self—talkative as ever. "So Alicia, I heard that your dad is going to Turkey to try and find Noah's Ark."

"Yes, he should be leaving in a few days. Wouldn't it be crazy if they really found it?"

"Oh yeah," answered Amanda, "It might make lots of skeptics reconsider their lack of faith."

"I don't know," replied Alicia, "Skeptics usually have the mentality like, 'Don't bother me with the facts and the evidence because my mind is already made up.' Even with all of the archaeological evidence we already have for the Bible, the skeptics still come up with excuses not to believe."

"That's true, Alicia. But still, if the Ark is found, a whole lot of people will have a lot more explaining away to do, and they even might have to apologize for all of the mean things they have said about believers."

"Oh, believe me, Amanda, skeptics specialize at explaining away the obvious. And they rarely apologize for their spiteful taunts."

Amanda tried to bring others into the conversation. "Hey Randy, what do you think about the Ark sighting in Turkey?"

"Only turkeys would actually think that Noah's Ark would have been preserved all these thousands of years—if it even existed in the first place. It's probably just some deformed rock sticking out of the mountain, like usual," answered Randy.

"I figured you'd say that," said Amanda.

Then Steve chimed in, "Or *maybe* they'll discover the tomb of Zeus and Aphrodite," with a sarcastic response.

Alicia was quick to intercept Steve's attempt at humor, "For your information Steve, the tomb of Zeus was claimed by the ancient Cretans to be in their possession!"

"*Really?*" asked Randy.

"Yes," answered Alicia. "Maybe by the time you boys get some edumacation you might know the difference between pagan myths and actual history. Who knows, you might even become Christians."

"That would be more miraculous than anything Jesus was ever said to have done," said Steve. "Besides, usually the more educated people get, the less likely they are to be Christians."

"That's not necessarily true Steve," said Amanda. "There are lots of educated Christians who are just as brilliant, if not more so, than the mainstream intellectuals that you hear about. The problem is the liberal, secular-humanistic bias in our educational system—a system that blackballs almost anyone who rejects Darwinian evolution. So in many intellectual circles, the conclusions about what is true and what is not true is reached by consensus rather than good research and sound reasoning."

"Wow! That was a mouthful," shouted Randy, as he winked at Steve.

"Sounds like con-spir-acy," sang Steve.

Just before the conversation became too colorful, Virgil announced, "Okay people. We're about halfway through our hike here at a scenic peak. Feel free to take pictures, and if anyone needs to go to the restroom, there's an outhouse behind that huge bolder by those giant trees. We'll continue in fifteen minutes."

"Outhouse?" said Amanda. "Are we still in stone age?"

"No. More like early 20th Century," joked Steve. Amanda crossed her eyes at him. It was obvious that Steve liked Amanda, but she had no interest in his goofy self. For Amanda, a man needed to at least *have* a serious side to compliment a sense of humor. With that, Amanda and Alicia walked to the outhouse. There were actually three outhouses, and to their surprise, they were fairly well maintained.

While Alicia and Amanda were sitting in their respective outhouses, the wooden sheds were hit by what seemed to be small rocks. Amanda finished her business and ran behind the outhouse. "Cut it out Steve," she yelled. But Steve was nowhere to be seen. "I know it's you," shouted Amanda. As soon as Alicia joined her, Amanda was struck in the arm with a rock, and it hurt!

"Ow! Stop it Steve—that hurt!" exclaimed Amanda.

"That's not funny Steve—knock it off!" yelled Alicia.

They heard a muffled laughing sound coming from the small hilltop behind the outhouses. They ladies looked up and saw the top of the head of a young, shirtless boy. When the boy saw that he had been discovered, his facial expression turned from delight into horror.

"Wait. Stop. Hello?" called Amanda and Alicia, as they walked up toward the hill. "We just wanna talk to you," they said. The boy shook his head in fear and then he ran away. Amanda said to Alicia, "Hurry, let's follow him."

"Shouldn't we be getting back to the group?" asked Alicia.

"We still have five minutes. Let's at least find out who the boy *is*."

"Okay," said Alicia, following Amanda.

When they finally got to the top of the small hill they could see the boy in the distance—walking now, and not running. Obviously, the boy assumed that the women would not follow him. Walking as quickly and quietly as they could, Amanda and Alicia gained ground on the young boy. He climbed up a narrow path and around a large rock. To the right of the path was a steep slope down the side of the cliff. Alicia and Amanda looked at each other as if to say, "Should we continue to pursue him?" Without speaking a word, they both agreed to continue, as their curiosity overcame their senses.

They carefully walked sideways around the big rock. "Don't look down," teased Amanda. "Yeah, yeah, yeah," answered Alicia, as they both giggled. As soon as they got past the big rock and into a clearing, they saw something that rocked their worlds! There was a large native standing before them, wearing nothing but a loincloth. He must have been between nine and ten feet tall! His skin was reddish-brown and his black, straight hair came down to his shoulders. His head was very large, but other than that, his body was well-proportioned with his stature. The only anomaly was that he had six fingers on each hand and six toes on each foot. His black eyes seemed to be bulging out at them in apparent disgust. He opened his mouth, as if to speak, and his large teeth were exposed in their many rows, and were frightful. The young boy stood right beside him—"probably the man's son," thought Alicia to herself. The giant said something to the boy in their native language, and the boy ran away toward the tree-line in the distance. Then the giant spoke to Alicia and Amanda in broken English, "Who-you? What you here for?"

His voice was very deep and there was a certain "growl" to it. The women looked at each other as they trembled in bewilderment. The giant spoke again, "You speak English?"

"Yes," answered Amanda. "We are students. We go to school. We are visiting Machu Picchu."

"Machu Picchu?" asked the giant. "Over there," he said, as he pointed toward the trail that the ladies should have been on.

"Who are you? Where do you live?" Amanda asked, boldly.

The giant answered, "No. You go now. You not be here, no come back no more!" The look on his face was stern and angry. Amanda and Alicia quickly turned back, crawled around the rock, and then ran as fast as they could back to the outhouse.

When they returned, all of the other students were scattered around looking for them. "There they are, Virgil," yelled Randy. Virgil stood with his hands on his hips, as Amanda and Alicia approached him. "Virgil, Virgil—we saw, we saw," uncharacteristically, Amanda could barely speak.

"What did you see?" asked Virgil.

"We saw a giant native," replied Alicia. "He was at least nine feet tall!"

"Oh boy, here we go again," Steve chimed in. "Not another one of their Bible stories coming to life."

"No Steve," answered Amanda. "We really did see him. A young boy was slinging rocks at us when we were in the outhouse, so we followed him up this hillside trail. Then we were stopped by this huge man who had six fingers and six toes on his hands and feet!" Amanda was nearly crying now.

"Well, they obviously saw *something* to be shaken up like this," said Virgil. "I'm going to radio back to the bus driver and see if he knows anything about this." He grabbed his walkie-talkie. "Chuco, this is Virgil, over."

"This is Chuco, go ahead."

"Chuco, do you know anything about tall natives around here? I mean *really* tall?

There was an odd silence for about five seconds.

"Chuco, are you there?"

"Yes, amigo," Chuco answered. "You all need to come back here right now. You might be in danger. Did they see you? Did anyone talk to them?"

Virgil answered, "Yes. Two of the students walked up a hillside…"

"Come back here pronto, amigo. Run as fast as you can before they get their friends. How far are you?

"A little more than a mile or so," said Virgil. "We're on our way now."

Virgil turned back toward the frightened students. "Did you all hear that? Now we need to stay calm and keep our heads. We're going to head back to the bus stop. It doesn't look like we're going to see Machu Picchu today."

"That's just great," said Steve. "Thanks a lot Amanda."

"This is no joking matter Steve," said Virgil, cutting off any chance of empty talk. "We need to get going. All right everybody--grab your gear, and let's go."

The group headed back towards the trail, now traveling more uphill than before. The forest seemed very still now, as the birds that once played, whistled, and chirped were now absent. As the group exited the first set of trees, they approached a narrow pass between two cliffs. The cliffs had rocks that slanted down in such a manner that it was hard to understand how they could remain on the cliffs without falling into the pass. All of the students hiked with a sense of urgency and nervous energy. Randy tried to get Amanda and Alicia to talk more about the giant that they saw, but they were too scared to speak, almost in shock!

Just then they all heard a loud rumbling sound. Up ahead of them the rocks were sliding down the cliffs into the pass. "Rockslide!" shouted Virgil. "Everybody run back this way!" The rocks ahead of them filled the pass so that it was impassible. So when everybody turned back towards Machu Picchu, they saw an entire tribe of giant natives waiting for them. When they turned back towards the pile of rocks, to their utter horror, they saw giants climbing down the cliffs as to surround them. At this point, all twelve of the students—and Virgil—were in a state of panic with shouts and screams. But there was no place to run. They were trapped on the trail surrounded by giants!

"Silencio!" one of them shouted. "Nobody hears you. You invade our land, now you come with us!"

Virgil interrupted, "No, wait a minute, sir, there's just a misunderstanding, see. One of your children was throwing rocks at us."

The same giant that spoke to Amanda stepped in front of the first giant that spoke. "My son plays. This his land, he plays here. You go too far. Now you come with us."

"But we're students. We have to get back or they'll come looking for us," insisted Virgil.

"No. They no see you no more. Come now," said the giant.

Before Virgil could plead their case once more, and by walking away from the giant spokesperson, a huge spear came soaring down into Virgil's chest from above. Virgil immediately fell to the ground, motionless. Crying, screaming, and weeping broke out from the remaining twelve students. "No more!" shouted another giant, as he pulled his spear from Virgil's lifeless body. "We go now." Another one of the giants brought a long rope and others helped him tie the hands and feet of the students. Then they were hung upside down onto a long pole and carried back toward the open end of the trail. All of the students were in shock and terrified. Not one spoke a word. Alicia began to pray silently to herself, "Oh God, please deliver your daughter from this evil. Do not let these wicked men triumph over us. In Jesus name, amen."

8

MULTIPLE PERSONALITIES

The six professors from Lakewood University met at the Igdir Inn Café at 6:45 to have breakfast. Five of the six slept extremely well, due to their exhaustion. It was Professor Richard Mockens who had trouble sleeping because of the theological conversation that he had with Dr. Christian Sage. To Richard, there was no running away from, no changing the subject, and definitely no intellectual answer he could give to ward off the verbal assault of Christian's theology and worldview.

"Could it actually be?" thought Richard, as he tossed and turned the night before. "Could this Bible actually be the personal revelation of the Creator of the universe?"

Even after trying to reassure himself intellectually and personally, Richard still could not fall into a deep sleep—as tired as he was. "Clearly, Dr. Sage won round one," thought Mockens to himself. "And it is unlikely that I could go toe-to-toe with him." By the middle of the night, Richard eventually planned to rekindle the fire publicly, in front of the other professors to see if maybe any of them could come to his aide and at least partially refute was Christian was trying to share with him. Richard's thoughts gained him only a couple of hours of good sleep—he longed for a few cups of coffee as soon as possible.

Five of the six professors waited anxiously outside of the Igdir Café for Dr. Norton, who was running late. When he finally showed up at 7:00, they went inside and sat down. "Sorry I'm late gentlemen, I forgot to pack my razors and the ones offered by the hotel aren't very sharp," said Dr. Norton, chuckling. "That's okay, Hank," replied Dr. Saal, "It's understandable how we can so easily forget how good we have it in America."

All six men sat down to bagels, pastries, and delicious Turkish coffee. Two taxis were supposed to pick them up around 8:00 and take them to a small airport, where they would board a helicopter to take them to a landing zone near the sighting on Mount Ararat. From there they would hike a few miles to the discovery zone, where a few international archaeologists and other scientists were already trying to dig out the alien object in the rock. While the men were waiting, Dr. Mockens thought it would be a good use of their time to continue the theological discussion that he had had with Dr. Sage the night before, only this time it would become a more public forum. The discussion went as follows:

Mockens: So, Christian, before we passed out last night, you were saying something to me about the overwhelming evidence for the resurrection of Jesus, right? Would you care to elaborate on that?

Goldberg: Oh, brother! Here we go again, (Rolling his eyes).

Norton: Do you really want to go there, Richard?

Mockens: What? You guys act as if this conversation were a rerun or something. I would actually like to hear this evidence. Usually, all I hear is, "You just have to believe and have faith, man." Or, "I know it's true in my heart because I have a personal relationship with God and he has changed my life," and other subjective nonsense. I have never really heard much objective evidence other than, "The Bible says this…", which is suspect in and of itself.

Saal: That's usually what I hear too, although we Muslims use similar arguments. So it really does come down to faith. I am interested in hearing about objective evidence too, Christian.

Sage: Ah ha! I see you've been strategizing, Richard—trying to use these gentlemen as your reinforcements. Well, the truth is, I have had such discussions with Dr. Goldberg and Dr. Norton, but not with Dr. Saal.

Mockens: What about Cliff?

Cooper: I'm a believer too, Richard.

Mockens: Are you serious? I have never met a geology professor who was a Christian, you know, with all of the scientific evidence contradicting the Bible and all.

Cooper: Actually, you'd be surprised of how many scientists are Christians. Most of them are "Old-earthers", but none-the-less they do believe in Jesus Christ and that the Bible is the Word of God.

Mockens: How is that possible?

Cooper: It really comes down to what a person's assumptions and presuppositions are. Any belief about the unobserved and unrecorded past requires some form of faith. The scientific method is limited by what can be observed and tested, and even then, at best we can only *assume* that the physical and geological processes that we presently observe are somewhat similar to the times of the ancient past. And that is a *huge* assumption—an assumption that is questionable at best, and somewhat easy to discredit by all of the past catastrophic events that are evident to us today.

Mockens: So, Cliff, are you telling me that you actually believe that it is possible that 98% of the scientific community is wrong in their assertion that the earth and the universe is billions of years old?

Cooper: I think it is a distinct possibility. I'm open to whatever the truth is—and I don't think the Bible is necessarily dependent on the age of the earth either way because time is relative to gravity and other elements of physics. But as far as I'm concerned, I haven't seen any conclusive evidence of billions or millions of years that doesn't come with several faulty assumptions—those which are held by faith. And it should be remembered that truth is *not* determined by consensus. Additionally, the scientific community has been wrong on several occasions about many things, so we should not put all of our eggs in the basket of any prevailing modern theory. Any scientific theory about the unobserved past is certainly fallible. Thus, I can say with just as much scientific certainty as any other scientist that it is possible that the earth is only thousands of years old, and not millions or billions. Perhaps, nobody can know for sure, but the methods that are currently used are not without problems, therefore their results cannot be absolutely conclusive by any stretch.

Norton: Astonishing!

Goldberg: Metaphysics can be a tricky thing. And while I disagree with Cliff's conclusion, I must admit that at least he's thought it through and his beliefs are coherent and logical.

Saal: I don't know whether or not the earth is billions or thousands of years old, and to me it's irrelevant. But I do know that Darwinian Evolutionary Theory has many problems that most evolutionists are afraid to declare publicly because of how it might effect their educational stronghold.

Norton: It sounds like you're yelling conspiracy, Jabari.

Saal: I'm not so much into conspiracy theories as much as I am into conspiracy *facts*. For years now, Westerners have been intentionally secularizing every aspect of education which has produced the gross immorality that we see today. Information without foundation or purpose is not real education, only ammunition for personal agendas. It leads to Postmodernism and Subjectivism, something that the Eastern philosophers brought to the West during the 1960's and 70's.

Sage: You know your history and philosophy well, Jabari. Watch out! You might become a Christian if you keep following this path.

Saal: We Muslims have many things in common with the Christians—we even worship the same god. We just have a more complete revelation of god in the Qur'an.

Sage: I know that you *believe* you worship the same God as I do, Jabari, but I respectfully disagree. The attributes of the god of the Qur'an are distinctively different than the God of the Bible. For example, the god of the Qur'an has no sons, but the God of the Bible has one very unique Son, Jesus Christ. The god of the Qur'an does not love sinners and unbelievers, but the God of the Bible loves every sinner so much that he sent Jesus Christ into the world to die in their place. I could go on and on about the differences of the deities of the two holy books, but I know what Islam teaches on the subject, and you will believe whatever the Qur'an says to believe.

Saal: I do know about the differences of our two holy books, but the Bible cannot be trusted in its entirety because it has been corrupted. There is only one god and the Qur'an has the most recent and truthful revelation of him.

Mockens: Dr. Saal, even though I agree with you that the Bible should not be considered the word of god, I do have to admit that the text itself shows no evidence of corruption based on the manuscript evidence.

Saal: I don't know about that, Richard. The whole reason why the angel Gabriel dictated the Qur'an to Muhammad was because the Bible had become corrupted by the Medieval Catholic monks.

Sage: But Jabari, how do you know that? And how do you know that the Qur'an is truly the word of God?

Saal: The Quran is true because it contains no errors. It is the word of Allah because it says that it is the word of Allah.

Sage: I can think of two errors the Qur'an has off of the top of my head, even though I admit that I have not studied the book in its entirety from a scholarly perspective. The first one is in Sura 18:86, where the conquest of a ruler, probably in reference to Alexander the Great, is said to have gone as far west as unto the place to where the sun sets into the earth. The second error is the statement that Jesus was not crucified, whereas the historical evidence, even by non-Christian accounts, verifies that he was indeed crucified. And to your last statement, saying that the Qur'an is the word of Allah because the Qur'an *says* it is the word of Allah is a circular argument. We need something outside the Qur'an to demonstrate its integrity. Would you trust that America has no governmental corruption just because the government tells you it has no corruption?

Saal: Ha ha ha! It is clear that you don't understand *how* to read the Qur'an. The 18:86 passage is written in a poetical language and should be understood figuratively.

Sage: But that particular passage is an historical account, not a poetic description. Besides, believing that the sun could set into the earth is not an absurd belief in 7th Century Arabia. Only in recent centuries do we know otherwise.

Saal: Well, doesn't the Bible teach that the sun goes around the earth in the Psalms?

Sage: Actually, it says that the sun moves within its circuit—not in a manner where it orbits the earth.

Cooper: Oh, and it should be noted that the sun actually does move in its own orbit throughout our galaxy.

Saal: You still don't understand that the Qur'an teaches about spiritual truths, not scientific ones.

Sage: You seem to be back-peddling on the issue. If the Qur'an is the word of God, how can it be so mistaken in an obvious scientific way?

Norton: Fascinating, fellows, fascinating, (clapping).

Saal: Well, concerning circular arguments, almost every argument will become circular if you deduct far enough to its original premise. So I am quite comfortable with the idea that the Qur'an is the word of Allah and that its proof is within the text itself. I do not require external evidence, and Allah will reward me for my faith. After all, having faith is an excellent virtue in any religion.

Sage: This is true, Jabari, but a person's faith is only as good as the *object* of that faith. So if you have faith in faith, then that faith is extremely fragile and can only go as far as that faith remains in that fallible person, and there is no true power that can be channeled from a god that is unknown to that person. So if Allah is not the true creator-God, then faith in him is powerless.

Saal: Well, we'll just have to agree to disagree as far as that's concerned. Allah will judge all of us at the end of the world. He will judge us according to our faith, our obedience, and our intentions. I feel that I have held up well so far, but I know that I have to depend on the mercy of Allah.

Sage: If you were to die today, do you think you would enter God's paradise?

Saal: I cannot be sure, for Allah is unknowable in his judgments. I believe that my good deeds have outweighed my bad deeds, though, I just pray that he shows me much mercy.

Sage: Well, according to the Bible, Christians can actually *know* whether or not they can go to heaven—and it has nothing to do with their good deeds being more than their bad deeds. The Bible tells us that there is not one human being that is righteous because all of us have sinned against God, and even one sin separates us from God for all eternity. It only took one bite of forbidden fruit for Adam and Eve to be expelled from the Garden of Eden. And since we are all related to Adam, we inherit his sinfulness and separation from God. It was for this reason that God sent Jesus into the world—to die on the cross as the final blood-sacrifice to die and experience God's judgment in our place, so that we may be reconciled to him through our faith in Jesus' atoning sacrifice. And once we believe in what Christ did for us on the cross, and we repent from our sins, and follow Jesus, we are promised by God that we will receive eternal life. So it's all about what Jesus did for us—living a sinless life and suffering the penalty for human sinfulness on the cross—it's not about us earning our way to heaven.

Saal: All of this sounds nice and comforting, but it seems to alleviate the human responsibility to worship and obey God. The Hadith teaches that Jesus did not die on a cross, that actually Allah fooled the people by giving them Judas to crucify instead of Jesus. Allah would never punish one of his prophets or allow Jesus to suffer such a humiliation.

Sage: The Bible does not let people off the hook as far as remaining obedient and to worship God appropriately. It only teaches that it is impossible for sinful humans to offer anything righteous to a holy God to please or appease him. The sin of a man separates him eternally from God, so he cannot even approach God without a spotless, blameless blood sacrifice. Jesus Christ came to mediate between sinful humanity and a holy and perfect God. He is that spotless lamb who takes away the sin of the world.

Saal: Blood sacrifice was an ancient practice. Allah requires no more blood, only obedience.

Sage: But how do you approach God as a sinner? You yourself even said that you have no assurance that God forgives you or that you will enter heaven. And as far as Jesus' crucifixion is concerned, it seems ironic and contradictory that an all-powerful God needs to *deceive* people into *thinking* that Jesus was crucified, when actually it was Judas. And to think that Jesus' followers, and even his enemies, acknowledge that he was crucified and this was the central teaching of the Church from the beginning—why would an all-powerful, all-knowing God allow his people to worship in ignorance for 600 years until Muhammad said otherwise? Like I said before, even the Romans and Jewish authorities recognized that it was indeed Jesus of Nazareth who was crucified.

Goldberg: Yes, it is quite an absurdity to think that Jesus did not die of crucifixion.

Norton: Yes, and His followers certainly *thought* they saw him alive again, with nail prints in his hands and feet, and a spear wound to his side, although I personally think they were hallucinating.

Sage: The Hallucination Theory, eh?

Saal: Allah allows unbelievers to follow their own delusions, so people believed whatever they wished to. And Allah is not required to immediately correct misunderstandings of humans—he acts how he wants and when he wants. Besides, since the Bible was corrupted, we only know what the disciples *allegedly* taught about Jesus—we do not have what they *really* taught. That's why Allah gave us the Qur'an.

Cooper: So we're circling back to that again, huh? Well, in science, if something is unable to be disproven, then we should be very skeptical of its truthfulness.

Saal: Like I said, it is about faith.

Sage: But why would a loving God keep such a vital truth from his people? Why would he allow so many people to live in spiritual darkness for so long? Biblically speaking, there has always been a remnant of people who truly belong to God and who live as his witnesses. This demonstrates God's love for the world, even if only a small percentage of people are true believers.

Norton: I believe that we are *all* God's children and that he loves us all, just how we are.

Sage: While I would agree that we are all God's *offspring*, we only *become* his children by being born-again through faith in Jesus Christ. Then, and only then, God adopts us as his children, while we were illegitimate when we were lost sinners.

Goldberg: Saved by the cab! Let's get our things together, our taxis are here.

Norton: Blasted! We were just beginning to have fun. Who are you riding with, Richard?

Mockens: I'm not sure. Are we assigned?

Cooper: No, it doesn't matter.

Norton: Okay, I will ride with you, Cliff. I am interested in hearing more about some of your scientific beliefs.

Goldberg: Yes, I would like to be entertained as well. I always like to hear something new.

Mockens: Well, I guess that leaves me with Jabari and Christian. Dr. Sage, will you do the Christian thing and pick up the tab?

Goldberg: Of course he would! But I tell you what, I will display the biblical virtue of sharing the tab, I'll go half with you, Christian.

Sage: Gee thanks, Geoffrey. How pious of you.

Saal: I'll pitch in too. I'm starting to feel like *I'm* the infidel!

Norton: Cliff, hold the cabs for us, this could take awhile.

9

CHUTES AND WATERS

The underground chute that Alex Sage and Kyle Sanchez had entered into came to a gradual, horizontal stop. Surprisingly, the chute was relatively clean for being embedded in a rocky cave. There was no evidence of any bugs, spiders, or rodents, and very little dirt or dust.

"Are you alright, Kyle?" asked Alex.

"Yeah, I think so. How about you?" replied Kyle.

"Well, I'm alive. All things considering, that's not too bad," responded Alex.

"I hear you, brotha. I guess we're going to have to crawl our way out of here. Do you think those people are going to follow us down here?"

"Naw, I don't think they can fit in this pipe, or at least not easily. But in any case, they probably know where we're at, so we better hurry."

As Alex and Kyle crawled toward the other end of the chute, they both noticed an eerie silence. There had been no apparent attempt by their pursuers to enter into the chute, nor could they hear any sounds coming from where they were crawling to. It was pitch black and the only things heard were the scooting sounds of Alex and Kyle crawling on their hands and knees. They couldn't help but notice how smooth the texture of the chute was. It was definitely something made with precision, not a natural tunnel.

Eventually, the two pilots began to hear what sounded like running water in the distance. This motivated them to accelerate the pace of their crawling, with which the water sounds increased. There came a point when the noise of the water became quite loud and it was clear that there was some sort of waterfall very near to where they were at. Alex wondered why he couldn't see any light at the end of the tunnel. "Perhaps this is a dead end," he thought to himself. That would spell certain doom if that were true!

Suddenly, Kyle spoke up—"Um, Alex?"

"Yeah, what is it Kyle?"

"I think we're at the end of the road. I think the chute goes back down again, but I can't see a thing! There might be a river directly below us—I can smell the water as good as we can hear it."

Alex answered, "Well, we don't have much choice do we? If we go back, we're dead for sure. So let's find out what's at the bottom."

Kyle gulped. Scared out of his wits, he turned his body around in the crowded space and prepared for another freefall. Kyle crossed himself, as suddenly the fear of God came over him as his early years of Catholic catechism flashed before his eyes. "Okay, here goes nothing Alex."

"Let's do it!" whispered Alex.

Kyle slipped down first, followed immediately by Alex. Both men were tempted to yell as they fell straight down, but fear of being discovered prevented them from doing so. The river beneath them welcomed them by submergence, as the body of water was plenty deep. Neither Kyle nor Alex hit the bottom of the river even though they fell over fifty feet straight down from the chute. Surprisingly, the water was relatively warm for a river—especially considering they were supposed to be somewhere near the Arctic Circle. When both men surfaced, they quickly gasped for air and grabbed a hold of one another as they treaded water. Apparently, they were now drifting in an underground river. The place was, somehow, dimly lighted. It was clear that they were in some kind of underground cave system. Other than the rushing water, there were no other sounds, and seemingly, no animal life. There was water falling from various places into the river. "Other pipes like the ones we just went down," thought Alex to himself.

The river had to be at least 50 yards wide. But before either of them thought about swimming to the shoreline, the flow of the water rapidly increased. Treading water became extremely difficult as both men struggled to keep their heads above water now. Suddenly, Alex and Kyle found themselves falling again—this time down a tremendous waterfall. "We will surely drown now," thought Alex, as he fell downward into another river. This time Kyle couldn't help but yell out as he fell. Surprisingly though, neither of them hit any rocks, nor did they touch the bottom of the river below. Not only did both of them survive, but neither of them took any water into their lungs either.

"Kyle, Kyle!" screamed Alex. We've got to swim to the side!"

"What?!" answered Kyle. "I can't hear you!"

Alex pointed toward the shoreline and began swimming, as the river's current began to subside somewhat, although they were still drifting downstream. Alex then saw the mouth of the river as another body of water intersected. Alex thought he heard a low humming sound, but he wasn't sure. Suddenly, a large vessel appeared from the adjacent river. The boat looked like an oversized canoe, constructed flawlessly by the finest wood. There were oars on the side of the vessel, but no one was using them. There were a number of large seats on board of the boat, but no one was sitting in them—at least Alex could not tell from where he was looking.

Once the vessel crossed over into the middle of the river that Alex and Kyle were drifting in, it stopped suddenly, as if the boat had breaks. Alex and Kyle began to try to swim around the vessel when suddenly several of the large, blonde giants appeared holding a large net. The net was thrown overboard entangling Alex and Kyle, as the large men began to cheer and celebrate. Alex and Kyle started shouting, "No! No! Let us go! We didn't do anything!" The giants just laughed as they pulled the two young pilots aboard their vessel.

When the two pilots were aboard the ship they looked up through the net and saw ten large, blonde giants looking down at them with contempt. Some of them had smirked, others only had hatred in their eyes. One of them, who was a head taller than the tallest of the rest of them and wearing a hat made of some type of animal skins, broke the ranks of the others. This man also had a large red beard which was much brighter than his long, blonde hair. He had a very muscular build and stood about 12 feet tall. His eyes were black and had several rows of teeth which were pointed at the end. On each hand and foot were six fingers and six toes, respectively. He easily grabbed the net which was holding Kyle and Alex, and lifted the net while the others tied it to a vertical beam aboard the vessel. Then the boat reversed itself and went back in the direction from which it came on the adjacent river. Alex and Kyle hung suspended inside of a net hanging from a wood beam. Both of them were terrified as several of the giants were staring at them and speaking in their native language. Alex began to pray silently.

10

TAXI CAB CONVICTION

Richard Mockens was beside himself. His plan of, "critique-by-committee" had failed miserably. Once again, thought Richard, Dr. Christian Sage seemed to have controlled the conversation, with the only strong objections coming from Dr. Saal—and religious objections at that! Nobody had confronted Dr. Sage at the philosophical, logical, or epistemological level. Dr. Goldberg and Dr. Norton seemed almost disinterested, but then again, they had probably had similar debates in the past with Christian. At any rate, those two were unconvinced at Dr. Sage's proclamation of Jesus Christ as Lord. Dr. Saal was obviously biased toward his own Islamic beliefs and it didn't seem that any amount of reasoning was going to alter his opinion. Professor Cooper seemed to be an intellectually-content Christian—even a scientifically-oriented one at that—very similar to that of Christian Sage. But Professor Richard Mockens could not easily dismiss the claims of Christianity like Dr. Goldberg or Dr. Norton did. He was deeply disturbed by the inability for these intellectual giants to repudiate anything Christian Sage was saying. They just chose to disagree for their own personal reasons. "So much for scholarship," thought Richard.

Professor Mockens smiled as he opened the door of the cab for Dr. Sage and Dr. Saal, although beneath the smile was intellectual and spiritual panic! When all three professors were in the back of the luxurious cab and the other cab, carrying the other professors were behind them following, Richard re-ignited the conversation again before the cab could travel only two blocks. The conversation went as follows:

Mockens: So, Christian, we never did get around to the evidence for Jesus' resurrection.

Sage: Oh, that's right. We seem to have been distracted by all of the collective thoughts on theology in general. That was a valiant attempt, Richard, of trying to rally the troops behind you in your objection of the Bible.

Saal: I can only imagine the conversation you two had last night, (laughing).

Mockens: I was just testing you, Christian. It's one thing to try to evangelize one person—and I'm admitting my lack of knowledge on several of these issues—but I wanted to see you in action when confronted by the collective wisdom of five other professors who might know something that you or I do not. But it didn't seem like everybody was eager to share, though.

Sage: Well, like we had alluded to, there have been quite a few of these conversations between myself and much of the Lakewood faculty. I have yet to hear of a really excellent reason from anybody to reject the testimony of the Bible concerning God and Jesus. Everybody seems to have their own subjective reasons for not believing.

Saal: Couldn't the same thing be said for your affirmation of the Bible?

Sage: In a sense, yes. I'm not going to lower myself to the standards of Naturalistic Evolutionists by make the false assertion that everything *must* be explained by objective evidence. Surely, there have been personal experiences of mine that confirm what I believe, and those are valid for me. But in a different sense, my faith in Christ can be founded on objective evidence and history that is true for everybody—even if they choose to ignore it or disbelieve it. That is something that not everybody can say. There are many Biblical teachings that I wish were not there and have no advantage for me personally. For example, Jesus taught that any man who lusted after a woman in his mind has committed adultery with her in his heart. Now what man would *invent* such a teaching as that?

Cab Driver: Maybe a eunuch, (everyone laughs).

Sage: Exactly! The answer is that no normal man would make up such a doctrine. People who start new religions generally are more sexually permissive than their predecessors, not more stringent! Mormonism would be a good example. Another thing that a person starting a new religion would not want to do is to claim that if a certain person did not come back from the dead then the whole thing is false. And that's exactly what the Apostle Paul did in 1 Corinthians 15. So basically, Christianity is the only religion or worldview that says that everything is determined by one historical fact—a person who died and came back to life—and if this is not true then we shouldn't believe none of this stuff. Additionally, if that person said that there are hundreds of people who are alive today that were eyewitnesses to the fact of this resurrection and that you can go and ask them about it—if this were not true then that person would have to pull off such a stunt to have any person become a follower of that religion. This is definitely not something that a charlatan would do, even condemning himself, if Jesus were not in fact resurrected.

Saal: The Bible teaches this?

Sage: Yes. And Paul's first letter to the Corinthians is one of the earliest documents of Christian history. Even most liberal experts agree that this epistle is early and legitimately Pauline. No other religion can make such a boast to the validity of the factuality of their faith. So if a person were an honest religious inquirer, it would make sense to begin with Christianity because it is certainly factual and falsifiable if the historical evidence is to the contrary.

Mockens: This sounds interesting, but is this all of the resurrection evidence that you spoke of?

Sage: My friend, this is only the beginning of the introductory material!

Saal: So quit teasing us already—let's hear some of this evidence. (Winking at Mockens).

Sage: Okay, okay. There actually was a scholar who did his dissertation on this topic, and what he did was interview several non-Christian scholars of first-century Palestine and Greco-Roman culture and gather all of the information that he could about what even *these* experts were in agreement with what Christians believe about the resurrection events. From these agreed facts, we can deductively come to the conclusion about the event that most likely caused these historical facts. Of course, this doesn't prove the resurrection beyond *all* doubt, but it certainly makes the resurrection of Jesus of Nazareth the most reasonable explanation.

Saal: Aahh, clever! So how much agreement is there between the liberal and conservative experts?

Mockens: Wait a minute! How come Christians always discard what 'liberals' say when it does *not* confirm their faith, but when it *does* it is all of the sudden admissible evidence?

Sage: Richard, while I agree with your assessment that some Christians are biased and sometimes too quickly disregard opposing opinions, or even refuse to hear them, this line of argument does not let anybody off of the hook from historical facts. So for the sake of argument, let's just assume that everybody here is open-minded and honest enough to at least consider what the facts are and we can come to our own conclusions. Okay?

Mockens: Fine.

Saal: You Christians sure are clever with your reasoning. So please, entertain us Dr. Sage.

Sage: Basically, there are twelve historical facts that Christian and non-Christian historians of the first-century agree on. Some of these will sound rather simple, but they are important: (1) Jesus of Nazareth died by Crucifixion...

Saal: But the Qur'an...

Sage: Wait, just hear me out Jabari, please. These are expert historical opinions, not necessarily religious ones. (2) Jesus was buried. (3) The death of Jesus caused his disciples to become saddened, lose hope, and believe that his life had ended. (4) A few days later, the tomb of Jesus was discovered empty. (5) His disciples had actual experiences of the resurrected Jesus being alive after his death and burial. (6) Based on these experiences, the disciples were transformed from fearful doubters who were afraid to identify themselves with Jesus to bold preachers of the death and resurrection of Jesus. (7) This message was central to the preaching and teaching in the early Church. (8) This message was especially proclaimed in Jerusalem, where Jesus had died and was buried shortly before he was seen alive again. (9) As the result of this preaching, the Church was born and increased in number. (10) Sunday became the primary day of worship—a change from over 1,500 years of Judaism. (11) James, the brother of Jesus, who was a skeptic, became converted to the faith when he believed he had an encounter with the resurrected Jesus. (12) A few years later, Paul, who had previously persecuted Christians, was also converted by an experience of the resurrected Jesus.

Saal: Wow! If these facts are reliable, these would be very convincing.

Mockens: Maybe, but experts are not always right. There are always more discoveries being found everyday—like the one we're here for. And often, these discoveries cause the so-called experts to reconsider their previous beliefs.

Sage: While this is true, it sounds like whatever evidence I suggest, you would not be satisfied. If the experts had evidence that directly refutes the resurrection, you would certainly consider their evidence as legitimate, but since the evidence actually supports the Christian faith, you're just closing your eyes and hoping that someone will find *something* that will justify your skepticism.

Saal: So if non-Christian experts believe all of these facts, why do they still not believe?

Sage: That's a great question! It is similar to the reasons why Richard won't believe—they don't *want* to. I have even heard of an attorney who studied the evidence for the resurrection based on the eyewitness testimony and come to the conclusion that Jesus probably did rise from the dead. But he said that he just *chooses* not to believe. And that's what it comes down to ultimately—free will. Now, true faith is not intellectual assent to evidence, but a volitional adherence to the God who has performed his act of atonement through Jesus on the cross. Faith is not a blind leap in the dark—God has provided more than enough evidence to believe. But because people are sinners, they prefer their darkness over the light because the light hurts their eyes and exposes their sinful deeds that condemn them.

Saal: This sounds very well put. So what do these twelve facts imply as far as what excuses that people might use to not believe?

Sage: Well, let me tell you some of the alternative theories of an actual resurrection that people have tried to come up with. First, the oldest one in the book, literally—because it's what the Jewish leadership claimed in the

Gospel of Matthew, is that the disciples stole the body. But it is extremely unlikely that the disciples, who were so afraid that they all abandoned Jesus and betrayed him, would muster up enough courage to attempt such a thing, when it would be so easy for the authorities to catch them or find out through investigation. Furthermore, many of Jesus' disciples were willing to endure severe suffering and persecution—even death—for their testimony of the risen Jesus. Why would any person die for a lie?

Saal: Lots of people do that all of the time! Look at the lunatics from my religious persuasion—not the true Islam, but the fanatical Jihadists. They fly planes into buildings, strap bombs to their chests and blow themselves up to kill their enemies because they think they will enter into paradise with all kinds of rewards.

Sage: Yes, but those people actually believe that it's true. In this case, if Jesus disciples' had actually stolen his body they would've known that the resurrection was a lie. What kind of person would die for something they *know* is a lie? Maybe a few crazies, but only in the most extreme cases. Besides, even opponents of Christianity would mostly admit that Jesus' followers were at least pious in their everyday living.

Mockens: Yeah, I wouldn't go with the stolen body theory either—it defies common sense.

Sage: Another popular theory is the hallucination theory.

Saal: Yes, I heard you briefly mention that before. What is that?

Sage: This is the belief that Jesus' disciples actually did have experiences of Jesus being alive again after his death, but that they were merely hallucinating.

Mockens: This sounds possible.

Sage: Really? Normally, groups of people do not all hallucinate the same experiences to where their stories would corroborate. Their experiences, assuming that more than one person would actually hallucinate anything similar to the others, would have inconsistencies and contradictions. This would hardly become a movement that would become an extension of a legitimate religion like Judaism. And besides, if a person even thought that they might be hallucinating, wouldn't they at least ask somebody to confirm reality for them?

Mockens: Yeah, but it is possible for one person to actually have strong hallucinations and if that person was influential, he could cause others to *want* to believe that as a reality so much that they could psychosomatically cause themselves to hallucinate too. Remember, the disciples really had their hopes up that Jesus would be their political deliverer from the Romans, and hope is a very strong emotion that can trigger hallucinations if that hope turns to severe grief.

Sage: (laughing) Richard, do you even hear yourself right now? Like I said before, these facts do not prove the resurrection beyond *all* doubt, but certainly reasonable doubt. The hallucination theory would require an elaborate conspiracy at some point, being able to overcome the mighty Roman Empire. This theory, while possible—and I mean winning-the-lottery possible—is certainly not very reasonable.

Mockens: Dead people coming back to life seems equally doubtful, though.

Sage: Not if you believe that God, who created the entire universe from nothing, exists. If a person believes Genesis 1:1, "In the beginning, God created the heavens and the earth...", then bringing back a person, especially the Son of God, from the dead is not a difficult task.

Saal: Yes, this makes sense. Not all of the hallucinating in the world would spark such a movement, and with God all things are possible!

Sage: Now you're talking!

Saal: What are some of the other theories?

Sage: Another popular one is called the Swoon Theory. This is the belief that Jesus did not actually die on the cross, but merely fainted. And later, while lying in the tomb, he woke-up, hence he appeared to his disciples after his crucifixion.

Mockens: But what about him being stabbed with the spear of the Roman?

Sage: While I believe that, not all secular experts believe the historical accuracy of the Gospel accounts. What can be known, though, is that the Romans were professional executioners. If a prisoner escaped, the person responsible for allowing him to escape would be put to death in his place. And even if Jesus were able to survive a crucifixion, which would have been practically miraculous in and of itself, freeing himself from a tomb, that was guarded by Roman soldiers—at least according to Matthew's Gospel—and then appearing to his disciples, nearly naked and severely wounded—this hardly would've inspired his disciples to say, "Oh my Lord and my God—you have come back to life!" Rather, they would try to get Jesus some medical attention! And if this is true, what became of Jesus? Certainly, a man of his fame could not have gone very far without being noticed—especially bearing the scars of crucifixion and then escaping the vast geographical region of the Roman Empire!

Mockens: Right. I'm surprised that an intelligent person could actually believe this.

Sage: You'd be surprised. But I say the same thing about a person believing anything *but* a resurrection, especially in light of this evidence. Some of the less-popular theories are even worse: the Wrong-Tomb Theory declares that the women went to the wrong tomb—and indeed it was empty!

Saal: Then the body would've still been in the right tomb.

Sage: Correct! Or the theory that says that Jesus *spiritually* resurrected and he now lives in the hearts of his followers.

Mockens: Then his body would still be in the tomb and Christianity would have nothing to go on.

Sage: Right again! Believe it or not, the Jehovah's Witnesses do not believe in a physical resurrection.

Mockens: Really? Don't they believe in the Bible?

Sage: Well, they have a certain translation of the Bible that fits their theology—and not a very good translation by-the-way.

Saal: Well, wouldn't Jesus' body still be in the tomb?

Sage: They believe that Jesus' body was burned up in a divine flame—even though nothing in Scripture even comes close to saying this.

Mockens: I used to have a neighbor who was a Watchtower guy. He had meetings all of the time and they used to come to my house at least every other week. After awhile, I started to just not answer the door or even hide behind the furniture. They are just out to lunch with some of their beliefs.

Sage: They mean well, but they have been deceived by a very well-organized cult. But back to our topic, it's ironic that the theory that is most taught by Religious Studies departments at universities is actually the theory with the least evidence to support it.

Saal: Which one is that?

Sage: It's what is often called the Legend Theory. Basically, it claims that the Christian movement began as a purely ethical movement about Jesus' teachings that evolved into an elaborate theology that ended up deifying Jesus as a response to Roman oppression. This view does not really consider much of the evidence that I have presented to you very seriously, but rather that the legend of Jesus distanced itself further and further away from the historical Jesus as time went on. This is just a lazy way of thinking that avoids having to answer any of the historical facts or the eyewitness accounts of Christians, Jews, and Romans.

Cab Driver: (holding back tears) I have never heard any of this before! I am so fed up with all of the Islamic fundamentalism in my country and I am depressed. I was approached by a Christian missionary last week, and I wanted to believe him, but I have been brainwashed by my culture for so long it's just so hard to believe the Christian message. Now that I have heard you speak, sir, I want to become a Christian now. What should I do?

Sage: Are there any churches close to where you live?

Cab Driver: The closest one is about five miles away. It's the same one that the missionary told me about.

Sage: Well, I think you should go and talk privately to a pastor there. He can lead you into the kingdom of God. But before that, you can pray to God and admit that you are a sinner and that you need his forgiveness. Confess that you believe that Jesus is the Son of God and that he died for your sins on the cross, and that he resurrected on the third day. Ask for God's Holy Spirit to enter into your heart so that he may begin your new relationship with God as his child through the blood of Jesus. You will be forgiven and you will be born-again—a new creation of God! Do these things and the Lord will guide you into all truth and into his kingdom.

Cab Driver: Thank you, sir, I will do that.

Sage: What about you, Jabari? Are you ready to become a Christian?

Saal: I'm not that simple to convert. I do believe that we worship the same god, but my faith is in the Qur'an and that Muhammad is Allah's prophet. Although you have been very persuasive with your information, I have to do some research myself before I can really consider such a radical move.

Sage: Well, at least you're open to it. What about you, Richard?

Mockens: Umm, I still think it's possible that the disciples halluci-
nated. They were definitely sincere in their beliefs, but they were mistaken
in their grief.

Sage: Would you at least admit that the resurrection is equally plau-
sible?

Mockens: Maybe, but coming back from the dead is not at all something that a human being can personally relate to, while hallucinating is
definitely something that many people experience and can at least fathom.

Sage: You have somewhat of a point, but again, it seems that you are
reverting back to subjectivism and not really taking into the historical facts
and evidence. It is as if you are saying, "Don't bother me with the facts and
the evidence because my mind is already made up." At this point I guess
there's not much else I can say to persuade you.

Mockens: Perhaps you're right. I definitely do not want to become
some religious person who never has any fun and is always telling other
people how they should live their life instead of the way that they seem is
more enjoyable.

Sage: Personally, I would have to say that I have lots of fun, and I
have not invaded your right to live however you want to live, I have only
given you some of the excellent reasons of why I believe the Bible is the
word of God and that Jesus Christ is the savior of the world. Of course, believing this does come with the responsibility of making personal, ethical
applications of what Scripture teaches and how we should live, so the two
cannot be divorced from one another.

Mockens: So the academic and apologetic reasoning you are giving
me is just a less offensive way of preaching to me and telling me that the
way I see the world and my personal beliefs about morality and the possibilities about God are wrong.

Sage: To me, it seems as if you are experiencing what we Christians
call the conviction of the Holy Spirit. I have hardly said anything about
ethics or how you live. Although you are correct in saying that a person's
worldview and beliefs about God inevitably relate to how they behave.
I'm not condemning you, I'm only sharing because I care about your soul
Richard, and you seemed to have been interested in what I believe. And

by the way, you haven't exactly articulated any particular worldview or ethical belief system that is very coherent to how you live personally.

Mockens: Christian, I'm flattered that you care about my soul. And you're correct that my worldview is limited to what I personally experience. This is partly because I do not trust religious institutions based on much of their history and seemingly contradictory behavior with their own proclaimed values. And I have not personally experienced anything spiritual enough for me to adhere to or follow as far as a theological belief system where its ethical values are absolutes. It would take an extraordinary event for me to change my attitude and my ways.

Sage: Now we're getting somewhere because you're finally being honest. Let me ask you, if the God of the Bible were to appear to you, or make himself real to you, would you then believe?

Mockens: You mean if all of the sudden there were lots of coincidences that I interpreted in a mystical way would I believe everything you've shared with me? I think a lot of so-called religious experiences are just that—circumstantial coincidences. And how would I *really* be able to know that God is manifesting himself to me? How could I be certain that *I* am not hallucinating, or having a dream, or a psychotic episode of sort?

Sage: Richard, now you are back to grasping at straws again! But I guess if your mentality is that you cannot be certain of anything, even what you sense to be reality should be in question then. If this is the case, you cannot be actually held morally responsible for anything—other than what civil laws dictate to you.

Cab Driver: Okay, gentlemen, we're here. Thank you for all of the great talking—I am greatly interested in learning more.

Sage: I really do pray that you will talk to a pastor at that church. You will see what great things the Lord has in store for you.

Cab Driver: Thank you, thank you. God bless you too.

11

UPSIDE DOWN AND BITTERSWEET

Alicia Sage had fainted from shock almost immediately after her prayer and being tied upside down onto the pole of the native giants. When she had regained her consciousness, it was as if she had not fainted as far as her memory was concerned. But now she was on a foreign path from which she could only describe from an upside down view. She could see the humongous bare feet, which bore six toes, of one of the natives who were carrying the pole full of students with apparent ease. A few minutes later she could discern that it was Amanda who was immediately tied up in front of her face.

"Pssst. Amanda," she whispered.

"Oh, you're back with us now," Amanda answered as she turned her head around, in somewhat of a louder whisper.

"How long have I been out?" asked Alicia.

"I don't know exactly, but it seems as if we have been marching for miles now. I can't see the sun in the sky anymore so I know it must be late afternoon now," responded Amanda.

"Is Virgil dead?" Alicia asked.

"I think so, although they tied him up too. I think he's at the front end of the pole. What do you think they're going to do with us?"

"I have no idea. I'm sure we're going back to wherever these people live. We need to avoid too many negative thoughts so we can keep our composure and not panic."

"I agree," said Amanda. "I hope the Lord will find it in his heart to rescue us from this mess—we need a miracle of biblical proportions!"

By this point she was speaking in her normal voice, which brought unwanted attention to herself. It seemed as if speaking of 'The Lord' caught the ear of one of the natives, because he quickly walked aside of Amanda and kicked her in the head.

"Your god no save you here—only our gods live here. Now quiet—no more talking!" yelled the giant.

Amanda could not help but softly sob at this point and Alicia was too terrified to say another word. At this point she could hear running water not too far from where they were at. Suddenly, a thick fog came upon the group and it was difficult to see further than ten feet from them. Then there was a steep incline as the students were being carried uphill through a fairly dense forest. There was no sign of physical challenge or fatigue of the natives who carried them. The sound of running water grew louder as the students began to be struck by branches of brush. Alicia's legs and arms began to bleed from the several scratches of the brush, but she could barely feel the pain. Then there was a sharp change of direction, about 90 degrees to Alicia's left. Now they were traveling parallel to a small stream.

A few minutes later they had arrived at a small waterfall and the entourage came to a halt. Alicia could hear some conversation between the giants in their native tongue. Two of them walked by Alicia, and apparently they walked into the stream due to the sound of feet splashing in the water. The next sound that Alicia heard was the apparent sound of a large stone being moved or scraped along another stone surface. Not too long afterward, the line began to move again. This time everyone was in the water. The stream was cool and refreshing to Alicia, cleansing her abrasions as they went. The only problem was that she could barely lift her head above the water. Most of the giant natives did not even get their knees wet. Alicia turned her head as far as she could behind her, for she was facing opposite from the direction of travel. She could see two natives holding a large stone which had apparently covered a hidden tunnel beneath the waterfall. It was evident that everyone was going to get drenched by gentle falls. When it was Alicia's turn to get immersed, again it was pleasantly refreshing on such a humid and tumultuous day.

When the group entered the tunnel, everything was pitch-black. Alicia was wondering how the natives could see anything at all—even if they were thoroughly familiar with the tunnel. There was some water covering the ground, although probably not more than three inches or so, according to how the splashing of the feet sounded. Most of the students hung about two feet from the ground. The next sound that Alicia heard was the scraping of another large stone being moved. Not long after, the sound of feet climbing up steps was discernible. The ascent was not steep but it must have been about 70 or 80 steps up and around. Finally, the total darkness began to subside gradually as the sound of other voices in the distance grew louder and echoed in the corridor. The first thing that Alicia was able to see was a dimly lit torch on the stone walls. She could scarcely see some ancient form of hieroglyphics carved along the wall as they traveled.

Suddenly, the natives who escorted the students came to a complete stop and began chanting about 5 -6 words repeatedly, in their native tongues. After about one minute of chanting, they entered into a large doorway which looked like an entrance to a sacred palace or temple. The lighting vastly improved inside of this palace, and there were people of all shapes and sizes moving about freely in this large room. The people hardly looked twice at the tied up students, as if this were a normal sight in this place. Alicia thought that it seemed like an ancient type of swap meet where goods were bought, sold and bargained for. The entourage that carried Alicia and her classmates walked without ceasing and eventually found their way to a wooden bridge that crossed a small chasm. Alicia tried to look down into the chasm but she could see nothing but darkness. Finally, the group came to a halt and each student was cut loose and escorted to an isolated place that was some sort of holding tank for captives.

Alicia could see some men carrying Virgil's lifeless body away from the others. The other twelve students were brought to what looked like a large sandbox that was dug into the ground. Each student was violently shoved into the sandbox, from which there was about a five foot drop from the edge to the bottom. And just in case anybody had any thought of escape, six giant natives approached the outskirts of the sandbox with wild jaguars on leashes and chained them to six 10-foot poles that surrounded the sandbox. The sandbox was circular in shape and had a diameter of about fifty feet. In the center of the sandbox was a small pool of not-so-clear water. Randy was the first to taste of the water, for apparently he was so thirsty that he didn't care how clean the water was.

Randy took a small drink from his cupped hands and appeared delighted at the taste. He followed by filling up his hands twice more and drinking before he shouted, "Hey guys, come and drink—the water is sweet as sugar!" Everybody hurried toward the pool of water and began drinking without any questions asked, including Alicia.

The twelve students enjoyed the water that they drank from so much it was as if they had forgotten what they had just experienced for the past four hours. They laughed and joked around with each other like they would at a frat-party. It was as if the water had been drugged with euphoric substances. Nobody spoke of any escape plans or exit strategies. Everyone seemed as festive as any of the people in the main room of the palace. There was no presence of danger, no more fear of dying, and no apparent memory of the loss of their group leader Virgil.

Everything had seemed even dreamlike to Alicia as she and Amanda giggled at each other's words. This was until Amanda grabbed her stomach in pain and hunched over as if to vomit. Soon everyone was filled with fear, and then one-by-one, each person began to be sick to their stomachs and was bent over facing the ground. No fluids escaped their mouths, though they wished they could give the water back. This was when Alicia began to see dark shadows flying above the sandbox, descending on the twelve students. Then it was Alicia's turn to be sick and she followed suit by doubling over. She could hear the whispers coming from the shadowy figures. She opened her eyes barely enough to see that most of the other students were lying motionless on the ground. Then, even Alicia lost consciousness—again.

12

WEIRD SCIENCE

While Dr. Sage was schooling Dr. Saal and Professor Mockens in their respective cab, Dr. Geoffrey Goldberg, Dr. Hank Norton, and Professor Cliff Cooper were in the cab behind them, on their way to the Mount Ararat dig site. Dr. Goldberg taught Jewish and Semitic Studies, Dr. Norton was the head of the English Literature department, and fittingly, was British as well. Professor Cooper had only been teaching Geology at Lakewood University for one year now, so he was the newest of the full-time faculty on staff. And just as the cab ahead of them was full of the most delightful of conversations, the taxi in the rear was no less amusing. The conversation went as follows:

Norton: So Cliff, when you were applying for your job, did you let it be known that you were a creation scientist?

Cooper: No, I did not volunteer that information. But if someone would've asked, I would've told them—I have nothing to be ashamed about.

Goldberg: It's a good thing nobody asked you. Most creation scientists get black-balled from the public educational system.

Cooper: That is true, and it is unfortunate. Creation scientists are just as adequate, if not more so, to teach science as mainstream scientists. We all practice science the same way—by observing, hypothesizing, testing, and concluding with the results, whatever they may be. The only difference is our assumptions about the unobserved past: I assume that God created all matter and all creatures in a purposeful way and that he was personally involved. Many of my colleagues assume that, "In the beginning there was nothing, and then it exploded. Over billions of years, the exploded matter cooled and randomly arranged itself. And then by chance, evolution occurred and the matter went from the goo-to the zoo-to you." I believe that by what can be observed today, namely complexity, order, and purpose, that my assumption is much more scientific than the assumptions of mainstream scientists.

Goldberg: I believe in God too, but I believe that God created all matter and then used evolution as the vehicle to which purpose and function came about. The descriptions in the Torah are spiritual and theological—not scientific.

Cooper: I agree that the Bible is spiritual and theological, but it doesn't necessarily have to be compartmentalized from what we humans call 'science' today. Certainly truth cannot contradict truth. And the God of the Bible is definitely not the god that used evolution to create. When God finished creating, he rested and called his creation 'very good'. Evolution maintains that life only comes about by death, and the advancement of life only comes about by much death and random error before a 'finished product' finally appears. The God of the Bible calls death an enemy and it was not according to his original plan for his creation.

Goldberg: Well, I believe the Bible teaches about God from the point of view of those who wrote it, but it is not necessarily absolutely true in a mystical-divine sense.

Norton: That's right. Men wrote the Bible, and since men are prone to error, then it can't be 100% accurate, especially in scientific matters.

Cooper: I will have to tell you, I am not as well versed in philosophy and history as say, Dr. Sage, but I do know this: If God is all-powerful and all-knowing then he could easily choose certain men to write his words accurately and without error. Now the god of evolution made lots of mistakes in his original creation—that's why he needed random mutations, errors, and death to come to a finished product—and millions of years too, by-the-way. In fact, if you study the basic tenets of ancient pagan beliefs about origins and modern biologists about origins, the two are eerily similar. They both believe in some primordial soup where life just "springs forth" out of the waters or from the "mound" of land that comes forth. I believe that Darwinian evolution is nothing more than modern paganism dressed in scientific jargon.

Norton: Unbelievable! People have advanced far from the days of believing in gods, demons, and spirits. Things that used to be attributed to supernatural powers have now been observed as naturally explained now. Just look at what people believed in the medieval times—it was just a bunch of superstitious nonsense!

Goldberg: Yes. And the Catholic Church persecuted many scientists and other professionals who went against their dogma—including many Jews.

Cooper: I agree with you both, for the most part. Many things that were believed to be supernatural were actually not. That doesn't mean that God cannot use nature to accomplish his plan. See, the Naturalist presupposes a closed universe where only the laws of nature occur, and, by-the-way, only in an uniformitarian manner. They say, "The present is the key to the past." I think it's the other way around: the past is the key to the present. In fact, many scientists today are abandoning the theory of uniformity and leaning more towards catastrophic theories.

Norton: Refresh my memory—what is the theory of uniformity?

Goldberg: It means that all physical forces have always worked at a similar rate as we observe them today.

Cooper: Right, Geoff. And we can easily observe today how many catastrophic events like earthquakes, floods, tsunamis, volcanoes, and hurricanes can quickly alter the geography and even tilt the axis of the earth. And say a meteor crashes into the earth, which has happened and is what many scientists believed caused the extinction of the dinosaurs—this would severely alter much of the environment, including the rate of decay, which would make carbon-dating and other radio-isotopic dating methods extremely suspect. But this line of reasoning is completely ignored in our educational system, and the students don't know any better, so they just believe it because it is in a textbook!

Norton: Interesting.

Goldberg: I recall that you said earlier that there was an abundance of evidence against the theory of uniformity. Is this it?

Cooper: No, this is only part of it. There are other things, like the moon moving further away from the earth every year by about three centimeters. I know that that's not much, but if our solar system were 14 billion years old, like some claim, then at one point the moon would actually make contact with the earth, much less be so close that the gravitational pull would be so tremendous that life would be impossible on earth and there would be numerous catastrophes by the tides and magnetism.

And speaking of magnetism, we can measure the annual decline in the earth's magnetism. So if the uniformitarian view is correct, and if the earth were 5 billion years old—or even many millions of years—the earth's magnetism would've been so great at one point that there could not have been any land animals whatsoever. And then there's the amount of helium still remaining in rock formations. We can measure how fast helium escapes from rocks and how long it stays in our atmosphere. If the earth were millions or billions of years old, we would have no helium left in the rocks and much more in the atmosphere. And then...

Goldberg: Okay, I think we get it, Cliff. So the theory of uniformity has some major flaws, but that does not necessarily prove a young earth.

Cooper: Correct. It only proves that you cannot assign long ages for the earth based on the methods that are used today because it comes with an uniformitarian assumption. But what it does is put the young earth theory on the same playing field as the old earth view, and it does make it a valid scientific theory and not just a religious point of view. It also creates a large measure of doubt on Darwinism.

Norton: How so? Haven't we found some fossils that show a variation of species?

Cooper: Well, in order for Darwin's Theory of Evolution to be true—and let me clarify—I'm speaking of *macro*-evolution, not minor variations within species—Darwin needs there to be millions of years for Natural Selection to use random chance for mutations to occur gradually so that species can evolve into something new. Without lots of time, it would be an absurd impossibility. In fact, Darwin's "Natural Selection" becomes sort of a deity in that it can choose favorable traits and discard unfavorable traits. All in the name of survival too, by-the-way. And no, Hank, there have been no fossils that have shown "missing links" or in-between creatures. There have been lots of intentional fabrications, and findings that have been interpreted with Darwinian assumptions, but nothing conclusive.

Goldberg: Wait a minute, don't we have evidence for the development of the horse from a small, donkey-like creature to the thoroughbreds we have today?

Cooper: The pictures in the textbooks show them that way intentionally to make it seem so. But there are still small horses today and there were large thoroughbreds in ancient times, and there is no evidence that horses were something else or ever evolved into a different creature. See, the educational system wants to deceive people into the progressive Darwinian worldview of the 'Survival of the Fittest.'

Norton: Are you crying conspiracy?

Cooper: Yes, it's obvious! Even Dr. Goldberg admitted that creation scientists get black-balled from the mainstream scientific community. In fact, Charles Darwin and his mentor, Charles Lyell purposely put forth these theories in an attempt to dismantle the dominion of the Judeo-Christian stronghold on history and science because of the ethical implications that are produced from them. You see, sinful humanity wants to alleviate itself from being accountable to a holy God, and by trying to convince ourselves that we are nothing more than highly evolved animals. And they think this gives us the justification to live however we want without any absolute consequences.

Goldberg: Are you saying that evolutionists are inherently immoral?

Cooper: Not necessarily. But absolute morality is a contraction in terms with the evolutionary worldview. In that worldview or philosophy, whatever the strongest creature desires and can accomplish is for the good of the species and its survival. So that means murder, rape, incest, pedophilia, theft, or you name it—it is not absolutely immoral if Darwinian Evolution is true! But it sure is funny, when an evolutionist is confronted with something evil, all of the sudden the image of God surfaces from within and they cry out, "Immorality! Immorality!"

Norton: Now we're going into philosophy and ethics, I want to hear more of the science.

Cooper: Yes, but you see, the science has ethical implications, and the two cannot be divorced. But strictly scientifically speaking, the scientific method cannot produce one positive shred of evidence for macro-evolution. We have not observed it in nature, although it can be produced in a lab—but only with human interference—definitely not Natural Selection! In fact, the irreducible complexity of a multitude of creatures demonstrate that it is impossible for them to have evolved from a simpler organism. If the all of the parts are not functioning correctly the first time, then the creature would die, and dead things can't evolve! Think of childbirth, woodpeckers, giraffes, you name it! There are so many examples that it would take a whole college course to go through all of them. The question I would ask an honest evolutionist, is why *do* you believe it? Just because it was taught to you? Where's the evidence? It's not science at all, it's a philosophy and a worldview—the only alternative to the Judeo-Christian worldview that is even slightly intellectual—emphasis on the slightly!

Goldberg: I freely admit that you might have a case, if all of what you just said is true. But going back to an earlier point, even though uniformity might have some problems, it's all we can scientifically go by because it would take speculation for us to assume that the laws of physics and the earth's environment was vastly different in the past. So basically we've got nothing concretely scientific.

Cooper: I would say that, for one thing, too much emphasis is being put on the scientific method as the measuring rod for truth. I know, I know, I'm a scientist by trade, but geology is just my personal hobby and my occupation. However, if we were to take what the Scriptures have to say about history seriously, then we can make some *reasonable* conjectures and assumptions about the ancient past.

Norton: Is this where you're going to tell me that you actually believe that people really lived to be over 900 years old and that a man built a big boat and put two of every king of animal—including the millions of species of insects and the sort—on the boat to avoid the worldwide flood that a loving God sent to destroy the earth?

Cooper: Is this where you are going to try to make me feel stupid if I truly believe this, even if there are excellent possibilities of it being true? Isn't this why we're here in the first place—to see if Noah's Ark still rests in the Ararat Mountains?

Norton: Aw, come on Cliff. Why is it so hard to believe that the early chapters of Genesis are nothing more than contemporary myths of the Ancient Near East. Almost every culture has similar stories to try to explain why things are the way they are.

Cooper: Exactly! The similarity in stories verifies the historicity of them. The reason why they are different is because people spread out in the world after the Tower of Babel incident and they took these accounts with them. With time and the diversifying of culture, some of the stories were altered. And besides, Jesus and his contemporaries believed that these were real historical accounts. And if Jesus is truly the Son of God then these accounts must be historical.

Goldberg: With all due respect, I believe Jesus was a trouble-making, false prophet. But it is true that the 1st Century Jews believed this was real history. But things have changed now; now we know about myths and fables and how ancient cultures passed down tradition.

Cooper: But if God truly exists, and he does actually communicate with his people, then he would not have deceived them with false information, and he would have preserved the true history about himself.

Norton: So how was it possible for people to live so long before and not now?

Cooper: Since God created everything perfect with the intention of all creatures living forever, the environment would've been pure and free from all toxins, UV sunrays, and other hazards that are threatening to life. God created Adam and Eve without any negative traits or self-destructive tendencies. Even the animals were all vegetarians because there was no death initially.

Norton: So are you saying that even the lions and the T-Rex and Great White Sharks were all vegetarians?

Cooper: I'm not saying it, the Scriptures are implying that God did not create his creatures to die, so animals were able to be sustained without killing other animals. I know it sounds crazy for us 21st Century folks, but if this were the case, the environment would be much different.

Norton: So you're saying, I mean you're claiming that the Bible is saying, that before Adam ate the forbidden fruit that everything was perfect, but the one little act of disobedience caused all of the evil that we see today?

Cooper: Sort of. All of the evil did not happen all at once, but gradually. Adam and Eve were kicked out of paradise and at that point they began to age and slowly die. In fact, God killed the first animal because the Bible says that he clothed the naked couple with animal skins. So even in the very beginning, a blood sacrifice was necessary to atone for sins.

Goldberg: Keep in mind that this was written by Jews who were trying to explain their religion by past justification.

Cooper: But how would you explain that every ancient civilization had some sort of animal sacrificial system in their religion? Only a real event, such as the Genesis 3 account, could explain the worldwide phenomenon of animal sacrifice. Of course, this eventually plummeted into human sacrifice in some cultures, but the essence of a blood sacrifice mysteriously permeated all cultures in the world. And of course, Jesus Christ was the final blood sacrifice and God destroyed the Temple in Jerusalem 40 years later to prove that point.

Goldberg: Hey, hey, watch the anti-Semitism.

Cooper: No offense to you, Dr. Goldberg, but the temple was destroyed, and if God exists then he allowed it to happen for a reason.

Norton: So why did people stop living to such long ages later?

Cooper: Many people continued to live up to long ages until the generations after the great Flood. Evidently, the worldwide catastrophe of Noah's Flood altered the environment so radically that people and animals began to die earlier. It might have to do with UV sunrays and the collapse of a vapor canopy, called the firmament in the Bible, or it might have to do with the water diminishing the nutritional value of vegetation, the oxygen content of a non-tropical atmosphere, the need for incest with the eight survivors of Noah's family—with this time the human gene pool being smaller and with more disease and infection because of sin, or there could be many other reasons as well. These are just some.

Norton: You believe that the pre-Flood world was entirely tropical?

Cooper: The earth probably did have a global greenhouse effect that enabled an oxygen-rich atmosphere where plant life could grow to tremendous sizes, which in turn would produce excellent nutrition and creatures that grow continually throughout their lifespan, such as reptiles, fish, and other insects, could grow to enormous sizes. And we have fossil evidence for all of this, hence the dinosaurs. Imagine a world with cockroaches growing up to one foot long! Such discoveries have been made. Plus, we have discovered reptile fossils near the north and south poles, which would be impossible if those regions had freezing temperatures.

Norton: Fascinating!

Goldberg: I'm not sold yet! How could Noah get all of the animals on board the ark? I mean we have millions of species of animals today.

Evolution explains this, but if the Flood was really worldwide, the animals that Noah could not fit on the ark would have died.

Cooper: Actually, Noah did not have a pair of every *species* of animal on the ark. The Bible says that he had two of every *kind*, including seven of certain kinds. So Noah did not have to have a pair of tigers, a pair of cheetahs, a pair of lions, etc. He only had to have a pair of prototypical felines. From this prototypical pair, the genetic variability within the gene pool could have easily produced all of the cat family that we see today. And this would be true for every type of animal, even dinosaurs.

Norton: How could creatures as big as dinosaurs have been on the ark?

Cooper: Well, most dinosaurs were relatively small, the size of sheep on the average. Besides, Noah could have put younger dinosaurs on the ark. Remember, reptiles continually grow as long as they live. So it is the dinosaurs that lived the longest that were the largest. And by-the-way, they didn't call them dinosaurs back then, that is a 19th Century term.

Norton: Right, in my English Literature studies there are lots of tales about dragons and other large creatures. I do believe these were real creatures because of the context of which they were written. And I do know about the current findings of dinosaur DNA being found in bones and eggs which would make it impossible for them to be millions of years old.

Cooper: Right! See, now you're with me!

Goldberg: Okay, I'll play along for a minute. So how did the animals get to the islands and far reaching places of the world from the ark on Mount Ararat? How did the animals get to Australia, for example. Australia has unique creatures that are found nowhere else in the world.

Cooper: Well, we do know that there were land bridges that once existed that are now under water. The sea level was also much lower in previous times too. The Flood is what brought about the large increase in sea level. And the apparent volcanism that occurred as both cause and effect of the Flood and which produced the subsequent Ice Age had a tremendous effect on sea levels, land bridges and the like. It is also probable that the continents were all connected prior to the Flood and that the earthquakes, flooding, and volcanoes are what caused them to drift apart more rapidly than what we observe today. So in effect, the Flood itself severely altered any possible way to measure the past by using the observed physical laws of today.

Goldberg: You're rabbit trailing now. Are you avoiding my Australian objection?

Cooper: Sorry, I just get a little excited about this stuff!

Norton: Obviously!

Cooper: Animals could've reached Australia by land bridges, being transported by people on vessels, or they could've migrated by what are called 'floating islands.'

Goldberg: Floating islands? What in the world are those?

Cooper: This is a phenomenon which has been observed even today. For example, a hurricane in the Caribbean region once caused a large landmass to be dislodged from the coast of Florida. This large piece of land had on it dozens of iguanas. The land mass finally reached one of the Caribbean islands—I forget which one—an island without *any* iguanas. Some of the iguanas from the floating island boarded the main island, they reproduced and now that particular island has a large population of iguanas! Something similar could've occurred in Australia and the other islands. And because of the remote geographical location, the animals adapted to their environment and are unique to their relatives in other parts of the world. However, the fossils of Australian animals are also found in India, so it is very likely that at one point in time that the two lands were connected and then severed and drifted apart.

Goldberg: Wow! You are impressive, Cooper. You might be on to something.

Norton: Indeed. I might have to rethink some things. So, Cliff, what do you think we will find here on Mount Ararat?

Cooper: I have no idea. I mean, if wooly mammoths can be preserved in ice with undigested food still in their stomachs, I supposed a wooden vessel could as well. Although, I have to admit that I am a bit skeptical that 4,500 years of decaying would make it unlikely for preservation unless there was a solid freeze.

Cab Driver: Okay, men, we are here.

Norton: Now our journey begins!

13

ARKAEOLOGY 101

Dr. Christian Sage and his five colleagues exited their vehicles at a small airport a few miles from Mount Ararat. A helicopter was waiting for their arrival, for they would be air-lifted up to a recently manufactured loading zone. After this they would have to hike about three miles to the dig site. At the actual dig site there would be a large camp ground where scientists and historians all over the world were staying while the large object was being dug out. Christian could only hope that he was among the first few entourages to arrive at the site. The original sighting was nearly three weeks old now, and the Turkish government worked tremendously hard to provide all of the necessities and collect the needed funds to accommodate this awesome new research.

As soon as the six gentlemen were seated in the military-style chopper the propellers immediately spun into action. Dust began to circle the chopper causing the passengers to cover their eyes and their faces. Professor Cooper's long blonde hair danced wildly, as Dr. Norton had to grab hold of his hat, which covered his completely bald head. Dr. Saal was glad that he had his contact lenses in instead of wearing his glasses, which probably would've been scratched by flying sand. Professor Mockens was trying to spit out some of the dust, and possibly a bug, which entered into his mouth. Dr. Goldberg smiled as he observed this, while stroking his grey beard. Dr. Sage seemed to be the only man not phased or amused at any of the activity—he was deep in thought—both from the conversations that had just taken place and the prospects of this archaeological find. His grayish-blue eyes were in a trance-like thousand-yard stare.

When the helicopter came to a stop at the landing zone, it was nearly 9:00 am. At that altitude, the air was briskly cool—probably in the high 30's. The six professors were adequately prepared for the weather and the hike. Each had two canteens of water attached to their belts and large backpacks full of clothing—warm and cold weather—enough for three days, tools for digging and measuring, personal hygienic items, and whatever other personal things that each man desired to bring and could fit in the rucksack. They were instructed that they would stay at the dig site for three days and then be air-lifted back down for two days of rest and renewal, and then back up for another three days. Lakewood University permitted these men to endure three cycles of this schedule—a total of 16 days and four additional days of round-trip travel.

Surprisingly, after all of the previous conversations, the men were relatively silent as they hiked the three miles to the dig sit campground. It was all business now. There were two five-minute breaks along the way so that the professors could drink water and eat granola bars and dehydrated fruit. When they finally reached the campground they were greeted by an administrator, who apparently was expecting their arrival. "Welcome, gentlemen," he said in his Turkish accent but in very good English. "We are glad you are here. What institution are you from?"

Dr. Goldberg answered, "Lakewood University in Oregon, United States."

"Ummm…oh—here you are," said the administrator as he scrolled down his chart. "Very well. By the way, my name is Sammi and I will show you your tent. Right this way."

It did not take long for the professors to stow away their personal belongings and gather all of the necessary tools for their dig. The spirit of excitement filled the camp. The six men then walked toward the trail that led to the actual dig site. It was not difficult to tell that the trail was very new because there were still lots of rocks, rubble, and even some trees and plant life that altered the course of the trail. The trail was not longer than a quarter of a mile, but the incline was very steep and the hike was difficult.

Dr. Norton, who was the second oldest at 44, had the most difficulty as he was continually out of breath.

After the hikers passed the final bend of rock they could see the large object protruding from the side of a large cliff of dismantled sediment. The bottom of the object rested on a large pile of rocks and from where the professors were, it appeared that about 25 feet in length of the object was totally exposed. There were several men digging about the rock formation trying to free up more space so that the object could be more accessible. There were also several men observing the digging and taking notes on clipboards. As the professors approached they all had a sense of awe. It was indeed a large, wooden vessel that was exposed out of the side of a mountain! Professor Cooper was the first to take his camera out of his rucksack and begin to take pictures. It did not take long for the others to follow suit.

After about three minutes of picture-taking, a young African security guard approached the awe-struck professors, asking, "Are you men English speaking?" in a Nigerian accent.

"Yes," answered Dr. Saal. "We are from Lakewood University in…"

"ID badges, please," said the security guard.

All six of the professors pulled out their badges from their pockets.

"Okay, good. You may proceed. There is a large ramp structure on the other side of the cliff that will give you the access you need to join the others. Any items that you bring back must be logged in at the booth over there and you are allowed no more than three items. Is this good to you?"

"Sure, fine," answered Dr. Norton. "Thank you."

The Nigerian smiled and nodded and stepped sideways out of the way, permitting the men to pass.

When the professors finally reached the apex of the digging cliff, they all pulled out their digging tools from their rucksacks: small shovels, trowels, pick-axes, and soil sifters were all that was necessary for this trip. There were about 18 other people who were digging along side of the vessel. Several small pieces of wood were removed to be tested and analyzed at a lab back at the camp. At this time there were no large pieces of wood removed as to enter the vessel because of the attempt to totally remove all of the surrounding sediment and capture the totality of the find. At a more isolated post, there were two men with jack-hammers attempting to remove larger sections of rock. The echo of metal striking stones was a constant. The only conversation to be heard was that of a face-to-face discussion, and there was not too much of that at the dig level. The six professors from Lakewood University spread out relatively close but each had their distinct space. There was more than enough room for the now 24 men who were digging.

After about six hours of digging, there was probably about 20 more feet of ancient wood now exposed as to when Dr. Sage and company first arrived. Much of the wood was already damaged and rotted. Somehow this vessel had been preserved—probably in solid ice for much of the time, according to most of the scientists present. Nobody knew yet how long the vessel was or how long it would take to totally recover it. As time went on that day, about 12 other men had joined the dig and many of the others had spread to other surrounding areas, hoping to discover something unique or exquisite. So far the only things found besides the vessel were a few fossils. Most of the fossils were marine invertebrates, but there were a few fish, plants, leaves, and even fossilized tree trunks. All of this pointed to a sudden catastrophe or catastrophes that demonstrated that sea life had once thrived at over 10,000 feet. But there were yet to be any significant discoveries of man-made tools, coins, pottery, or other utensils.

About forty-five minutes after the sun had sunken beyond sight, a series of whistles began to ring the ears of the diggers. Security issued a five-minute warning for people to gather their things and return to the camp. Just like a group of disciplined soldiers, most of the diggers immediately jumped up from their positions, gathered their tools and began walking down toward the trail as if they were eager to return to camp. Many of them were probably starving after a long day of hard work at such a high altitude. Perhaps it was the American individualism of the group from Lakewood University that caused them to look at one another with such a gleaming rebellious glance. Or perhaps it was the hearty meals that they had already partaken in, but each of the six American diggers was determined to put in some overtime. Dr. Sage directed the plans.

"Okay here's the plan," said Christian Sage in a low voice a little louder than a whisper. "We will gather our tools and climb up above that rock over there on the other side of that slanted tree. The rock looks flat enough for us to lay flat on our stomachs and the branches of the tree should hide us from plain sight."

"What if they find us? Won't they expel us from the dig site?" asked Professor Cooper.

Christian replied, "I doubt it. After all, our university has given them quite a bit of money and it would do the whole project no good if exploration and discovery were discouraged."

Professor Mockens protested, "Wait a minute—what happened to Christian ethics?"

"Richard please—this is not the time for letter-of-the-law gotcha statements! Don't you want to be the first to solve this riddle?"

"Of course," answered Professor Mockens, "I just wanted to make sure that you had enough selfishness to be on board with the rest of us."

"Well," said Dr. Sage, "If trying to find a discovery that would vindicate a Biblical position and bring glory to my God is selfish, then go ahead and brand me a staunch ego-maniac. Besides, my name won't be the only one in lights if we find something, it will be all of us—our team—that will be credited for the find."

"Well put, Christian," responded Dr. Norton, Britishly. "I'm in. Is anybody not?"

"Of course not!" exclaimed Dr. Goldberg. "Quickly, let us get going to our hiding place."

One-by-one, each of the six professors from Lakewood University quietly and unnoticeably retreated to the rallying point that Dr. Sage had spoken of. The fact that darkness had begun to set in made it more difficult to be spotted—especially since most of the diggers wore dark clothing. As soon as the last evidence for non-Lakewood diggers was absent from the dig site, each of the men retrieved flash lights from their backpacks. They began back down towards the vessel, trying not to make too much noise as they went.

"So what's the plan now, Christian?" asked Dr. Saal.

Dr. Sage answered, "How about lowering me onto the top of the vessel with this rope. I'm shocked that nobody has tried this yet."

"What are you going to do then?" inquired Professor Cooper.

"I want to see if I can find an entrance into the vessel," answered Dr. Sage.

"But won't that damage the vessel? Aren't we trying to avoid that?" protested Professor Mockens.

Dr. Sage responded, "Overall, yes. I will try to minimize the damage, I promise. But if this is Noah's ark then this thing is about 450 feet long, and at this rate it won't be completely dug out of the mountainside until next year!"

Dr. Goldberg interrupted, "How can you be so sure that this *is* Noah's Ark, Dr. Sage?"

"Well," said Christian, "The height of the vessel is about forty-five feet high, which corresponds with the Biblical account nicely. Plus, the fact that we are indeed on Mount Ararat suggests the tremendous possibility that this is Noah's Ark. I mean how many large boats do you expect to find at 12,000 feet?"

With that, Professor Cooper and Dr. Saal began to lower Christian Sage onto the top of the vessel with a rope. Dr. Sage had his flashlight secured in his armpit while he held a small pick-axe and shovel with his hands. When he landed on the surface, he heard the wood crack beneath him, and he could feel the feebleness of the deck. He would have to be very careful not to break the wooden surface, or was that not the idea in the first place? Perhaps the ark could be broken into without the use of any sharp tools whatsoever. "So much for government oversight," whispered Christian to himself. "These geniuses thought to escape from the obvious and chisel their way in. Or perhaps they wished to frustrate people so they could have the ark to themselves."

"Who are you talking to, Christian?" asked Professor Mockens, as he laughed.

"Just thinking out loud," replied Dr. Sage. "Why don't you come down here and join me, Richard. The water's fine!"

"Don't mind if I do. Geoffrey, lower me down now," said Professor Mockens.

Christian carefully walked over to where Richard was being lowered down to. Dr. Sage was hoping that the weight of both of them would be enough to send them crashing down. But what if there was nothing to break their fall for the entire forty-five feet, thought Christian to himself. This could be very painful. But it was all worth it to him. This was his life, and the totality of his life was worth finding out. Besides, he sincerely trusted the Lord that he was exactly where he was supposed to be for this very purpose. Once Richard Mockens landed on the deck, there was another series of cracks in the wood and there was also a subtle sink on the surface.

"My god, Christian. We're going to fall through!" said Richard.

"That's the idea, Richard," answered Dr. Sage. "But I think we need more people aboard. Hey Cliff, you're next. Come on down."

"Okay. Here I come," said Professor Cooper, as Dr. Saal lowered him down. As soon as Cliff Cooper hit the surface, a very loud crackling sound came from the surface of the vessel.

Dr. Goldberg shouted down to them, "You guys are going to fall in. I think it's time to take a different angle to the boat. It's getting too dangerous. I'm going to lower the rope and bring you guys back up."

"That's right. This is going too far," added Dr. Norton. "I want to go back to camp. I'm tired."

Dr. Saal interrupted them, "No. Wait a minute. I've come this far, I do not want to retreat now. I'm going down next. We need to see what is inside."

"Dr. Saal, would you listen to yourself—you are going mad!" exclaimed Dr. Norton.

"No, come on Dr. Norton. Lower me now!" yelled Dr. Saal. But Dr. Norton was gathering his things to head back to camp.

"How about you, Dr. Goldberg?" pleaded Jabari Saal.

"No, I think I've had enough as well. If you all want to raid Noah's Ark, I will not be a part of it. You will go at it alone. This is getting too creepy for me now. Good night," said Geoffrey Goldberg, as he walked away from his colleagues to join Dr. Norton.

"So who's going to lower me down?" cried Dr. Saal.

"Jabari, you can scoot down the rock slowly over there. Shine your light to your left. Can you see over there—it is not as steep," Dr. Sage directed.

"Oh, yes," replied Dr. Saal. "I will try there."

With that being said, Dr. Jabari Saal slid down an adjacent rock formation, but he was still about fifteen feet above where Richard, Cliff, and Christian stood.

"Just jump now, Jabari, we'll catch you," promised Richard.

"Yeah, we got you," agreed Cliff.

Dr. Saal closed his eyes and slowly lowered himself as far as he could without falling before taking his final plunge. He fell into the arms of the three men below, and indeed they caught him. It just so happened that the weight of four men could not be supported by the ancient wood at their feet and the deck of the vessel collapsed beneath them. There was a loud crackling sound followed by a sudden crash and the men went falling down a long distance, with several other wooden structures breaking their fall as they hit the bottom of the vessel. The vessel was completely dark accompanied by an unspeakable stench that was foreign to the nostrils of modern man. Each man survived the crash but not without a few injuries. Dr. Sage had lots of scrapes and bruises, Dr. Saal dislocated his shoulder, Professor Cooper bruised his tailbone, and Professor Mockens apparently broke his left pinky finger as well as bruising his ribs. The men lay silently in the dark for several minutes without much movement at all. Dr. Saal wondered if anyone had heard them crash. Dr. Sage wondered what in the world that terrible smell was. Professor Mockens, for some reason, thought about his ex-wife. And Professor Cooper just thought about how much his butt hurt! To top it off, all four men heard was sounded like the moving of furniture within the vessel. Not one of them had their flashlight in hand, and suddenly terror filled their souls as something unknown was apparently upon them and there might not be anyone to help. Christian Sage began to pray to the Lord, silently, in the shadows of Noah's Ark.

14

DUNGEONS OF DARKNESS

Alex Sage and Kyle Sanchez were barely conscious when the large wooden vessel finally came to a sudden halt in the middle of the river. Neither of them could even estimate how long they were hanging upside down in that net. The deep, horrifying voice of the large, red-bearded giant quickly brought sober reality back into the minds of Alex and Kyle. He stared up at them and smiled malevolently. Then he began barking orders to his subordinates and pointing in several directions. One of the blonde men jumped up and snatched the net from the mast. Without looking at either Alex or Kyle, the man walked to the side of the ship and easily tossed the net to another of his mates who stood at the shoreline. It seemed as easy as tossing a pillow across the living room, although Alex and Kyle felt more like beanbags being tossed to and fro.

The large blonde who caught Kyle and Alex carried them in their net to a nearby cave. He was accompanied by two of his ship mates, who moved aside a large stone blocking the entrance to the cave. As they walked through a corridor of the dark cave, automatic motion-detecting lights sprung on, but neither Kyle nor Alex could discern the source of the light. The three giants were met by an associate—although this one had dark hair and no beard, but he was equally tall. The beardless giant led the other three into an isolated chamber where a door of infra-red light blocked the entrance. The beardless giant, who apparently acted as a prison warden, spoke to them, saying, "You two will stay here for now."

"You speak English?" asked Kyle.

"We speak every tongue," answered the warden. We have been here for thousands of your years. But no more questions. Walk through the light."

They hesitated and looked at each other.

"Now!" he screamed, with the growl of a beast, as he pushed them through the laser door.

The two of them had been pushed to the ground. They looked back from where they were pushed. The entrance to their prison cell was evidently blocked by some electronic, infra-red door. Kyle tried to run back through it, but he was zapped immediately, and he flew backward about five feet. "Kyle! Are you okay?" asked Alex.

"Man! Have you ever grabbed a live wire when you thought you turned off the breaker switch? That's what my whole body feels like right now," answered Kyle. Alex helped Kyle off of the ground and then slowly walked toward the entrance to try to catch a glimpse of landscape outside of the prison cell. He could not see anything but the infra-red light, which acted somewhat like a curtain made out of red fog. Kyle had begun to walk the other way, towards the back of the cell. "Hey, wait for me," said Alex.

The lighting inside of the cell was also red, but very dim. It was difficult to see anything with any clarity. The walls of the cell were of relatively smooth stone and there appeared to be some sort of writing engraved on some parts of the walls, though writing was indeterminable. As they walked back about 20 feet they discovered a small set of steps descending to a lower level.

"This is certainly better than a 6 X 9 cell," commented Alex.

"This must be the luxury dungeon," answered Kyle.

Just then they heard someone moan in a deep, but quiet fashion. "What was that?" whispered Kyle.

"Oh crap! I think some one is here with us," Alex answered. His assumption was confirmed with a voice, saying, "Why are you whispering?

Obviously you two have made enough noise to give away your location by now. If you wish to speak, do so firmly with confidence."

"Where are you, sir?" asked Alex, as he turned to seek the voice that seemed to be about 20 feet to his right.

"I am here," said the man, as he appeared right behind Alex and Kyle, putting his hands on their shoulders.

Kyle screamed, "Aaah! Man, you scared us. Please don't creep up on us like that, we can barely see anything."

The man replied, "My apologies. You two are of the created earth, are you not?"

Alex hesitantly answered, "Yeeaah. Where else would we be from?"

The man laughed, "You do not know where you are, do you?"

"Do you care to fill us in stranger?" answered Kyle, not so jokingly.

This stranger was not of giant stature, standing at about six feet tall, but his features were difficult to make out because he seemed to be covered in a dark substance, similar to tar. His voice was also deep, but not nearly so as the red-bearded giant. His head appeared shaved bald and there was no evidence of any clothing on him. His shape was shadowy and his eyes were dimly glowing in a yellowish-orange color. The stranger began to answer Kyle's question, "You have entered a portal into what you would call the spiritual realm—which is actually the realm of ultimate reality. This happens on occasion, but usually humans re-enter their own domain within seconds. Somehow, you have remained here, which is extremely rare."

Kyle interrupted, "Wait a minute. Aren't you human too? You look just like us."

The man answered, "I am not human. I am of the heavenly realm of the hosts of the Father Almighty. My name is Sarakiel the archangel. I only appear human to you, for if you saw me as I really am, you would faint in terror."

Alex responded, "Aren't you supposed to have like six wings and four faces or something?"

Sarakiel answered, "Very good, I see you have read your Scriptures. Is your name in the Book of Life sealed by the blood of the Son of God?"

Alex answered, "I think so. I mean, yes. Well, I know I have back-slidden off course a bit, mostly due to my mother being killed by a drunk driver too early before her time. I am having a tough time dealing with that. But I still believe in Jesus."

Sarakiel responded, "Well that is good. And I know that pain and suffering can be difficult to overcome for you humans, but I can tell you for certain that your God is abundant in grace and mercy to your kind. As long as you continue in faith you can overcome your troubles and enter into the glory of our Master."

Kyle cut in, "So what happened to your wings? And what are you doing in this dungeon if you are so powerful? How do we know that you are not with those other things out there?"

Sarakiel said to him, "You are just full of questions and doubt, are you not? It seems that you are ignorant of the war of the spiritual hosts. You see, us who are in the angelic order cannot be killed, but we do feel pain and we can be captured and incarcerated for a time. I have been captured over 75 times in my existence. And every time, my brethren come to my aide, so I am just waiting out my time. The Fallen Ones have temporarily severed my wings, which diminishes my power, and they have covered me with watery pitch so that my motions are slower than normal. But as you have witnessed, I can still move much quicker than any human. And as far as my allegiance to Yahweh, I guess you cannot be certain, but you will have to take it on faith."

Kyle turned to Alex and asked, "Who is Yahweh?"

"That's the Hebrew name for the Lord," answered Alex.

Sarakiel interrupted, "What are your names?"

"My name is Alex Sage," answered Alex. Kyle pulled Alex's shoulder back and uttered, "Sshhh. I don't trust this guy. We shouldn't give him our names."

Sarakiel interrupted again, "Oh, I know who you are now. You are the son of Christian Sage, my fellow heir of the kingdom of the Almighty. You live at 4998 Cherry Street, Oregon. I have seen you quite often." He then turned to Kyle, "And you are Kyle Sanchez of Phoenix, Arizona. You serve your nation with Alex in your Air Force."

"How did you know that?" yelled Kyle.

Sarakiel answered, "Because I am the archangel Sarakiel, an angelic being of the Second Order. My name means, 'The Command of God.' I am a protector of the heavenly realm against Satan and his Fallen Ones. I am the Chief General over the order of the Watchers. I protect children and record the sinful deeds of humanity into the divine records of the Almighty. I can instantly access billions of files on millions of humans at any time. I am a fellow servant of the one you call Christ Jesus, although I am currently a prisoner of angelic warfare. I will soon be rescued and will re-engage in this war until the Day of the Almighty when the Son of God will return to the earth and permanently establish the fullness of his kingdom. And I do know about you, Kyle Sanchez. You used to believe when you were a young child, and you still nominally acknowledge the existence of God, although you are currently unredeemed and are in rebellion against him. Ultimately, you are just as the Fallen Ones out there who have imprisoned you."

"I am not with them, sir," said Kyle, assuredly. "I may not be sure of which religion is the right one, and I might have my doubts about my Catholic upbringing, but I am not on the same side as one of those things out there."

Sarakiel responded, "I know that you believe that, but you are mistaken. Your friend Alex has his name in the Book of Life because he has trusted Jesus to save him from his sinfulness by believing that Christ died for his sins on the cross. This is the only way unto salvation—the Almighty has made no other provision for humanity. If you refuse this Lamb of God, who is Jesus, then you are still an enemy of God. Even though you do not follow after Satan directly, you are following in his footsteps by going your own way and relying upon your own understanding."

"So how did Satan fall anyway?" interrupted Alex. "The Bible does not clearly describe the event, and my dad says that scholars are in disagreement about the few parts of the Bible that allegedly speak of it."

Sarakiel replied, "Oh yes. I am well aware of the fallible interpretations of man. I could tell you the account of how it happened, but it would take some time."

"Well, I don't think we'll be going anywhere anytime soon," said Alex with a grin.

"I suppose I could tell you, but it is extremely difficult to describe in human language, even a language as exquisite as English," said Sarakiel.

"Obviously, the Almighty has permitted you to enter into this realm for his mysterious purposes, so that is the permission that I need. But I will warn you this: once I have revealed even one thing unknown to most mortals, you will be held to an extremely high level of accountability. Especially you, Kyle, because you are not yet of the Kingdom of God. Are you both in agreement?"

Alex and Kyle both nodded.

"Let us sit down over here," continued Sarakiel. Before they sat, Sarakiel gently grabbed both of their ears and withdrew drops of blood from their earlobes. He sprinkled the blood on the seat which they would soon sit.

"Why did you do that?" Kyle protested.

"This is the blood of our agreement for you to hear what I am about to share with you, answered Sarakiel. "Your blood is a witness to your accountability for this divine knowledge. So if you have two good ears, listen to what I will now share."

In the meantime, the red-bearded giant returned to a port with his vessel. He and his men dismounted and walked toward a large crater in the ground. One of them whistled and an aircraft quickly ascended to their ground level from the abyss. Three of the giants, including the red-bearded one, boarded the aircraft. This aircraft looked much like a raft with metal beams as the foundation, enclosed by a five foot steel wall. About half of the bodies of the giants were exposed over this wall, once the three men boarded. The aircraft quickly descended back down the abyss. It stopped immediately at the proper level. One of the giants reached out with his arm and pulled it back into his body. With this motion, a stone land bridge rolled out toward the aircraft to enable the giants to walk into the entrance of the cave.

The three giants entered the cave and descended down a steep stairwell that wound around the circular chamber. After about a thousand steps, they gathered around an enormous, circular moat of water, which was enclosed by a brick-like stony wall, forming somewhat of a large aquarium. The diameter of the moat was nearly 100 feet. Right above the water was a glowing orange vapor that gave off a considerable amount of light. The three giants knelt beside the body of water, prostrated themselves, and began to chant, "Tamiel, Tamiel, Tamiel, rise up Lord Tamiel. Our Pefection of our god, Tamiel."

After repeating the chant for nearly five minutes, a large being flew up from beneath the water and hovered, nearly five feet above the water. He had six wings—three on each side of his body. The upper and lower sets of wings flapped as he hovered, while the middle set wrapped around his body as to conceal it from his worshippers. The creature's eyes were red and large. Its head was disproportionately large to the size of its body. Its body was a grayish-green and it appeared to be void of feet, ears, a nose, or a mouth. The bottom of its body formed what looked like a large tail. Its tail was pierced by a large chain, which apparently kept it confined to its watery habitat.

"Why have you disturbed me, my children?" shouted the creature of the deep in his own language.

The red-bearded giant answered him, "Lord Tamiel, we have captured two humans who have entered into our domain through a portal. We have them imprisoned and we await your verdict on what we shall do with them.

"Where are they now, Aegir?" asked Tamiel.

"They are imprisoned in the Door of Demise for now," said the red-bearded giant.

"Aegir, you fool!" exclaimed Tamiel. "Are you not aware that Sarakiel is also imprisoned there?"

"Yes, my Lord," answered Aegir. "I was not expecting them. I did not know what to do with them and I did not want to bring them to you without your consent. Besides, I would not worry about Sarakiel. The Door of Demise is heavily guarded and Sarakiel's wings are severed. He can do them no good."

Tamiel responded, "Do not underestimate Michael and his legions. They have sprung him from many prisons before and we cannot afford to lose our stronghold here, for my time to be freed from my dungeon is almost upon us, and I need to have our armies strong and fortified at the time and event of my release."

"Yes, Master," said Aegir. "So what would you have me do with the humans?"

"Are they members of the Body of Christ?" asked Tamiel.

"We do not know, my Lord," answered Aegir. "We have not interrogated them yet. We want them to remain in confusion as much as possible."

"But you put them with Sarakiel?" responded Tamiel, with disgust. "Here is the strategy we will use: the worship of humans increases our strength—especially those of my Order. If I can get both of them to worship me, as you do, then the time of my release will hasten. We will now separate the two humans—bring me one of them—and we will tell them that they can return to their natural lives if they will bow down and worship me. After they worship me, they shall become your slaves for eternity and we can use them to win our war against that disgusting, two-faced, human-loving Yahweh! We will defeat him when our Lord Satan gathers all of his armies in such high numbers that even that lucky divinity on the throne cannot endure the assault!"

"Amen, Tamiel. Amen, Tamiel," chanted Aegir and his two helpers, worshipping, as Tamiel descended back into his watery abyss. The three giants went back on their way to gather one of the human prisoners for their master, Tamiel. A new phase of the battle was to begin.

15

PRIESTS OF THE UNHOLY

When Alicia Sage had regained her consciousness for the second time that day she found herself in a cage that was suspended from the ceiling. Lying down next to her was Amanda, still unconscious. Both of them had apparently been stripped of their clothing and then redressed with large leaves that wrapped around their chests and pelvic areas. From what Alicia could tell, they were in some sort of sacred sanctuary or temple of worship. The temple was lit by torches which surrounded the altar in a circular fashion. Lying on the altar, totally nude, unconscious, and with her wrists tied, was one of Alicia's classmates, Nancy Dollar. On the backdrop of the altar was a painted wall that depicted the constellations. On the top of that wall were three stone models of what looked like extraterrestrial deities that were looking down upon the altar.

At this time, the temple was absolutely empty and silent. Aside from Nancy Dollar on the altar, only Alicia and Amanda were present, locked up in their cage. There were five other cages that hung from the ceiling by some sort of vine, but the other cages were empty. The cages were in a formation as if to be observation posts to whatever type of activities occurred in this sanctuary. About five minutes after Alicia had regained her consciousness, Amanda began to stir about. Alicia was petrified. She tried to yell out to try to wake up Nancy, but nothing came out of her mouth. She looked around and could see nothing but vague objects immersed in darkness. She decided to try to wake up Amanda. She grabbed her shoulder and shook it, saying, "Amanda, Amanda, wake up. We're trapped in a cage."

Amanda opened her eyes and then rubbed them with her hands. After looking around for a few seconds, she asked Alicia, "Where are we?"

"I don't know," Alicia answered. "It looks like an ancient temple or something. Look—over there—Nancy is tied up on that altar."

"Oh my gosh! We have to get out of here!" exclaimed Amanda. "Nancy! Nancy! Wake up!"

Nancy remained asleep. Amanda's yelling did get somebody's attention, however. The sound of a large door opening echoed in the temple. Footsteps followed methodically. "It has to be two or three men," thought Alicia to herself. The footsteps continued to sound closer to them, but Alicia could still see nothing. Then suddenly, a whole row of torches that descended down the steps below the altar lit up the entire temple. Another row of torches that intersected the first row were lit immediately after. The rows of torches resembled an Egyptian ankh with the circle on top of the cross shape surrounding the actual altar. Now Alicia could clearly see two very tall men wearing priestly robes with hoods covering their heads. They both stood over Nancy's unconscious body and said a few muddled words. Next they turned around toward where Alicia and Amanda were hanging. They stood about fifty feet from the cage and then began walking toward it. One of the men removed his hood, exposing his long black hair. The other man kept his hood on, and from what Alicia could tell, it seemed as if his eyes were a glowing orange color.

When the two giants were about ten feet from the cage, the hoodless man spoke to them, "I see that you have awakened. Welcome to our world."

"How do you speak English so well?" asked Amanda.

"We are actually speaking our own language, but you hear English," the man said. "The water that you drank—it was prepared by our shaman here—this man, standing next to me. The potion allows us to communicate despite our differing tongues. It is an undoing of the curse of Babel. The potion also allows us to see into your souls so that we may know you better."

"What are you going to do to us?" Alicia interrupted.

The shaman removed his hood and his eyes lost some of their glow. The shaman's skin was either painted or naturally blue with many red wrinkles—Alicia could not tell. He was not as tall as his partner, but he still stood at about eight feet tall. Both of their robes were a dark green color and hosted a series of gems and colorful stones. The shaman's head was shaved and his many rows of teeth were a rotting yellowish color. He spoke to them, saying, "We wanted to offer you as sacrifices to the gods because you are both virgins." Both Alicia and Amanda simultaneously looked down at their leafy underwear realizing that they had been checked for their virgin status.

"It is becoming very difficult to find virgins at your age," the shaman continued, "But we did find two others: the woman on the altar and another one of your men. The gods told us that you two were sealed and protected by your God and so we cannot harm you, but we will keep you as our prisoners and make you watch our sacred ritual."

"What are you going to do with the others?" asked Alicia.

The shaman answered her, "They will be part of our ceremony. You will soon see. The ceremony will begin in two hours."

Amanda butted in, "Who are you guys?"

The taller man with the long hair answered, "My name is Hunahpu, and our shaman is Xbalque. We are priests of the gods."

Alicia questioned them further, "Where did you come from, and why are you so tall?"

The two men looked at each other for a few seconds, and Xbalque nodded at Hunahpu approvingly. Hunahpu, who stood almost ten feet tall, did have his face painted with many eyes, what looked like swastikas, and other sacred symbols including ankhs. He faced the frightened women and told them, "We are the remnant of the ancient heroes from the old world. Since you are protected by your God and you probably already know a little about us, we see no harm in sharing with you.

"When the gods—those whom you call the Fallen Ones or Nephilim--came down to this planet they lusted after many beautiful human women. They rebelled against your God because they wanted to have their own dominion on earth and to have offspring just like humans do. The Fallen Ones, who are our fathers, they planned this out carefully. They studied human behavior, reproductive organs, and what you call genetics and DNA very closely. They figured out how to possess human bodies—those who were willing to cooperate and allow them to possess their bodies—and how to intermingle their essential sky-bodies with human DNA. The gods impregnated many thousands of earth women. Some of them were taken by force, others were even willing to produce these beings—part human, part god.

"The sacred rituals that were performed, much like what you will witness this evening, were actual marriage ceremonies bringing forth the volunteering god into the human body and to enter into the bride to produce an offspring. This practice has been going on for thousands of years—even way before the Flood, although there have been many times where the practice was almost lost because of the angelic hosts of your God who is jealous of us and wishes to destroy us."

"Wait a minute," challenged Amanda. "I was always taught that the 'Sons of God' and the 'Daughters of men' were just the promised line of Seth intermarrying with the cursed women of Cain. I thought that Jesus taught that angels cannot marry or have sexual relations."

Hunahpu answered quickly, "No ,that was the misguided teaching of later men. How could Seth's sons and Cain's daughters produce giants like us? This is a gift from the gods. Your Jesus did teach correctly, but he spoke of the angels in heaven who did not need to marry because they had no need to multiply their numbers because they already dwell with your God in harmony. The Fallen Ones desire to overthrow your God and they are outnumbered two-to-one, so they need to increase their numbers and they also need to defile all aspects of the cosmos—things that are living and even things that are not.

"Like we said before, we are going to continue our sacred ceremony, and your friend, Nancy, is fortunate to have such an honor. She has kept her body pure from human defilement, and she will bring another one of us into our world."

Alicia interrupted, "You don't have to do this. You can let us go—we will go back home and we won't tell anybody about this—we promise!"

Xbalque responded, "No, our decision is final. You should be happy that we cannot use you two in our ceremony, so you will live. But you will be our prisoners and our slaves forever!"

"Why can't you let us go—we didn't hurt you!" cried Amanda.

Xbalque answered, "You intruded into our domain, so you are now ours. We are involved with a cosmic war against your evil God. He says that he created us with love and with the ability to make decisions, but he does not approve of our decisions so he punishes us. That is not good, but evil."

Alicia answered him, bravely, "If God allowed you to do whatever you wanted to then you would also be co-equals with him in exercising your sovereignty."

Xbalque angrily responded, "Shut up! You assume that your God is the creator, but there is no proof of that except what you humans have written in books. Our high god is just as wonderful as your God, and he says that all of the gods came from the same primordial waters that were in the heavens, but it just so happened that your God randomly evolved first before our high god did. However, our high god will soon evolve to such a high position not even your evil God will be able to subdue him any longer.

"That is why we wage war against your God—we believe that with proper studies of the universe—that universe which is eternal and without beginning or end, and all of that which exists is really one—we can evolve into a more prolific entity than your God can ever imagine! That is why our gods defile what is called his creation. They create the religious systems of the world, they create pleasures and pastimes that keep humans so busy that they do not even wish to care if your God really even cares about them—and he doesn't by the way!

"And those people who do seek religion, our gods create better religions that allow people to worship them in their own ways and according to their own desires—we do not discriminate or exclude anybody, or even worse—say that there is only one way to achieve the ultimate goal—immortality! Now think about it, this is much better and non-judgmental that the religion of your God and your Savior. Your God is a bigoted, hate-filled, glory-hog who cannot stand for others to make their own decisions and determine for themselves what is right and what is wrong. Your God is jealous and insecure so he makes up rules that go against how you naturally feel and then tells you that it is wrong so that you feel guilty, so that you will come crying back to him! You should recant and reject your silly, narrow-minded God and come with us—we can make you powerful beyond anything you have ever dreamed of!"

Alicia Sage could not take any more of Xbalque's blasphemies, so she cut him off, yelling as loud as she could, "Enough! In the name of Jesus Christ, I command you to be silent and to leave us alone!"

Xbalque flinched at her commanded and covered his eyes for a moment. Hunahpu looked at him and then back at the women, with his eyes bulging almost out of their sockets with stunning surprise. Xbalque regained his composure and then sneered at the women, saying, "Fine, have it your way. You will be on the losing side of this war. We are taking over the world, you know. Our gods have established strongholds over nearly every nation of the world, every religion of the world. We have control over your banking system, your educational system, politics, militaries, and many other secret groups who pull the strings in your so-called societies. Your race and your God are through—face it! We will win. Now we must be going—come on Hunahpu. We have a wedding ceremony to prepare for."

Alicia and Amanda sighed in relief, as they sat in their cage. They both were glad that the two priests were gone, but they had hoped that they were in some crazy nightmare. But it wasn't—this was real, and it was really terrible. There was no way out. At that point Alicia and Amanda decided to lay hands on one another's shoulder and begin to pray. At the sound of their prayers, Hunahpu hastily returned with a large black sheet and covered their cage like that of a bird that needed to be silenced. "There. That should do it," growled Hunahpu. Then he walked away to begin preparations for the ceremony.

16

THE MISSION OF THE SACRED SCROLLS

For a moment, Dr. Sage and his colleagues forgot all about the pain of their injuries as they were terrified at the sound of movement within the darkness of the vessel. Almost five minutes had passed since they heard any movement, but it seemed as if hours had passed and each man controlled his breathing to a minimum. Professor Mockens finally had the courage to whisper, "It was probably nothing. Just the shifting of ancient objects that have not been disturbed for a long time until we fell through the roof."

Professor Cooper responded in a normal voice, "Does anybody have their flashlight on them?"

Just then a bright, blinding light suddenly was upon them from within the vessel. Within the light was an extra-terrestrial being whose head spun around in circles but whose face seemed to be on every side of its head. Its eyes were a glowing bright blue as well as the opening of its mouth. This being had two arms where they would normally be. Above and below its arms were a pair of wings, with the bottom pair covering its mid-section and the upper pair standing upright. Its feet were not visible and it appeared as if the creature were hovering about four feet above the ground. The amazing thing was that the rest of the room remained completely dark—the light only exposed the creature. The details of the rest of its body were difficult to discern, as the light blurred the ability to describe it.

All four men screamed in terror at the sight of this being. They huddled and hugged each other like a bunch of frightened children. The creature leaned down upon them and looked at them angrily. The four professors all put their heads down and closed their eyes, hopelessly. Then they heard a loud buzzing sound for about ten seconds, and then silence again. The four men lifted up their heads and noticed the room had returned to its previous darkness. Then a more mild light spread across the spacious vessel and everything became visible. Then an old man appeared in the middle of the floor. The man was dressed in a gleaming white robe with precious stones on the breastplate. The robe covered his whole body except his forearms. His head was completely bald but his beard was long and grey. His eyes were the darkest brown known to man and his skin was a bronze color. The old man said to them, "Do not be afraid, men. You are here by divine appointment."

The four men stood speechless for about a minute, before Dr. Saal spoke to the creature, "Who are you? Are you a jihn?"

The being answered, "Sort of, but not in the Arabian sense. I am the Archangel Pravuil, the Chief of Divine Records. I record every deed of the Father Almighty and every word of the Holy Spirit of God. You—Richard!" he shouted, pointing at Professor Mockens. "Do you believe that you are having a psychotic episode now?"

"N-n-n-n—no. I don't think so," answered Richard Mockens, stuttering and trembling.

"Good," said Pravuil. "If you did I would have to destroy you on the spot. I already wanted to do that concerning your previous blasphemy, but the Lord would not permit it in his mercifulness."

Dr. Saal boldly interrupted Pravuil, saying, "Are you a messenger of Allah?"

The old man answered, "No. Allah is an ancient Arabian moon-god— he is not the Almighty. Yahweh is God and there is no other. The one called Jesus Christ is his Son and is the incarnation of your creator. The Holy Spirit is the omnipresent manifestation of God who indwells the believers of Jesus and also convicts individuals of sin and enables unbelievers to believe. The Holy Spirit dwells in two of you, as of now, but you other two are yet to be sealed by him."

Professor Cooper then asked him, "Why did you change from your previous form into a human?"

Pravuil answered, "You all seemed to be terrified at the sight of me so I manifested a more acceptable human form. I am here because you four have been chosen to participate directly in the Battle of Pneumatika."

"The battle of what?" asked Dr. Saal.

"Spiritual hosts," answered Dr. Sage. "Pneumatika is Greek for spiritual hosts, or angelic beings."

"Very good," commended Pravuil. "The relative brilliance and devotion of Christian Sage is one of the reasons you four have been chosen, but also it is by the grace of our Father primarily. For reasons unknown even to me, The Almighty has desired that you four have privileged inside information about the nature of the battle of ages that has been going on even before humanity was created. This precious ark of wood on which we stand, is one of many doorways into the angelic dimensions of creation. I am one of many of the keepers of this door. There are several such portals throughout the universe, and even many on this earth. Some of the portals even shift and are mobile, opening up on occasions depending on the positions of the stars and a variety of manipulations.

"The angelic majesties are all very much aware of these openings, whereas humanity is almost completely ignorant—and for good reason. The wickedness of the human race cannot handle the information in their current condition without totally destroying itself. Some of your great scientists, like Einstein, understood that these dimensions existed, but even he could not comprehend the logistics of them. Most of what you humans call UFOs and extra-terrestrial encounters are nothing more than angelic, inter-dimensional phenomena."

Professor Mockens asked, "Are you saying that life does not exist on other planets? I mean, there are so many of them. There must be life elsewhere."

Pravuil answered him, "The Father did not create life on other planets, although the angelic majesties do have access to the entire universe. You are thinking in terms of the human invention of naturalistic evolution. Our Creator specifically created every being for a purpose, not by random chance or mutation. Earth is the center of the universe as far as mankind is concerned. The other orbits in the universe declare God's glorious handiwork and are accessible primarily for the angelic majesties. Just because there are millions of planets does not necessitate that organic life exists on them in the way that you imagine. It takes much more than just water or oxygen—there are many factors that are needed for your type of life to exist, and no other planets in the universe have the conditions necessary for your type of life except the earth. Indeed, you live on a privileged planet, which glorifies our Creator even more so."

Dr. Saal then asked, "So what is this battle that you speak of? What do we have to do with it?"

Pravuil responded, "The battle is ultimately over the souls of humanity—at least as far as you are concerned. On a much larger scale, the very existence of the universe is at stake and over who will control the cosmos. I will soon tell you very much about how it all began, but come and walk with me over here."

The four men followed Pravuil deeper into the part of the ark that was still covered by the mountain overhead. As Pravuil walked the room lit up as if by motion-detecting light bulbs, but no light fixtures were evident. The inside of the ark was enormous, but there was not much to look at other than the walls and a few of the stalls that once kept the animals and other storage items in place which remained, but they were in very poor condition. The decay of time affected even a vessel where an inter-dimensional portal existed. But considering the many thousands of years that this vessel had been here, it was amazing that it was still kept as good as it was.

As Pravuil walked with the four men he would briefly put one of his hands on the shoulder of each man. He did this with each individual and the injuries sustained in the falling through of the ark were immediately healed at the touch of Pravuil. It was obvious that this man meant no harm to any of them. Pravuil walked them all the way to the back of the ark and into a cavern that extended through the end of the vessel. There was a small room hewn out of a rock, which the men entered into. The room had many shelves cut into the rocky wall. On these shelves were large clay jars.

Pravuil stood in the middle of the room and began to speak, "Please have a seat against the wall and I will explain much to you. You are now sitting in the oldest library that currently exists in the world. In these jars are several scrolls that date all the way back to Adam and the first generations of humans. There are several copies of each, and within the year they will be discovered by your archaeologists. Although the language is unknown to man, within a few years they will be able to understand some of the scrolls by linguistic comparison.

"However, there is an easier way that I will allow each of you to understand what is written in the scrolls. If you are to eat and ingest the scrolls, you will have a vision of what is written—much like how your technology allows you to digitally download videos and information. You will see what is written much like you would see a movie. After all, the universe is nothing more than a complex, digital simulation of the ultimate reality. The reality that humans experience is only but a portion of the ultimate reality. The angelic realm offers more of a totality of the reality, although there are even areas that are forbidden even to us—only The Almighty can access those.

"Each of you will be allowed to choose one scroll to eat and ingest. With the information that you gather, you must use it to help redeem humanity and prepare people for the coming of the end of the age. Most people will not believe you, but you must continue with your mission. You will be held responsible and accountable for the access to the private information contained in these scrolls. If you misuse or abuse your privilege, the results could be disastrous—not only for you but to all with whom you are affiliated with. If you carry out your mission properly and in obedience to God, then you will reap the heavenly rewards that await the saints of our Father. You will be allowed to choose one scroll at a time, but I will not be present—for you must choose on your own. I have put a hologram of an English label on each scroll for your convenience, so that you will be able to choose, but the archaeologists will not be able to see them. But before this I must give you the backdrop and the origin of the war that we are engaged in, for the beginning of this war is forbidden to be written on a scroll—I must tell it to you. Do you understand and do you accept this mission?"

The four men nodded. "Good," said Pravuil. "Now repeat this oath after me: 'I solemnly swear by Yahweh our Creator and by the precious blood of his Son Jesus Christ, that I fully acknowledge and accept the responsibility invested in me in the understanding of these scrolls, and the carrying out of the divine mandate of evangelism and preparing all of mankind for the conclusion of this age of human history, which will be upon us shortly. I am fully aware of the penalties and curses for abusing and misusing the information contained in these scrolls. I am also fully aware of the magnificent rewards that await me in the heavenly places for fulfilling my mission. I fully believe and accept the atoning sacrifice that Jesus Christ made on the cross for us, and that he was buried, and on the third day he was made alive again. I desire to walk with Jesus and be his disciple. I fully accept the Holy Scriptures of the Bible as the Word of God and will gladly submit to that word as the ultimate authority for my life.'"

All four men repeated the oath, although one of the four men was insincere. Pravuil did not know which one, only God knew. Pravuil then continued, "Okay, now I must tell you the origins of the Battle of Pneumatika. If you have two good ears, listen to my words." Dr. Sage and his colleagues were as attentive as they had ever been in their lives.

17

TO BOW OR NOT TO BOW?

Within the dungeon of the Door of Demise, Sarakiel began to tell Alex Sage and Kyle Sanchez about the Fall of Satan and the rebellious angelic order. "When we were first created," began Sarakiel, "The Godhead was already in perfect tri-unity—Yahweh the Father, the one you call Jesus the Lamb of God, who is the Son, and the Holy Spirit who is the perpetual witness of the Godhead to all of creation. All of the angelic order was created simultaneously along with the heavens and the earth. The heavens becoming what you call the universe—they were created by the utterance of the Godhead. It began small and expanded outward at tremendously high speeds.

"Each individual angelic host, which make up the Archangels, the Stars, the Seraphim, the Cherubim, the Ophanim, and the Watchers—we were created fully mature, ageless, sexless, and with the full potential of knowledge that is required for our distinctive order. Our heavenly gifts were ingrained in our inmost being. Thus, we have learned nothing as far as our duties are concerned and it is not possible for us to improve or deteriorate, nor do we age. We can improve our understanding in other aspects of creation though. Especially in human affairs and everything concerning what was created after us. And much like humans, we were created with emotions and free will. We can choose to obey our Father the Almighty or we can rebel. For the most part, we have maintained our holiness before our Creator. But there have been two major revolts against the Lord of Hosts. This particular order of beings, which we are dealing with here, are of the second rebellion."

Kyle Sanchez chimed in, "You said when you were created that God already existed in perfect unity. Who created God then and how did he become as he is now?"

Sarakiel frowned at Kyle and answered, "You humans think you are so intelligent with your criticism, but your thinking is severely flawed. God is eternal—much more so than the angelic orders are. God did not begin to exist nor will he cease to exist. Unlike myself, he cannot learn anything nor can he be surprised by choices made by created beings. It is unfathomable for a created being to comprehend a being without beginning or end, so therefore it is used as an excuse not to believe the obvious. God exists outside of time or space and this is inherently necessary for him to create in the first place. He is not part of his own creation, but he can and does intervene constantly."

Just as Sarakiel finished his last sentence, the sound of footsteps entered the corridor outside of the cell. The sound of the red-bearded giant speaking to the beardless warden echoed throughout the corridor. "I must vanish," Sarakiel told Alex and Kyle. "Have faith and do not listen to them. May the peace of The Almighty be with you."

Aegir, the red-bearded giant, waved his hand and the infra-red force field disappeared from the entrance of the cell. The warden walked in and grabbed Kyle by the arm and walked him out. Aegir did likewise with Alex, as he prayed silently in his head. Each giant took their prisoner in opposite directions. Aegir walked with Alex about fifty feet before he brought him to an isolated room with a table in the middle of the room. Aegir brought Alex to the table and ordered him to sit on a flat stone that was to be used like a short chair. Then Aegir left Alex alone sitting at the table, and as Aegir left the room another infra-red laser light blocked the entrance to that cell. This cell appeared much smaller than the one he was previously in, but the dim red glowing left the cell just as dark.

Alex was extremely terrified now. He knew that what Sarakiel had told him was real, and suddenly his childhood faith had returned to him. He now began to pray out loud, "God, I'm sorry for doubting you. I know that you took my mother for a reason, and I do want to be reunited with her again someday. I put my complete trust in you and I pray that it is your will that I would be delivered out of this demonic hell-hole. In Jesus' name I pray, Amen."

Just as Alex finished his prayer, the room filled with light, and a beautiful woman walked through the walls. Her hair was golden and several sparkling jewels were adorned across the top of her chest. She wore a golden dress which covered her body entirely. Her eyes were a lively purple and her lips were also purple. In her hands she brought a plate full of delicious looking fruit—a medley of every fruit imaginable. She put the plate on the table and spoke to Alex, saying, "Your prayer has been heard and I am here to deliver you. My name is Ran and I am an angel of God. I have brought you something to eat to strengthen you. Please eat."

Alex was extremely hungry, but he wasn't sure about this woman. Although she did come immediately after his prayer, he never heard of angels being women in the Bible. The name 'Ran' also seemed to be a strange name for one of God's angels. Alex thought that surely this must be a test from God to see if his prior confession and claim to trust was authentic. Alex told Ran, "No thank you, I'm not hungry."

Ran replied, "Okay, you don't have to eat if you don't want to." She picked up a peach and began to eat it right in front of Alex's face. "Mmmm, it sure is tasty. You're missing out. So Alex, I heard your prayer and I want to reunite you with your mother—she's here with us you know."

Alex answered, "Well, where am I? I know this is not heaven and that's where my mother would be, and those things out there are demonic. I don't get it."

Ran responded, "The spiritual realm is a difficult thing for you to understand, but I am here to deliver you. I can show you your mother *and* I can help you get back home. How does that sound?"

"It *sounds* good," said Alex, "But how do I know that you're not with those giants out there? I mean how can I know for sure that you are from God?"

"Do I look evil to you?" asked Ran. "I am not a giant, and you can see how beautiful I am. Demonic beings are ugly and gruesome, not beings of light and as beautiful as I am."

"I don't know about that," replied Alex. "I think I remember a passage of Scripture that says that Satan masquerades as an angel of light in order to deceive people, and that he has ministers that do likewise."

Ran answered a bit more passionately now, "I can assure you that I do not serve Satan. Look over there—I can see your mother coming now."

Alex turned around and saw a vision of another woman descending from a light in the ceiling. His mother indeed appeared before him and smiled. She put her hand on his chin and said to him, "Everything is okay Alex. I'm having a great time here in heaven. Just do what the angel says and you can return home and I will come and visit you when you get there. I love you son."

"I love you too, Mom," answered Alex, now trying not to cry.

Alex's mother said to him, "I must go back to my mansion in heaven now, but just do what Ran says to, okay? I will watch over you and everything will be all right."

Alex nodded, and his mother ascended back into the light in the ceiling and then she disappeared along with the light. Alex's attention returned to Ran again. He noticed that the food was gone now. "So are you ready to get back home now?" asked Ran.

"Yes," answered Alex. "What do I do?"

Ran said to him, "I must take you to my superior angel, Tamiel. You must pay a tribute to him by bowing and singing to him. After that I will take you back home to Oregon."

Now Alex knew for sure that this was a satanic deception. If there is one thing that Alex remembered about the Bible is that only God can be worshipped and bowed down to—not even the angels could receive worship from humans. Alex knew he had to buy some time somehow, so he inquired further, saying, "Why can't Tamiel come to me as you have?"

Ran answered him, "Tamiel is a very busy angel and he is stationed elsewhere. It will not take long to take you to him. Are you ready?"

"No, I've changed my mind," replied Alex. "I kind of like it here, I think I will stay a while."

Ran's facial expression instantly became unfriendly for a split second and then became somewhat exotic. She licked her lips and said to Alex, "Oooh, Alex. You sure are a brave soldier! Listen: I don't think we need to see Tamiel after all. I think I can take you home all by myself."

Ran approached Alex seductively and sat on the table above him. She untied her hair that was up in a bun, and her golden hair fell down near her waist. She removed her top, exposing her whole chest to Alex. "Don't be afraid, Alex. I'm real—go ahead and touch me and I'll take you home," said Ran as she leaned down to kiss Alex, who was still seated on his stool.

Alex's heart was beating a million times per second, as he was terrified and excited at the same time. He knew what he had to do, as he shouted, "No!" He pushed her face away from his with his hand. "In the name of Jesus Christ, get away from me you devil!"

Ran's beautiful appearance instantaneously transformed into a hideous, reptilian figure, with large fangs, and she hissed at him. "You will surely perish here Alex Sage!" she growled at him, and then she disappeared. The room returned as it was before with the infra-red force field blocking the entrance of the room. The dim red light that partially illumined the cell was all that Alex could see. There was now complete silence. He had passed the test, and it was an extremely difficult test indeed.

Meanwhile, the beardless warden had escorted Kyle to a room similar to that of Alex. He was also seated at a table, and a woman also appeared to him with a plate of fruit medley. "Greetings, Kyle! My name is Bara and I am an angel of the most high god. I have brought you delicious fruit to eat. Please feel free."

"Thank you," responded Kyle, as he thought nothing of it. He hadn't eaten anything for almost a day now, and he was quite hungry. "Are you one of the good angels or one of the bad angels?" asked Kyle, as he bit into an apple.

Bara giggled and untied her long red hair, which fell at her waist, as she sat on the table next to the plate of fruit. "Do I look like an evil angel?" asked Bara, as she stroked her hair. "I have come to rescue you from this awful place. You do want to go back home, right?"

"Yes!" answered Kyle. "But how do I know that you're not with those giants out there? Sarakiel told me not to believe anything that is told to us."

Bara replied to him, "We're with Sarakiel. We have already rescued him and he is outside waiting for us. We need you to eat so you can be strengthened. Then we must go pay tribute to another angel, Tamiel, who is also a prisoner here. We need to bow to him and sing him a song so that he may be released and then we can go home."

"What about the giants?" Kyle asked her. "Won't they be out there waiting for us?"

Bara answered him, "We have already subdued the giants. They are tied up for the moment, so you must quickly eat and then come with me." She smiled at Kyle and stroked his young face with her soft hand. Kyle blushed and then grabbed a cluster of grapes and said, "Okay, let's go. I can eat on the way."

"Very good," replied Bara. "Come right this way."

Bara waved her hand and the infra-red force field vanished. She took Kyle by the hand and led him to the crater in the earth. "Where's my friend Alex?" asked Kyle, with a mouth full of grapes.

"He's coming too," answered Bara. "Another angel has already rescued him and he is probably already paying tribute to Tamiel as we speak."

"Okay, good," said Kyle.

They both stepped aboard the elevator-type aircraft that led them down into the abyss. The craft hastily sped down unto the level where Tamiel was chained to his holding tank. Bara knelt beside the moat of water where Tamiel dwelt beneath. She lit two large candles which stood on each side of Bara and Kyle. Bara instructed Kyle to kneel beside her and to repeat her chant after her, "Tamiel, Tamiel. Oh come Lord Tamiel—oh perfection of god."

After three consecutive mantras, Tamiel burst upward out of the water and was hovering with his wings. His skin was a glowing orange color and he had a satisfied grin on his face. He said to Bara and Kyle, "I am so glad that you are here to rescue me. Please, sing me a song of tribute, a hymn of praise so that I can be released from this prison."

With this, Bara grabbed hold of Kyle's hand and instructed him, "Okay, Kyle, repeat and sing after me:

Oh glorious Tamiel! Oh glorious Tamiel!

Perfection of god! Pefection of god!

Conductor of the deep, Watcher of the sheep.

How many maidens do you seek?

Oh their souls do you keep!

Teacher of the sun,

Keeper of medi-cine,

Who summons the divine,

To capture human kind,

Oh Tamiel, Oh Tamiel

Oh perfection of god!

Kyle had sung the song in harmony with Bara, and somehow there was background music of many harps, flutes, and drums. Kyle had felt all right about singing until he repeated the part about capturing human kind. This made him feel very nervous, as if he had been deceived. Tamiel had thoroughly enjoyed the hymn, and at the song's finish, there was a standing ovation from many of the giants who had appeared behind Bara and Kyle—many of which held musical instruments.

Tamiel's wings fluttered about at high speed, as he said to Bara and Kyle, "Thank you for that marvelous tribute of praise and worship. My strength is almost full now and my time of release is imminent. I do not know how you got here, Kyle, but you are now officially part of our kingdom. Welcome home, son."

Tamiel laughed in an evil manner and the surrounding giants laughed with him. Just then two large giants grabbed the arms of Kyle Sanchez and dragged him away from Bara, who blew Kyle a kiss as he left her. Kyle shouted in horror, "No! No! You tricked me! It's not fair! Let me go!"

The two giants brought Kyle to Aegir who slit Kyle's throat with a dagger while another giant captured Kyle's blood in a chalice. Kyle's physical body instantly died, while his spirit tried to ascend up and out of the cavern to escape but there were other evil spirits there waiting for him. They captured Kyle's spirit and took him to an aircraft that was waiting beside the moat of Tamiel.

Aegir spoke to Tamiel, "Lord, we will transfer his spirit to the abode of transformation so that he will become our slave, just as you instructed. We have kept his blood in this chalice for a sacrificial rite in the near future."

"Good," applauded Tamiel. "The time is almost near—I can feel it!" A thunderous howl followed Tamiel's statement—even Alex could hear the loud shouts and feel the vibrations. He never felt so alone in his life—but yet he knew that the peace of the Lord was with him and that things would work out for his benefit. He just didn't know how.

18

THE RITES OF THE DAMNED

Alicia and Amanda began to hear numerous footsteps entering into the temple. Several conversations were being had, although none of them were discernible to either of the American women. Soon a series of drums began to pound the atmosphere, followed by several different sounding flutes and piccolos. Then the harpists began to play, followed by a stringed instrument that was foreign to the ears of Alicia Sage. It was obvious that the temple was filling up with people and they were being entertained by the music and some singing as well. It sounded like there was some dancing going on as well, and then a widespread clapping that was in sync with the drums.

All of the celebration and commotion came to a complete halt when a loud gong rang out three times. Other than the echo of the third gong in the temple, there was complete silence. Two large men proceeded to remove the large, black sheet from over Alicia and Amanda's cage. Alicia could now see everything. The other cages that were suspended from the ceiling now contained the rest of her classmates, minus Nancy and Steve, but they were unaware of Alicia and Amanda—their eyes were fixed on the ankh-formation of torches surrounding the altar. At the moment, the altar was vacant. "What happened to Nancy?" whispered Amanda. Alicia shrugged her shoulders. She did not want to make a sound in fear of gaining unwanted attention.

Behind the altar and tied to a wooden cross, the lifeless body of Virgil hung. In blood, there were several occult symbols painted on his body, including the symbol of the yin and the yang on his forehead. Xbalque, the head shaman, ascended up the steps and stood in front of the altar. He began to speak, "Welcome my brothers and sisters. Tonight we have a special occasion in which we will unite the bodies of one of our gods and with a human virgin. The stars and the planets are in perfect position, and the proper intercession will be made. First we will partake in our sacrificial mass of human flesh."

Xbalque pointed back toward Virgil and suddenly six priests or perhaps "altar boys" (for they were smaller in stature) took Virgil's body down from the cross and began to cut the flesh from his bones and poured what remained of his blood into chalices. Xbalque continued, "While we await the body to be broken, we will have our sister Copil play a song on her flute. Copil, please come forth."

Copil stood in front of the altar and began to play. Again, the drums took rhythm and the people began to clap in unison. Within two minutes, some people began to chant strange mantras while stomping their feet and dancing in place. When Copil finished her song, she received a standing ovation and the people began to shout and howl. By that time, enough of Virgil's body had been cut up to begin the unholy mass. Xbalque returned to the front of the altar, replacing Copil. This time Hunahpu joined him at his side. Xbalque began the ceremony, "Let us pray." He then chanted the "Our Father" prayer backwards, and finished the prayer by saying, "We shall do what we will: this is the whole of our law. Amen." At the closing of the prayer, Xbalque held pieces of Virgil's flesh in a bowl and Hunahpu held the chalice of his blood. The people—giants, men, women, and children—lined up to eat Virgil's flesh and to drink his blood. As they lined up and partook of the mass, a soloist strummed the harp in an eerie fashion.

When the last person partook of the wicked mass, Xbalque and Hunahpu partook of the body and blood themselves, kissed each other on the mouth, and then set the bowl and the chalice beneath the altar. At that moment, a blast of thunder erupted and a lightning bolt touched the ground just outside of the temple, causing a flash of light to illuminate the temple through the openings in the roof. At this point, one of the giants pulled Steve by a chain that was around his neck into the altar area. Hunahpu removed the collar from Steve's neck and forced him to crawl upon the altar on his hands and knees, facing the crowd. Steve seemed like he was in a catatonic trance. Xbalque shouted out, "Behold—the male virgin of sacrifice!" The crowd responded by roaring and howling along with their applause.

The entire orchestra of music began to play again with the crowd clapping and dancing in place with the beat of the drums. Hunahpu then walked behind the altar and tore Steve's clothes off with a dagger. Then Hunahpu removed his robe and his loincloth and spread a substance on his genitals. Not long after, Hunahpu growled loudly and shouted to the heavens and then violated Steve. Amanda and Alicia could not bear to watch their friend be tortured and who knew what else. When Hunahpu was finished, he put his loincloth and his priestly robe back on. The crowd was now in a frenzy, and some of them were even cutting themselves with knives and slamming their bodies into one another.

This frenzy was again interrupted by three gongs, and again there was silence. Xbalque stood in front of Steve, who was now laying flat on his belly on the altar and Hunahpu was still behind him, fully dressed. Xbalque now held in his hand a long pointed stick. He lifted his eyes to the sky and pointed his stick upwards, saying, "Abigrael! Oh Abigrael! I summon thee to this sacred ritual and offer unto thee the blood of this virgin male. I now call from the gods four witnesses: Ixchel, for wind. Xquil, for fire. Cihuacoatil, for soil. And Tezcatlipoca, for water."

At each of these names, Xbalque pointed to each of the four cardinal directions respectively with his wand. When he finished, he knelt down in front of the altar, looked again to the sky, and then took a dagger from his belt, and slit Steve's throat. He collected his blood in a different chalice—this one was made of shiny brass, whereas the one used for Virgil's blood was made of clay. The altar boys then took six of the torches that surrounded the altar and moved them back about 15 feet. Xbalque gave the brazen chalice to Hunahpu, who proceeded to use Steve's blood to paint an inverted pentagram around the altar. When Steve's body was well-drained from much of its blood, it was his body that was now tied to the wooden cross on the backdrop, against the painting of the constellations.

The same giant that had brought Steve to the altar was now bringing Nancy Dollar on stage. Nancy was dressed in an all-white robe with a wreath of leaves in her hair. Her face was painted with heavy make-up, which also included some occult symbols. Around her neck was a golden ankh. Unlike Steve, she was not catatonic. She even resisted somewhat, until a native pointed a spear at her as she walked down the center aisle. After that, she submitted, although with a petrified look on her face. At this time, the rest of Alicia's classmates were released from their cages and were escorted onto the altar stage. Each of them laid down flat on their backs, and they also seemed catatonic. Nancy was now laying flat on her back on the altar, with Hunahpu standing behind her head, and Xbalque standing in front of her feet, facing the crowd.

Xbalque now knelt in front of the altar again, saying, "I now offer my prayer of silence." This was followed by about a minute of silence where each person bowed their heads. Alicia also prayed, "Lord Jesus, please come and deliver us from this evil." Amanda joined her in prayer again.

Xbalque now stood up and again looked to the heavens, saying, "Oh Abigrael, I humbly beseech thee—the time is almost upon us. Which name should I call upon from the people to offer his body to the gods and create a new offspring? Who should be joined with this woman to form an inter-terrestrial marriage?" His question was followed by another blast of thunder, and then lightning, which illuminated the temple. Xbalque then turned his face to the crowd and yelled, "I call upon Nahual! Nahual— please come forth and enter into the sacrament of this marriage."

Nahual, who looked no older than 17 years old, walked up to Xbalque and stood beside him facing Nancy. Again, Xbalque faced the sky and said, "Abigrael, please send forth Itzamna. I call upon the god Itzamna!" Then the music started up again, full-blast. The crowd began chanting, "It-zam-na! It-zam-na! It-zam-na!" to the beat of the drums. They began to cut themselves with knives again and dancing in a frenzy. Just then, a loud humming sound came from up above the temple and bright lights shone down upon the altar from the sky window. Xbalque then shouted over the music and the humming sound from above, "Oh Itzamna! Majestic is your beauty, you have knowledge without end, awesome is your power, and merciful to your subjects are you forever and for eternity! Itzamna— thee—thee do I invoke! Behold! I am Yesterday, Today, and the brother of Tomorrow! Therefore, in all things I do obey and you shall come forth from my word."

A series of lights descended upon Nahual as he lifted his hands up. He then turned to the crowd, and his facial expressions transformed to that of an angry animal! As much as Alicia and Amanda did not wish to look, they were captivated by what was going on and could not help themselves. Nahual's eyes then turned bright red, and his long, straight hair began to curl up. His muscles began to bulge out of his body and then he arched his back in a manner that is not possible for normal people. He began to foam at the mouth for a moment before he wiped it with his forearm. Again he turned toward the altar, lifted up his head and growled to the sky. He turned back around to the crowd and yelled, "Behold! He is in me, and I in him! Mine is the radiance, wherein Lucifer floats over the firmament. I travel upon high! I tread upon the firmament of Amun-Ra! I raise a flashing flame, with the lightning of my eye! Ever rushing on, in the splendor of the sun glorified in Lucifer who gives life to the gods who dwell in the heavens and upon the Nephilim who give life to the dwellers of the earth!"

With that last statement, Xbalque passed out unconscious. Several orbs of light began to fill the room. Alicia and Amanda now closed their eyes and held each other tight, yelling to each other, "Don't look! Don't look! God save us!"

The frenzied crowd was even more out of control now, as several demons entered into their bodies. Two of the altar boys held the frantic Nancy down on the altar as she was now screaming. Nahual turned to Nancy and ripped the robe off of Nancy and began to rape her, while the music continued to drive the demonic frenzy. Even the other American students who were lying on stage were involved in the mass-orgy of demon-possessed Peruvian natives—giants, men, women, and children. The body of Steve was torn down and eaten by hand and mouth. Even with their eyes closed, Alicia and Amanda spewed vomit outside of their cage and their vomit was consumed by a few people of the crowd as they danced around naked. "How are we going to escape this," though Alicia to herself. "If we are truly protected, why have we witnessed this? What is going to happen to us?" It was not long before Alicia and Amanda passed out from shock and exhaustion.

19

A CREATIVE EXPLANATION

After Dr. Christian Sage and his three colleagues had finished swearing their oaths, they all sat on the ground as Pravuil began to tell them about how the Battle of Pneumatika came about. Pravuil stroked his long, gray beard as he also sat on the ground of the ancient library. He looked upward and spoke an angelic dialect, which apparently was a prayer of some sort. Then he returned his gaze upon the four men and spoke to them, "Let me begin by telling you that things in the heavenly realm work differently than they do in the earthly realm. For instance, on earth you humans are bound by time and space, whereas time and space function very differently for us. For our Creator time is a non-category essentially, although he operates within time and occasionally enters into it. This is difficult for the human mind to fathom and I will try to explain things to you in the best way possible.

"In the beginning, when the Godhead began to create, he brought what you call *matter* into existence all at once, albeit in forms that are very different than they are presently. When God created the *heavens*, it included all of the heavenly beings simultaneously—including myself. We were all created with full maturity, our personalities, and our potential understanding and ability, although we continue to increase our skills and knowledge to this very day. All of the orbiting stars and planets existed but were not visible as they now are because light did not exist immediately. When we were created, the Godhead already was—and we dwelt with him in the angelic dimensions only at that time.

"There was great heavenly fellowship between all of the angelic orders, even though we were without sight at that time, for there was not yet light. We could hear each other, and we could hear the discussions of the Godhead concerning us. Our Father foretold us all that he was going to do concerning creation and explained to us what all of our original duties were to consist of. He also spoke to us concerning our personal holiness and that we were to remain obedient to his commands and decrees, despite having the ability to rebel against him if we so chose. He told us that the moment that we sinned against him that we would be condemned to die and expelled from our proper habitation. Many of us were immediately concerned with the implications for our freedom of volition—this would mean that potentially much evil could result from the goodness of God's creation and ordination of being agents of holy morality. But the Son of God, knowing our thoughts explained that without the ability to choose evil and to be tested according to this ability, then true heavenly virtue, goodness and morality could not exist in any meaningful way and that there could not be such virtues as love and adoration, which results in worship. Although we could hear the words of our Father, we did not understand anything yet, because we had not vision without light.

"While Yahweh was explaining much to us at this juncture, he had sent his Holy Spirit to inspect the dark, formless mass of the earth and to prepare it for its proper formation. When the Holy Spirit returned unto the Father, we heard a great rumbling of sound. Then we heard the most lovely of all voices imagined, say, 'Let there be light!" Then immediately the light of the God himself shone upon all of us, and then our individual lights also shone forth. We could see the glory of the Godhead in perfect tri-unity, and we could also see each other. Suddenly, everything that the Almighty had told us made complete sense because we had vision now— our minds were enlightened. The Godhead then distinguished the light apart from the dark—the former was declared, 'Good'. Then immediately, one of the most beautiful of the angels, named Lucifer, began to play the musical instruments that were created as a part of his being, and he led us in worship, singing, 'Holy, holy, holy is our Creator and blessed is his name forever!' Many others began to play instruments and to sing, as well.

All of this occurred in a time period, which in human terms, is called, 'The First Day.'"

Professor Clifford Cooper interjected politely, asking, "Do you mean that the *days* of Genesis were not literal days? How are we to understand this?"

Pravuil promptly answered, "Remember, the sun and the other heavenly lights had not been given their proper function as intended yet. The days of Genesis 1 do not represent what you call geological time periods, nor were they literal 24-hour days as you understand them. Rather, the human 'week' is modeled after what you humans call, 'Functional ontology.' Functional ontology refers to each aspect of creation being officially 'created' only after its function was declared and given by God. Since time is relative to many physical forces, such as gravity and reference points of heavenly orbits, it would be impossible to precisely describe the time of the Genesis 1 days in a way that is comprehensible to humans. It is also important to understand—and many Western Christians seem ignorant of this—that the proper interpretation of the Scriptures must always be primarily understood from the perspective of the original, intended human audience. The ancient Near Eastern audience did not view creation in the same way modern Westerners do, namely matter being created out of nothing in a chronological sequence. Ancient Near Eastern peoples understood something being created only if it had a purposeful function. Therefore, when our Holy Father gave each part of creation its function—and remember, these were already created materially—it was seen by the original audience as 'created'. If something did not have purpose or was disorderly, it was considered not a part of the creation—at least in the divine sense. So all of the modern Western theories of Genesis 1 are typically way off because they begin with an inappropriate hermeneutic with many flawed assumptions. Are there any more questions regarding this matter?" asked Pravuil.

Everybody simultaneously shook their heads, as the looks on their faces were utterly in awe, with their jaws hanging low and their mouths open. "Good," Pravuil said. "I shall continue: the Godhead continued to create and to mold the universe into its intended form. At the next command of our Creator, the waters of the sky were separated from the waters of the earth, thus creating distinct atmospheric conditions for the earth, and divisions of the heavens in what you call 'outer space' and also in the angelic dimensions. In your Genesis, Day 2 seems somewhat simplistic, but let me tell you, the divisions of the heavenly dimensions and the separation of waters are quite exquisite and detailed for those of us who know them. It is also important to know that whatever The Almighty created for you humans, there is a correspondence of that creation in the angelic realm. Our dimensions are like a reverse negative, equivalent to a digital mirroring of your world. When God created light to be seen on earth, that light is even more impressive and radiant to us. When he created the waters for you, the waters that existed and still exist to some extent, were evermore fabulous than anything fathomable to the human mind. And so it became for everything that the Godhead created—that is why the heavenly dimensions are the ultimate reality compared to what The Almighty gave to humans for their stewardship.

"Then the Creator made an earthly distinction between the oceans and the land. The earth, as many humans have postulated, was originally one continent, so there was only one distinction. On the dry land, the seeds of the earth were caused to sprout its vegetation at the command of the Creator. This did not happen immediately, but over your human time. That is why it is written in your Genesis chapter two, verse five that no bush had sprouted in the field yet. You see, Genesis 1 was written primarily about function and not chronology. Genesis 2 is actually closer to what you humans call, 'chronology' than Genesis 1 is, but that is not the entire focus either. Anyhow, Yahweh also caused the earth to tremble so that mountains could be uplifted over time. These too began to sprout vegetation and trees. Eventually, the earth was beautifully decorated with greenery, flowery, and luscious food to eat, but some of this happened rather suddenly after Adam was created—again, detailed in your Genesis 2. Simultaneously, the angelic vegetation of the spiritual dimensions also sprouted. We all had a magnificent feast of heavenly fruits, vegetables, and bread. Lucifer and his musicians led the worship of our feast. Everything that was created, at that point, was exceedingly good, and our Father declared it so.

"My personal favorite part of creation came on your Day 4—the luminaries!" shouted Pravuil, with an obvious look of excitement on his face. "For the first time, a distinguishable night and day was apparent from an earthly perspective. This was for the purpose of telling time for the future humans. You see, this part of creation chronologically preceded the creation of vegetation or any creature. Yahweh created new light that emanated from what you call stars. Essentially, this light is merely a dim reflection of *the* light, namely the Son of God for you humans. Yahweh moved a distant star and brought it forth to govern the day of your planet. Your moon was formed by a piece of floating space debris that was reserved for that very moment. This would enable you to discern monthly cycles of time. Only later would you humans discover the true nature of the sun in which you could accurately determine annual cycles of time. So through your sun, moon, and the stars of the galaxy, you humans could determine the times and seasons, which would become an important point of reference for your activities and for your observations of the creation."

At this, Richard Mockens could be silent no more. He politely interrupted, "Why would God create the sun *after* he created light? I've always been mystified over this?"

Pravuil answered, "Morally speaking, he did this so that humans would understand that light does not ultimately come from the sun, but rather from God himself. Our Father did not desire for you humans to worship the sun as the source of light and life so he purposely waited for a period of time to create the luminaries, or rather give them their functions. The error of your assumption, again, is that you are assuming that the Genesis audience thought scientifically and chronologically as you modern Westerners do. You are thinking in terms of material creation rather than functional. Back to the theological illustration though, after the Fall of Humanity humans wanted to escape their moral accountability to their Creator and wished to rule over themselves, thus they created other systems of worship to suit their fallen desires. But Yahweh did preserve a remnant of true followers that would preserve the true records of history, and this special occasion is proof of that and you all are also called to become a part of God's remnant people."

At this point, Christian Sage asked a question: "How do angels tell time?"

Pravuil responded by saying, "The time that we keep is largely ingrained in our created being. We can also determine times based on our knowledge of all of the stars in the universe, but it is very complex and incomprehensible to humans at this point. Just know that we have an internal clock, if you will, that lets us know exactly when to execute the commands of our Father.

"With the creation and placement of the rest of the luminaries of the universe, the Godhead also established the portals of angelic travel according to specific places on the stars and planets and throughout the spaces of the universe. Black holes would be one example, but those did not exist originally. They came about after the Fall of the Angelic Majesties. But in the meantime, we hosts of The Almighty were having another celebratory banquet in our Father's honor. Again, Lucifer and the musicians led the worship of the Godhead, and the rest of us joined in the singing and dancing. We moved about freely throughout the universe and throughout the heavenly dimensions. We began to create chariots, vessels, and aerodynamic forms of travel. We did this to increase our speed and as a form of artistic beauty! We were able to take substances from the planets, moons, comets, asteroids, and stars and make these vehicles. The time of angelic exploration, study, and experimentation was officially underway. Yahweh also assigned each of us a stewardship of certain parts of the universe. And since the universe has been expanding since the creation, our jurisdiction has also expanded. The fact that several of us are no longer serving our Father has also increased the jurisdiction of each one of us. The Fallen Ones are always trying to steal the dominion of the faithful.

"Anyhow, as described during your Day 5, after a period of time the Godhead again began to create. All sea creatures, birds, and other creatures that fly were created by the word of the Creator's mouth. The Godhead also spoke to them and commanded them to procreate and fill the earth. And again, our Lord determined that his creation was good. This is important because in the beginning, there was no death. Every creature was a vegetarian and peaceful by nature."

With that being said, Richard Mockens interjected, "Wait a minute. Are you telling me that carnivorous creatures like lions and great white sharks did not eat other animals? How is that possible?"

Pravuil answered, "Yes. Even the great cats and sea monsters—and even dragons—ate from the produce of the earth."

Professor Mockens asked again, "Then why do some animals have canine teeth? Isn't that proof of adaptation?"

Pravuil frowned at Richard, and then replied, "One major obstacle that many people have to believing the truth is that they assume that things have always been as they are presently. One of your philosophers, posing as a scientist, coined the phrase, 'The present is the key to the past.' In actuality, the past is the key to the present! Every adaptation of every living thing—including plant life—was built in by the Creator. Remember, God has complete foreknowledge and he foresaw everything that would eventually happen, even evil. So yes, all creatures were originally herbivores and that should not be problematic because even large carnivores today are capable of eating vegetation. This is just an excuse that is posed by mockers and skeptics."

Professor Cooper smiled and looked around at his colleagues. Then Dr. Jabari Saal chimed in, "You said something about dragons? Were they real?"

"Yes," Pravuil responded. "What you call dinosaurs were first called dragons by you humans. And yes, they did live alongside humans up until only a few hundred human years ago. This is a well-documented fact, but the scoffers and mockers try to downplay this as fantasy."

Dr. Saal then asked, "When did the creatures begin to eat meat then?"

Pravuil replied, "Death came about as a result of the sin and rebellion of humanity, as a curse. The entire creation began to gradually become un-done and the good environment became polluted with evil, causing death. In fact, many of us hosts were surprised that our Father did not just destroy most of it and start over, but he has such a love for you that is unfathom-able. He is truly the God of redemption. But I do not wish to get ahead of myself—I must tell you how the war began."

20

THE GIANT ESCAPE

An eerie silence was felt by Alex Sage, as he sat quietly in his cell, praying. Suddenly, the room became very cold. The drop in temperature was accompanied by a foul stench—something like a mixture of blood and rotten eggs. Then Alex heard footsteps. It was Aegir, the red-bearded giant. He waved his hand and the infra-red force field disappeared from the entrance of the cell. Aegir's eyes began to give off a red glow as he approached Alex inside of the cell. "Your friend Kyle is now with us," he said in a very deep and disturbing voice. "If you want to be freed, you must come and worship Tamiel as well."

Alex noticed a bit of splattered blood on Aegir's arm. "You've killed him, haven't you?" shouted Alex. "Well, you're going to have to kill me too because I refuse to worship you evil devils!"

"Have it your way," replied Aegir. He pulled out his dagger and grabbed Alex by the hair to bring his head closer to the dagger. Alex closed his eyes and uttered, "Lord Jesus, into your hands I commit my spirit."

With those words, Aegir let go of Alex's head and put his dagger back into his waistband. "Oh, now you believe in him all of the sudden?" mocked Aegir, sarcastically. "Well he is not here with us and you have no hope of escape. He doesn't care about you either, otherwise he would have rescued you by now, right? Or maybe he is too weak to do it? Either way, you have no hope. You might as well join us in our revolution. We will overturn the decrees of your evil god, for we are gaining in strength and numbers. We also have much influence over the whole world. Face it: you cannot win! The entire planet is joining us in our rebellion against your god. So even if you were to return to your normal dimension, you will become an outcast and our followers will reject you and persecute you. It's much easier to just join us, for we can grant you a much better life than what is in store for you."

Alex replied, "You guys are a bunch of liars! Whatever temporary benefits that you can give me will cost me my soul in the end, so it's not worth it."

"No!" shouted Aegir. "We will win! Our god is becoming much more powerful by the minute and we will overcome that bigoted Yahweh!"

Just then, a loud, thunderous sound came from up above. Both Alex and Aegir looked up toward the ceiling. As a few seconds passed, the sound became more evident. It sounded like a roar of rushing water—or even an ocean—washing over the surface level of this cave system. Aegir growled, and a facial expression that was even more sinister overtook his usual gaze. "I will be back," he told Alex, angrily. Aegir walked quickly out of the cell, and as soon as he was in the corridor Alex could hear him running. Then Alex heard other footsteps running, and then much shouting, as the environment grew very chaotic.

Several of the giants were now gathered at the surface level of their domain. Many of them had their small portable aircrafts. They were armed with their crossbows and shooting into the sky. The object they were shooting at was a round, wheel-like aircraft that moved in a circular fashion. This aircraft hovered about 200 feet above the ground level, and was a glowing orange color. After the giants began shooting at the craft with their laser-like arrows, the bottom of the large aircraft opened up and several creatures descended upon them in small, portable aircrafts of their own. They returned fire with their own laser-like weapons of projectile. Some of the attackers were hit by the giants' assault, and consequently fell to the ground. Some of the giants ran over to them to engage them in hand-to-hand combat.

Many of the giants were also hit with the electronic weapons of the visitors. There were several large explosions, as some of the weapons hit the surrounding mountains, rocks, and trees. As the battled ensued on the ground, the large craft then positioned itself directly above a certain mountain. An electronic blast of lightning came from beneath the aircraft. The explosion was extremely loud and awesome! There was now a large opening in the mountain—the diameter of which was about 75 feet. Three other visitors jumped directly down into the hole in the mountain—they did not have portable aircraft.

As the chaos level steadily increased and loud explosions could be heard, Alex Sage became antsy. He began to pace back and forth, praying in the process. Suddenly, a bright light overcame the infra-red door that blocked the cell entrance. There stood a creature with a cubed head and four faces. Its body was human-like, but its feet were like calf hooves that were a glowing bronze color. On each side of its head there were different faces. Each had a face similar to a man's face, but on the rear side there was also the face of an eagle. On its right side there was the face of a lion, and on the left side there was the face of a bull. The creature had two arms where arms would normally be. Above its arms were two wings that touched each other behind its head. Below its arms there were also two wings that covered the midsection. And even beneath the wings of its midsection, there was a bright orange glow as if a fire were perpetually burning from its belly.

Alex was terrified and he ran to the corner of the cell and hid his face in his hands. The creature slowly approached Alex and said softly, "Do not be afraid, Alex Sage. I am Phanuel, a servant of our Lord Jesus Christ and I am here to rescue you."

In the middle of the sentence, Alex looked up at him. When he spoke, his wings moved apart horizontally and his head spun in a circle.

"How do I know that you aren't with them and trying to deceive me as they are?" asked Alex, meekly.

Phanuel responded, "Who is it that died on the cross for your sins and has redeemed you?"

"The Lord Jesus Christ!" replied Alex

"Yes. He is Lord of all," said Phanuel back to him. "If I were of the enemy I would not be able to say that while still remaining in a peaceful state of being. The sound of the name of the Son of God literally hurts the hearing of the Fallen Ones, that is why they do not mention his name and they become very agitated whenever you say it. Now come with me, I will get you out of here."

Alex followed Phanuel out of his cell. There were two others like him waiting in the corridor. Phanuel grabbed Alex by the hand and pulled him upward, as he flew, as soon as space permitted it. They got to the top of the mountain's new opening. But waiting for them were several of the blonde giants with their electronic crossbows in hand. Phanuel and his fellow angels quickly flew over their heads and Alex was safely dropped in a remote spot. The giants began shooting at them rapidly. Phanuel and company drew out swords that appeared to be made of lightning. They deflected several of the fiery arrows in their defense. The crossbows of the giants were destroyed by the deflection and return of their own fiery arrows. Then the giants also pulled out shiny, shortened swords that were a glowing bronze color.

There were five giants now engaging in hand-to-hand combat against the three angels. The swords of the giants were no match for the angelic lightning swords. The giants' swords were broken quickly, as one of Phanuel's friends kicked two of the giants down the cliff. Now it was three-on-three, but the giants were without any weapons. They began to retreat, and as they did, Phanuel put his hand inside of his midsection and pulled out a ball of fire. He hurled it at the running giants and it struck all three of them. They fell to the ground and were writhing in agony. Phanuel then went over to where Alex sat and observed this short fight, if it could even be called that. Phanuel reached out his hand and said, "Time to go home."

Alex obeyed without saying a word. Phanuel grabbed a hold of Alex around the waist and carried him up into the aircraft and they sped off into the sky. Alex briefly took a look down at the aftermath of the battle that took place. He could see several giants rolling around on the ground in pain, several of them were burned. Inside of the aircraft were other creatures similar to Phanuel. Some of them had been wounded in the battle, and their injuries were being attended to. Surrounding the inside of the aircraft were several large eyes on its walls. The eyes even blinked as if they were literally watching Alex.

"Welcome to our domain," Phanuel told Alex.

Another creature approached Alex and said in a familiar voice, "It is good to see that you are okay."

"Is that you Sarakiel?" asked Alex.

"Yes," replied Sarakiel. "This is my true form, wings in all."

Alex responded, "Wow! This is amazing. I didn't know you guys traveled in space ships. And thank you very much for rescuing me, by the way."

"Do not mention it," said Phanuel. "We are servants of Christ, just as you are. It is our duty to serve you and do the will of our Father. But we do not call our chariots 'spaceships.' We do not travel in space as you imagine and we do not come from other planets, although we do have dwellings on some planets, but on the spiritual dimensions of them. It's kind of like an inside-out universe in the angelic dimensions. There are certain pockets and portals that allow us to travel faster than your 'speed of light', but there are rules that govern our abilities to use them, as the Godhead decreed."

"So am I in the spiritual dimension now, or the physical world?" asked Alex.

"As of now you are officially in the spiritual dimension," answered Sarakiel. "Everything you've witnessed was of the spiritual realm. Even the death of your friend Kyle, although his body was literally slain, it occurred in one the angelic dimensions."

"Do you mean there are multiple angelic dimensions?" asked Alex

"Oh yes," answered Phanuel. "There are many dimensions. You and Kyle just so happened to be at the right place at the right time when your jets entered into a mobile, inter-dimensional portal into the angelic realm. If you would have kept flying straight, you probably would have exited through the other side. But since you flew your plane in circles, you remained with us longer than usual."

"So it's my fault that Kyle is dead?" asked Alex, sadly.

"No, not at all," answered Sarakiel. "I tried to warn him not to listen to the Fallen Ones, but his desire to escape his reality overcame his ability to have faith. Kyle was unredeemed at the time, so he was especially susceptible to the demonic deception. Our Creator has bestowed upon us the freedom of volition. It was by Kyle's own will that he chose wrongly and those choices result in the consequences that are."

"So is he in hell?" asked Alex, sobbing now.

Phanuel responded quickly, "You should not be concerned about that which cannot be overturned. Every angel and every man was created with the unique ability to choose his destiny: either according to the will of his Creator, or according to his own will, which is contrary to that of God—especially in the sinful nature that your kind is currently under. Kyle's fate is of his own doing. But you have the opportunity to choose wisely now. Remember, that our Father is a good and righteous judge and there is no fault in him. What you should be concerned with is what you need to do now."

"So what *do* I need to do now?" asked Alex, wiping tears away from his face. "Are you going to take me back to Oregon now?"

Phanuel answered him, "No, you will be returned to the place on earth where your aircraft last left off. Of course, your aircraft will not be there because it was ruined in the angelic realm. Your body will be placed on a floating block of ice, just north of Iceland. A rescue unit will find you there and you will be admitted into a hospital and be treated for hypothermia and a broken wrist. You will not remember any of this at first. But while you are recovering in the hospital, every memory will be restored to you in a dream. A local journalist will then interview you and you will tell him everything that happened to you. That is all that I have been allowed to tell you at this point."

"Do you mean there's more?" asked Alex. "Can you see into my future?"

"No we cannot," answered Phanuel. "We have been instructed by Yahweh about these things. This is all according to his wonderful plan."

"Why didn't he save Kyle?" asked Alex. "And why didn't you guys come rescue us earlier?"

"I'll take this one," said Sarakiel to Phanuel. Then he replied to Alex, "Us angels are in just as much awe and are just as curious about the Godhead as you are about many things—just in a different way. You see, we dwell in his presence eternally and yet there are still mysteries about him that we cannot even know. Considering the greatness of the wickedness of the human rebellion against God, us angels are even amazed that our Holy Father even desires to save *any* of you humans at all. The Godhead has allowed a way out--the atonement for all people through the Lamb of God who takes away the sins of the world. Even though most humans reject God's means of salvation, it is all the more precious whenever a person repents of evil and puts their trust in the blood of the Christ. Whenever this happens, there is a great banquet and feast in the heavens and we angels rejoice greatly that the family of our Father is increased.

"We could not come to your aid until a certain confession of your sinfulness occurred, as well as a public proclamation of faith in the face of danger. We were all ready to come to your aid, but we were under strict orders to wait for that moment. Then, as we left, several of the Fallen Ones confronted us and we had to engage in a battle of wits. This is not a physical fight, but more of a battle of intelligence—similar to how you humans have debates. I know that must sound strange to you, but this is one method of warfare that angels engage in. So once our battalion outwitted our enemies, we quickly came to your aid. We are truly sorry that you mourn over your friend, but I can assure you, our Creator has great things in store for you, provided that you remain faithful."

Even though Alex Sage was extremely sad at the death of Kyle Sanchez, he was glad to be in good hands. The answers of the angels were intellectually satisfying, but Alex was still very nervous about what he would encounter now. Just then another angel approached Alex with a bowl of food, saying, "Please eat this. You will be strengthened." The food looked something like oatmeal, but it smelled absolutely wonderful. He took a bite and amazing flavor aroused his taste buds. He ate the entire bowl of this angelic delicacy, as he was starving at this point. Soon after his meal, Alex began to become drowsy. It did not take very long before he was sound asleep on a comfortable, supernatural couch.

21

IT'S A JUNGLE OUT THERE

Alicia Sage woke up in a cold sweat. She had hoped that she had been having a horrific nightmare, but the reality of the bars of her cage confirmed the actuality of what she had witnessed. Amanda had already awakened. When Alicia looked at her, Amanda put her finger to her lips to silence any potential speech. She then pointed to the altar. The rest of their classmates were lying on the floor of the altar, naked, wounded, and dead. All of them, that is, except for Nancy, who presumably was in the captivity of the native devil-worshippers. There were a few of the natives passed out drunk on the floor beneath the cages and throughout the court of the temple. Dried blood was splattered everywhere. The temple was lighted by the morning sun, which shone through the openings of the temple ceiling. The torches of the temple lacked their fire.

Alicia and Amanda were completely silent for about ten minutes. They looked all around as if expecting Xbalque or Hunahpu to show up, but they did not. Alicia had wondered if anybody from the hotel or even the bus driver had reported them missing to any of the authorities. She had remembered hearing the bus driver warn Virgil to run away as fast as possible, as if the bus driver knew about these people. "Who else knew about these people?" thought Alicia to herself.

Just then a gust of wind entered into the temple, blowing Alicia and Amanda's hair back. A bright light suddenly appeared right in front of their cage, and the door of the cage opened. The women covered their faces from the blinding light. They both heard a whisper saying, "Go. Get out of here and do not even turn to look back. Take the trail and travel northeast. Help will be sent to you." And just as fast as the wind and the light entered the temple, it was gone. Amanda held on to the bottom of the cage and lowered her body, hanging on to the cage with her feet about twelve feet from the ground. She released her grip from the cage and fell to the ground, bruising her hip in the process. By the time she got up, Alicia was already dangling from the cage as well. Amanda helped her out of the cage without injury. A few of the drunken natives began to stir a bit. Alicia and Amanda tip-toed past them on their way to the temple entrance with Amanda slightly limping. The entire temple "mall" was completely empty, in contrast to the busyness that they had witnessed the day before.

Neither of the women were exactly sure which way was the entrance. They came to a place where there were two possibilities of the exit. Suddenly, the same voice that spoke in the light before whispered to them again, "Take the door on the right." They both looked around the room to try to find the source of the voice, but they saw nothing. Without much hesitation, they walked toward the large wooden door on the right. Amanda pulled it open, and it creaked slightly. They both looked around behind them to see if anybody had heard them. So far, there was no sign of anyone. Inside of this door there was a narrow corridor with stone walls on each side. Alicia and Amanda almost had to walk sideways to get through. On the walls graffiti of occult symbols were painted everywhere. Skulls, mutilated bodies, sexual content, and even what looked like UFO spacecraft and the worship thereof by the land's inhabitants were some of the depicted items on the walls.

The corridor widened slightly toward the end, of which there was a vine hanging from an opening in the ceiling. Amanda began to climb up the vine, as Alicia pushed her feet up in assistance. As Amanda reached the top of the opening, which was about 25 feet from the ground, Alicia began to climb as well. Suddenly she heard the slight murmur of voices coming from the other side of the wooden door from which they came. The door creaked open and the sound of footsteps followed. Alicia was a little more than halfway up when she heard the voices shout at her with urgency. She hurried up to the surface to meet Amanda. "Quick! Pull up the vine," yelled Alicia to Amanda. They both hurriedly pulled the vine up.

Just as they had finished, they saw a young, skinny man look up at them in contempt, shaking his fist and shouting angrily at them.

Both of the women turned around to run. They were actually in a small village. There were children who were playing amongst themselves who stopped what they were doing to observe the two strangers who suddenly appeared in their home. The sun had not yet shown itself above the trees of the jungle, but the women could sense its general direction and ran toward that particular tree line. As they ran, a couple of the village women came out of their huts, bewildered. One of the village women whistled. Alicia spotted the trail that the voice had spoken of near the tree line and ran toward it, leading Amanda. Amanda looked back and saw one of the village men running toward them with a spear. "Hurry!" shouted Amanda. "Someone's coming." Alicia then took a quick peek and she saw two men running toward them now.

Just as Alicia entered the trail, she heard the sound of a spear just missing her head, and landing in front of her. She ran past the spear and took another peek behind her as she ran. Amanda was falling behind and limping badly. They were both running on the trail now and had entered the tree line. The two village men were gaining on them, and one of them, who had already thrown his spear, was about 15 feet behind Amanda. "Come on, Amanda, run!" shouted Alicia.

"I can't go any faster, go on without me," responded Amanda. "Get help."

Just as the front-running villager was about to grab a hold of Amanda, out of nowhere a jaguar sprung forth from the brush and attacked the villager. The other villager stopped dead in his tracks and just stared at the two women who were going to escape them. He then used his spear to fight off the jaguar that had saved the lives of Alicia and Amanda, and help his fellow villager.

"Keep running," said Alicia. "We don't know if more will come after us."

"Okay, but can you slow down a little," replied Amanda.

At that point the women slowed down into a trot, panting frantically. "We need water," said Amanda. "We've gone hours without a drink or a bite to eat. We will pass out if we go on much longer."

Alicia responded, "Yeah, I know, but the voice told us to stay on the trail and help would be sent to us. So if we look for water, we can't stray too much."

Amanda replied, "Do you think we can trust that voice? I mean, I know that whatever it was—a guardian angel or whatever—helped us escape. But does that voice have the ability to keep us safe?"

"Well," said Alicia, "We don't have too many options, and if it was an angel then God sent him and that means we must have faith that things will be okay. I mean, what are the odds of a jaguar just so happening to be right where he was to attack our pursuers? The natives live with these animals, but yet—I mean, it's just too coincidental to be a coincidence, don't you think?"

"Yeah, you're probably right," answered Amanda. "So we'll stick to the trail and hope that it comes across a stream or something."

At that point Amanda and Alicia had slowed to a walk. The fear had almost completely left them when they began to talk about faith in God and the miraculous escape from their captivity from the most gruesome evil that either of them had ever encountered. As they walked, they talked about some of the things they witnessed. They hoped that Nancy was okay, and they mourned their fellow classmates.

As they walked the trail, they occasionally stumbled upon trees and plants that had fruit, vegetables, and nuts—but still no water. They ate as they walked. The day grew hotter and more humid, and dehydration began to set in. Both of them became lightheaded. "We should sit down and take a break now," Amanda told Alicia. "I think I'm going to faint."

"Okay, I guess we can do that," replied Alicia.

They both found a large tree on the side of the trail to sit under. It wasn't long before both of them fell asleep. A couple of hours later they were awakened by drops of rain. "Water!" yelled Alicia. Lightning and thunder began to sound as the downpour increased. The cool water felt good on the sweaty skin of the women, which was still covered by the large leaves that the natives had sewn together for them. They returned to the trail and lifted their faces to the sky and allowed the water to drain down their dry throats. After about five minutes of intense downpour, the rain stopped. Alicia and Amanda felt refreshed and began walking again.

After a few more hours of walking, and occasionally taking a break, the trail began to ascend upward upon a hill. The sun had begun to set behind the trees to the west, and the light of the skies began to wane, as the moon showed its face. When they got to the top of the hill, which turned out to be a plateau, there was a small, stone monument that stood between four tall trees. Alicia and Amanda went into the stony shack and noticed more native graffiti. This time, the emphasis of the graffiti was much more on encounters with demonic extra-terrestrials. And this time, the graffiti was not painted, but carved into the stone. "I wonder how old these carvings are?" asked Alicia.

"I don't know," answered Amanda, "But they sure are creepy. Do you think this has something to do with what happened last night?"

"Oh, I'm sure of it," replied Alicia. "What most people call a mystery is actually an ancient, demonic phenomenon. It seems that we have stumbled right into the thick of it too. God must be trying to show us something. We should sit down, pray, and meditate on these things and see if that voice will return to us."

"Good idea," said Amanda. So they both sat upon the wall of the stony, UFO shack. They prayed and meditated for about an hour, and then they both fell asleep again, leaning against each others' backs. The evening was upon them and the full moon illuminated the jungle.

Meanwhile, the impregnated Nancy Dollar was laying on a cot in the village that Alicia and Amanda ran past. She had been sound asleep at the time Alicia and Amanda ran by. She was now officially the wife of Nahual, whether she liked it or not. Nahual had another wife, but she was his spiritual and ceremonial wife. Nancy had been left alone for most of the day, with which she cried most of the time. All of her classmates were either dead or gone, and she had never felt so alone in her life. Somehow, she had felt that she was responsible for bringing this tragedy upon them. Outside of her hut were two giant men watching over her to make sure she did not escape or try to hurt herself. If she could, she would surely end her life right now. She did not want to have the baby of these beasts! She felt dirty, violated, and torn apart. She was too terrified to sleep now, and it would be a long night indeed.

22

THE IMAGE OF GOD

The messenger Pravuil continued the history lesson to Christian Sage, Cliff Cooper, Jabari Saal, and Richard Mockens. His brazen face seemed to emit a glow as he said, "As it is written, 'A day is as a thousand years to the Lord, and a thousand years is as a day.' While it is true that this primarily speaks of the infinitude of God—being outside of time and space—it also has a practical sense in some regards. It is not a secret formula for prophetic predictions as some charlatans have attempted, but as far as creation goes, the human *days* or time in general, were similar to millenniums in the angelic realm. We had been carrying on in perfect harmony, studying the nature of the creation, the physical laws, the character of the Godhead. We would also carefully observe how our Father would create according to earth time. As multi-dimensional beings, we have the ability to exist in our own dimension but yet see how things occur chronologically according to earth time. Now I am speaking of actual chronology, not of each "day" of Genesis 1 being actual chronology.

"And just when many of us thought we had it down, our Father would again begin to create on the earth and more would be added within the angelic realm. In the Kingdom of Heaven, there are similar creatures as were created on the earth, but they are even more magnificent. Some of the bodily features are combinations of the earth-creatures' features. Some of us angelic beings even borrowed animal-like features from the newer heavenly creatures. It would be comparable to how humans change clothes and have different wardrobes. That brings us to your Genesis Day 6.

"The pinnacle of all creation came from the dust of the earth: but first, our Father created all land creatures—and yes—including dragons. He blessed the animals and commanded them to be fruitful, multiply, and fill the face of the earth. He immediately declared this as good, and the corresponding creatures in the Kingdom of Heaven were also available to us. Then, after more earth-time passed, the Holy Spirit made an announcement in all of the heavens: the archangel Michael blew his trumpet to silence every activity of the angelic order in order to witness what the Godhead was about to do. So as every one of us stopped what we were doing, we looked closely upon the earth, and the Godhead spoke, 'Let us make humankind in our image, according to our likeness; and let them rule over the fish of the sea and over the birds of the sky and over the cattle over all the earth, and over every creeping thing that crawls across the earth.'

"And out of the dust from the ground, the Godhead formed the man in his own image. The Holy Spirit was blown into the nostrils of Adam by Yahweh and the man became a living being. We angels looked at one another in amazement, for we did not know what to make of this. We did not know what it meant to be created in the image of God, and we began to question amongst ourselves. The Son of God, knowing our thoughts, came to us and asked, 'What is troubling all of you?' Lucifer was the first to respond, 'Why is it that the earth creature, who is limited to such a small domain is honored above the angelic majesties by being created in the image of God? Are not we worthy of such a title?'

"The Son of God answered him, 'You all have been given much to govern over—the entirety of the heavenly luminaries are yours to keep forever. You have free access to the very throne of God whenever you please to worship and fellowship. All that the Father has belongs to you all and you are his children. You have vast knowledge--of both good and evil, whereas the man on earth has just enough knowledge to suit his stewardship. He is created lower than you, so there should be no covetousness among any of you. Beware, lest you fall into temptation and think evil of the Father or that you should be his equal in understanding and power. This is a real temptation, but you must master your wills and overcome such a temptation. Do not be saddened by this, but rejoice! Come, let us have a feast of celebration!'

"This was a satisfactory answer for most of us. We replied to the Son of God by singing, 'Amen, amen! Holy, holy, holy is the Godhead!' Then a celebration broke out indeed. The food was gathered from the trees of the heavenly gardens. There were many trees from which to eat from. All of us angels had eaten many times from the tree of knowledge. In fact, the trees of the heavenly realm provide fruit that, when eaten, the contents therein provide us not nourishment, as if we needed bodily nourishment, but certain attributes of immortality. The food from these was especially good this time around, and the heavenly bread was also extraordinarily tasty.

"As Lucifer and the heavenly choir sang and played their instruments, the Son of God stood in the midst of the assembly and said, 'Now there will be a contest amongst us: there has been a new tree planted in a new garden of the kingdom. This tree is called, "The Tree of Life." The fruit of this tree will ensure your immortality in that however your development takes you—whether it be knowledge, virtue, skills, talents, or character—these attributes will remain with you for all of eternity. They will be unchangeable and undeletable. So understand that with these awesome benefits come the incredible responsibility to maintain your personal holiness and your allegiance to the holy throne of the Godhead. The first of you to locate this tree and bring its fruit to the midst of this assembly will acquire a special privilege of authority over your brethren. Likewise, the man of earth will also have the opportunity to locate a tree of life in the Garden of Paradise in his own domain. He too, has the chance to gain immortality and become likened unto you as well. If that happens, he will be able to join us and communicate with us freely, just as you have access to the throne of the Godhead at your pleasure. Thus, the contest is begun.'

"As the Son of God made that announcement, the feast was put on hold as the hosts of heaven hurriedly scattered throughout the universe in search of the hidden tree of life. As this was happening in the heavens, on earth the Son of God also planted a garden to the east of where the man was and called it Eden. Meanwhile, the man was enjoying the scenic beauty of the creation, playing with the animals, running wildly without a care in the world. The mist which came up from the ground and watered the plants sprang up, and Adam was fascinated by this. He splashed the water on his face and then began splashing some of the other creatures with water, while chasing them around.

"While this was going on, the Father had finished creating the Garden of Eden. Next, the Son of God descended upon Adam and picked him up off the ground and carried him through the air to where the garden was.

He told Adam, 'Your job will be to cultivate the ground and its produce and keep guard of it. The animals will try to eat its produce, but you must limit them and manage the garden. Look around at the abundance of trees in this garden.' Adam lifted his head and observed every tree with a look of awe in his face.

"As Adam looked around, smiling, the Son of God left his physical presence. Then Yahweh spoke to Adam from the heavens, 'You may eat freely from any of these trees. Only the tree of knowledge—both of good and evil—you shall not eat from that one. The day that you eat of it, while eating it you shall experience the awful process of death.'

"Adam understood and said, 'Yes, my Lord.' Adam began to observe the garden and make measurements in his head and began to calculate how to begin his work of stewardship in the garden. Meanwhile, Yahweh took council with the Son of God and the Holy Spirit. He spoke to them, saying, 'It is not good for the man to be alone. We will make him a helper that corresponds to his likeness.' There was agreement within the Godhead, as always. And out of the dust of the Garden of Eden, Yahweh created specific animals—the prototypes of every kind of animal—and they went to Adam. Adam began to give names to every type of animal—and he was very fond of each one of them—but he discovered that there was not one animal that was like he was.

"The Godhead saw this, and even though Adam was perfectly content with his environment and his job, they decided to give the ultimate gift to Adam—a woman. The Father caused a deep sleep to come over Adam, and while he was sleeping, the Father took a piece of rib from Adam and formed the woman and breathed life into her nostrils. Adam woke up and saw the most beautiful of all the earthly creations with her eyes fixed on him. He immediately looked up into the heavens and gave thanks to his Creator, and said, 'This is now bone of my bones, and flesh of my flesh; this one shall be called woman because she was taken out of man.'

"After exploring one another's anatomy, they consummated the first marriage of all creation, and became one flesh. The Godhead blessed them with the decree telling them to be fruitful and to multiply. They would have stewardship over every living thing and creature of the earth. They would be able to eat any plant or herb for food. Together—male and female—they constituted the fullness of the image of God.

"The man and woman cooled themselves off in each of the four surrounding rivers, which Adam named—the Pishon, the Gihon, the Tigris, and the Euphrates. The water refreshed their naked bodies—and they were unaware of their lack of covering because there was no shame in their perfect condition. Not long after, there was evening and then morning upon the earth. The Godhead saw everything that they had created and declared it complete and very good."

Dr. Jabari Saal raised his hand as if he were in a classroom. Pravuil pointed to him, and Jabari asked, "Are those rivers the same as the Tigris and the Euphrates that go through Iraq today?"

Pravuil answered, "No. The original rivers were destroyed in the Flood. The rivers so named today were renamed after the original rivers by the post-Flood patriarchs."

Dr. Saal asked another question, "Where on earth was the Garden of Eden created exactly?"

To that, Pravuil replied, "Keep in mind that there was only one continent at that time. But to answer your question directly, it would be the region of modern-day Jerusalem. That is one reason why that city has always been a sought-after and fought-after parcel of land because of its holiness and spiritual value. The Fallen Ones are forever trying to dispossess the people of God from that land and take it for themselves, and at times have been successful."

Richard Mockens chimed in, "So what did Adam and Eve look like?"

Pravuil smiled and said, "Oh yes, the apparently most important question to humans, even in its shallowness. Well, think in terms of your genetic laws. Since all of humanity has what you call DNA from the gene pool of Adam, and all humans are his descendants, that means that in the genetic makeup of Adam, every trait of humanity must have been present. That means he could not have been blonde haired and blue eyed, and he could not have been extremely dark skinned and dark eyed. His hair could not be extremely straight or extremely curled. He was the perfect medium—as perfect as a human can be—in all of its genetic character. His skin was the perfect medium brown. His eyes were what you call hazel. His hair was wavy. His voice was the perfect medium. He was without defect whatsoever, and his gene pool was humungous in terms of the possible variety that which could spring forth from him.

"He was the perfect man—a direct creation of God, in his image. And with the angels, who are also direct creations of The Almighty, he was also called a son of God. The paradox was this: he was created a little lower than the angels, but yet he was distinguished as being created in the divine image, along with his wife, and angels were not. This idea was so mysterious amongst the host of heaven that it is what caused the initial thoughts that led to the rebellion, which led to the Battle of Pneumatika. Let me tell you."

23

MEMORY LANE

Alex Sage woke up all alone in a dark room. He was lying down on an elevated bed and he could vaguely see the shadow of a door about 15 feet in front of him. He tried to get up but the cords and wires that were connected to his arm and chest pinched his skin hard enough to keep from rising up. Pain shot through his left wrist, and he noticed that a cast covered his entire forearm. He looked to his left and then recognized by the machinery and the beeping of his pulse that he was in a hospital. "What in the world happened to me?" he thought to himself. He looked around for a signal to call the nurse. On the armrest there was a red button that looked fitting, so he pressed it. Moments later there was a knock at the door. "Come in," yelled Alex.

A heavy set woman turned a light switch on that allowed a dim but sufficient set of lights to illuminate the room. "Hello, lad, how are you feeling?" asked the nurse in a Scottish accent.

"I'd be a heck of a lot better if I knew where I was and what happened to me," answered Alex.

"Well, lad, I can answer the first question certainly, but the second I do not know," replied the nurse. "You are in the ICU of Reykjavik hospital in Iceland. You arrived here about ten hours ago suffering from extreme hypothermia that almost killed you. The Almighty must have found favor with you, for I sure did not expect you to survive. You also broke your wrist somehow. Tell me, lad, do you not remember anything?"

"No, I can't remember," answered Alex. "The last thing I remember was flying over the Arctic Circle with my squad and...um, I think I remember a violent hailstorm knocking out our communications. Now I have waken up here."

"That sounds strange indeed," said the nurse. "Hailstorms are not frequent in the Arctic Circle. Are you sure that's where you were flying?"

Alex responded, "Yeah, I'm sure. The one thing I do remember was our training exercise and specifically my plane being pelted with ice."

"Well, my name's Annie," said the nurse. "Can I do anything for you right now?"

"Does anyone know I'm here?" asked Alex.

"Oh yes, lad," answered Annie. "We got your information from your dog tags. We have contacted your headquarters in Germany and they are sending an envoy to take you home. And to answer your other question, apparently your jet crashed into the ocean, but somehow your body was found on a floating piece of ice about 4 miles off our northern coast by one of our helicopters."

"I don't, I don't remember the crash," said Alex, sadly. "How about the others? Did they find any other of our pilots? What about my partner Sanchez?"

"No, you were all alone," answered Annie. "You're lucky to be alive—count your blessings. Is there anything I can get you, lad?"

"No. I think I'll just get some more sleep—the meds are making me drowsy," replied Alex.

"Okay, just give me a ring if you need me," said Annie.

"All right, I'll do that," Alex responded.

Alex slept throughout the night, and he was not awakened until 6:00 am the next morning by his new nurse. "Good morning, Alex. My name is Laura and I'll be your nurse this morning. Are you hungry? Would you like some breakfast?" asked the young red-headed nurse.

"Uh, okay. What do you have?" asked Alex.

"We have either a pancake breakfast or an omelet."

"I'll take the pancakes."

"All righty, coming right up."

Alex thoroughly enjoyed his pancake breakfast as if he had not eaten a meal for a week. He was immediately sleepy again from his hearty meal. Again he fell into a deep sleep. This time he began to dream—vividly! Everything that he had experienced was being replayed by his memory and this time it would remain with him as any other actual experience. At the end of his dream, he saw an angelic figure that was not in the dream. Alex saw himself ask the angel, "Is this real?" Then his father appeared in place of the angel and answered him, "Yes, son. All of this is real. I know it, you know, and your sister knows it too."

"Alex, Alex", a voice from outside of his vision called, interrupting his dream. Alex opened his eyes and saw Laura standing next to a man wearing a cheap suit and a leather hat, holding a briefcase. Laura said again, "Sorry to wake you, Alex, but this is Philip Heath from the local newspaper, "Today's Iceland." He is covering your story and would like to interview you."

Suddenly, Alex had an epiphany. He remembered that the angel Phanuel had predicted that he would be without memory for awhile and then he would remember everything in a dream and then tell the story to a reporter. Alex's face gleamed with joy, as he looked at Philip Heath and said, "I'd be glad to give you my story."

Laura looked puzzled and then asked, "Alex! Do you remember what happened to you now?"

"Yes," answered Alex. "I just had a dream right now, and suddenly I can remember everything in detail."

"Well that's great!" said Laura. Just then, Laura was being paged to another room. At that point, Philip sat down next to Alex and said, "So how are you feeling Alex?"

"I'm actually feeling much better than yesterday," answered Alex.

"Well that's good. Since you can remember in such great detail now, I'm going to record our interview rather than take notes," said Philip. "At first I was under the impression that you couldn't remember, but now I'm going to need to record our interview and take this story back to the office."

"That's fine," replied Alex.

"Good," said Philip. He then reached into his briefcase and pulled out a tiny recording device. "You may begin," said Philip.

Philip listened carefully and wide-eyed as Alex retold his bizarre story to him. Once Alex had finished his account of the events, Philip turned off the recording device and put it back into his briefcase. His facial expression was as though he wasted an hour of his life listening to Alex's recall of his experience. Alex noticed that and said, "I know all of this must be hard to believe. I mean, I probably wouldn't believe it either if it didn't happen to me—but it did happen! I can assure you that this is as real as you sitting here in the room with me!"

Philip responded with a compassionate, but cynical, "I know you've been through a lot kid. And I know that the extreme temperatures that your body has been through has caused you to go into shock and your brain is hallucinating these images—as awesome as they are—to try to give you an explanation of how you got here."

Alex was not surprised that Philip was skeptical, but he still felt insulted. He responded by saying, "Some people never recover their memories and live their whole lives with unknown events that are mysterious to them all the way to their graves. And usually when people hallucinate they hallucinate about things that they already know about. Why would I, or even *how* could I make this stuff up? How could my brain conjure up unknown images with such detail if they were not true?"

Philip was perplexed by such an articulate objection to his skepticism. "I don't know, Alex," answered Philip. "I'm just not apt to believe in blonde giants living beneath the North Pole with six-winged, four-faced angels who go to war against them with lightning swords and flying saucers. I don't know you personally, and I don't know what you're into—your hobbies and obsessions—but I just can't come to grips with all of that being real—not in my world. I wish I could believe you—and I want to—but, come on Alex, do you even hear what you're suggesting to me?"

"I understand," said Alex. "I was told that my message would not be accepted, so I don't blame you."

"Well, good luck to you Alex—I mean that," said Philip. "I'm glad that you're okay and I wish you a good life. Take care."

"You too," answered Alex, feeling embarrassed and humiliated.

Philip exited the room and was approached by Nurse Laura in the hallway. She asked him, "So what happened? Did you get an interesting story?"

"The story is very interesting," answered Philip. "But I think he's still in shock or something because the story is just, 'out there!' Too out there to put in a legitimate newspaper. Maybe The Sun or The Enquirer would be interested."

As Philip Heath left the hospital, Lieutenant Alex Sage's envoy had arrived to be checked into the hospital. All of the necessary paperwork for Alex to be discharged from the hospital was taken care of. Staff Sergeant Bill Ross entered into his room and said to him, "How are you doing, sir? Are you ready to go back to base?"

"Doing okay Sergeant Ross, all things considering," answered Alex. "But yeah, getting back to normal doesn't sound too bad."

Nurse Laura interrupted briefly to remove his IV tube and the other wires that recorded his vitals. She said to him, "All of your paperwork is complete, Alex. You can go as soon as you're ready. All of us here hope that your stay here was as comforting as possible, and we wish you the best from here on out."

Alex responded, "Well thanks, Laura. You've all been so kind to me, and the food was great! Take care of yourself." Nurse Laura smiled as she exited the room. Sergeant Ross had brought a change of Alex's uniform from his barracks in Germany. Alex went into the bathroom to change into them. As he closed the bathroom door behind him, he was startled as he looked into the bathroom mirror and saw the reflection of Aegir the red bearded giant. The image was there for only a split second. Alex flinched at this gruesome sight, but when he blinked it was only Alex in the mirror. He looked all around him and saw nothing. He turned on the light—still nothing. He decided that his mind was playing tricks on him and thought nothing else of it. "Did I really dream about what happened or *is* my mind really playing tricks on me?" Alex wondered to himself.

After he was dressed, it was obvious that he had lost considerable weight since the last time he put on his uniform. His shirt and his pants were very baggy on him. But he had only been in the hospital for two days—how could he possibly lose that much weight in so short a time? He walked out of the bathroom in full uniform. Sergeant Ross was standing there waiting for him. He looked astonished when he saw Alex. "Sir," he said, "You sure did lose a lot of weight since the last time I saw you—have you been eating?

Alex responded, "I was just about to ask you if this is really my uniform. Did you get it from my wall locker?"

"Yes sir," answered Sergeant Ross. "There are not that many Sages in the Air Force. You lost weight."

Alex looked puzzled. "Hmm," he said. "Oh well, at least I'm alive. Let's go."

As they left the room, Alex noticed a very foul stench that was not there before. He asked, "What's that smell Sergeant Ross?"

"What smell? I don't smell anything," answered Sergeant Ross. "Maybe it's your upper lip, sir. Did they give you a bath?"

Alex smiled, "Oh yeah—that must be it." When they got to the bottom floor and to the front desk, there were two other airmen waiting for them. They saluted Alex and he saluted back. "Good to see you, sir," said Airman Richmond.

"Likewise, Richmond," replied Alex. All six of them walked out of the hospital doors. There was a Hum V waiting for them with another airman in the driver's seat. It was just beginning to get dark now. As they were about to enter the vehicle, they all heard a loud explosion come from the direction of the hospital. They turned and saw flames coming out of one of the rooms on the second floor. "Holy smoke! We were just on the second floor!" exclaimed Sergeant Ross.

"I think that might be the room where I was staying," said Alex. "Let's go back and see what happened."

"I can't let you do that, sir," said Sergeant Ross. "I'm under strict orders to bring you back—and safely might I add. You're not well enough to be out here in the cold or in there with all of that smoke, so let's get in. We can find out what happened later."

Alex followed the advice of Sergeant Ross. He looked back one more time at the burning room, and he could have sworn he saw a dim-red glow that was distinct from any flame come from the room. He could hear sirens as the fire department was surely on its way. The Hum V took off and headed for the airport, which was only about ten minutes away. Alex was in a daze, and it seemed like they were at the airport within seconds. They boarded a M.A.C. flight back to Germany. Sergeant Ross finally broke the ice concerning what had happened to Alex, "So what the hell happened to you, sir?"

Alex thought about telling him what he had told Philip Heath, but thought better of it. Instead he played dumb and said, "You know Sergeant Ross, I really don't remember much. It all happened so fast. One minute everything was fine, then a vicious hail storm took out our commo, and then we went down. That's all I remember."

"You didn't see Lieutenant Sanchez?" asked Sergeant Ross.

Alex's countenance fell, as he looked at the floor of the aircraft. In a low voice he answered, "No. He must have drowned or something. I don't even remember landing or how I got on a piece of floating ice. I don't even remember being rescued. It's all a blur to me."

Sergeant Ross nodded and looked to the other men with them. The plane's engine started up, and then it was difficult to hear anything then. The back of the military plane was freezing cold, and the men wrapped blankets around their bodies to keep warm. Alex felt guilty about the answer he gave Sergeant Ross. He wanted to tell the truth, but he was afraid that he would be treated even crazier than how Philip Heath treated him. He thought deeply about how he was going to treat this situation from here on out. How could things ever return to normal? Why did this happen to him? All of these types of thoughts kept racing through Alex's mind throughout the flight, while the other men slept comfortably.

They returned to Germany in the middle of the night on a Saturday morning. He would not have to report to duty until Monday. It only took a few seconds for Alex to fall asleep once his face hit the pillow. He began to dream about his experiences again—very vividly. This time he began to sleepwalk. Since he did not lock his door, he turned the knob and walked outside into the corridor of the barracks. He was mumbling as he walked. One of the other Lieutenants walked by him with a beer in his hand. "Sage? Is that you?" he asked. Sage turned to him, with his eyes still closed. He stopped his mumbling for a second and spoke clearly to him, "The Fallen Ones are here."

The other Lieutenant looked puzzled at that statement. He put his hand on Alex's shoulder, and said, "Dude, what did you say? Are you toasted, man?"

Alex smiled, but his eyes were still closed. He repeated himself, louder this time, "The Fallen Ones are here! The Fallen Ones are here!"

Lieutenant Daniels laughed this time and asked, "Are you *that* drunk, Sage?" Daniels looked over his shoulder and called to Lieutenant Calvin, "Calvin! Hey come over here and check this out. Sage is totally wasted! I've never seen him like this."

Lieutenant Calvin did come over to see what the commotion was about. He looked at the two men and asked Alex, "Sage! Are you okay, man?"

Alex answered, "The Fallen Ones are here!" He repeated himself again, this time shouting, "THE FALLEN ONES ARE HERE!"

Calvin replied, "Who? Who are the Fallen Ones?" Alex just smiled, while keeping his eyes closed. He then turned away from the two men and began to walk back to his room and began mumbling again. By this time a couple of other men who were awakened out of their sleep opened their doors and were asking what in the world was going on. Calvin told them, "I think Lieutenant Sage is sleepwalking. It's nothing." Daniels and Calvin then helped Alex get back into his bed. Nothing was heard from Alex Sage for the rest of the weekend.

24

THE DOORS TO THE OTHER SIDE

The sound of footsteps startled Alicia Sage and Amanda Day out of their sleep. Alicia got up from the ground and looked outside of the stony shack's doorway. She saw nothing. Amanda quickly joined her. The only thing that could be heard now was the sounds of the nearby jungle—night birds singing, the croaking of frogs, the chirp of crickets, and other bugs. Even though it was completely dark, the full moon lit up the night sky and the tops of the jungle trees. Amanda broke the silence, "Did you hear footsteps or was that just me?"

"I thought I heard them too," answered Alicia.

Both of them walked around the perimeter of the plateau's edge looking down at the terrain beneath and beyond them. Alicia spotted a clearing in the jungle with torches illuminating the clearing area. There were people moving within the clearing, but Alicia could not see who they were in detail. She summoned Amanda, "Come over here and check this out Amanda."

Amanda walked over to Alicia and observed the clearing with her. "Oh my gosh! What's going on?" she asked Alicia. "Do you think they're searching for us?"

151

"I don't know," answered Alicia.

"We should go and see," said Amanda.

"Wait! We need to be careful. They might be the same people that we just escaped from," replied Alicia.

"Yeah, you're right," Amanda answered back.

Both of them turned around to the shocking horror of a tribe of giants that now had them surrounded. For being such large men, their stealth was amazing. The two women opened their mouths to scream but nothing came out. Terror gripped their hearts as two of the giants grabbed Amanda and Alicia by the arms and pulled them toward the group. Another man tied ropes to the wrists of the women and pulled them in the direction of the formation of giants who were now marching downhill. Alicia and Amanda walked in silence with their heads down. The pain from the cuts and scrapes of their bare feet suddenly came to their awareness with great intensity. Alicia began to wonder why the angelic voice sent them in this direction only to be recaptured by these satanic men. Where was the help that was promised? Amanda was too frightened to even think along these lines.

The giants led the women to the clearing in the jungle. Apparently Alicia and Amanda had been spotted hours earlier, and a new unholy ritual site had been set up in the clearing. This time there were other people present—even those who were obviously not from Peru. There were men and women present—some of whom wore casual business suits, others in casual-dress attire. The different ethnicities and nationalities of the people intrigued Alicia; it looked like some sort of United Nations gathering in a jungle of Peru.

All of the people stared at Alicia and Amanda as they were brought into the center of the clearing. The looks in their eyes were that of murderous contempt. Amanda swore that she saw the bus driver amongst the crowd, and Alicia thought she saw the manager of the hotel in attendance as well. There was a large tree in the center of the clearing. One of the giants tied Alicia and Amanda to the tree facing opposite one another. Just then, Xbalque and Hunahpu emerged from the crowd. They both had evil smirks on their faces and spoke to the women in their native language. Apparently, the potion of hearing one tongue had worn off. At the command of Xbalque several torches were brought to the center of the clearing. One by one, torches were strategically placed around the tree on which Alicia and Amanda were tied. Alicia could not tell what sort of pagan symbol the torches were set in place to represent, but it was obvious that another type of sacrifice or ritual would take place.

Amanda yelled to Alicia from her side of the tree, "I thought they said that we were protected by our God. So what's going on?"

"Just be patient and have faith," responded Alicia. "They might be trying to scare us into denouncing our Lord. We need to pass this test. Hold on and pray!"

Xbalque stood in front of Alicia and spoke to the crowd. They cheered and began to take off their clothes without any shame whatsoever. A native band began playing music again—very similar to that which took place the evening before. At the sound of the drums, the naked people began to dance and run around the women in a circle. Alicia could not be certain, but she swore that she saw a couple of recognizable American politicians amongst the crazed assembly. Then suddenly the music stopped and every person prostrated themselves to the ground. Xbalque stood next to Hunahpu and he began an incantation just like he had done before. This time no person from the crowd was chosen to come forth. When Xbalque finished his mantra, with which the prostrated assembly responded by chanting, "Ommm, Ommm," a light appeared in the sky above them. The light was exceedingly bright so that the source of the light was indiscernible. Orbs of lesser light descended from the greater light and began to fly around the torch formation. Amanda began to sob but Alicia maintained her composure and observed carefully.

The orbs of light kept their distance from where Alicia and Amanda were, but they seemed to be interacting with the members of this unholy assembly. The crowd became ecstatic and they began to babble in unknown languages. Some of them began to laugh uncontrollably, others began barking like dogs. Other people began to engage in sexual activity with other members. Just when things seemed hopeless, the voice returned to the women, saying, "Shhh. Open your eyes and see the salvation of the Lord."

At that word, immediately Amanda and Alicia saw several winged angelic beings appear in the distance of the tree line. They began moving toward the clearing and it appeared that they were carrying swords of light. Seconds later, the orbs left the assembly and rushed quickly towards the angels as if to engage them in combat. One of the more powerful of the angels of light stepped forward and struck many of the orbs with his sword. The orbs flew up into the sky like baseballs hit by a major league slugger. Another angel stepped forward and shouted to the orbs and pointed to the sky. At that command the remaining orbs flew back to the main source of light and then the light disappeared.

Xbalque and Hunahpu shouted to the assembly and suddenly panic and chaos filled the clearing of the jungle. People began running about aimlessly and shouting. Some people began to put their clothes back on. Two angels came into the clearing striking several of the people with their swords. One of the angels spewed a fireball from its mouth and the fireball consumed Xbalque. He screamed in agony as his body went up in flames. The other angel grabbed Hunahpu by the throat and lifted him up. The angel opened his mouth wide and put Hunahpu's giant head into his mouth. Hunahpu's head was removed from his body and spit onto the ground. It was not long before every member of the assembly was dead. Suddenly all of the angelic beings vanished from the sight of the women, who were now free from their ropes.

Alicia and Amanda looked around them and then at their hands, astounded at what just took place. Even Amanda was speechless. They looked at all of the dead bodies that were scattered about in the jungle's clearing. Suddenly they heard the voice again, behind them, saying, "Fear not, the Lord is with you." Both women were startled and turned around. They saw a young, dark-skinned man wearing a white robe. His face had a huge, friendly smile on it and his voice was full of compassion and genuine concern. Amanda asked him, "Who are you?"

The man answered, "I am Asphael the Cherub of Yahweh the Most High. I am the chief of 1,000 guardians and one of the main destroyers of God's enemies."

"Where are your wings?" asked Alicia.

Asphael smiled and said, "I have chosen a less frightening form so that I may comfort you. Here—I have chosen some clothing for you two. The women who wore them a few minutes ago will not be in need of them any longer." Asphael turned his back, giving the women dignity as they removed their garments of sewn leaves and putting on the clothes that were given them, which included comfortable shoes. All of the clothing fit perfectly for the petite women.

When the women finished dressing Asphael turned back around and faced them. "Much better?" he asked.

"Yes, thank you," answered Alicia.

"So what in the world is going on, sir?" asked Amanda, bluntly.

Asphael smiled gently at her, with his hands behind his back, walking slowly to her side. He began pacing in steps of four and began to speak, "You two have been chosen by the Almighty to be active participants in the Battle of Spiritual Hosts, also known as Pneumatika in the Greek tongue. It was necessary for you to be exposed to this evil so that you understand the severity of what we are up against. It is also a good indicator of where the human race stands at in the final times of your age, even though these types of practices have been going on for thousands of your years. You two have proven to be faithful even in these instances of extreme danger and your reward will be great. At the same time, your paths will be difficult and you will face great tribulation. But be of good cheer: the Holy Spirit will empower you and enable you to persevere until your duty is complete. This is all according to the plan of our sovereign Lord."

Asphael paused with that last statement, and Amanda took advantage by asking, "Well what about Nancy? And Steve? And all of the others?"

The look on Asphael's face suddenly became serious and saddened. He shook his head and sucked his teeth three times. He said to them, "Nancy and Steve brought this upon themselves. Steve has been involved in several séances during the past six months. Nancy and her friend Valerie have been calling upon evil spirits using a Ouija Board for over three months now. All three of them have been calling on the names of ancient Incan gods during their occult practices—which are an abomination to our Creator. They have allowed their studies of ancient culture to overwhelm their sinful imaginations and have made contacts to the actual demons who were worshipped by the Incans. These Fallen Ones were waiting for the time when your study group would come visit this place. These demons are worshipped and are in constant contact with the remnant of the mighty ones who seized you. They alerted them of your presence and that is how these events have come about. But at the same time, The Almighty has permitted it to be so, and his sovereignty has rule over even the most evil of choices that any person or groups of people can make. Yahweh and his Son will prevail, as you will see."

Amanda then asked, "So do you mean that this is not really anybody's fault? God planned that all of this would happen?"

Asphael answered, "God is not willing that any person should perish but that all would come to the knowledge of his goodness. However, he permits people to choose their own fate, and in this case, Nancy and Steve—as well as the others—chose to rebel, so they reaped the consequences of their actions. It is not part of Yahweh's perfect will, but he does always leave a redemptive option open to those who are in rebellion, even according to his marvelous grace to you humans. Believe it or not, all of your classmates were enabled by the Holy Spirit to repent in their final moments of their lives. They all were given thoughts to call on the name of Jesus to save them—but their stubbornness overtook them and they went with their default, sinful instincts and faced their consequences as they were."

Alicia then asked, "Is Nancy still alive? We didn't see her body in the temple."

Asphael answered, "Nancy is still alive. She is wedded to Nahual and is pregnant with his twin sons. I have not received instruction or information of her final fate other than that."

"Well can you save her?" asked Amanda.

"As of right now, I cannot. She is still in rebellion. That is all I know."

Alicia then asked, "I don't mean to change the subject or anything, but who were these other people that died tonight that are not from here? I thought that I recognized a couple of them"

Asphael looked keenly at Alicia and said, "Those people were members of what you call 'secret societies' from around the world. Every year they meet at certain places and worship the Fallen Ones and other evil spirits. And yes, you probably did recognize a few of them. Many of them are prominent members of world governments and people in high places."

"Wait a minute," said Alicia. "You said Fallen Ones and *other* evil spirits. I thought that all evil spirits are demons."

"Well, that is partially true," answered Asphael. "The Fallen Ones include the original angels who rebelled with Lucifer, as well as the Watchers who lusted after human women in the centuries before the Flood of Noah. The other evil spirits are those of the humans before the Flood that were not part of the Covenant of Yahweh's faithful, or what you might call 'saved' people. What you call 'hell' did not exist before the Flood, so when unrighteous or unfaithful humans that lived before the Flood died, their spirits were left to wander the earth aimlessly until the end of the age of humanity. They have been judged and condemned, and on that final Day of Yahweh where all of humanity and the angelic realm will be judged, the unredeemed humans will all enter into the Lake of Fire along with the angels who rebelled.

"The lesser evil spirits do the bidding of the Fallen Ones, but they are much weaker and have less influence on human activity. They are involved in what you might call 'hauntings' or they might masquerade as other deceased people to deceive their mourning loved ones so that they might believe things that are not true of the spiritual realm. Their main objective is to deceive as many people as possible so that they will not come to the knowledge of the truth of Yahweh and his Son Jesus Christ. They want as many people to remain spiritually dead, as they are, so that they may accompany them in the Lake of Fire on Judgment Day. The same can be said of the Fallen Ones, but the rebellious angels are much more powerful and influential on human civilization than the lesser evil spirits of the deceased men who lived during the first epoch of humanity."

Alicia and Amanda stood in silence as they were both in deep thought now. Amanda then asked, "So what happens to us now?"

"You must continue on the Northeastern trail," answered Asphael. "After a couple of days of travel, you will come upon a small town where you must report everything that you have witnessed to the authorities. That is all I am permitted to share with you as of now. Do not worry and do not fear—you will have guardians protecting you until your missions are complete."

"What is our mission?" interrupted Amanda.

"I cannot say nor do I know the details," answered Asphael. "Just remain faithful and your reward will be great. Peace be with you."

With those last words, Asphael vanished from their sight. "O-kay." Amanda responded. "I guess we're on our own now—at least practically speaking."

Alicia replied, "Since we have a couple of days of walking I think we should get some sleep."

"Good idea," said Amanda.

They both walked back up to the stony hut on the hilltop where they were asleep before. Again, they leaned upon one another's back. Amanda fell asleep almost immediately. Alicia could not sleep, for she was deep in thought. She remembered a time when she was fifteen years old and she, along with two of her schoolmates, also experimented with an Ouija Board, out of curiosity. They were at Gina's house, where Gina had found the board game in her mother's closet. Alicia had tried to warn her friends that the Ouija Board was evil—at least that's what her father had told her. But peer pressure and her own curiosity of the supernatural had gotten the best of her.

The three of them had sat down in front of the Board on the carpet of Gina's bedroom. They held hands and invited the spirit of the Ouija Board into the room. Gina and her friend Michelle began to ask the spirit of the board general questions. Gina asked the spirit, "Who are you?" The plastic tear-shaped pointer was in Gina's hands and it began to spell out, "S-P-I-R-I-T", but Alicia could not tell if Gina was moving the planchette or if a genuine spirit guided the plastic piece.

Then Michelle asked the spirit where it was from. Again, the planchette now in Michelle's hand, spelled out, "H-E-A-V-E-N."

Then it was Alicia's turn. She wanted more specifics, so she asked the spirit what its name was. Suddenly, a supernatural force gripped Alicia's hand and moved the planchette and spelled out, "N-O-O-N-E." Alicia could feel what felt like real fingers on her hand as the plastic pieced moved to each letter.

Alicia remembered Michelle asking Gina, "What is Noone?" Alicia had answered the question for Gina, saying, "I think it is saying that it is no one, stupid! I'll try again."

Alicia asked the spirit again what its name was, but this time the planchette did not move at all. The other girls laughed out loud and Gina said, "I don't think the spirit likes you. Let me ask something now."

"No. Wait," replied Alicia. "Let me try something." This time Alicia would ask some theological questions from her Christian upbringing. She then asked the spirit, "Were you there when Jesus Christ died on the cross?"

The spirit moved Alicia's hand to the sign, "YES".

Gina and Michelle looked at one another in shock and bewilderment. Then Alicia asked a similar question, "Were you present at Jesus' tomb when Christ resurrected?"

The spirit again moved Alicia's hand to the sign, "YES".

Alicia asked another question, "What did you feel when Jesus was raised from the dead?"

There was a three-second moment of silence. Then the spirit's grip tightened on Alicia's hand and spelled out, "F-E-A-R." Gina and Michelle gasped out loud, with Michelle saying, "Oh my God! This is crazy!" Alicia looked at her and put her index finger on her mouth to silence her, as she was working methodically.

The next question Alicia asked the spirit was: "How do you feel towards me?"

The spirit squeezed Alicia's hand even tighter now, even to the point where the marks of actual fingers made four red spots on Alicia's hand. The spirit spelled out, "H-A-T-E."

"What do you think about the Bible," Alicia asked immediately.

The spirit spelled out the four-lettered F-word on the board. Alicia had asked Gina if she had a Bible. Gina replied, "Yeah, my Dad has one in his bookshelf." She left and returned with a Bible about 15 seconds later. Alicia took the Bible and placed it on top of the Ouija Board. Almost immediately, the Ouija Board levitated off of the floor about three feet. The Board tossed the Bible across the room where it hit a replica painting of Van Gogh's "Starry Night" and knocked it to the floor. Gina and Michelle screamed in nervous fear and Alicia had felt a hand slap her in the face and knock her to the floor. Gina's bedroom door which was left halfway open slammed shut as the spirit apparently left the room. A red hand-mark was visible on Alicia's face. The girls had learned their lesson, and Gina and Michelle went with Alicia to church the next week and soon became Christians after witnessing the evil spirit that entered into the human realm. Just as Alicia's father had often told her, "Jim Morrison was right: there really are doors that 'Break on through to the other side'. But the doorknobs are on our side—we are the ones who open those doors and invite the demons to our world.

25

THE SEEDS OF DOUBT

With the four professors still sitting perfectly still in the ancient library, Pravuil continued his heavenly recall of pre-history. He told them, "All of the hosts of heaven were desperately searching the universe for the heavenly tree of life to receive the reward of authority. Even Adam and Eve could see an extraordinary amount of activity in the skies up above from where they were. Finally, Archangel Michael found the Tree of Life located in a distant dimension of a remote galaxy. The tree stood out amongst the several trees of that particular spiritual forest. Once Michael found the forest within that dimension, the tree itself was easy to spot. The tree's trunk was shining brightly as precious metals decorated the tree and its fruit was pleasing to the eye and delicious when Michael shared it with the rest of us. He brought the tree to the throne of the Almighty. As promised, Yahweh rewarded him by giving him authority over all angelic beings as the Head Archangel as well as a seat at the Table of the Godhead. There was a celebration and a feast in Michael's honor and all of the other angels rejoiced and were happy for his accomplishment.

"During that feast for Michael, the Holy Spirit made another announcement: 'At the end of this feast we declare a new project for all—

you will gather materials that will be used to build a holy city of the God-head, surrounding his throne.'

"All of us cheered loudly, as we continued to celebrate—eating, drinking, and the playing of angelic games. We quizzed each other about our knowledge. We challenged each other to debates. We made predictions about when the humans would find the tree of life and what would become of them. It was all a good time in a perfect universe and the splendor of God's goodness permeated the entire creation.

"After the feast was over it was back to work for us. We traveled throughout all of creation to gather materials for the heavenly City of God. When all of the materials were gathered we all began building the city together. Several of us had distinct responsibilities: Lucifer built the mountain of God that was to stand on the outskirts of the city walls. He decorated the mountain with several precious stones and caused fire to come from within the stones. Whenever he walked through the fiery stones, beautiful music came from them—indescribable to the human ear. Raphael, Akibeal, and Zateel constructed the walls of the city. Uriel, Gedaeyal, Ertael, and Meliyel collected and arranged many sparkling stones and shining lights that decorated the walls. Narel, Heloyalef, Samsaveel, and Indu constructed the twelve gates that surrounded the holy city and inscribed the appropriate names on each gate. Raguel, Zelsabel, Samyaza, and Hallah paved the transparent-golden street that led up to the throne of the Godhead. Rakael, Adnorel, Zaveba, and Yekun formed the River of Life that flowed from the throne, as Michael planted the Tree of Life on the side of the river before the bottom steps of the throne. Several of the other angels constructed many fabulous and remarkable buildings, structures, pieces of artwork that replicated the creation, as well as beautiful parks and beaches for us to lounge and engage in games, debate, and have discussions.

"The most magnificent of all structures was the worship sanctuary. The sanctuary stood in the middle of the city with the River of Life running through the middle of the building. The bricks were made of the finest gold that can be found as well as precious metals that are foreign to human knowledge. For a reason unknown to us at the time, the Son of God instructed us to mold a golden lamb on the altar of the holy place within the sanctuary. Beneath the feet of the lamb was a bronze serpent that bit one of the feet of the lamb but the lamb had its front hoof on top of the serpent's head. Before the altar there were seven golden lamp stands that corresponded to the seven days of creation along with the sacred day of rest. Before the altar and the lamp stand was a stage of performance where Lucifer and the heavenly worship team could perform songs that glorified the Godhead on the days of celebration. Several of the angels contributed to the Sanctuary of Worship including Lucifer, Michael, Gabriel, Raphael, Azazel, Sarakiel, Phanuel, and Tamiel. These were the chiefs of construction of this sanctuary. Even so, all of God's angels had their names inscribed on the walls of the sanctuary. With the completion of the Sanctuary of Worship, the city was completed and absolutely beautiful!

"When the heavenly City of God was completed, the Age of Sabbath was upon us in the heavenly realm. This angelic day corresponded with the first Sabbath Day on earth. Adam and Eve rested from all of their duties in the Garden of Eden and only focused on enjoying each other's company. The Son of God also came down and fellowshipped with them as he did regularly, teaching him some of the secrets of keeping the Garden of God. While the humans were enjoying their day of rest on earth, we angels were enjoying the Age of Sabbath in the heavenly places. Each son of God was assigned specific territories throughout the universe by the Godhead. This included places within the angelic dimensions with access to a variety of planets, moons, stars, and even certain places on and in the earth.

"Almost every one of us was extremely pleased with The Almighty's good creation and we were enjoying our Age of Sabbath and the rest that accompanied it. The storehouses were filled with enough of the heavenly fruit, bread, wine, and water so that we had no need to gather them. We were allowed to explore our individual domains but we were not permitted to labor during this epoch of angelic time. While peace and joy were abundant throughout all of the creation, there was one angelic being who was less than satisfied.

"The Anointed Cherub Lucifer was an extremely talented angel with much power and influence amongst the sons of God. Yahweh had given him the entire estate of the Mountain of God that surrounded the walls of the heavenly city. Additionally, Lucifer was given complete access to your planet Venus, the morning star, with which he was the only angel to have his own planet. Most planets had at least three angels who shared access and dominion over it. Lucifer was probably the most beautiful of all of God's creation and his wisdom was second to none. He was articulate, poetic, and his voice was as attractive as the music that came from his bodily members. And while most angels preferred donning the appearance of many different animals of the creation—and remember, this is similar to your human wardrobes—Lucifer only liked the appearance of serpents when he was not in his original appearance. He was a master of blending many different shades of coloring on his heavenly scales, and even though he only used serpentine appearances, his diversity of coloring was more glorious than any other angelic appearance. This gave his musical performances even greater value to the hearer. And most importantly, he had the greatest love and respect from the persons of the Godhead, which gave him even more confidence in his abilities.

"During this Age of Sabbath, Lucifer was taking his rest on his holy mountain, eating delicious grapes and drinking the purest of water imaginable. He still could not get over the fact that the earth dwellers were created in the image of God but yet were created beneath the angelic majesties. He thought to himself, 'How could this be? I am way more beautiful than they! I have much more brilliance, wisdom, and ability than they! How could the Godhead favor Adam over me!'

"With this line of reasoning, Lucifer flung his grapes into another dimension and poured his chalice of water over his head in disgust. He then thought to himself, 'Perhaps I am not a created being after all. Maybe the Godhead is holding back the truth from us because they do not want any of us to advance past them. Ha! What if the universe is itself eternal instead of the Godhead? What if the universe created God rather than God creating the universe? What if we all randomly sprang forth from the heavenly waters of the firmament by mere chance and evolved into what we have become now? With enough time and all of the material elements just so happening to come together at the right time and place it *is* possible! Ha! Yahweh, the Son of God, and the Holy Spirit were just luckier than the rest of us—that is all! With enough time and steady improvement any of us can become creators of our own. We can even surpass the Godhead with enough toil and practice. Besides the creation what has The Almighty done anyway? We are the ones doing all of the work now!'

"Lucifer had convinced himself that he himself could dethrone the Creator himself. His beauty, intelligence, wisdom, and abilities corrupted his soul and his thinking and his jealousy over the humans caused pride to swell in his innermost being. At this stage he began planning a rebellion. He had several loyalists amongst the angelic majesties—most of which played music with him, others who were in love with his lyrical and musical abilities. He held a private party within the spiritual dimension of your planet Venus and he only invited a select few: Hallah, Moroni, Indu, Avatarael, Mohammael, Butah, Mastema, Jinhael, Ananel, Maijan, and

Ahuramahz. Lucifer knew that these were absolutely loyal to him so he confided in them his plan to overthrow the throne of God.

"When the confidants of Lucifer arrived at his private party in their chariot, they dismounted and sat upon the fiery couch of the Venusian Dimension. Avatarael opened the conversation by asking him, 'So what is on your mind, brother?'"

"Lucifer grinned devilishly and said in his normal sing-song voice, 'After much study and thought, I have stumbled upon a discovery: Yahweh is not who he claims to be—he has been deceiving us and holding back on us all along.'"

"Butah interjected, 'What do you mean, Lucifer? I thought The Almighty is incapable of such an evil.'"

"Lucifer replied, 'As did I for the longest time. But I have been doing extensive study of the heavenly waters of the firmament and they contain many particles and properties that make up our angelic bodies and much of the other material that exists in the universe. I have calculated that it was not the alleged eternal Godhead that created the universe, but the universe is the eternal one and it gave birth to the waters of the firmament which by random chance created the persons of the Godhead first, and then us sometime after. The Godhead evolved the ability to think, will, see, and then create. Think about it: did any of us actually *see* Yahweh create any of us? Of course not! We saw him create other things of the universe, including those pathetic humans, but there is no evidence that God is eternal, almighty, or even that he created us. He was just lucky enough to be created first by the cosmos and then have the additional time to develop more fully than we have as of yet. Now he tells us this lie about how we are his children and how he loves us and wants to cherish us. The worst part of it is that he wants us to worship him, as if he were inherently better than us!'"

"Hallah interrupted, 'Are you sure about this? And if so, how do you plan to conquer the King who sits on the throne. He is more powerful than any of us.'"

"Lucifer answered, 'He is more powerful than any of us *individually*, yes. But collectively there is no telling what we can accomplish if we can gather enough support. We need to take advantage of this Age of Sabbath and improve our understanding of the universe and our skills. We must manipulate the materials of creation, just like we did when we made tools. This time we will make tools of destruction that will injure anyone who gets in our way. We will then subjugate those we overcome and use them as hostages to blackmail and leave the Godhead no other choice but to vacate their throne and become my subjects.'"

"Moroni smiled said to Lucifer, 'It sounds like you have been planning this for some time. I think you might be right about the possibility of the eternal universe creating the Godhead first by chance. But what if you are wrong and then Yahweh destroys us for insurrection?'"

"Lucifer responded by saying, 'I am not wrong—for I have studied these things closely. Even if our mission falls short, Yahweh does not have it in him to destroy us—look how beautiful we are. And consider how unfair it was to create the humans in his image when we are so much more advanced and wonderful than they are. The Son of God does not understand what it is like to be humiliated in such a way as we have. We are entitled to more than what we have been given and Yahweh owes us at least the chance to debate this issue publicly. And if he will not give us this chance, then we will be forced to take his throne by violence.'"

"Mohammael then spoke, 'I believe that you speak truth, Lucifer. I will submit to your rule and follow you no matter what.' The others soon were convinced as well, so they made a pact. They planned to propagate accusations against our Father, questioning his goodness to each angel individually, at first. They did not do so in a rash manner, but with subtlety and with the appearance of honest inquiry. Many of the angelic majesties rejected the proposition outright, but some at least thought about and considered the possibilities and their ramifications. Many seeds of doubt were implanted in the souls of many of the angelic hosts. Lucifer's quest had a significant impact and small victories were won in the minds of many of his brethren."

Professor Cooper briefly interrupted Pravuil by asking, "How many angels did God create, anyway?"

Pravuil answered, "As many stars that you can count in the heavens—they are as many as we are."

"But we can't count all of them," replied Professor Mockens.

"Exactly," said Christian Sage.

Dr. Saal chimed in, "Please, continue to tell us more—this is fascinating!"

Pravuil smiled, stroked his beard and then looked up towards the roof of the cavern, as if silently requesting permission from his Father. He returned his gaze upon his students and said, "Okay, it began like this…"

26

ARRESTED DEVELOPMENT

When Lieutenant Alex Sage lined up with his unit for P.T. on Monday morning at 0545 hours, he was greeted with a celebrity's welcome. He received hugs and handshakes from practically the entire platoon. Once the platoon sergeant ordered them to "fall-in", however, it was business as usual. They were going on a run for about three miles. Once the run began, the thoughts of the supernatural events again filled Alex's mind. He did not feel the brisk morning air on his face or the exhaustion that normally plagued him during these runs, for Alex normally hated running. The three miles went by like three blocks because of Lt. Sage's preoccupation of last week's events.

While Alex was eating breakfast in the mess hall, his platoon sergeant, Master Sergeant Gerald Wilford, told him that the company commander requested his presence as soon as he was finished eating. Alex had expected as much, and was actually surprised that he had not been summoned the day before, considering the nature of the events that he was involved in. Alex nodded politely to Sergeant Wilford, in agreement. Immediately, nervousness befell Alex. He did not know what to tell Captain Moore regarding what had recently happened to him. The truth sounded way too crazy for anyone to believe, but yet if he pretended not to remember then his own conscience would nag him for the rest of his life. Additionally, what if some sort of evidence emerged to reveal Alex's lack of integrity? This moral dilemma completely removed his appetite, as Alex threw away his breakfast before finishing half of it. "This had to have happened to me for a reason," whispered Alex to himself, as he walked toward Captain Moore's office.

The skepticism of the reporter in Iceland really had a negative impact of how Alex saw himself and the events that he allegedly had experienced. He was unsure if he had just dreamt up all of these things, as Mr. Heath had suggested, or if these things had really taken place as his memory seemed to authenticate. Since Alex could not determine that actual reality, he decided to stay "below the radar" and to play it safe by claiming a loss of memory—which was originally the case anyway. Alex was able to satisfy his conscience by this reasoning until further clarification was realized. He walked into platoon headquarters nervous, but yet with this tentative game plan. Senior Airman Jones, who was on duty for Charge of Quarters at that time, greeted him, "L-T Sage, good to see you, sir."

"Thank you, Jones," answered Lt. Sage. "I'm here to see the Captain."

"Oh yes, he's expecting you. Go ahead and go right in."

Alex approached Captain Moore's door and knocked.

"Enter!" shouted Captain Moore, in his deep, raspy voice. "Please have a seat, Lieutenant."

Alex sat down, trying to hide his nervousness. Captain Moore put aside one stack of papers by his computer and then reached into his desk and pulled out a few other pieces of paper. He skimmed down them for about ten seconds and then returned his gaze to Alex. "Well, well, well," he said to Alex. "You've had quite a time haven't you, Lieutenant?"

"Yes sir," answered Alex. "Too bad I can't remember much of it at all."

Captain Moore continued as if Alex's words meant nothing, "It says here that you were on a training exercise over the Arctic Circle, and according to the other pilots, that you and your partner, Lieutenant Sanchez, just disappeared and that you did not answer your radio. The other pilots circled the area for an hour and could not locate you by sight, radio, or satellite. Then, about six hours later, the Icelandic authorities find you, alone, floating on a piece of ice. Do you remember any of this?"

Alex tried to swallow the lump in his throat. He thought he would improvise his original plan somewhat, responding, "Well sir, the only thing that I remember was being caught in an ice storm. Lightning had nearly struck us, or so it seemed, and then our aircraft was being pelted by large hailstones. After that I blacked out. The next thing I remember is waking up in a hospital bed, and now here I am."

"Hmm," Captain Moore sounded in response to Lt. Sage's answer. "Well, I'm no meteorologist, but according to the reports there was a snowstorm that was nearby, but hailstorms are not compatible with snowstorms, nor are they common in the Arctic Circle. What you are telling me doesn't make any sense."

"Maybe it wasn't a hailstorm, sir," answered Alex, "But I do remember our plane being struck by several small objects. We must've crashed afterward, although I don't remember specifically."

"Are you sure that you didn't fly off course?" suggested Captain Moore.

"No, sir, I did not."

Captain Moore then said, "And what about Lieutenant Sanchez? We have not recovered his body yet. Hell, we haven't even recovered your plane yet or found any evidence of a crash. This is all so odd—and I hate oddities! Your lack of recollection only makes things even more complex."

Alex answered, "I don't know what to tell you, sir. I don't know what happened to Sanchez or where his body is. And I certainly don't know where the plane fell either. I wish I could be more helpful, but I'm still trying to get things straight in my own head."

"That's understandable," replied Captain Moore. "And I apologize for showing my frustration—but the Colonel is demanding more info. Just be aware, Lieutenant, that a formal investigation is underway, so expect to be questioned by more people then just myself."

"I understand, sir," Alex said.

"Okay. Dismissed," said Captain Moore. As Alex was about to exit, Captain Moore said one more thing, "Oh, by the way, Sage, I'm glad that you're okay."

"Thank you, sir—I appreciate that," replied Alex, as he exited his company commander's office. He headed back to his barracks so that he could change into his basic duty uniform. The rest of his day was as normal as could be, apart from a few conversations that he had about his "crash" with his fellow airmen. Alex did not give out any new information other than what he had told Captain Moore. His conscience still was not at ease from his withholding of information to his superior officer. Eventually, he had to tell someone—otherwise he would go crazy.

That evening when he had slept, he saw the angel Sarakiel in a vision. Sarakiel seemed to have personally visited his room in his glorious form, sat on the bed next to Alex, and told him, "Do not be afraid to give the truth to the next person that asks you. The truth will set you free. Trust in the Lord with all of your heart, and do not be supported by your own understanding of how things will work out. The upright must walk by faith."

Alex woke up from that dream at 3:00 am. He was unable to go back to sleep, so he spent the next couple of hours reading the Gospel of Matthew in the New Testament. It was obvious that he needed to deepen his faith in Christ if he was to overcome these sudden obstacles in his life. He knew that God had allowed them to happen for a reason—he was sure of this now. Lieutenant Sage went through another uneventful day at work. Almost immediately after his platoon was dismissed for the evening, he was greeted by a journalist of the USA Today newspaper, which sells its media on every U.S. military base.

"Excuse me, Lieutenant Sage?" asked the reporter.

"Yes, that's me," answered Alex.

The reporter continued, "My name is Arnold Dixon from USA Today. Is there somewhere we can meet privately?"

Alex replied surprisingly, "Uhh, I guess we can go to Sed's Burgers down the street. I'm kind of hungry, plus they have some booths that are isolated from the rest of the restaurant."

"Okay. That'll do," Arnold said, in his southern, Georgian accent.

Lieutenant Alex Sage got into Arnold Dixon's Mercedes Benz and they drove five blocks to get to Sed's Burgers. After they ordered their food, they sat down at one of the more isolated booths of the restaurant so that Alex could tell his story freely without much interruption or other people overhearing. While they were eating, Arnold took out a renowned tabloid magazine that featured part of Alex's bizarre experience on the front cover. Alex was taken back at the sight of the imagined blonde giants aboard a typical UFO. Arnold read the article on page 5 that allegedly corresponded with the front page story—the bottom right-corner part of the front page to be specific. Alex couldn't help but laugh at the revised edition of what he had told Philip Heath during his last day at the hospital in Iceland. Alex asked Arnold humorously, "How could they mess up the story that bad? What I told that guy was way different then what is being said in this article."

"Evidently, the person who interviewed you sold your story for a few quick bucks," answered Arnold. "Since your name was not given, they were not obligated to be factual but whatever can generate enough sensationalism to sell magazines. The reason that I am here right now is to find out whether or not there is anything to this story—if there is anything true about it whatsoever—and if not, what really happened to you last week."

Alex was naturally reluctant to be as open with Arnold as he was with Philip Heath, but he remembered his dream the night before with Sarakiel's instructions to speak freely with the next person who asked of him. He would have to put his complete trust in God's plan for his life. And at this point, his conscience could not bear to conceal the truth any longer. After a brief moment of silence, as Alex chewed on his burger, he said to Arnold, "There is an actual story to report to you, but before I tell you I would like to voice a few concerns."

"Okay, shoot," Arnold said to him."

Alex continued, "Officially, as to what I reported to my superior officer yesterday, I do not remember the events that I experienced last week. So anything that I tell you will contradict the answer that I have already given to my company commander. If this story gets out in a popular way, I could get into a lot of trouble."

Arnold replied, "Well, I don't imagine your story being on the front page or any widely read portion of our paper. I'm a small-time reporter and most of my articles are on the last few pages if they even make the paper at all. The fact that I'm doing a follow up on a tabloid article is already laughable according to the standards of reliable sources, so you shouldn't worry too much about any of this getting back to your superior officers."

That sounded reasonable enough to Alex, once he thought about it, taking the final bite of his burger. Arnold then asked, "What are your other concerns about giving me your story?"

Alex thought about this, while he finished chewing the last bite of his burger. He then said, "When I gave my story before, the reporter looked at me as if I were a lunatic hallucinating on mushrooms or something. I didn't like that look at all—in fact, I began to doubt myself and thinking that maybe that my brain did make up the story to explain what was forgotten or perhaps too horrific to remember. But I can be absolutely sure that what happened to me and Kyle was real—and there is not any evidence to the contrary!"

Alex began to raise his voice a little to the point where a few others of Sed's customers turned their heads to look at him. He returned a look to them as to apologize, holding up his hand and bowing his head. To this, Arnold said to him, "Look, Alex, I'm not here to judge you in any way. I'm just doing a follow-up to a peculiar story that—at most—will get maybe two paragraphs on page 13 of our paper. Yeah, many people will read it, but if your story is too weird then those people will probably be skeptical anyway—just as they already are with much of the news. We're in this business to sell stories to the public to keep them buying our newspaper, and if your story is interesting they will continue to buy our paper to read about more interesting stories—even if they are unbelievable. And look, I have paperwork here that will pay you a percentage of whatever revenue our paper will get on that particular day that your story will be in the fold—if it even makes it."

Alex looked over the paperwork. He began to reason to himself, "Well, I have been instructed from above to tell my story. And if I can make some money in the process, then why not?" Alex didn't take long to think things over before he signed his name on the contract. He then went on to tell Arnold everything that he had told Philip Heath, and his memory did not fail him at all. Unlike Philip, Arnold kept an objective, poker-face while writing down the details. Several times, he would ask Alex to repeat certain details because, unlike Philip, he did not have a recording device but took down the notes manually. When Alex had finished telling Arnold everything there was to know about what he had experienced the previous week, Arnold drove him back to his barracks and promised Alex that he would be the first to know if his story made the paper or not. Alex believed Arnold because he seemed like a sincere fellow. He went to sleep that night without any worries or anxiety.

The rest of the week was about as routine as weeks go by military standard—until Friday. When Lieutenant Alex Sage lined up for physical training at 6:00 on Friday morning, Captain Moore was there to greet him: "Good morning, Lieutenant Sage. How are you feeling this morning?"

Alex replied, "Okay, sir. Is everything all right? I don't usually see you out here this early."

Captain Moore chuckled and said, "Yeah, you're right about that. Listen, we need to have a talk about what we discussed on Monday. I need you to run back upstairs, get your uniform on, and come to my office—ASAP!"

"Yes sir!" answered Lt. Sage. Alex did as he was commanded. He was slightly nervous, but yet reassured that things were going to work out. He walked into Captain Moore's office upbeat and with a smile on his face. Captain Moore's face did not show as much optimism. Alex sat before his commanding officer as he had done five days earlier, when Captain Moore began his speech:

"Lieutenant Sage—I'm not sure what to make of your selective *amnesia* about what happened to you last week. I wanted to believe what you told me on Monday about you not remembering what happened, but the testimony of the other pilots and some of the other events that followed have given me a reason to be suspicious. For example, immediately after you checked out of the hospital in Iceland, a small explosive detonated in the very room that you stayed in. Nobody knows where it came from and there were no witnesses of any strange visitors coming into your room. Obviously, *somebody* wanted *somebody* dead, and that somebody knows *something* about what happened to you. Now let me ask you, straight up—are you a spy?"

"No way, sir!" exclaimed Alex. "I would never betray my country."

"Good answer," said Captain Moore. "At least one investigator is suspicious that you took your plane to a foreign nation and that you were followed to Iceland—but that can't be proven. And normally, I would tell that investigator to go jump in a lake because you have an outstanding record here with our company, Sage. But I can't vouch for you any more, Lieutenant, do you know why?"

"No, why is that sir?" replied Alex.

"Because now I know that I can't trust your word as gospel truth," answered Captain Moore. "You lied to me, and if there's one thing I cannot stand is a liar who betrays the trust of his superior officer. Doggone it, Sage, we're supposed to be a family here!"

Alex sat there speechless. He thought to himself, "Does Captain Moore know something that I don't know? Did someone tell him something about what happened? But who? Arnold had promised to let him know if anything became of his story." Alex just shrugged his shoulders and said, "I don't understand, sir."

Captain Moore continued, "Another example would be the testimony of several officers in your barracks who said that you came back last Saturday night drunk and babbling about, uh…what was it? Falling stars are coming? Or something of that nature. Is that some kind of code language for terrorists or something? Sage, you had better come clean or you will be in a world of hurt! Do you understand, Lieutenant?"

Alex was puzzled. He had not remembered being drunk or saying anything to anyone when he returned early on Sunday morning. He said to Captain Moore, "I understand the implications of falsifying a report, sir. But I don't know what you're talking about getting drunk or talking about falling stars or terrorists or whatever you're referring to. I hardly ever drink, sir."

Captain Moore was un-phased about Alex's last statement. He continued on with his rant, "And then I wake up yesterday morning and grab my paper like I always do. I skim through the articles to see if there is anything relatively related to our mission, or something interesting worth spending my precious time reading. I get to the third page and I see this: Captain Moore showed Alex an article on the third page that read, AIR FORCE PILOT CLAIMS EXTRA-TERRESTRIAL ENCOUNTER OVER ARTIC CIRCLE.

Alex could not believe it! That liar Arnold betrayed him! He began to quickly read the article, which included his name and where he was stationed. Not only was the article not in the back pages and not a mere paragraph or two, it was on the same page as a story of the U.S. President, featured in an article that was about twelve paragraphs long! And sure enough, Arnold Dixon's name was attributed to the article. When Alex looked up, he saw Captain Moore's dark brown eyes bulging out of its sockets in apparent rage. Alex could tell that he was doing his best to keep calm and not to raise his voice too much, but he couldn't help from yelling somewhat, "Is there a reason, Lieutenant, that you told me that you did not remember what happened to you, but you were able to *suddenly* remember all of these details when confronted by the media? You make me sick!"

At this point, Alex began to panic, "Wa-wa-wa-well, you see, sir, I was afraid to tell you because I thought you would think I was crazy or something and lock me up. I actually told this story to a reporter in Iceland and he blew me off and sold my story to some tabloid. So this other guy from USA Today came to me on Tuesday and promised to keep my story low-key and he convinced me to come out with the story."

"Bad move, Lieutenant," answered Captain Moore. "For one thing, you can never trust the media—that's a cut-throat business and they'll say anything and do anything to get their story in the headlines. You can't give them squat! Even more serious, is that you lied to a U.S. Air Force officer during an investigation. I can't cover for you anymore, Sage, and my boss tore me a new one last night! I have to turn you over to the MPs, Lieutenant Sage. They should be here any minute. You will be given representation, and you will tell your story to a judge. As for now, you are officially under arrest."

"What!" exclaimed Alex. "Sir, you can't do this. I was confused and scared, I didn't mean to deceive you or to hold out on an investigation. I didn't know it was that serious."

"Not serious?!" yelled Captain Moore. "Sage, we have lost the life of a fellow soldier—Lieutenant Sanchez. And we have lost on of our aircraft—of course this is serious! Like I said, I can't help you anymore, Lieutenant—I'm in a mess of my own and I'm sure the media will be knocking at my door any minute, as well as my own superior officers giving me grief."

There was a knock at the door.

"Who is it?" asked Captain Moore.

"MPs," said the military police officer.

"We'll be right out," answered the Captain.

Alex Sage was now visibly shaken up and holding back tears. Captain Moore did show some compassion. He put his hand on Alex's shoulder and said, "Look, Sage, I'll see what I can do to put in a good word for you. I know sometimes there are gray areas in some of these unique situations. But you have to level with me from here on out, okay?"

Alex looked up and nodded. Then Captain Moore walked him out into the hallway where the Military Police handcuffed Lieutenant Alex Sage and placed him into the back of their squad car and drove him into a holding tank at the station. He was booked for lying to an Air Force officer and for insubordination. They fed him a hearty breakfast and were kind to him. Alex would wait for an attorney to show up for the next few hours. Until then, he dozed off in his jail cell.

27

SQUARE ONE

It was an uneventful two days of walking for Alicia and Amanda on the Northeastern trail. The two women were grateful to have on real clothing and comfortable shoes now. The weather was consistently warm, even at night, so sleeping was not difficult—even leaning against rocks and trees. Much of the trail paralleled a small stream so drinking water was available most of the time. A variety of fruits and vegetables were also easily accessible so that the nutrition of the two women was sustained. Alicia and Amanda spoke a lot about their recent experiences as well as other times in their lives where they believed that God had intervened and done many marvelous works.

After two days of walking the women finally spotted a small town on the top of a small hill, just like Asphael had told them. Excited, Alicia and Amanda quickened their pace up the hill. As the two women entered into the town the passersby looked at them as the outsiders they were. Both of them had taken two Spanish classes from high school to college, but they were far from fluent. They did greet people who walked close enough to them with, "Buenas tardes," as it was about two hours from sunset. The buildings were old and run down, but still a considerable upgrade from the village they escaped from a few days earlier. Fortunately for them, they spotted a police station where they encountered a deputy who spoke very good English. The deputy who worked at the front desk saw them and greeted them, "Hello, young ladies, how may I help you?"

Amanda responded, "Sir, we would like to report a series of kidnappings, rapes, and murders by an evil cult of people."

The deputy, now looking alarmed, said to them, "Wait over there and have a seat. Someone will be with you shortly."

He then got on the phone and spoke with somebody in Spanish, as Alicia and Amanda sat down on a couple of very uncomfortable chairs. About five minutes later, a young man who looked like he was in his late teens or early twenties came out and introduced himself, "Hello, my name is Carlos and I am here to take down your report. Please, come with me."

Amanda and Alicia followed Carlos into his office. The seats in his office were much more comfortable, and from the pictures on his walls, Carlos was a family man with two children and was fairly decorated in his profession. Amanda and Alicia began to tell them their story without omitting any of the extraordinary details. Alicia noticed that Carlos' facial expression was that of fascination and not of disbelief or skepticism. He asked additional questions to bring out the details about physical descriptions, names, places, times of day, and any quotations that people made. Carlos was very professional, but surprisingly, none of this seemed shocking or out of place to him.

When Carlos was finished gathering all of the information for his report he got up out of his chair and said, "Okay, I am going to run this report to my boss and I'll be right back."

Amanda quickly interjected, "Wait, what's going to happen to us? How are we going to get back home?"

"Don't worry, we will get you home," answered Carlos. "Give me a couple of minutes, I'll be right back."

Carlos returned about fifteen minutes later with good news. He told the women, "Well, it looks like we have two plane tickets for you to get back home. In a few minutes, one of our deputies will be here to take you to the airport. Is there anything else I can help you with?"

Alicia replied, "No Carlos, you have been very helpful to us. Thank you so much, and God bless you."

"Thank you. I wish the same to you and that all will be well," said Carlos.

So Alicia and Amanda returned to the uncomfortable seats in the front waiting area. They waited for about ten minutes and then a deputy, who spoke very little English, came through the door. He smiled at the women, evidently confirmed with the front desk deputy about his mission, and then invited them to follow him into his squad car. At this time the sun had begun setting and darkness began to dominate the evening sky. There was no conversation between the women and this deputy, as they rode in the back of his car. It took about fifteen minutes of driving before Amanda dozed off. Alicia was deep in thought. They drove for another hour or so when finally Alicia asked the deputy, "Excuse me sir, about how much longer before we get to the airport?"

The deputy answered, "Sorry, me no understand English."

Alicia tried again, "Cuantos minutos a la aeropuerto?"

He answered in Spanish that it would be about another twenty minutes.

Almost immediately after that short conversation, two military jeeps sped ahead of their squad car, skidded sideways, and blocked the road ahead of them. The deputy slammed on his brakes to stop his car and told the women, "Stay here," in his thick accent. He got out of the car and unsnapped his holster and kept his right hand near his pistol. Then four men jumped out of each jeep dressed in all black tactical military uniforms with machine guns drawn. Alicia could tell there was a short conversation between them and the deputy, which resulted with the deputy sliding his pistol towards the men on the ground and dropping to his knees. One of the military men picked up the deputy's pistol and handed it to another person who stayed in one of the jeeps. Meanwhile, Amanda began to wake up from her nap. "What's going on?" she asked Alicia.

"I don't know, but I don't think we should stay here and find out," answered Alicia.

Two of the military men grabbed the deputy and began to tie his hands and feet. This is when Alicia and Amanda quickly opened the car doors and ran towards the side of the road. Three men began to pursue them down the side of the road and into an open field. It didn't take long for the men to catch the women. They tied their hands and two of them carried them over their backs as they climbed back up to the road. Alicia and

Amanda were each put in the back of one of the jeeps, separated for the time being. The jeeps drove off back to the direction from which the women came, with the deputy tied up and laying in the middle of the street. A couple of minutes later, the jeep went off road and into a dirt road through a forest. About an hour later, they arrived at a military outpost that was hidden by camouflaged netting. Alicia and Amanda were taken out of the jeeps and put in separate jail cells within the outpost prison. There they spent the night hungry and alone in the dark.

Alicia had been awakened early the next morning by the opening of her cell. A man in an expensive, white suit brought her half a loaf of bread and a large bottle of water. He spoke to her, "This is what you will have for the rest of the day, so don't consume it all at once." She nodded and began to eat and drink to satisfy her desperate hunger. The man watched as she ate with a smile on his face. This man was clean shaven, wore glasses, and had light brown skin. The fragrance of his elegant cologne filled the air.

After Alicia had ate and drank what she would for that time he began to speak again, "You and your friend have witnessed activities that you were not intended see and live to tell about it. Apparently, you are divinely protected, so we will not kill you. So if we cannot harm you, we will seek to be accommodated for our loss of people and your witness. We will hold you hostage and seek a ransom from your country for your release. But let me tell you this: if you ever go public with what you saw, we will find you and we will make your life a living hell. Do you understand?"

Alicia nodded, as she was astounded that a man could say such things in such a polite manner. She was about to ask him how they could make her life a living hell if she was divinely protected, but she thought better of it and kept that thought to herself. The man continued, "Just as we have people in our government who are with us and willing to give us the information for your whereabouts, we have people in your country in high places that would do the same. So I beg of you, keep your experience in a personal diary and share it with no one, for your own safety. I would hate to have to track you down again because I will not be as polite, I can assure you. I am sincerely sorry that you had to be involved in this, but we can't change that now, can we?"

Alicia nodded again and asked, "Who exactly are you?"

The man answered, "We are the people in the shadows who pull the strings of the world system. We are untouchable and untraceable. Let's just keep it at that."

"Is Amanda going to be okay?" asked Alicia.

"Her fate will be the same as yours," the man replied. "Good day."

The man closed the cell door and left the outpost. Alicia could hear a helicopter engine starting and then pulling up from the ground. Apparently, this was the mode of travel that the man in the white suit went about his business. Alicia had been in this situation a lot during this past week, but unlike the other times she was in perfect peace because of what Asphael had told her. And if she knew anything at all, it was that if God is with you, who can be against you? She began to hum hymns at that moment and she spent the rest of her day in prayer and meditation, as she rationed her bread and water.

28

THE FIRSTFRUITS
OF THE FALLEN

Dr. Christian Sage, Professor Richard Mockens, Dr. Jabari Saal, and Professor Cliff Cooper were on the edge of their seats, as they sat on the floor of the prehistoric library listening intently to the angel Pravuil. He was giving them the unknown account of the origin of evil that began in the angelic realm. Hours had gone by but they seemed like merely minutes. Each of the four men were like children listening to the story of Santa Claus for the first time—but this was real. To the men it was surreal—almost like an out of body experience. Sitting on the floor for hours would normally be very uncomfortable, but the story that Pravuil gave them made it seem like they were not physically in the room.

Pravuil continued, "Lucifer and his cohort had subtly influenced a large enough number of their angelic brethren to join in their conspiracy against the Godhead. Others were not convinced but were still uncertain. However, most of the sons of God maintained their absolute loyalty to Yahweh. The undercover rebels had quietly gathered enough materials to make potent weapons, if needed. Lucifer had still wanted to usurp the throne in a more democratic way though, through the art of persuasion and reason. The number of Yahweh loyalists still bothered him enough to conjure up a contingency plan.

"A secret meeting of the eleven loyalists to Lucifer took place at his estate in the angelic realm of Venus. When the last of the twelve angels was present, Lucifer laid out his plan. He said, 'Look: although our secret campaign has received a significant amount of support, we are still out-numbered more than 2-to-1. Maijan, how does our weaponry fare against such odds?'"

"Maijan answered, 'Lord Lucifer, our weapons would fare well in an even match up of a hand-to-hand assault, but against such odds it is far from certain.'"

"Lucifer responded, 'Thank you for your realism, Maijan, that's what I figured. And that is exactly why I called this meeting. I have a plan that just might inspire more of our brethren to join us, and if not, then we can perhaps put ourselves in a position to where our voice can at least be heard where then reasonable souls can decide for themselves the truth.'"

"Indu replied, 'Excellent, Lord Lucifer. What is the plan?'"

"Lucifer gave a sly glance toward Indu and then to the rest of his coun-cil. He said to them, 'On the next feast day coming up when we will per-form our songs of worship, we will begin our praise like we normally do. After we have our brethren in an emotional state of ecstasy, we will then perform a new song that will establish our ideas. When we merely speak the words to our angelic brethren, they are able to use their reason. And since they are not as advanced as us, they still believe the word of Yahweh with a pathetic sense of blind faith and obedience. But when souls are under a more emotional state of being, their reason begins to subside and they think with their feelings rather than their logic or intellect. So when our worship songs have brought them to the highest point of exhilaration, we will strike with our music and I guarantee that we will persuade many more of our brethren to our side.'

"Lucifer continued, 'In addition, we will conceal our weapons within our bodies behind our instrumental anatomy. If we need to, we will subdue any resistance and take them hostage up to the throne of the Godhead. If they will not hear us, we will threaten our way to victory!'"

"The other eleven all sighed out, 'Yes! Aaah, yes, Lord Lucifer, hail!' Lucifer then told them the new song they would perform with the sounds that would amplify their rebellious ideas. Out of his eyes he projected the blueprint onto the wall of the meeting hall. The twelve rebels took a few moments to study the plan and then they all absorbed the information and were excited about finally taking their plan into action.

"Finally, the time came to perform in the holy sanctuary before the throne of the Godhead. Every angelic being in existence was present. Our Father Yahweh, the Son of God, and the Holy Spirit were all present on the holy throne with Michael on their right, and Gabriel on their left. Lucifer and his eleven loyalists took the stage. None of the others knew about the plan, except for the Godhead, of course. Yahweh purposely did not reveal anything to anyone, including Michael or Gabriel. He wanted them to demonstrate the loyalty that he foreknew them to possess. None of the angels that remained strict loyalists to Yahweh had any idea of what could happen, even though many of them had heard Lucifer and his council had given them their reasons of doubting the lordship of the Godhead. Most of them thought that Lucifer had allowed his brilliance to get the best of his reasoning at times, but none of them thought that he would be actually foolish enough to think that he could dethrone the Godhead, or that he could even plan anything in secret that Yahweh would not know about.

"The worship began as usual. Many of the angels flew around the sanctuary in an awesome display of light-work and artistry. All of them sang along the familiar songs of worship, making complimentary sounds of their own. Some of them thought that Lucifer and company had never been better and that he had vastly improved his skills, as talented as they were already. The spirits of the angelic hosts were as highly ecstatic as they had ever been and the Godhead was glorified magnificently.

"Immediately after the last of the worship songs, Lucifer led with his stringed instruments a new tune that had never been heard before. The other musicians also played accordingly with their harps and other various stringed instruments, piano-type instruments, flutes and other various instruments of breath, and finally the drum-playing of Indu was most excellent. The angelic brethren looked at each other with awe and their eyes wide with excitement! They began moving about to the drum beat and corresponding with the most excellent of sounds as well. When it came time to sing, the instrumentals quieted down enough for Lucifer's beautiful voice to be heard. Lucifer sang,

Waters of the cosmos I do wonder,

How we all came asunder,

We were all once yoked as one,

Now we worship Yahweh and his Son,

And the Holy Spirit—to all we sing,

O Eternal waters who produced the king,

Eternal universe, without beginning or an end,

By random chance his power does depend,

O why was I not created first,

That I should make decrees for the universe,

My misfortune has reached its end, now it's time,

My evolution is has reached its peak, time to climb,

Demonstrate how I can reign with awesome power,

The throne of Yahweh will become my tower,

Beauty perfected, surely full of wisdom,

A light-bearer, given as my position,

Anointed Cherub covering the throne,

I filled my mountain with every precious stone,

I breathe the flute and strum the tambourine,

With my beauty there's not a thing I can't achieve,

It can't be treason, as any can see--perfected reason,

Naturally selected to rule—it's now the season,

Listen to my voice, enjoy the noise my brethren,

I am predestined to ascend to heaven,

I will raise my throne above the stars of Elohim,

It is written in the heavenlies that I will be the king,

I will sit in charge in the assemblies of the stars,

On my mountain—a god—to all, whoever you are,

I will ascend above the heights of the clouds,

I have evolved, don't ask me how—the time is now,

Oh my, oh my, I shall become like the Most High,

Oh my, oh my, join my revolution against the Most High!

"With that last line, Lucifer took a bow as his fellow band members played their instruments at their highest pitch. Many of the angels who had already pledged loyalty to Lucifer applauded and sung words of praise towards him. Many others who had not been previously persuaded, now joined the revolt of heaven and also gave praise to Lucifer. The majority of the angels who remained loyal to Yahweh looked at each other in bewilderment! Michael and Gabriel who sat on each side of the throne of the Godhead asked Yahweh, 'What shall we do about this blasphemy?'

"Yahweh answered them, 'Have patience my sons.' The Son of God had secretly left them while Lucifer played his final song in the sanctuary. He suddenly descended on the throne and appeared with what looked like lightning in his hands. He gave weapons to Michael and Gabriel and said to them, 'Behold, there has begun a war in heaven. The period of goodness and perfect righteousness has ended and now we begin the Battle of Pneumatka. I have given you swords from the Almighty. Take these and multiply them to give to your brethren. Do not fear, you are eternal beings who have tasted of the tree of life—you cannot be destroyed, nor can the rebels. These weapons can stun you, though, and cause temporary impotence, so beware.'

"With that, Michael and Gabriel quickly descended down to the sanctuary. By that time, Lucifer had gathered his followers and began marching up the steps to the throne of the Godhead. Michael and Gabriel gathered many of the faithful and quickly explained the situation and transferred the power of the majestic weaponry. They had to move quickly because the rebels were moving rapidly toward them. Michael then assembled the armed angels and led them down toward Lucifer. A dark cloud soon covered the area and the lights and the brightness of the precious jewels of the sanctuary were now dimmed. Only a faint light from the throne illuminated the street of gold, as thunder clapped from the cloud above. Soon, snow began falling upon the angels. They all looked up for a moment and then returned their gaze upon their opponents.

"Michael, who was now face to face with Lucifer, said to him, 'I should have predicted such a folly from you. Many of us had begun to think that your vast talents have gotten the best of you and some of us heard your ridiculous theory of eternal matter giving birth to us by random chance. Ha! Do you really think you can overthrow the Almighty?'"

"Lucifer looked at him with a straight, evil face for a few moments and then let out a sinister laugh and turned around to face his loyalists, who also began laughing. He returned his face to Michael and said, 'You ignorant do-gooder! If you had only investigated the cosmos as closely as I have instead of going on that wild hunt for a foolish tree—you would have come to the same conclusion as me! Deep down inside I think you already believe what I believe, you are just too scared and weak to act upon it. I think you know that it is true, and that is why you are trying to kiss up to the king until your own opportunity arises—but too late—I have beat you to it! I will reign over you unless—unless you join me, and then we can rule the universe, side-by-side. How does that sound to you, Michael?'"

"Michael looked down for a moment, and then back up to Lucifer. Gabriel and Raphael now joined him at each side. Michael answered him, 'We will not join you Lucifer, and you have deceived yourself into thinking you can overcome the one who gave you life! Think about it: how can nothing, or a mindless piece of universe, accidentally create a thinking, volitional being along with an orderly universe where everything is so perfect?'"

"A few of the less-loyal angelic majesties behind Lucifer began to grumble amongst themselves at Michael's statement. Lucifer, recognizing that Michael's reasoning had been a striking blow against his theory, turned around at his followers and shouted, 'Silence! Do not be fooled by Michael's trickery, he knows fully well that he does not stand a chance against us, that is why he is stalling and trying to buy time so he can think of what to do next.'"

"The rebels regained their silence and their composure. Lucifer then said to Michael, 'Brother, brother, brother: why are you making things more difficult than they have to be? You see, we have been planning this coup for quite awhile now. We have access to powers that you have yet to discover. I suggest you all return to your domains before we destroy you. Besides, if Yahweh is truly all-powerful, why does he need you to protect him? Can he not defend himself against an alleged created being? You fool! You are being used to do Yahweh's dirty work. He is a lazy deity who is making us his slaves and sending us on these silly missions. I bet that the Godhead are laughing their heads off watching us scramble around looking for magic trees and wasting our intelligence on serving the throne and bowing and worshiping them! It makes me sick! And it is even more pathetic that you are so narrow-minded as to believe everything he says without questioning any of it. You see, I am an independent thinker who has discovered how to defeat that holy slave master! Join us and we can all have independence and true freedom of being and create our own identities and become gods ourselves!'"

"Michael had had enough of Lucifer's rant. He then pulled out his sword of lightning and held it across his breastplate. He looked into the red eyes of Lucifer, which was deeply hidden beneath his serpentine mask, decorated in bright yellow, purple, and lime green. He said to Lucifer, 'Your blasphemies will no longer be tolerated on this holy mountain. If you do not vacate immediately, we will take action against you. Take a close look—you are outnumbered and we have a superior position over you. We also have our Father Almighty behind us. You have no chance. Turn around and be banished from this holy place, you enemy of the Most High!'"

"When Michael finished speaking those words, the holy angels behind him all drew their swords and yelled out a great cry. Lucifer then drew his sword and raised it above his head. He sang out, 'This is what we have been waiting for my brethren. Let us partake in our victory and overrun this holy mountain and take the throne of the Godhead. Engage! Engage!'"

"With that, the steps of the holy mountain of the Godhead immediately began to be filled with hand-to-hand combat with swords of lightning. There were angelic majesties flying all over the place. Bright flashes of light filled the heavenly places. Many angels were struck and stunned by the weapons. Some of the Luciferians unleashed cosmic bow-and-arrows and began shooting down many of the holy ones. Lucifer had tried to side step Michael and ascend up the mountain. Along the way, he struck down many of the holy ones with his splendid power and precise abilities. Eventually, Michael had caught up to him just before he reached the actual throne of the Godhead. 'Not so fast, you shining serpent!' shouted Michael. 'You must get by me first.'

'With pleasure,' replied Lucifer with a devilish grin.

"The two went at it for a great length of time. Eventually, the holy angels of the Almighty had subdued the Luciferians and bound them with chains. They were soon at Michael's side to assist him. Lucifer stopped for a moment to look around and notice that he was surrounded. He had not been able to advance past Michael, and their one-on-one battle ended in a stalemate. Lucifer saw beyond the holy ones and noticed that his loyalists had been defeated. He looked down with sorrow, but his pride would not allow him to surrender. He scowled and looked up again and pointed his sword at Michael, and then to the rest of the holy ones who surrounded him. He began to circle in place, looking at his foes, daring any one of them to make the first move. Just then, the Son of God descended with a flash of light upon the battleground. His eyes were fiery orange and out of His mouth came the sound of roaring waters. He spoke to Lucifer, 'Put down your weapon and come with me.' Then he looked at Michael and said, 'Bring the rest of the rebels up to the throne.' Michael nodded and then carried out the order. Lucifer also obeyed the order of the Son of God and walked with him up the steps to the throne of the Godhead.

"When the Son of God and Lucifer approached the throne, the mere presence of Yahweh caused Lucifer to kneel before the throne, against his will. The Son of God kept moving up toward the throne and became part of the light that sat on the throne. There was another that joined the light that sat upon the throne. Soon after, the defeated Luciferians were brought before the throne also, bound with supernatural chains. And even though Lucifer was not bound with chains, he was unable to stand against the throne of judgment, as much as he tried to. Michael and Gabriel sat in their honorary seats on each side of the throne.

"Once Michael and Gabriel had taken their seat, a voice came forth from the throne, saying, 'You had the seal of perfection, full of wisdom and perfect in beauty. You were in the garden of God and every precious stone was your covering. You had access to nearly every part of creation. Your instruments were built in for the purpose of worship and song, and you played wonderfully! On the day you were created they were prepared. You were the anointed cherub who covers the sanctuary. I placed you on the holy mountain of God and you walked in the midst of the stones of fire. You were blameless in your ways from the day you were created until unrighteousness was found in you. By the abundance of your talents you were internally filled with jealousy and violence, and you sinned in your soul. Therefore I declare you as profane from the mountain of God, and you will be destroyed, O covering cherub, from the midst of the stones of fire! Your heart was lifted up because of your beauty, and you corrupted your wisdom by reason of your splendor. I will cast you to the ground and you will be accursed. By the multitude of your iniquities and in the unrighteousness of your abilities, you have profaned your sanctuaries, therefore I will bring a fire from the midst of you and it will consume you and turn you to ashes before all who will see you—you will be a terror no more.'

"Lucifer meekly raised his hand as to speak. The voice of the Godhead graciously allowed him, saying, 'You may speak for yourself, cherub.'"

"Lucifer looked up and said, 'Thank you my Lord. Forgive me for being so brash with my actions, but I got caught up in the moment. I had meant to come and speak with you peaceably about my grievances and my curiosity of the origin of all things. But have you even considered my proposal and all that of which I have studied about the cosmos?'"

"The Almighty answered, 'O cherub, who are you to accuse the Most High? You are but a created being and a rightful subject, as are your brethren. I have been a loving father to you and have given you much. But yet, you are not satisfied and your jealousy of the humans is completely unreasonable and outrageous. You are not a god and you cannot create. You can only manipulate that which already is---that which I have created for you to have stewardship over. What is your complaint?'"

"Lucifer replied, 'Well, when you put it like that it makes things seem like your way is the only righteous path of divinity. How do you know that I cannot rule the cosmos better than you can? Are you afraid of letting one of us try—even for a season? Are you such a control-oriented being that you cannot let things go and function on their own, or let another try to practice sovereignty over creation?'"

"The Son of God appeared out from the light and descended upon Lucifer. 'O cherub, do you seriously think you can reign in my place?'"

"Lucifer answered, 'If I was given the opportunity, I do believe I can surpass you, with all due respect. Your power is awesome, but I truly think that it occurred by chance, time, and with more practice and opportunity than any of us have had. I beg of you, give me a dominion over the earth for a time, and I will show you my strength and splendor and how much more advanced I can become with the natural process of cosmic evolution.'"

"The Son of God laughed, which caused Lucifer's countenance to show an intense hatred never before seen on an angelic being. Then the Son of God spoke again, 'Since you are sincere in your belief, albeit sincerely delusional, I will play a game with you and give you an opportunity to prove your theory. Here is how the game will be played: I will grant you a limited rule over the earth and the power of the air over the earth. I will allow you to attempt to persuade the humans to join your rebellion. I will even allow your fellow rebels to join you on the earth. You will be surely cast out of your rightful place in the heavenly realms and be disinherited from your estate, but you will still be granted limited access. You will have the opportunity to defeat me, but I know you will fail—I have already foreseen it! The penalty of your failure will be eternal suffering in the Lake of Fire, which I have created especially for you and your loyalists, as I foresaw your attempted revolt. If I wanted to, I could banish you into the Lake of Fire right this moment and your evil would be ended right now. However, I have already lost 1/3 of my sons, whom I love. And I desire my kingdom to be overcrowded with the souls of the holy. Because of this, I will allow the humans to procreate and their offspring will have the opportunity to join the holy angels in my kingdom at the appropriate time. The Father, the Holy Spirit, and I have foreseen it, we have decreed it, and it will come to pass.

"'You will cause tremendous chaos, pain, and suffering. But I will bring redemption, justice, peace, and righteousness. I will fill the heavens with the saints of the Most High. My kingdom will be restored with the perfect goodness with which I originally intended it. Now, therefore I cast you down to the earth with your limited and temporary rule. Since you believe in luck and chance, may you perish with them, and witness the futility of your thinking! Be gone!'"

"With the final word of the Son of God, Lucifer was immediately cast down to the earth, with his Fallen Ones with him. They landed in the far north of the earth and it took them a great while to gather their bearings and to figure out exactly where they were. Once they regained their proper consciousness and gathered their strength, they began to plot about how they would go about defiling the humans who were created in the image of God."

29

CAPTIVE CAPTURE

Lieutenant Alex Sage was awakened by the sound of his jail cell opening. He lifted up his head to see who it was. A short and stocky military police officer walked in with a tray of food. "Aaah, you're awake this time, huh Lieutenant? Supper time!"

"Dinner?" Alex responded. "What happened to lunch?"

The officer replied, "We came in with lunch five hours ago, but we couldn't wake you up, sir, so we let you sleep."

Alex did not say anything to that, but he was curious as to why an attorney had not visited him yet. "Let us know if you need anything else, sir," the officer said as he left the cell. Alex nodded as he began to stuff scalloped potatoes down his hungry throat. Next, the barbequed chicken was devoured before everything was washed down with a bottle of water. Alex was confused as to why he was so tired as to have been asleep all day, and as to why no legal representation had been appointed unto him yet. These things, as well as the events of the past week and a half raced through Alex's head all of the sleepless night. Just before dawn, Alex began to read a Bible that was in his cell. He read Paul's epistle to the Romans. He had read 8:28 which says, "We know that all things work together for good for those who love God, who are called according to his purpose." He thought to himself, "*All* things? Even my situation?" He began to meditate on the outrageous notion that his situation was working out for good, even though he had previously dreamt of the angel telling him the same thing. It just seemed too good to be true.

He began to fall asleep again, with the Bible on his chest. Just as Alex began to enter into his deeper sleep, he heard his cell open again, waking him. Alex sat up, with blurred vision from being half asleep. He saw two men in black suits wearing sunglasses and having earpieces in their ears. Alex asked them sleepily, "Are you my attorneys?"

"No," one of them answered. "We're from the U.S. Department of Homeland Security. You will have to come with us."

"Wait a minute," said Alex. "I know my rights. I want to speak to my defense counsel, right now! And I'm not going anywhere until then!"

The other one spoke now, "Lieutenant Sage, what you have claimed to have witnessed is far beyond any normal circumstance. Therefore, normal protocol is out of the question. You will come with us, be it voluntarily or otherwise. Which will it be?"

Alex ignored the man, stood on his tippy-toes, and looked above his head and yelled, "Guard! Guard! Help me! Call my attorney! I want to speak with counsel!"

As Alex was yelling, the two men aggressively walked toward him and grabbed at his arms. Alex shook himself free and tried to push past the two men. One of the men put Alex into a wrestling submission hold while the other man used a tazer on him. Alex convulsed as the electricity ran through him, and one of the men put handcuffs on Lt. Sage. Then the two men lifted Alex off of the ground and carried him on their shoulders out of his cell and through the corridor. Alex's body was tingling from the electricity that ran through his body. They passed through the booking area and out the front door where there was a black armored truck waiting for them. Alex was placed into the back area that was caged off from the passenger section. A driver and a passenger awaited the other two men who had subdued Alex. As soon as everybody was seated, the truck peeled out of the parking lot and onto the highway.

For the first twenty minutes there was complete silence. There was no radio playing, no walkie-talkie transmissions, no cell phone calls, and no discussion between any of the four men in the passenger section of the truck. Finally, Alex built up the courage to ask, "Where are you taking me?" The men looked at each other, when the one who tazed him earlier answered, "To headquarters."

"Headquarters of what?" asked Alex.

The man in the front passenger seat turned around to face Alex and said, "Lieutenant Sage, I apologize the lack of manners of my colleagues. My name is Chief Officer Peter Griffin from the U.S. Department of Homeland Security. Upon reading your article in the USA Today, we were given orders to disrupt the normal proceedings of the justice system to intercept and detain you until further notice. You will be interviewed several times by several different interrogators until we can fully investigate the events that you have been a part of. So the more you cooperate with us, the faster we can get you back to base. If we find no fault in you, then all charges will be dropped. But if you screw with us or refuse to cooperate, then this will be a very lengthy and unpleasant experience. Do you have any other questions?"

"Where exactly are your headquarters?" Alex asked. "I was unaware that we had any of your offices here in Germany."

Everyone laughed. Griffin answered, "We don't—at least not officially. The exact location is not important, and you will not be able to remember how to get there or find your way out—so don't bother trying. Our headquarters is in a very secure place. Don't worry—you'll be well taken care of."

The others laughed again. Then Griffin's cell phone beeped and he answered. He said, "We're in route. Be there before your break...roger that....out." Griffin looked back at Alex again and smiled. He then turned on classical music. Alex thought it was Mozart or Beethoven—he couldn't tell the difference. He just sighed and put his head back against the chair. He began to relax just a little, when all of the sudden, he saw a bright flash appear in the road ahead of them. The driver slammed on the breaks and covered his face with his hands. An extremely loud and low humming sound boomed from the area of the flash. The four men screamed in agony as their flesh began to melt as if being cooked in a microwave oven. The handcuffs on Alex's wrists also melted off of his hands, but Alex felt no pain—only warm melted steel. The back doors of the truck flew open and Alex was sucked into another bright light like a dust bunny by a vacuum cleaner. Alex felt just as light as he was shot through a tunnel of light, or so he thought. And just as quickly as the flash of light had appeared, just as quickly it vanished and Alex was in complete darkness. The darkness was so completely dark that he could not see his hand in front of his face.

He shouted, "Hello? Anybody there?"

"Sleep, my son," a voice whispered in his ear.

He turned to look and saw nothing but darkness. He then felt extremely drowsy. He felt himself fall to the ground. It felt like concrete. He crawled around trying to feel for any familiar objects, but he found nothing. Finally, his face hit the pavement as he passed out.

30

A CRY FOR HELP

Many days had passed since Alicia Sage and Amanda Day had been captured by Peruvian guerilla elitists. Alicia had been keeping count of the days by making tally marks with a stone, but there had been a couple of times when she had passed out from exhaustion and malnourishment and been asleep for what seemed like more than a day. This caused Alicia to stop trying to keep track of time. She had noticed that she had lost a significant amount of weight. The Peruvian captors occasionally had her prepare meals for the troops stationed at that post, and sometimes an officer named Alberto gave her some additional rations to keep her nourished as well as keeping her in good spirits. Alicia often sang hymns as she worked, and a couple of times Alberto asked her questions about God and her faith. One day Alicia even shared with Alberto about her recent experiences, for he spoke and understood English perfectly. When Alicia asked Alberto about how Amanda was doing, Alberto had told her that she was in a different location that he was unaware of.

Amanda Day was awakened in the middle of the night by her body freezing and shivering. Ironically, her clothes were drenched with sweat. She had been extremely ill for over two weeks now. A doctor was sent in to examine her and he offered her some medicine, but Amanda refused to take it. She did not trust the people who had kidnapped her and kept her imprisoned for so many days with only a loaf of bread and a bottle of water to live on every three days. She trusted that if God wanted her well then she would be well and she would not compromise with the enemy. Unfortunately, Amanda had been unable to keep down any food or water for about five days now. Her fever had been constant and her throat was so dry that she was unable to speak. She prayed silently in her head, "Lord Jesus, please allow me to escape this terrible place. Send an angel to rescue me like what happened with your servant Peter. But let your will be done. I beg of you, to alleviate my suffering and take me home if you do not wish me to escape. Please Lord, save me from this dungeon! Amen."

When she finished her prayer, she closed her eyes for about five seconds and then opened them again. A man dressed in a brilliant white robe was sitting in front of her. Amanda tried to speak but no words came out from her dry throat. The man put his index finger on her lips and said, "Amanda, the Lord has found favor with you and has heard your prayer. I have been sent to bring you home. Well done, good and faithful servant. Now, take my hand and let us return to the Father."

Without hesitation, Amanda grabbed the man's hand and immediately his skin became as a bright light and angelic wings emerged from his back. The angel lifted her up from the ground. Amanda briefly looked down upon her lifeless body which was wrapped by the filthy blanket that refused to comfort her. In the blink of an eye, Amanda Day was greeted by the singing of heavenly hosts in the most dazzling of any paradise she could ever imagine. She heard a voice that sounded like the rushing waters of Niagara Falls, saying, "Welcome, daughter, and enter into your rest which has been prepared for you since the foundation of the world."

The next morning, Alberto had brought a loaf of bread and a bottle of water for Amanda. He saw her body lying down motionless in her blanket. Her normally dark brown skin was now a pale-bluish gray and her hands and feet were swollen beyond their normal size. Her emaciated body was stiff as he tried to nudge her with his foot. He was filled with grief, for he admired her for her faith in God and her unwillingness to compromise. He knew that she had been very sick for several days now. That is why he told Alicia that he did not know where she was because he did not believe that she would live much longer. But Alberto did not know whether or not he could keep such a secret from Alicia now. Their conversations about Jesus had given him a new outlook on life and he was hopeful to become a better person and eventually, witness a better world to come. For these past several days since he first spoke with Alicia, he has felt like a different person, despite being in a very difficult situation himself. He could not blow his cover, but he knew that the time was coming when he had to act soon—he now needed to be on the alert for the opportunity to fulfill his mission.

Late in the evening, Alberto was on his way to the outhouses. He was off-duty at that time, but he was still wearing his uniform with his sidearm holstered in his belt, as well as his radio. He passed the guards, as they saluted him. He went into the outhouse shed like he normally would. This time he quietly removed the wooden back panel from the shed, which he had loosened some time earlier for this precise situation. At this time of night, he thought, there would unlikely any other people at the outhouse. Behind the shed was a barbed fence with a steep hill immediately behind the fence. At the top of the hill was a forest which would conceal him until he was able to reach his place of communication. Alberto pulled out his wire-cutters from his pocket and quietly began to snip away at the fence so he could escape.

He was a little more than halfway through when he heard footsteps approaching the outhouses. He stopped and got facedown on the ground. He hoped that whoever was coming would not enter into the same stall where he had just been. Alberto had put the back panel back into place, but it was not perfectly flush. All someone had to do was shine their flashlight on the back wall and they would be able to tell that the back panel was out of place. Alberto heard someone enter and sit down. It did not seem like it was the same stall. It seemed like forever had passed, but the man was still there. Alberto was growing impatient. He slowly got up and began to cut more of the chain-link fence apart. Just as he began to cut the first link he heard the man get up. The door opened and the man seemed to be looking for something—or *someone*. Had he heard Alberto? The next thing Alberto heard was the man's walkie-talkie go off and apparently, one of the two guards that Alberto had passed was in front of the outhouses now. The other guard was asking his location. The guard at the outhouse had told him that he thought he heard something behind the shed.

At that moment, Alberto reacted impulsively. He began to finish cutting the fence so he could make his escape. The guard called into base to affirm that someone was indeed behind the shed, as he simultaneously began to come around to the back. Just as Alberto had cut the final link of the fence necessary for him to escape, the guard shot at him and missed. Alberto ran uphill and avoided the next three shots fired at him. Alberto pulled his pistol and fired back, and the guard ducked behind the shed for cover. By the time the other guards had arrived, Alberto was into the tree line and out of the guards' sight. Alberto could hear dogs barking now and people yelling. He kept running through the forest. Soon, he knew there would be a manhunt. He had to reach his acquaintance in town so he could make his call to C.I.A. headquarters for reinforcements. It would be another two miles of running for Alberto, but he made it to Manny's safe house. He made his phone call and help would be on the way.

31

THE BLUEPRINT OF DECEPTION

As Pravuil continued his story of the originality of evil, he could tell that Professor Richard Mockens was itching to ask him a question, so he paused and allowed him to speak. Richard politely asked, "I don't mean to interrupt or anything—because this is fascinating stuff—but how long have we been sitting here? Won't this place be swarming with security and scientists pretty soon?"

Pravuil answered him, "Do not worry, Richard. You are in a dimensional holding space right now, thus the time of the earth is much slower than what you have experienced here this evening. This event has been foreseen and it will not be thwarted by human efforts. So now, shall I continue?"

All four of them nodded. So then Pravuil continued to speak of the fall of Lucifer, hardly changing the tone in his voice. He said to them, "The Luciferian rebels fell to the earth like lightning, and it was quite a display of spectacular lights when they hit the ground in the middle of the earth night. They crashed in the midst of a jungle, creating actual physical craters—about 150 feet in diameter each. The creatures of the jungle had never experienced an interruption of the peace that they had enjoyed up to that moment. They had all lived in harmony with one another—only feeding on the earth's vegetation. This is when fear first struck the earth.

"Lucifer was the first on his feet. He looked around, trying to peer through the smoke of the explosion and of the dust of the earth. He choked and coughed as he inhaled the dust. For him, this was the first moment that he had felt physical displeasure—physical in the angelic sense, of course. The anger and bitterness that he had allowed to engulf him had now intensified a thousand times over. His hatred for God and his creation would be the fuel that motivated his new destructive nature. As he hovered over to each fallen one he shouted, 'Get up! Get up! We have work to do! We will meet immediately before the giant rock 800 cubits to the northeast of here!'

"Lucifer's inner circle of rebels were the first to the giant rock: Hallah, Moroni, Indu, Avatarael, Mohammael, Butah, Mastemah, Jinhael, Ananel, Ahuramahz, and Maijan were all anxiously waiting upon the others. A beautiful angel named Zenshinto was the next to arrive. His face was glowing orange with a sinister grin on his face. Lucifer looked upon him and within him and asked, 'How would you like to join my inner circle— my 12th apprentice in this circle of 13?'"

"Zenshinto answered, 'Gladly,' in a soft but deep voice. Within moments, all of the other fallen stars appeared almost simultaneously. A greenish-orange glow surrounded the fallen in a way that could be seen light years away from the earth. A low humming sound could also be heard in the heavens. Lucifer began to direct them, saying, 'Okay, so the game has officially begun. The Son of God has given us this opportunity to rule and overthrow the Father, so we must act quickly and effectively. We cannot allow the humans to multiply at the rate of the other animals or else our job will be much more difficult. We must get them to join our rebellion very soon! Does anyone here have any ideas?'

"Hallah said, 'We can write a divine book that is beautifully written— poetically and lyrically—and we can sing it to the humans and tell them that it is from God. In the book, we can communicate to them that they must face a certain direction—a holy mountain that we can possess—yes! And they must bow and worship us at certain times of the day.'

"Moroni nodded his head and applauded, 'Yes—that's a great idea!'

"Lucifer thought about it for a few seconds, 'Hmm…That is not a bad idea, Hallah, but we must remember that the Son of God meets with them on a daily basis and has already instructed them on how to worship. The humans may be animals like the rest of these earth-creatures, but they're not stupid. Let me hear some more ideas.'

"Indu was the next to make a proposal. He said, 'We should approach the humans and tell them that there is one supreme God who oversees all activity, but ultimately that we are all gods and that the creation and universe itself is all one ultimate god that we are all a part of. Us heavenly beings, humans, animals, trees, rocks, the dust, the water—all things constitute the god consciousness. That will elevate their sense of independence from the creator and choose to go their own way and create their own truth according to their own likeness.'

"Lucifer smiled and said, 'Indu—I like that idea—but it is a bit too complex for the humans at this stage of their development. I think we can use the independent thinking and the aspiration to godhood idea though.'

"Moroni agreed exuberantly again, shouting, 'Yes! Let's do that!' Lucifer turned and looked at him and Moroni's countenance and enthusiasm subsided. Lucifer continued, 'Here is what we will do. We must split up for the time being and study the environment for the next few days. Whoever finds the humans first must call to the rest of us so that we may observe them together. Of course, we must hide our earthly visibility until the right time. Remember, Yahweh told them that they can eat freely of any tree except for one—the tree of the knowledge of good and evil. If they eat of that tree Yahweh told them that they would die. When that happens, the humans will be cut off like the rest of us here. Then they will have no choice but to join us. We can then show them the tree of life that will give them the immortality that is like what we posses. Then their fate will be sealed forever!'

"The rebels roared in applause, and the sound of it was as the roaring of the seas during a massive storm. When the noise had died down, Lucifer continued, 'So the humans must eat of the forbidden tree *first*—before they eat of the tree of life. One of us must find the tree of life and guard it and keep them from approaching it—and without being seen. As far as getting them to disobey God—leave that up to me. I have a plan. Now, let us get going on our mission. Does anyone have any questions or thoughts on the matter?' Every one of them shook their heads and then they again applauded Lucifer's speech. Then they all hid their earthly visibility and scattered from that place.

"Meanwhile, up on the throne of God, the holy ones were watching and listening to the entire plan. Michael asked the Son of God, 'Lord, why did you not destroy them for their insubordination? How can you allow them to even think about destroying your beautiful creation and all that we have worked for?'

"The Son of God answered him, 'Michael, all of this has been foreseen. We created so that the multiplication of this wondrous cosmos can increase so that there may be even more of us to celebrate the love of life. This cannot happen in this cosmos without the ability to choose the good. Of course, having freedom and volition comes with the possibility to choose other than good, which will have negative results, evil, sadness, despair, and destruction. But without these bad things, the good cannot increase and virtues like beauty, love, fellowship, and life are not possible. The rebels will have a certain degree of success even—and this will puff up their pride and hatred of the good even more. But the sovereignty of the Godhead cannot be undone or overtaken by that which is created. It is impossible. We will watch and be patient and allow choices and consequences to take place. And you will see that the plans of Lucifer, who is now The Adversary or Satan, will be frustrated and futile. This *game*, as he calls it, will bear witness to the truth that God is good and he will prevail.'

"At those words, the holy sons of God fell on their many faces and began to worship the Son of God before his throne."

32

BREAK FAST IN GERMANY

Alex Sage woke up the next morning on an unfamiliar couch in a foreign basement. The peculiarity immediately energized him to sit up and look around frantically. There were shelves covering three walls with books and other memorabilia on them. Behind the couch was a stairwell to the main floor to whatever house he was in. He looked down at his beige Air Force shirt. There were dried drops of blood over it. He put his hand up to his nose and felt the dried blood on his nose, which apparently was the source of the bleeding. He had minor scrapes and bruises on his arms and elbows. His broken wrist ached severely. His flight jacket had been used as his pillow, and his camouflaged pants and boots were still on. Faint footsteps could be heard above him now. Alex did not know what to do. Since he had no idea where he was, it was dangerous to just walk up the stairs to wherever they led to. If he yelled out, there was no telling if the people upstairs were friendly or dangerous. If he just stayed where he was he would die from the anxiety. Alex decided to walk over to the stairwell and politely yell, "Hello? Anybody here?"

After a few seconds, Alex heard footsteps coming closer to the door atop of the stairwell. The door opened, and a heavyset blonde woman in her fifties appeared and spoke German to him. Since Alex did not know very much German, he politely asked, "Do you speak English?"

The woman replied in a heavy German accent, "Oh, I am sorry. Good morning to you. My name is Karla. I found you lying on the ground in the alley behind my house early this morning, so I brought you inside to rest. Would you like something to eat? I just made eggs and sausage."

Alex eyes brightened up, "Yes, of course. I would be very thankful."

Karla then said, "Well then come up and wash yourself in the bathroom. It is over here to your right. Then come and sit with me and eat."

As Alex walked up the stairs and over to the bathroom, he saw pictures on the wall of the lady and her husband. There were no pictures of any children. The bathroom was very clean and well kept. The fragrances refreshed Alex's nostrils. He washed the blood off of his nose and cleaned his hands for breakfast. He looked in the mirror and saw the redness of his tired eyes and two days of unshaven face. When he returned to the dining area, Karla was already sitting down with more than half of her plate empty. Alex was tired, dehydrated, hungry, and with a headache. Karla asked him, "Would you like Apple Juice, Cranberry Juice, or a glass of milk?"

Alex answered, "May I have a glass of iced water?"

"Sure," Karla said. She immediately got out of her seat to oblige.

Alex consumed his meal at a boot camp pace. By then Karla had begun washing dishes. In the corner of the dining area was a small, flat screen TV that was mounted on the upper wall near the ceiling. The news was on, but the volume was very low. Karla had looked back at him to see how much he had eaten. When she saw that he was almost done, she asked, "Do you want more? I still have some left over."

Alex replied, "If it is not too much to ask, I would love some more—this is good!"

As Karla served Alex seconds, she asked him, "So, what is your name, soldier?"

Alex told her.

She then asked, "So what happened to you? Why were you lying on the street in the alley?"

"Well," Alex responded, "It's a long story. But to make it short, I was kidnapped, and the van I was in got into an accident and I was flung to the street. That's the last thing I remember before waking up in your basement."

"Do you know who it was who kidnapped you?"

"Not exactly. But they said they were part of U.S. Homeland Security, but they didn't show me any I.D. or anything—so who knows?"

Alex was unsure if he should have told her this much or if he would regret it. Somehow, he felt comfortable around her. After all, she could have left him in the alley, or at best just called the authorities where he might have ended up back in custody.

Karla responded somewhat sarcastically, "Really? That is quite a fancy story. Are you sure you just did not have too much to drink?"

"No, honest. That's all I remember."

Karla smiled and said, "I see."

She went back to doing the dishes, and Alex went back to eating. He was about to ask her why she was so brave as to take a strange man into her house when he happened to glance at the new and saw his face on the TV screen. He dropped his fork on his plate noticeably as his draw dropped just as fast. Karla turned around and asked, "What is wrong, Alex?"

Alex's faced quickly returned to normalcy, as he answered quickly, "Nothing," and began to eat at an even faster and nervous pace. Karla noticed his front. She glanced around the room until her eyes met the TV screen. She saw a truck on fire in the middle of a road with firefighters trying to extinguish it. She walked over to the TV with the remote in her hand to turn it up. The reporter spoke in German, of course. Alex pretended to be disinterested and kept his head down while he continued to eat. Karla looked at Alex and quickly back to the TV—and repeated twice. It was evident to Alex that he was now a wanted fugitive. He was probably blamed for the explosion of the vehicle as well. A nervous knot began to twist in his stomach. He wondered if the woman's husband was in the house somewhere, or if he was at work, or perhaps deceased. Out of his peripheral vision, Alex began to scan the place and plan an escape route if necessary. He would have to go back through the hallway where the bathroom was and venture into unknown parts of the house—that much was certain.

Karla gave one last glance at Alex and their eyes met. She began to walk toward the hallway, subtly faster than normal. Now she was between Alex and the exit. Alex heard her now speaking in German in a low pitched voice, as if trying not to be heard. Alex got up from his seat and wiped his mouth with his napkin. He yelled out, "Thank you for everything, Karla, but I really must be going now. Where is the door?"

He heard her speaking faster now. He walked toward her. He saw her on her cell phone and she walked away from him, still speaking. Alex could now see the living room past the hallway, Karla had gone into another room. Alex hurriedly headed for the door. It was locked, bolted, and chained. He began to unlock the door when he heard the familiar sound of a pistol being cocked. He turned around and saw Karla holding a black revolver. "Stop right there!" she said nervously. Alex put up his hands. He began to speak, "You don't understand, I am being framed."

Karla interrupted, "No more talking. The police are on their way."

Alex could see Karla's frail hands shaking with the revolver in them. He then spoke softly, "Karla, I am not the type of man that would hurt anybody, and I know that you don't want to shoot me. I don't know what is going on, but I do not trust whoever is trying to capture me. Please...let me go. The police already know about where I am—let them chase me and you do not have to worry about anything."

Karla's hands stopped shaking as she considered his offer. Thirty seconds went by. The faint sounds of sirens could be heard in the background. Karla told Alex, "Unlock the door behind you and walk out."

Alex slowly turned around and began unlocking the door. Alex heard Karla sniffle. He turned back around halfway through the process of unlocking the door. He could see Karla holding back tears. As he opened the door to exit, Karla said warmly, "Be careful, Alex, and may God be with you."

As soon as Alex closed the door, he heard a gunshot go off. Karla had shot a hole in her wall next to the door. Alex quickly jumped off of the front porch and began running down the busy street. There were a few people walking up and down the sidewalk of the downtown area. Alex had to sidestep them. He began to hear louder sirens in the distance. He ran between two buildings—one was a barber's shop and the other one was a dental office. To the rear of the buildings was a parking lot which was surrounded by a chain linked fence. By that time, a chubby police officer darted at him from the back parking lot. Alex easily jumped over the chain link fence. The officer was about 15 steps behind him. He also tried to climb the fence after Alex, but his foot slipped and he fell back down.

Alex was now running parallel to railroad tracks. The sirens were loud now, surely in front of the buildings which he ran through. He looked back and saw several officers running after him now. In the distance, a police helicopter could be heard. In front of Alex, he could see a freight train slowly moving toward him. The police behind him began to fire their pistols at him. Alex could hear the rocks of the train tracks being hit by bullets and flying through the air. Some of the bullets hit the train tracks. The train was about 75 yards and approaching now. Alex would have to board the train—he hoped that it was not moving too fast, but it was his only hope. Just then, a bullet grazed Alex's left ear. He grabbed it with fingers of his casted left hand, but oh how his ear now burned and his eardrum now humming from the sound of the bullet. His fingers were now full of blood. His right ear caught the sound of the train's whistle blowing loudly now. He could no longer hear shots being fired—he didn't know if it was because of the loudness of the train or if the police did not want to fire in that direction.

Alex allowed the first few train cars to pass him. He then saw a ladder about 50 feet from him. He guessed that the train was moving above 20 mph. Alex then turned and changed his direction as to run along with the train before he boarded it. Alex could also now see at least 4 police officers running toward him with pistols in hand. They were about 150 yards from him though. When the ladder was close enough, Alex grabbed a hold of it and began to climb to the top of the car. Once he was on top, he ran to the back of the car. The next car was only separated by about four feet. He was hesitant to jump, though, because what if he miscalculated? He looked back and saw the police ready to board the train in a matter of seconds. Alex jumped easily to the next train—thanks to the adrenaline. He ran to the back of that car and jumped to the next one. The car that Alex was on now had a small hatch on the top of it. Alex bent down to try to open it. He unlatched the hatch and saw that it was about a 14 foot drop to the floor. He didn't think twice this time—he jumped and hit the floor hard, spraining his ankle. The hatch had a spring on it so it closed by itself.

Alex looked around the dark room. He could hear the persistence of the train's wheels hitting the tracks. There were several barrels of cargo filling up half of the car. Alex opened one of the barrels, and then another. They were filled with some sort of grain. Suddenly, Alex heard the footsteps of the policemen on top of the car. Quickly, Alex buried himself in the grain of one of the middle barrels. Alex could hear the hatch open again, but he could not see the glow of the police flashlights searching the room. He could hear shouting in the German language, but he could not see the looks of disgraced frustration on the faces of the officers. Alex heard the hatch close again. Then he heard footsteps above continuing to move further to the back of the train. It seemed for now that Alex had escaped danger again. He thanked God.

33

COMPOUND FRACTURED

Alicia Sage awoke out of her sleep that morning with a familiar face hovering over her cot. It was the man in the white suit—only this time, his suit was gray. "Buenos dias, Alicia," the man said. Alicia sat up quickly, covering herself with her itchy blanket. "What are you doing here?" Alicia asked defiantly.

The man chuckled and said, "Apparently, your country has no interest in you and is not willing to make any agreements with us. They say that they don't negotiate with terrorists. It is ironic that we do not do anything that your country does not do, but anyway—that's another story. What brings me here is that you are going to be moved."

"Moved? Moved where?" shouted Alicia, angrily.

"Since we cannot get any value for you from your own country, we have decided to sell you to the Columbians—they pay quite well for little gringas like yourself," the man said smiling. "You see, last night we learned that we had an informant among the people here who escaped. And now this entire compound is compromised, so we must all leave this place soon. The Columbians will be here in a few hours, so we need you to get cleaned up and looking pretty."

"I am not merchandise to be sold—I am a human being created in the image of God—just as you are!" Alicia responded.

"Yes, I have heard of your religiosity and we understand that you are divinely protected, but nevertheless you will be sold as a—can we say—a religious relic."

Alicia did not appreciate the man's vile sense of humor. She had nothing left to say. The man then got serious and sternly said, "Here is a clean towel. I will escort you to the private shower where you will find a new set of clothes, jewelry, lotions, and perfume. You will put all of it on—it is not optional."

Alicia tried to hold back her tears as she followed the man out of her cell. The man's entourage had been waiting outside. Alicia prayed as she showered. It did feel good to be thoroughly clean again. She reluctantly complied with the man's wishes. Afterward, Alicia accompanied the man as he sat with his bodyguards on the porch of the big house, waiting for the Columbians to arrive. The man tried to engage in small talk with Alicia. "You are truly a beautiful woman, Alicia," he said, smiling. She ignored him entirely. After three or four attempts at conversation, the man became silent as well, and drank his lemonade.

After sitting on the porch for almost an hour, three Humm V's pulled up to the big house—about 40 feet from the porch. The man turned to Alicia and said, "Aaah, here are the Columbians." Two men exited the Hummer that was in the middle and walked toward the man. One of the Columbians greeted the man in Spanish and handed over a briefcase. The man opened the briefcase and eyeballed the currency before closing it again. The man then asked the Columbian spokesperson, "Do you happen to speak English?" The Columbian answered, "A little bit."

The man's facial expression turned mildly sour. He then told the Columbian, "Your accent is not from Columbia. Where are you from?" The Columbian looked astonished, "Perdon?"

The man said again, "Your accent—it is not Columbian, so please—do not act like you do not know what I am talking about. Who are you?"

"I am sorry, sir, you are mistaken."

"No! You are!"

With that, one of the man's bodyguards drew his pistol and shot the Columbian in the head. The rest of the bodyguards immediately began to fire at the other Hummers, and some of the other Columbians also returned fire. Alicia ducked down and tried to crawl back into the big house. The man was way ahead of her, as he was already in the house trying to gather reinforcements on his phone. Alicia finally made it into the house as well, between gun shots. By now both sides had fully automatic weaponry firing at each other. One of the Hummers drove away, but the other two were entirely shot up and totaled. Just then, Alicia saw one of the Hummers explode out of the upstairs window. Alicia could also see helicopters coming from afar off. The man came upstairs to grab Alicia. "Come with me," he said. He grabbed Alicia with one hand and held the brief case in the other hand, and was being escorted by one of his bodyguards. He went out the back door where his jeep was parked. The bodyguard opened the door but looked into the ignition where the keys were supposed to be. He looked at the man and said, "The keys are not here!"

The man was stunned, "What?!" he exclaimed.

"The keys—they are missing!"

"That's impossible, you idiot! Where did you put them last?"

Before the man could answer, he fell to the ground as a bullet went through his head. Alicia fell to the ground in fear, and the man hunched down, using his jeep as a shield and began to look around for a shooter, but he saw no one. At this point, the man forgot about Alicia and he tried to make a run for it back to the big house with the briefcase in hand. But another shot rang out and hit the ground in front of him, narrowly missing him, as dirt flew into the air. The man returned to Alicia's side, with sweat profusely running down his face. His glasses had fallen off, and the man looked completely perplexed.

After he caught his breath, he grabbed Alicia and put her in front of him as a shield. Alicia screamed her head off, but the man jabbed her in the lower back with his elbow. He was dragging Alicia with him back to the big house. When they were about 30 feet from the house, a grenade exploded near the back door. Then two Hummers pulled to each side of the man. Men exited the Hummers and drew down on the man with AR-15 rifles, using the doors as shields. At that the man let Alicia go and placed his hands in the air. Alicia ran to one of the Hummers where one of the CIA agents was her friend Alberto. Another agent hit the man in the forehead with a bullet and he collapsed to the ground. Alicia hugged Alberto and asked, "Why didn't you arrest him?"

Alberto answered, "He was way too dangerous to keep in any prison—including Guantanamo Bay."

"Who was he?" asked Alicia.

"He is one of the leaders of one of the largest mafias in South America as well as a high ranking member of several secret societies," answered Alberto. "He goes by several names, but one of his more infamous aliases is Jorge Espinosa. But he won't be kidnapping any more Americans or partaking of any more human sacrificial rituals."

Alicia gave him that look that said, "Oh, you know about that too" (She had not shared with him about that part of her experience). Alberto looked upon Alicia with affectionate concern, and Alicia returned his gaze. He said to her, "Well, I am very thankful that you are okay. Come, I will take you to our base and we will fly you back home."

As they drove off in the Humm-V, Alicia thought about home—she had been gone for so long, it seemed like a foreign idea to her now. She thought about her brother and how he was doing in Germany. She also thought about her father and wondered if he had indeed found Noah's long lost Ark. She missed her family, but she was also comforted by Alberto's presence. As the CIA agents vacated the premises, an attack helicopter flew by and bombed the complex completely as to annihilate any evidence of its existence.

34

THE FALL OF HUMANITY

While the angel Pravuil was coming to the conclusion of his story about the origin of evil and the Battle of Pneumatika, the sun was peeking its head above the eastern horizon on the mountains of Ararat. A few of the scientists were awake, but most of them were still lying in bed—if not asleep—due to the exhaustion from the previous day. Additional security forces were also in route. All of the regional activity was going according to plan, as Pravuil continued his narrating:

"The fallen angelic beings were still somewhat unfamiliar with the earth when they were first flung to it from heaven. Because of this, it took them awhile to find the Garden of Eden. Naturally, Lucifer was the first to find it. He summoned his inner-twelve to join him in observation. The other demons were traveling throughout the earth and some of them were even distracted as to descend into the depths of the ocean waters. Their impulse to observe, study, and attempt to manipulate the creation caused them to behave as such.

"Meanwhile, at the Garden of Eden, Lucifer and his twelve disciples were observing Adam and Eve playing flirtatiously in a shallow brook. Jinhael, Moroni, Maijain, and Ananel lusted after the beauty of Eve and the nakedness of both of their bodies. They witnessed desires and sensa-

214

tions that angels were not designed to experience. It was because of their corrupted and rebellious nature that caused them to lust after humans uncharacteristically. Maijan was the first to speak, 'I wish to take Eve away from Adam and to join with her in body and defile her humanness.'

"Lucifer replied, 'Maijan, I also agree that she is beautiful, but we must not abandon our mission and what we have agreed to. In fact, I want you to find the tree of life and guard it from the humans. Go now.'

"Maijan nodded in agreement and left the other twelve. When the humans exited the brook, they next went to eat from the trees. Eve had taken a piece of fruit from two trees, and Adam trailed behind her and took from the same trees that Eve had. They ate the fruit as they were walking in the garden. As they had passed the forbidden tree of the knowledge of good and evil, Eve took a long, hard look at it and gazed at its fruit. Adam called to her with the sound of his voice startling her and breaking her concentration, 'Eve—look at these monkeys! Look how they are playing in that tree over there. Even the jaguars are climbing after them and playing with them as well.'

"Eve looked over to where Adam was pointing, giggling along with him. They walked a bit further and they came across two beautiful serpents which stood upright about 5 feet tall each. The serpents wrapped and intertwined their bodies around each other and appeared to be dancing. Eve said to Adam, 'Look, Adam—those two serpents are celebrating God's precious gift of life with a dance. Let us dance with them.' Adam then grabbed Eve by the hands and they emulated the serpents standing about 7 feet away from them. The serpents hissed affectionately at one another and then the human couple hissed at one another as well, and then laughed as they embraced and then kissed.

"Lucifer turned to the other eleven angels and said, 'Did you notice how Eve had her eyes fixed on the only tree that she was not permitted to eat from?' The others replied, 'Yes, you are correct.'

"Lucifer added, 'Did you notice anything else?'

"Ahuramahz answered, 'I noticed that Adam ate everything that Eve ate, as if to win her affection ever the more.'

"'Excellent, Ahuramahz,' Lucifer responded. 'I was also intrigued about Eve's fascination with serpents, while Adam preferred the monkeys—being the overgrown monkey that he is! Even so, Adam abandoned his monkey-watching to join Eve's engagement with the serpents. This job will be oh so easy my brothers! We will return a day from now when the earth-star is one quarter of its path above the horizon. I will lead and you shall observe and learn how to deceive a human.'

"The other eleven laughed and howled, causing the earth to tremble slightly. Adam and Even stopped dancing and held each other tightly looking around as if they knew someone was watching them. 'Elohim, is that you?' asked Adam. After five seconds of silence, his anxiety subsided and he continued with Eve in their walk in the garden. Lucifer and the other eleven departed to the large rock to meet with the others.

"When the full moon was directly over the dark sky, Lucifer addressed his audience of angelic beings, 'I see that everyone is here except two of my brethren—who would that be?'

"Zenshinto answered him, 'I believe that to be Hallah and Mohamma-el, master.'

"'Well, where are they?' Lucifer responded.

"An angel named Baalzebub replied, 'They went up to the earth-moon to do exploration and analysis, my lord.'

"Lucifer put one of his hands over his face in disgust, saying, 'Well, then we will begin without them since they wish to be moon gods.' The others laughed. He continued, 'Brothers, listen to my voice. Tomorrow will be the day that we will persuade the humans to follow us in our rebellion against Yahweh. I have observed some natural tendencies in the humans and I will manipulate those inclinations to our advantage. Here are the coordinates to the Garden of Eden.' (Out of Lucifer's mouth projected a beam of light that resembled a map of the earth).

"Lucifer continued, 'All of you will watch my masterful performance as I will utilize the potential flaw of God in allowing humans to have free will. Humanity's lack of complete knowledge and virtual absence of divine wisdom will play into the trap that I have plotted against them.'

"Baalzebub interrupted, 'What is your plan, master?'

"Lucifer became irritated and satirically answered, 'That is for me to know and for you to find out tomorrow! I want all of you to have front row seats to this cosmic event. Each of you, make sure that you hide all visibility and any traceable signs you might give away. Choose a tree to occupy while I handle the rest. When the earth-star rises you are to go to your tree of choice. That is all—you may disperse to your own doing until then.'

"The other angels applauded loudly and created the sound of thunder. Adam and Eve were awakened out of their sleep momentarily. They looked at each other and Adam whispered, 'Was I dreaming or was that sound real?'

"'I heard it too,' replied Eve. They stood up and looked around. Suddenly there was a light show in the sky above them. It was as if there were falling stars going in reverse back up into the skies. Adam said, 'Elohim must have his messengers performing tonight. I have seen this before.' Eve just nodded, and soon they laid back down and returned to their slumber.

"When Adam awoke in the morning, it was similar to any other morning. He took some of the tools that he had made to tend the garden. He pruned the vines and the plants to trim the excess leaves and branches. Eve irrigated a canal in her section of the garden so that the water would run like a creek giving nutrition to the vegetation in a beautiful-like manner. After their morning chores, they began to take another walk in the garden. They held hands and took the same route as the day before. They remembered God saying long before about a tree of life somewhere in the garden. This was a tree that supposedly granted them immortality like God and his angels. They did not understand the difference between immortality and mortality at this point. They had searched all over and apparently had yet to find this tree.

"Eve took Adam by the hand and they went a little bit off course from their walk the day before. There was a tree that stood in the middle of a series of trees that formed a perimeter. The center tree was smaller and punier than any of the others. There was one humungous orange that hung from one of its branches, but other than that there was no fruit. Adam went to grab the orange, but he noticed an unfamiliar odor coming from the tree. There was a sudden drop in temperature surrounding the tree as well. This caused Adam to change his mind and retreat. He did not know that it was Maijan who was preventing him from eating of the tree of life.

"As the human couple walked in the garden they began speaking of the day when Eve would give birth to their first child. God had told them that this would be a tremendous blessing and that it was a gift that he had given the woman. Eve had no idea that she was three days pregnant during this conversation. Adam reminded Eve of God's command to be fruitful and multiply. Up to this point, both of them had observed other creatures procreate and give birth to offspring, but these first many days they had yet to do so.

"As they approached the rear side of the forbidden tree of the knowledge of good and evil, Eve gazed at its unique fruit as she had done for many days before. As her hazel eyes had ascended up its branches, she noticed a bright orange, red, and blue serpent descending down the tree. She grabbed Adam's arm and pulled his gaze away from the baboons who were playing in the opposite direction. She pointed to the serpent and they both approached the tree. The serpent dropped to the lowest branch of the tree which was about four feet off of the ground, just as Eve and Adam approached (Eve stood in front of Adam). Eve noticed that this serpent was different than any of the others that she had seen. This serpent had shiny, red eyes and its scales looked magnificently polished and bright. What happened next shocked Eve even more—the serpent spoke to her.

"The serpent's body was wrapped around one of the pieces of forbidden fruit. It said to her, 'Here, try some of *this* fruit—it is the best tasting of any in this garden. I should know because I have been here long before you have.'

"Eve and Adam both shook their heads rapidly. The serpent then continued its discourse, 'Did not God say that you can eat from any tree from the garden?'

"Adam began to walk away, pulling Eve by the hand. However, Eve broke loose of Adam's grip and responded to the serpent, 'We may eat of the fruit of the trees of the garden, but God said that we cannot eat of the fruit of the tree that is in the middle of the garden. We cannot even touch it—or else we will die.'

"The serpent laughed and then sank its fangs into the fruit, taking a large bite and swallowing it whole. The serpent then said to Eve, 'You will not die. The reason why God told you not to eat of this fruit is because that he knows that when you do eat of it your eyes will finally be opened, and you will be like God by knowing the difference between good and evil, even mortality and immortality. Look at me: I have been eating of this fruit since day one, and I have not died. In fact, I have become more beautiful, wiser, and more godlike everyday. I am becoming a god myself, and you can too. Elohim realizes that some of us might one day become just as wise and as awesome as he is—but he does not want that because he is afraid of having an equal. In fact, he does not want any of us to even get close to his splendor, so that is why he is keeping this excellent fruit from your lips, so as to keep you subordinate under him.'

"Eve took a long and hard look at the tree, inspecting its every detail. She agreed that the tree and its fruit was the best looking in the garden and able to make one wise. She had never thought of things the way this serpent had explained to her. He must be divine—after all, no other creature of this garden was able to speak. He must be speaking truthfully. Just then, Eve reached up and grabbed the unique purple fruit and took a large bite. Indeed, it was the best tasting fruit she had ever tried before! She then grabbed another piece of fruit from the branch and gave it to Adam, who ate along with her.

"After Adam and Eve had eaten their fill from that tree, Eve searched everywhere for the serpent, but he was no where to be found. At that point, the other fallen angels—filled with awe—decided to vacate the Garden of Eden, just as Lucifer had just done. At their departure, a very cold wind came upon the place, causing Adam and Eve to shiver for the first time ever. In fact, their bones even ached, and a burning pain was felt in their genitals and in the breasts of Eve. They also became nauseated. They each looked down upon their naked bodies, and perceived that they had changed. They felt ashamed for disobeying God and their newfound nakedness seemed to epitomize that shame. Eve wondered to herself, 'Is this what dying was? That serpent tricked me! I am not any more god-like than I was before. The only difference is now I know what it feels like to have betrayed my creator. How can I ever face him again?'

"Adam had similar thoughts racing through his mind. Later that day, Elohim was supposed to descend and meet with them, but would he come as a destroyer this time? Adam ran away from Eve into the thickness of the bushes. Eve ran after him, calling his name. 'Get away from me, woman!' shouted Adam.

"Eve responded, 'Wait, Adam, I am afraid. Do not leave me alone. I feel shame.'

"Adam turned and answered her soft reply with two eyes full of tears, 'I feel shame as well. Help me find covering for our nakedness.'

"Eve spotted a fig tree with very large leaves and pointed it out to Adam. They both gathered as many leaves as they could hold and took them to a secluded place by one of the rivers. Adam and Eve sewed the leaves together and made aprons to cover their naked bodies. When they were finished, they were exhausted from their experience and their bodies ached all over. They fell into a deep sleep beside the river. They had never felt so alone before this time.

"Meanwhile, Lucifer and his rebels were having a meeting by the large rock. He said to his comrades, 'Brethren, the time is near when the humans will join our rebellion. They will produce offspring and greatly multiply our numbers, so that the heavenly host will not stand a chance! We will allow the guilt and shame the humans are experiencing transform into bitterness and hatred toward God for allowing them to have such a horrible experience. Then we will go and show ourselves unto them and unite as one. We will form one army and prepare to do battle against Yahweh's hosts at the appropriate time!'

"Satan's minions shouted with joy and they were able for the first time to possess the bodies of the surrounding animals of the earth, for now the entire creation had been defiled and was undergoing decay, death, and the process of aging. Many of the animals that were possessed began to devour one another, with the demons enjoying the taste of blood and enjoying the sight of death on the earth. The other creatures that were not possessed were now filled with fear, for they innately knew that something was definitely wrong, although they did not have the capacity to understand what.

"Meanwhile, the heavenly hosts of angels had just witnessed the second rebellion against Yahweh in a relatively short time period. When they saw the catastrophic events upon the earth, many thousands of them gathered at the throne of the Godhead to complain to Yahweh. Gabriel asked, 'Lord, your creation is becoming undone and chaos is now filling your earth. Will you not intercede and crush this rebellion? Even the humans have betrayed you and will surely join Lucifer. They must all die!'

"The Son of God descended from the throne and spoke to the distraught Gabriel, saying, 'Do not worry my son. All of this has been foreseen. And though it seems as if the humans might join Lucifer, and have indeed somewhat followed in his footsteps, they will not choose to join his rebellion—at least not Adam or Eve. But you are correct that they must be judged and punished, just as the rest of my creation has already begun experiencing the consequences of sin, namely the process of death and decay. At the right time, we will go down and confront the humans, as well as that devil Lucifer. Pay close attention and be watchful. Whoever has the ability to hear, let him hear.'"

35

A SAGE AND A PRIEST
WERE IN THIS CAR...

The remainder of Alex Sage's train ride was tranquil and uneventful. Of course, Alex had no idea where this train was destined. But the lack of restraints, explosions, and gunfire was a nice change of pace. He had removed himself from the barrel of grain once he was certain that the German police were long gone. The thoughts of what had transpired the past few days occupied Alex's mind to the extent that the next six hours on the train felt more like 60 minutes. All of the sudden, a new thought entered Alex's mind: what if the German authorities had alerted the train station of every destination about him being a fugitive? If that was the case, then Alex might have to make an early exit from this train. He decided it was about that time. Alex opened the hatch of the train car, popped his head out and looked around. He was traveling in the middle of the European countryside right now. The fast air hitting his face felt refreshing. Alex lifted his body back on top of the train car and then lowered himself down the ladder on the side of the car. The train was moving at about 20 mph, but to Alex it seemed much faster. As afraid as he was, he closed his eyes and jumped into the hard rocks and gravel of the train tracks, scraping his elbows as he fell.

Alex got up from the ground, spit on his hands, and then rubbed his burning elbows with his moist hands. He began walking in the general direction of the train tracks for the time being—at least until he got to the upcoming hills to see if he could survey the terrain a little better. Luckily for him, it was the beginning of June, and it was not too hot, nor was it in the freezing winter months. Equally fortunate for Alex was that he ate a hearty breakfast and was adequately hydrated.

Once Alex came close to the hills he noticed that they were not too steep. Rather than walk between the hills along the route of the train tracks, Alex decided to climb uphill so that he could have more of a bird's eye view of what was in front of him. It took about 30 minutes to get to the top of the grassy hill. From what Alex could see, there appeared to be a few small towns about 3-5 miles from the bottom of the hill. He figured it would take about an hour and a half to get to the first town. Hopefully, these towns would not have been alerted as to his situation. Lieutenant Alex Sage began his descent.

About halfway to the first town a two-lane highway intersected Alex's line of travel. He walked alongside of this road until he reached the first landmark of civilization—a gas station. He approached the gas station clerk and said, "Good morning, sir." The clerk returned a serious stare for a couple of seconds and then muttered, "Good *afternoon*," in a broken accent. This less-than-friendly response almost caused Alex to turn around and walk out, but none-the-less Alex overcame his timidity and asked, embarrassingly, "Could you tell me where I am? What country is this?"

The clerk gave a slight grin and asked, "You do not know what country this is? Do you want to know what year it is too?"

Alex's face began to turn red, but he swallowed his pride and answered, "Sir, I have had a rough couple of days and I have been on the road for a long time—I just need to know where I am at so I know what I should do next."

The clerk erased his grin and replied more seriously, "You are a few miles north of Udine, Italy. Does this help?"

"Yes, very much," answered Alex. "Thank you." He turned around and walked back outside. He stood just beyond the door gazing intently at the road into town. Just then, a man (who happened to be in line behind Alex inside of the gas station) approached Alex and said, "Hello, young man. Would you like a ride into town?"

"Sure, thank you," replied Alex.

"Anytime," said the man. "My name is Giovanni, by the way. And you are?"

Alex was hesitant to give his real name, but he didn't have an alias handy, so he would offer his first name at least. He responded by saying, "My name is Alex, and I really appreciate your offer, thank you so much."

Giovanni smiled. He was an older man with olive colored skin, hair that used to be darker black but now was graying—that which was left of his hair, for his baldness took up most of his headspace. His moustache was black and thick. His brown eyes were shielded with spectacles and surrounded with a friendly face. Giovanni proceeded to put gas in his Volkswagen Jetta and gestured to Alex to sit in the passenger seat. The inside of Giovanni's car was impeccably clean and had the scent of the pine air freshener that hung from the rear view mirror. Giovanni finished fueling the car and then joined Alex. Giovanni turned the ignition, looked at Alex and gave a friendly smile and asked, "Are you hungry for supper? I have prepared some delicious pasta at my home and you are welcome to eat with me."

"Sounds great," Alex answered. "I have no where to go anytime soon."

As the Jetta pulled onto the two-lane highway, Giovanni—obviously noticing Alex's G.I. pants, T-shirt, and flight jacket—asked, "So are you military?"

"Yes," replied Alex. "At least, I was until recently."

"So what happened—if you don't mind me asking?"

"Oh, that's a long story. Let's just say that my destiny is no longer with the U.S. Air Force."

"So you are American? I thought so."

"Yeah, I was stationed in Germany. Now that I'm out, I'm just doing some traveling in the meantime, but I hit a few bumps in the road, so now I'm stranded," Alex told him.

Giovanni nodded. Alex then asked him, "So what do you do for a living, Giovanni?"

"I used to be a priest—a Catholic priest. But let's just say that my destiny is no longer with the Vatican," answered Giovanni. "Now I just live off of the farmland that my father left me."

"Mmmm," Alex responded, nodding. A couple of minutes of silence followed. Then Alex asked, "How many years were you a priest for?"

Giovanni answered, "Thirty-five years. Mostly in Italy, but I also served in a parish in Egypt for ten of those years in between."

"How many languages do you speak?" asked Alex.

"I can speak Italian, Spanish, English, French, German, Latin, and Coptic fluently—but I am also familiar with Greek, Hebrew, Russian, and Arabic as well," replied Giovanni.

"Wow!" exclaimed Alex. "Did you learn all of those growing up as a child? Or did you learn them after you became a priest?"

Giovanni answered, "The European languages I learned throughout my childhood, but the Latin, Greek, Hebrew, Arabic, and Coptic I had to learn in my fields of study. You will soon begin to learn a few of them yourself."

The last statement threw Alex off-guard, "Excuse me, Giovanni?"

"Please, call me Gio"

"Okay, Gio, what did you mean that I will learn some of these languages—please explain. I've been through quite a lot and I don't know who I can trust."

Gio could no longer keep his mission a secret. He sighed and began to explain, "Mr. Alex Sage—that is your name, correct?"

Alex's eyes widened due to the fact that he had not given Gio his last name. He nodded accordingly.

Gio continued, "You do not need to worry—you are in good hands. Right before I came to the gas station, I was taking a nap and I had this vivid dream. An angel from the Lord appeared to me and told me that I was to come to that gas station and pick you up. The angel also told me that I was supposed to train you in theology and biblical studies so that you will be prepared for the mission that God has chosen for you."

Alex interrupted, "Mission? What mission? I never said I wanted to be a priest or a pastor or anything. You must be mistaken."

"Trust me," said Gio. "This is not the first time the Lord has spoken to me in a dream. What he said will come to pass. If you try to run away from your destiny, you will fail miserably. It is no use to run from the one who created your legs! It is much better to surrender and trust in the power of the Lord. He will equip you. And besides, you are not the only one who was chosen for a mission here. I have also been chosen as the instrument of teaching in this situation. I have learned over the years not to resist God's will. Submission and obedience are not easy but the blessings that come with them far outweigh the burdens."

Still stunned, Alex said quietly, "I wonder why my dad wasn't chosen to teach me—he is a theology professor, after all. Huh, I wonder where my dad is. Do you have a cell phone, Gio."

"No, I am sorry, I do not," answered Gio. "I have a telephone at my home, though, and you are welcome to use it."

"That sounds great, Gio, thanks," said Alex. "I think my dad is in Turkey right now, excavating at that site where they think Noah's Ark might have been found."

"Oh, yes!" said Gio, excitedly. "It was on the news last week, but I have not heard anything in the last few days."

Alex added, "Have you seen anything about me on the news today?"

"No, I have not watched the television today," replied Gio. "Why? Are you famous?"

"Not exactly," said Alex. "I was kidnapped by people that said they worked for the U.S. Government. But something happened while they were driving me somewhere. The van flipped and exploded and I escaped. I think the media was blaming me for the explosion though, because the police were trying to come after me, but I escaped, and here I am."

"Oh," Gio responded, with a concerned look on his face. "So I am harboring a fugitive. Well that is just great! The Lord has not given me anything exciting to do in a very long time—I need some extra spices in my life!"

Alex laughed as Gio pulled his Jetta into a long driveway that led to his house. They entered his home which was furnished with antique furniture. As far as cleanliness was concerned, Alex had never seen a cleaner and more organized home. Gio took Alex into the living room and had him sit on an old, but very comfortable couch. "Would you like something to drink, Alex? Tea, coffee, water, or home grown grape juice?"

"Oooh, I'll try some of your grape juice, please," answered Alex. Gio turned on the television for Alex before he left to get the juice. Alex had never seen such an old TV in his life, but the picture was relatively good. The news was on, but nothing about him was showing at that time—only local crimes. A few minutes later, Gio returned with the grape juice and a half a loaf of bread with some dipping sauce. He then said, "Oh, let me turn to the international news station for you. Perhaps there might be something about Turkey or even about your escape from prison."

Even though Gio laughed at his last statement, Alex did not find it particularly funny—although he knew that Gio had not intended to be offensive. After Gio switched the channel he said, "Okay, I will go and prepare the pasta and the sauce. It will be ready in about 25-30 minutes. Just make yourself comfortable, and feel free to read any books or magazines from the bookcase over there."

"Okay, thanks, Gio," responded Alex. For a few moments, the news was saying something about European Union currency and certain nations going bankrupt. Then all of the sudden, the news changed to what had happened to him earlier in Germany. "Gio—come quick!" exclaimed Alex. "I'm on the news again."

Alex could hear Gio's feet shuffling as fast as his 65 year-old body could move them. Gio and Alex both watched as the media portrayed Alex Sage as an international terrorist who was responsible for gunning down a U.S. Air Force aircraft over the Arctic Circle, as well as planting a bomb in a hospital in Iceland and a U.S. Homeland Security vehicle in Germany that killed three federal agents. Alex's Air Force photo was used to identify him to the viewers, and a phone number to contact authorities if there was any information leading to Alex's whereabouts.

"Liars! They are so lying, Gio—you can't believe them!" yelled Alex.

Gio said assuredly, "Don't worry Alex, I am well aware of the lies of the media. Remember, the Lord himself gave me instructions regarding you, so I will not turn you in. And this farm is two miles away from the next neighbor, so you do not have to worry about being seen around here. Besides, what more do I have to live for other than this farm? I have a brother and sister, and four nieces and two nephews who live in Southern Italy. Other than that, I have no family, no children. Training you in the ways of the Lord is my primary focus now—that and dinner—speaking of which, I must go and stir the sauce. So if you will excuse me, Alex."

Gio shuffled himself back into the kitchen. They ate a very tasty dinner with some home-made wine as well. Alex told Gio everything that had happened since his Arctic Circle adventure. They both agreed to get their rest and begin the theological training in the morning—right after Alex would try to call his father in Turkey. It was a long and tiring day for both of them—they had earned the right for a good night's sleep.

36

STATESIDE DRAMA

Alicia Sage was being escorted to her college dorm by the CIA agent and her friend, Alberto, in a government Ford Taurus. Alicia was supposed to go and gather a few things and then they would drive back up to her home in Lakewood, Oregon. They were about 30 miles from the Pepperdine campus when Alicia, gazing at the 33 year-old Alberto asked him, "So Alberto, how long have you been in the CIA?"

"A little more than two years," answered Alberto. "I worked in the FBI for five years—and I was good at what I did—so when the opportunity to be recruited came along, I jumped on it!"

Alicia continued, "So I am assuming that your name is not *really* Alberto, right?"

"You are correct," answered Alberto, grinning.

"So are you going to tell me your name?"

"Well, it's not really protocol to do so. But since I like you, I'll think about it."

"Ha! The fact that you're willing to break protocol tells me that you want to already. You're just toying with me."

"So let us toy for a while longer, shall we?"

Alicia smiled, but said nothing. A few minutes later, Alicia decided to break the ice and share with Alberto everything that she had witnessed in Peru. Alberto's face increasingly displayed shock as the story continued. Before that Alicia had merely given another CIA agent a statement as far as being kidnapped and detained by Jorge Espinosa, but this was the first time she shared the fullness of her Peruvian experience with anyone. She remembered Espinosa's warning about telling anyone what she had seen, but he was dead now, and even Espinosa admitted that Alicia was divinely protected—so why not get this heavy burden off of her chest? And even more than that, the entire world needed to know what goes on behind closed doors and in the deepest, darkest jungles of the world.

As Alicia finished her story, they were approaching the Pepperdine campus. It was Saturday, so there was much less traffic and congestion than normal. Alberto asked Alicia, "Would you like me to accompany you to your dorm room?"

"No," Alicia answered sassily. "I will only be a few minutes. And besides, I shouldn't be walking with a man who refuses to tell me is real name." Alberto laughed at her sarcasm.

Alicia walked into her empty dorm room. Her roommates, Kristen and Kim, must have went home for the weekend—they were usually still asleep at 11:00 a.m. on a Saturday. Alicia grabbed a week's worth of clothes and stuffed them in her suitcase. She also gathered all of her personal hygiene items, her cosmetics, and her Bible.

When Alicia walked out of her dorm, locking the door on the way out, she was startled by a young woman who ambushed her, saying, "Good morning, my name is Susan Gil from CBS News. Can I ask you a few questions?"

"What for?" asked Alicia. "Did I do something wrong?"

"No, not at all," said Susan. "Your experience of being held a political prisoner for ransom in Peru has been a hot story for weeks now, and the word just came in this morning that you were rescued and returned home—we'd like to hear all about it!"

"Well, not right now," replied Alicia. "I'm very tired, and I just got back. I just want to get situated first." Alicia began to walk back to Alberto's car.

Susan walked beside her and said, "Well, I understand that—and I don't want to interfere. Here is my card—call me when you're ready, okay?"

"Sure," answered Alicia. "Have a nice day." At that point Susan stopped walking with her, but all of the sudden, several news reporters and cameramen bombarded the Pepperdine sidewalks trying to get a word from Alicia. Every time Alicia would try to turn around and run with her suitcase, another news team cut off her path to the car. Finally, Alberto came running, holding up a badge and shouting, "FBI, you need to leave her alone—she's still in our custody."

Some of the news reporters backed off, but yet still others tried to press in. Alberto grabbed Alicia's suitcase and then picked up Alicia and carried her back to the car in his arms in a quick jog. He had left the car running, so he peeled out of the parking lot as soon as they were both in the car, fastening their seatbelts as they took off. The reporters ate their dust—but they both knew they would be back.

Alicia, who was holding her tears back, yelled at Alberto, "Why didn't you tell me that my situation was a big deal?"

"I didn't think they knew you were back, Alicia," responded Alberto. "Someone must have leaked that information out."

"That doesn't answer my question!" said Alicia, angrily.

Alberto's brown eyes compassionately looked into Alicia's green eyes. He answered by saying, "My real name is Ben Torres and I was born and raised in San Antonio, Texas. I'm 33 years old, single with no kids, engaged once, and I currently live in a 2 bedroom apartment in Richmond, Virginia—although I'm hardly ever there."

Ben's honesty comforted Alicia. "Well, nice to meet you, Ben," she responded. They both laughed and then engaged in personal dialogue for the next several hours on their way up to Oregon. They stopped in San Francisco for the evening, staying in two separate hotel rooms. The next day they had breakfast together at a local Denny's. When they were almost finished with their breakfast, Ben asked her, "When everything gets settled and back to normal, would you ever consider allowing me to take you out on a real date?"

Alicia almost spit out her orange juice. "Are you serious?" she whispered.

"Of course I am," answered Ben. "I don't know—there's just something about you that makes me feel alive and warm inside. In my line of work, that doesn't happen very often." Alicia began to speak, but Ben interrupted her, "I know that I'm ten years older than you and that I travel a lot, and all of that stuff, but I'm just asking for a date or two."

When Alicia was given the opportunity to speak, she answered, "Well, Ben, as a Christian woman I will only date men who are also Christians. And I don't want you to *say* that you are a Christian just because you want to go out with me. I want you to really get serious with the Lord *first*. I want to be able to see your faith with much more than just words. Believe me, I live in the dormitories of Pepperdine—I know phonies when I see them."

Somewhat disappointed, Ben said, "Wow, I'm really impressed with your commitment to God and your principles. I just thought I'd ask. I mean, I definitely believe that God exists—especially since I have known you. But the whole organized religion thing and putting God in the box of human customs and traditions—I can't say that I am ready to make a blind commitment right this moment."

Alicia replied, "Well, I admire your honesty, Ben. And I completely understand everything that you just said—and you're right—you should do your searching and allow God to reveal himself to you. And I know you went out on a limb to ask me out, risking an awkwardness for the rest of our trip. But don't worry about that—I do find you attractive as well, but now is not the time. We can keep in touch, though, if you'd like. You can call me or email me whenever you have time to."

"Thanks Alicia," said Ben. "You really know how to reject a man with style and grace!" They both laughed. The rest of their trip was pleasant and fun.

Ben pulled into the driveway of the home of Christian Sage. "I guess this is it," Ben told Alicia.

"For now," Alicia completed the statement.

Ben walked Alicia up to the front porch. Alicia did not have any keys, but she remembered that the spare was beneath the soil of the planter inside of a phony rock. She turned and saw Ben smiling at her. She embraced Ben with a squeezing, long hug and they said their good byes. As soon as Alicia stepped inside of her father's empty house, she grabbed the family phone book in the drawer beneath the living room lamp, picked up the phone and called her father.

37

THE CURSE THAT SIN BROUGHT

Pravuil, realizing that his time was almost up, began to haste in his storytelling:

"During the cool part of the late afternoon, Adam and Eve were preparing their evening meal from the delicious vegetables, fruits, and herbs of the garden."

Professor Richard Mockens interrupted, "Did they innately know how to use the garden to prepare their meals and make recipes, was it trial-and-error, or were they shown how to do it?"

Pravuil gave an annoyed glance at Richard and said, "Many things they knew how to do innately because they were created in the image and likeness of God, but God also instructed them of better ways—which leads us into the next part of the story. The Son of God came down to visit them in the Garden of Eden—as he had done many times before. Their meetings consisted of teaching and general fellowship—a relationship between the Creator and his special creatures, God and humanity. You see, Yahweh had always intended for Adam and Eve to have knowledge of good and evil, but he wanted them to learn in maturity as they grew—not learning in their own way and apart from God. The forbidden tree was a test to see if the humans would trust that God's way was better than their own. And of course, they failed the test.

"Anyhow, Adam and Eve heard the footsteps of the Son of God and they looked at each other fearfully. Adam said to Eve, 'I will hide myself between those two rocks over there, and you find refuge in that bush over there. Perhaps the Master will not find us and keep walking.' So they both hid from God.

"The Son of God called out to them, 'Where are you? I know that you are here.'

"Adam's stomach knotted up and he spoke from between the rocks, 'I heard the sound of your steps in the garden and I was afraid because I am naked—so I am hiding.'

"The Lord replied, 'Who told you that you were naked? Have you eaten from the tree of which I commanded you not to eat?'

"Adam came out from between the rocks, and when Eve saw Adam come out into the open, she poked her head up from the bush. Adam approached the Son of God and kneeled before him from about five paces away. He pointed at Eve and said, 'The woman—whom you gave to be with me—she gave the fruit from that tree to me, and yes I did eat it.'

"The Son of God summoned Eve to come near with his hand and she came forward and kneeled next to Adam. From the corner of her eye she saw a serpent making its way through the grass casually. Then the Lord said to Eve, 'What is this that you have done, daughter?'

"Eve felt terrible about the entire thing, and it showed on her face. She held back tears and spoke emotionally, pointing at the serpent, 'I was tricked by a serpent, and yes, I ate the fruit as well.'

"The serpent was minding its own business until it heard Eve's voice. The serpent was curious as to all of the commotion and it also recognized its creator, so it scooted, upright, over to the meeting. The Lord turned to the serpent and said, 'Because you have done this you are now cursed more than all cattle and more than every beast of the field. You will crawl on your belly from now on. You will inhale the dust for the rest of your existence, and I will put hatred between you and this woman, and between your offspring and her seed. It shall crush your head and you shall injure him on the heel.'

"Immediately, the serpent fell flat on its belly and slithered away, hissing. Adam and Eve looked at one another in confusion. The Son of God was fully aware of the fact that that particular serpent was innocent of any wrongdoing, but his cursing of the serpent was symbolic of future events involving the coming Messiah. In a more practical way, it also explained why snakes crawled on their bellies and why humans and snakes did not get along very well. The Lord was also aware of how Adam and Eve each deferred the blame of their own sinful decisions upon another and did not own up to their individual responsibility. Even more so, Adam being the husband and being created first, was supposed to protect Eve from such a deception and guide her away from disobedience, but he too was disobedient as far as his role and eating of the fruit.

"The Son of God turned to Eve and said, 'Because you have disobeyed, I will greatly increase the pain when you give birth to children. Sin has entered into your body and your mind: now you will have a desire to please your husband and to prove yourself worthy of him—but he shall rule over you in strength and in social status.' Eve's head dropped and she began weeping.

"The Lord then turned to Adam and said, 'Because you listened to the voice of your wife, and have eaten from the tree which I commanded you not to eat from, the ground is now cursed because of you. You will continue to eat from the ground, but you will have a great struggle bringing forth food and harvest for the rest of your days. The ground will now produce thorns and thistles when you try to cultivate it. Your body will suffer aches and pains and you will work hard and the sweat will drip from your face as you eat your bread from the fields. And though I told you the penalty for disobedience was death, I will suspend the immediate consequence of death—out of my mercy. But you will experience pain and frustration, and you will slowly begin to die. And one day you will return from the dust from which you were created. I am the Lord of creation. The creation as a whole is now cursed and will also begin to decay and die—death will be experienced by all because of you. Furthermore, you cannot cover your own nakedness by your own efforts. Your nakedness symbolizes your new sinful nature. You will no longer be needing those leaves.'

"The Son of God waved his hand and the fig leaved garments that Adam and Eve had sewn together and worn crumbled into small pieces. Adam and Eve tried to cover their genitals with their hands and legs. Just then, a lamb was passing through the field—it too recognized its maker and came to the Lord. The Son of God petted the lamb on its head and looked upon the first couple and said, 'I shall now show you what you must do to cover your sinfulness. You must perform this rite continually on a weekly basis—the day before the Sabbath.'

"The Son of God looked around on the ground and leaned over to pick up a small rock with a jagged edge. The Lord slit the throat of the lamb and its blood poured out to the ground. Eve let out a scream, 'No!' and Adam hugged her, also weeping and covering his eyes. The Son of God said, 'This is necessary to cover your sins. It is not what I intended but is a result of your rebellious act.' The Lord then tore apart the skin of the lamb from its body and divided the skin into two. He fashioned it to fit the bodies of Adam and Eve and then walked over to them and handed them their new garments. 'Here, put these on. Your sin will be covered for now until a savior is sent from your own seed. He shall totally redeem you. But until then, a blood sacrifice must be made continually. Only by the shedding of blood is there forgiveness of sins because life is in the blood.'

"Adam and Eve put on their new sheep-skin garments—they fit perfectly around their waists and half of their torsos. At that moment, Yahweh spoke from the heavens to the Son of God. Adam and Eve heard only thunder, but the Son of God heard the Father say, 'Look, the humans have become like one of us, knowing good and evil. Now, lest they stretch out their hands and take also from the tree of life and live perpetually in their sinful condition, drive them out of the Garden of Eden and into the world.'

"The Son of God did as the Father had instructed. He walked with them to the outer limits of the garden—a place where the humans had never went to, where the trees stopped growing. The Lord said to them, 'I will not abandon you, but you must now find a new place to till the ground and live. You must never return to this garden. Be fruitful and multiply and you will receive a blessing.'

"Adam and Eve slowly walked out of the Garden of Eden with their heads down and out into the barren field which had yellow grass and was full of rocks and thorny brush. As the Son of God watched them walk out of paradise, two of the Cherubim came to his side. Their names were Zateel and Uriel. The Lord commanded them, 'You are to guard this eastern entrance to the Garden of Eden until the appointed time. You must make sure that no human ever comes into this place again—and you must especially make sure they do not eat of the tree of life and live eternally in their sinful state. It is because they have not eaten from the tree of life that they will have the opportunity for redemption—unlike your brethren who have sinned *after* consuming from the tree of life.'

"Zateel and Uriel said, 'Yes, master,' and they drew out their flaming swords which spun in every direction to guard the eastern entrance. They remained there day and night until the hour before the great flood of Noah's time which destroyed the Garden of Eden. And this is the story of the origin of evil in God's good creation. Now, it is time for you to consume your scrolls and to gather the other items that I will give to you. The time is almost near for the others to join you."

38

ITALIAN SAUSAGE AND SIBLING SAGES

Alex Sage did not get much sleep that night—how could he? He was sleeping in the guest bedroom of a virtual stranger—someone who used to work for the Vatican. And Alex was aware of the many suspicions involved with Vatican politics. He did manage to get a few hours of quality sleep, nonetheless. He woke up early—6:10 according to the clock on the wall. He went into the bathroom to use it. As he was washing his hands, he noticed an unused toothbrush still in its package next to a traveler's tube of mini-toothpaste. Alex got the hint.

Alex left the bathroom, refreshed and rested. He saw Gio cooking breakfast in the distance. Gio looked and said, "Good morning, Alex. How did you sleep?"

"Very well—all things considering," Alex replied. "Gio, do you mind if I use your phone?"

"Sure, you can use it," Gio answered. "Let me show you where it is."

Gio left the pan that was frying Italian sausage, and walked into the study room where the telephone was. There was even more books on the walls of that room. Gio brought Alex to the phone that was on the study desk and said, "Feel free to call whoever you wish and speak for as long as you wish."

"Thanks, Gio," Alex responded. Gio nodded.

As Gio left the room, Alex began dialing his father's cell phone number. Unlike Alicia, Alex had an incredible memory when it came to numbers—so he had no problem calling his father. The phone rang twice and then went straight to voicemail in the manner that usually meant that the recipient of the call pushed the "ignore" button. "Hmm, must've called at a bad time," Alex muttered to himself. Alex then dialed his sister's cell phone number to find out that the number had been disconnected. Finally, he tried calling the number to his father's house. After three rings he was surprised to hear Alicia's voice say, "Hello."

"Alicia!" Alex said excitedly. "What's up? How've you been?"

"Alex?" Alicia asked. "Oh my gosh! Is that you?"

"Yes! Yes! I'm so glad to hear your voice—you won't believe what I've been through!"

"Oh you think that *you* have been through something? Wait 'till you hear what *I* have to share!"

"Huh!" Alex exclaimed. "It couldn't *possibly* measure up to my experience!"

"Oh yeah? Wanna bet?" retorted Alicia.

"Ha ha! You're so full of drama, Alicia. What is it—are your little boy school mates betting on who will take you out first again?"

"That is so old news, Alex. Let me tell you…"

Alicia began from the beginning about her class trip to Machu Picchu and everything that had happened since. Once Alicia finished her story, Alex was stunned and was completely speechless for a few seconds. Alicia even had to double check and make sure he was still on the line, saying, "Hello, Alex? Are you still there?"

"Yeah, I'm here," responded Alex. "It's just that your story is so unbelievable."

"Well, it really did happen!" said Alicia, slightly angry.

"No, it's not that I don't believe you," replied Alex. "It's just that it is so eerily similar to what I've experienced too."

Alicia's jaw dropped. *What possibly could he be talking about,* thought Alicia to herself instantaneously. She begged Alex, "Please do not tease me, brother—I've been through a lot."

"No, I'm serious, Alicia," said Alex. "Let me tell you what happened to me..."

Alex then began to tell Alicia everything that happened to him, beginning with that fateful air exercise over the Arctic Circle. As Alex told the story, Alicia's eyes began to tear up. When Alex finished telling his story, including the fact that he was now in Italy about to undergo theological training, Alicia asked emotionally, "What do you think this all means, Alex? Is this the end of the world or something?"

"I don't know," answered Alex. "I'm still in shock myself."

Alicia replied, "It seems like God is doing some major things right now—not only in our lives—but it feels like the world is about to shift in a significant way. Have you tried to call dad?"

Alex said, "Yes, I tried to call him right before you. Turkey is only a couple of hours ahead of me so I know he's awake, but I think he ignored my call. He must be very busy or something."

Alicia said, "Yes, I hope *busy* is what is going on and not something terrible like what happened to us."

"Don't worry, Alicia. I'm sure dad will call us sometime today—although he wouldn't recognize the number that I'm calling from," responded Alex.

The conversation went on for another hour before they hung up. Alicia began to try and put a meal together as well as collecting loose change and recyclables around the house so that she could produce some petty cash that would last for a few days until everything got straightened out. Alex began his theological training with Gio and remained under the radar of the international community that sought to bring him to the world's justice system. For the remainder of the week, Alicia and Alex experienced more peace and rest than they had for quite awhile—well, at least Alex did.

39

MOUNTAIN DO-NOT

The sound of Dr. Christian Sage's cell phone disrupted the intense concentration of Professor Richard Mockens, Dr. Jabari Saal, and Professor Cooper upon the words of Pravuil. As Christian dug in his pocket for his phone, Pravuil said to him, "Please shut if off, the time is short and we must go."

Dr. Sage quickly glanced at it and saw that it was an unknown international number. He hurriedly pressed the ignore button and then turned his phone off. Pravuil walked over to where the clay jars were and pulled out two dozen scrolls and caused them to be suspended in the air. He then said to them, "Each of you may choose one."

As the men drew near, Pravuil disappeared, but the scrolls remained floating in the air at eye level. Dr. Saal was the first to choose: his scroll had been marked, 'The Book of Methuselah.' Next, Professor Cooper chose the scroll marked, 'The Book of Shem.' Then, Professor Richard Mockens chose the scroll marked, 'The Book of Mahalalel.' Then finally, Dr. Christian Sage chose the scroll marked, 'The Book of Adam.' After they all had chosen their scrolls, they heard the voice of the absent Pravuil say, "Now eat your scrolls."

Each man ate their respective scrolls like giant burritos. The texture was like carpet, but the scrolls had the taste of honey. After each scroll was totally consumed, a loud, thunderous sound came from below and the ground shook violently. Richard Mockens tripped over his own feet and fell backward, while Chrisitan and Cliff Cooper leaned against the ancient walls trying to balance themselves. Jabari Saal also fell into another jar of scrolls and the jar broke—unnoticed by the others. When the earthquake stopped, Dr. Sage and Professor Cooper attended to Professor Mockens who had hit his head fairly hard on the ground. While Richard was receiving that attention, Dr. Jabari saw three more scrolls entitled, *The Book of Cain, The Book of Ham,* and, *Summoning the Stars.* He quickly devoured those scrolls before anyone else could notice.

By the time Christian and Cliff had helped Richard to his feet, Jabari had joined them, still chewing on his final scroll. Suddenly, the terrible stench that was first noticed when they fell into the Ark returned—twice as bad now. The voice of Pravuil again announced, "Quickly, go under the shelf beneath the jars and take what is there. Soon you will rejoin the others. May the grace of Yahweh be with you."

The four men did as instructed. Jabari grabbed a small clay tablet that looked like an ancient calendar of sorts, including engraved sketches of what looked like constellations. Richard picked up a strange object that looked like ancient pliers and another tool that had a flat hammer's head on one side, and a pointy sharp end on the other. Cliff took a small box that appeared to be fashioned out of shiny black rock. It had what appeared to be two drilled holes on each side of the cube. Christian took another jar—although this one was much smaller. This jar actually had an angelic hologram with his name on it. He did not open the jar, but only took and held it under his arm. After the professors had all of their gifts in their possession, they suddenly felt nauseous, having a bitter aftertaste in their mouths. Then a cold breeze entered the ark and the four men became dizzy. As they began to lose consciousness, they heard the distant voices of the other archaeologists outside of the ark.

Dr. Hank Norton and Dr. Geoffrey Goldberg were looking down upon their four colleagues, who were asleep on the ground using their rucksacks as pillows. Christian, Richard, Jabari, and Cliff simultaneously awakened to see Hank and Geoffrey hovering over them looking at their faces. Dr. Norton began the rebuke, saying in his British accent, "You guys stayed up here all night and didn't get anything accomplished? What is the matter with you?"

Dr. Goldberg answered for them, "They must've got scared and ran away by these trees."

"But how?" asked Dr. Norton. "How were they able to climb off of the vessel?"

Dr. Sage interrupted, "Very carefully—that's how." The other three looked at each other, amused.

Dr. Saal began to speak, "We actually accomplished many things..."

Both Dr. Sage and Professor Cooper looked at him sternly and quieted him.

"And what did you accomplish, exactly?" asked Dr. Norton.

Dr. Jabari looked at his three accomplices nervously and they offered him no help. He then said to Dr. Norton, "We found out that it was much too dangerous to try to enter the ark with the limited tools that we had— that's what. As a wise man once said, failure is progress because you now know that a greater effort is required for success."

Cliff and Christian looked at each other and tried their best to hold their laughter in. Dr. Goldberg interjected, "So are you going to join us now? Or are you going to sleep all day?"

Dr. Saal began to say, "Well, we are kind of sleepy..." Cliff poked Jabari in the side with his elbow. So Dr. Saal finished his sentence by saying, "But how can we possibly pass up such an opportunity to look into such a mysterious finding." So with that, they all walked together toward the ark. There were now about 40 other diggers at the site. Amazingly, Dr. Sage looked down upon the top of the ark and found that there was no evidence that he and his colleagues had ever fallen into the vessel. It looked exactly how it was before they fell into it. Dr. Saal, Professor Mockens, and Professor Cooper all looked at each other in astonishment, but said nothing. Each one of them also wondered about the extra items that Pravuil allowed them to take—where were they now?

It wasn't until after a full day of digging and they were all back in their tent later that evening that Dr. Sage, Dr. Saal, Professor Mockens, and Professor Cooper realized that their "extra" items given by Pravuil had been neatly stowed away inside of their rucksacks. They were careful not to expose them to Dr. Norton or Dr. Goldberg. They all ate a light dinner and fell asleep quite easily from their exhausting day of digging. There were no major discoveries that day either, but more of the same minor fossil finds. Two out of the six men began to wonder if this trip was a waste of time and money. It was apparent that it would take a significantly longer time to unravel the truth of this mysterious vessel.

During that night, Dr. Jabari Saal began to have vivid nightmares. He saw visions of people drowning in rapid water. He heard screams of those being killed and even murdered. He heard unintelligible chanting. He also saw visions of lightning striking the ground and then people walking through fire. After those visions and auditory experiences, Dr. Saal woke up out of his sleep drenched in sweat, despite being in an extremely dry environment. He wiped his face with his bed sheet. Then his nose began to bleed. He reached for a tissue and used one to plug the bleeding. Then the room became extremely cold, despite the heat lamps remaining lit. Jabari could see his breath. Then he heard a low humming sound coming from outside the tent.

Jabari Saal walked outside of the tent with his wool socks on and a tissue hanging from his bleeding nose. He saw a circular light descending upon him slowly. He tried to turn and run back to the tent but he found himself unable to move as if paralyzed. The light became so bright that he became temporarily blind and he felt as if he were being lifted outside of his body. He then saw a vision of a bluish-gray face with large, black eyes staring into his eyes. When that face disappeared, he found himself standing inside of the ark, alone. He felt compelled to walk back into the ancient library. As he walked he heard faint whispering calling his name, "Jabari, Jabari, set us free."

As he entered the ancient library he was suddenly aware of the fact that he was walking in complete darkness but yet stepped with precision. This time, there was a small portion of the rock wall within the library that had been removed. Jabari walked inside of the wall's opening and saw a stony stairwell that led downward. Dr. Saal walked downward and he saw light at the bottom of the stairwell. When he got to the bottom he noticed some sort of altar in a small, carved-out room. He knelt at the altar and could vaguely see what looked like an engraved eye—similar to the all-seeing eye of ancient Egypt—in the middle of the rock altar. He placed his eye upon that eye and saw a vision of a large, towering temple and people ascending and descending upon it. Sacrifices were offered at the pinnacle of this tremendous structure by some sort of ancient priests. He could hear chanting and then he saw lights descending from the sky that frightened him.

Jabari withdrew his eye from the eye of the altar. He looked to his right and noticed a small scroll with unintelligible letters written on the animal skin in what looked like dried blood. He heard a whisper saying, "Eat!" Dr. Saal also ate this scroll, and immediately he saw an alien being walk into the room behind him. It appeared to be the same bluish-gray being he saw earlier. This time it opened its mouth and revealed what looked to be fiery teeth. Its eyes then went from black to red. Then the being appeared to vaporize into smoke. Suddenly, Jabari felt a tremendous force push him into the ground and it felt like a heavy weight was pressing upon his chest. He then began to convulse violently and foam at the mouth. This happened for the next five minutes.

Meanwhile, every other scientist was sleeping soundly at the camp site until they heard the sound of helicopters in the distance. A few of the scientists woke up and wondered what could be happening at this hour of the early morning. Then the helicopter sounds went away. About an hour and a half later, the sounds of screaming and yelling awoke the entire camp. Then gunshots rang out. Now everybody was awake and putting on their clothes and trying to figure out what was going on. Then a series of explosions echoed throughout the mountainous region. Dr. Sage recognized that the shouting was in Arabic. He peeked out of the tent and saw several men dressed in all black and carrying assault rifles. He saw several of the security personnel lying on the ground motionless. It became evident to Christian that the entire camp was under a terrorist attack.

As soon as Christian and his colleagues were all dressed, they made a run for it back down to the landing zone. Each professor had his rucksack and a full canteen of water. As they began to make their stealthy escape, Dr. Goldberg asked, "Where is Jabari?"

Dr. Norton replied, "I don't know. Has anybody seen him?" They all shook their heads. As an explosive went off not too far from them causing them all to duck and cover, Professor Mockens announced, "We can't worry about Jabari right now—it's too chaotic. We must get going. He's a big boy—if he's able to escape he'll make it." They all nodded in agreement. They were about halfway down the trail to the landing zone when they heard a huge explosion followed by what sounded like a large rockslide. They turn to see if they could catch a glimpse of what it was, but it was too dark to see anything.

Dr. Sage and company were nearly at the landing zone of the Mount Ararat dig site when they heard fighter jets and military helicopters fly over their heads. They wondered if these were more terrorists or if they were the "good guys". Soon after, the group heard a fierce fire fight and a multitude of explosions. They saw flashes of light from where they stood, but nothing definitive. They decided to huddle up together for the remainder of the morning until sunlight so they could better discern what was going on. They were at the landing zone, so if any other helicopters were coming to land, they would be the first to know.

40

PUBLIC RELATIONS

Alicia Sage was awakened at 8:30 in the morning by the ring of the landline telephone. Thinking that it could be her father, she hurriedly got out of her bed to pick up the cordless phone. Instead of her father, it was a local news reporter who greeted her, "Hello, may I speak to Alicia Sage?"

"This is her," answered Alicia, wiping the cold from her eyes.

The reporter then said cheerfully, "Hi, my name is Cheryl Brown from the Oregon Cable News Channel. How are you doing this morning, Alicia?"

Alicia replied, "I'm doing well. How may I help you?"

"Well, there are many Americans who would like to hear your story, and I would like to give you the opportunity to tell that story on a television interview. Are you available sometime today?" Cheryl asked.

Alicia hesitated.

"Hello? Are you still there?" Cheryl intruded.

"Yes, I'm still here," answered Alicia. "I just don't know what to think of all of this."

Cheryl then said, "Well, I can understand that—I know that being kidnapped and held for ransom can be very traumatizing. But sharing your experience would be very therapeutic and it could potentially help other travelers to avoid the kind of things that you have experienced."

"Not to mention give you a good story to increase your social status," responded Alicia.

"Well, yes, I won't lie," replied Cheryl. "I'm always looking for a good story. It's how I pay the bills, honey. But I also try to make a positive contribution to society at the same time. So what do you say, Alicia? Would you be willing to do an interview with me?"

Another few seconds of silence went by. Cheryl waited nervously for an answer while listening to Alicia's breath over the phone. Finally, Alicia answered, "Okay. I don't see why not."

"Great!" Cheryl exclaimed. "When would be the most convenient time and place?"

Alicia almost invited her to her home, but she thought better of it and said, "Let's meet at Willow Park at two o'clock." Alicia thought that a public place where people would be present was a good idea considering what she had been through in recent weeks.

"That sounds good, Alicia," Cheryl replied. "We will be there an hour early to set up. I will give you my personal cell phone number just in case something comes up. Do you have a pen ready?"

"Hold on just a second," said Alicia. Once she found a pen she took down Cheryl's number and then hung up. Alicia had no idea what would come of this. She missed her father intensely and wondered if he was okay. She looked out of the window and saw nothing unusual. The press had access to her locally listed phone number but either did not have their home address or for some reason chose not to intrude. Alicia assumed the former rather than the latter.

Alicia got into her dusty Ford Focus, hoping that the few weeks of inactivity would not prevent it from starting. If it wouldn't start, she would have to have Cheryl pick her up. She had thought of calling Ben to take her, but she did not want to burden him or lead him on. She did feel comforted by his presence, though. Alicia turned the ignition and the engine coughed for two seconds before finally turning over and starting. She gave the pedal some gas. Apparently, her car had no problem with the time off, so she exited the garage and proceeded to Willow Park.

Willow Park was not a small park, but not huge either. It had two small ponds for fishing, a playground for big kids and one for younger kids. It had two parking lots, the first of which hosted two news vans. Alicia correctly assumed that Cheryl would be near one of the vans. The parking space between the two news vans was reserved for Alicia and she pulled in. The news crew gave Alicia sufficient space so as to not make her feel uncomfortable. Alicia opened her door, closed it and locked it. A smiling, light brown face greeted her, saying, "Hi Alicia, I'm Cheryl," extending her arm to shake hands.

Alicia took Cheryl's hand in hers and responded, "Nice to meet you, Cheryl."

Cheryl slowly led Alicia to the back of her van and began to explain how the interview would take place. She said, "Okay, Alicia, this will not be a live interview, so there is no need to feel nervous. Anything that will help you feel relaxed and comfortable, you just let us know."

Alicia nodded.

Cheryl continued, "We will sit on those benches over there," pointing to the north picnic area. "We have arranged with the park manager to have that section closed off so we will be undisturbed. I want you to speak as freely as you wish. Don't worry about making mistakes or misspeaking. The interview will be edited and we will make you look even more fabulous than you already are! Do you have any questions?"

Alicia responded, "Umm, does anybody else know that we are here? I mean do they know about me personally? I just don't want to be followed home or anything like that. I also don't want to be bombarded by other media as soon as our interview is over."

Cheryl assured her that they were the only news crew at the facility, and the interview commenced immediately afterward. Now Cheryl had only known about the kidnapping and the political extortion part of Alicia's story. She had no idea about the entirety of her experience. So when Alicia began to tell her everything that happened, Cheryl's face was frozen, awestruck, and horrified! Occasionally, Cheryl would politely interject with a question to gather more details. But for the most part, Alicia spoke in monologue for almost an hour.

When the interview was over, Cheryl took Alicia aside and spoke to her alone, saying, "Alicia—I had no idea that you went through all of that! I mean, if I were to hear your story by a secondhand source or read about it, I would be skeptical. But I can see into your eyes that you are telling the truth. I deal with a lot of phonies in this business, but I can tell that you're not lying. I'm so sorry—especially for your friend Amanda."

"Yeah, I know," Alicia replied. "I miss her so much. I wonder how her family is doing. Do you think they even know?"

"I'm not sure," answered Cheryl. "But I would expect that a government official would be in contact with her family. Do you happen to know them?"

"No, I don't," answered Alicia. "We were only schoolmates for a couple of semesters."

Cheryl said to her, "I can try and find out for you, if you want."

"That would be nice," said Alicia. "On another note, when will this interview be aired?"

"I would expect it to be within the week," answered Cheryl. "I will definitely give you a call and let you know."

"That sounds good. Thank you Cheryl."

Cheryl Brown hugged Alicia Sage, and they parted ways. When Alicia got home she tried to call her dad again, but his phone went straight to voice mail. She left him another message. Then she called her brother, Alex. They spoke for about an hour about how their day went. Alex was unable to reach their dad as well.

Meanwhile, back at the O.C.N.C. headquarters, Cheryl Brown had submitted her videotaped interview to her chief editor, Mark Sandberg. His jaw dropped as he listened and watched Alicia's testimony. Mark asked Cheryl, "I wonder if this girl, Alicia, is related to that Air Force pilot, Alex Sage. Do you know who I'm talking about?"

"No, Mark," Cheryl answered. "Who is that?"

Mark opened his mini-file cabinet at his desk and searched for a file. As he looked, he told Cheryl, "This Alex Sage had told a German newspaper a story that is similar to Alicia's story—with the giant men and their supernatural powers." He chuckled as he continued, "I thought it was pure sensational baloney—someone trying to get attention. And as it turns out, this officer is wanted for terrorism and espionage. They last saw him heading south on a train in Germany. But as I watched this Alicia Sage woman, she seemed very sincere about her story. It makes me wonder, Cheryl—if perhaps this Alex character's story might have a grain of truth. Perhaps he knows a deep, dirty military secret and now the powers that be are trying to frame him to shut him up."

"I thought that you were not into conspiracy theories," interrupted Cheryl.

"I'm not," replied Mark. "But can it be a coincidence that we have two stories—bizarre stories—on the opposite ends of the earth that are similar in nature and just so happened to be told be two people with the same last name? Or are they both college pranksters who have collaborated to give the world a big laugh?"

"Alicia doesn't seem to be the type," responded Cheryl.

"I know," said Mark. "And I sincerely doubt that an Air Force officer would jeopardize his military career—in fact his very life—with such a fanciful tale to only end up being an international fugitive. This is truly incredible!"

Cheryl said nothing, for she was deep in thought.

"Cheryl!" said Mark, raising his voice.

"Yes, sir?"

"I'm assigning you this case. I want you to do research on these two Sage characters. Find out who their family members are, what they do for a living, and what in the possible world-of-worlds is going on with super giants that practice sorcery in isolated places!"

"I will get on it right away, Mark. When will we air Alicia's interview?"

"I don't know yet. I wouldn't want to air it too prematurely before we investigate these incidents."

"But on the other hand, Mark, we wouldn't want our competitors to publish them first."

"Right you are, Cheryl! That's why you'll be working overtime until we can get some answers."

"Sounds good, chief. I'll let you know when I put something together."

"I know you will, Cheryl. Good night."

41

THE DREAM TEAM

Five of the six professors from Lakewood University sat on large rocks as the sun peaked over the mountains. Huge clouds of smoke covered the atmosphere and the smell of sulfur and gunpowder was ever present. Dr. Hank Norton and Dr. Geoffrey Goldberg were still unaware of the events that Dr. Christian Sage, Dr. Jabari Saal, Professor Cliff Cooper, and Professor Richard Mockens experienced. The latter had agreed to keep it secret for now because Hank and Geoffrey would probably not believe them if they were told. They kept waiting for a friendly helicopter to come and take them away from this war zone, but silence was all the help that was available.

It was nearly noon when the first evidence of civilization presented itself to the five men. It was not a plane or a chopper and it did not come from below. Footsteps from a group of people were heard descending upon the professors. "Do you think they are U.S. soldiers?" asked Richard. Everyone lifted up their heads as to discern the sound. A few muttered voices could be heard ever so slightly. Hank Norton could stand the suspense no longer, so he shouted out, "We're down here! Over here, gentlemen!"

Suddenly, the footsteps stopped. Then shouting in a foreign language echoed throughout the mountain pass, followed by running footsteps. Cliff said to them, "I don't think those people are here to rescue us—let's go!" The five professors all got up and mounted their backpacks and quickly began to descend on the rugged terrain. The footsteps and the shouting grew louder. Geoffrey slipped and fell, sliding down a trail of gravel and brush. Christian stopped and turned to help Geoffrey. As he approached Dr. Goldberg to help him up he could see the men in a distance, dressed up in desert fatigues and all holding machine guns or rifles. Shots began to ring out toward them. Dust blew up into the air as bullets ricocheted throughout the landscape. Finally, the professors all came to the edge of a cliff surrounded by steep rocks on the adjacent sides. They were trapped.

Soon the pursuers surrounded the professors, as they put their hands up in response to the weapons drawn upon them. The armed men wore long beards and appeared to be a local militia of some sort. "Please don't shoot us," pleaded Cliff. "We do not have weapons." The men laughed.

One of them stepped forward and spoke in broken English, "You are Americans, are you?"

The professors looked at one another. Finally Christian volunteered to speak, saying, "Yes, we are American teachers. We came to study Noah's Ark. You didn't blow it up, did you?"

The militia leader responded, "We did not blow it up—you did! Your planes dropped bombs on the boat and now it is destroyed!"

"Wait a minute," Hank chimed in. "Everything was peaceful until you people came with your weapons and began shooting."

The militia leader scowled at Hank. He then told them, "We only came because we intercepted a radio frequency that said the Americans will blow up the boat. We tried to stop them, but it was too late. We are Muslims. We believe that Noah was a prophet of Allah. We do not wish for Noah's boat to be destroyed. It was you American infidels who do not believe and want to destroy the things of Allah."

The professors looked at each other in confusion. Then Dr. Sage spoke up again, "We are teachers who came to learn about Noah's Ark. We did not wish to see the ark destroyed either. We are saddened by what has happened."

The militia leader threw up his hand in disgust. "It matters not! You will pay for this. Come! Follow us. We will take you back to our camp as our prisoners."

The professors did as instructed. Their bruised and scraped bodies now had to ascend back to where they came from. The Muslims had set up their camp where the archaeologists had originally set up camp. When they arrived, it was nearly dark again. The ground was filled with dried blood, but there were no dead bodies present. There was no sign of Dr. Jabari Saal either. The Muslims were kind enough to ration out military MREs for a satisfying dinner. Christian and Cliff ended their evenings in prayer, while Hank and Geoffrey were filled with fear and grief, struggling to sleep. Richard did not know what to feel. He was confused. He believed in God for the first time in a long time—but this particular scenario was troubling. Nevertheless, he fell asleep without prayer or overwhelming fear.

The dreams of two men, that night, were invaded by divine messengers. Pravuil appeared in Dr. Sage's dream and told him that he would give a speech at breakfast the next morning that would determine the fate of many. The words would be inspired by God the Holy Spirit who would speak directly through Christian to their Muslim captors. The militia leader who spoke to the professors, whose name was Sharif, was also visited by an angel who did not give his name. The angel said to Sharif, "Do not be afraid. I am a messenger of the Most High God. A foreigner will speak to you tomorrow. His words must be heard and you must listen and do what he says. Do not fear what the others say or do—you must take courage and trust God."

Early the next morning, Sharif was awakened by one of his fellow soldiers who was talking in his sleep. In Arabic, he was saying, "Jesus is the Son of God, Jesus is Allah's prophet..." Another man got out of his cot and slapped the dreamer in the head and whispered, "Stop blaspheming and go back to sleep. Allah has no sons and Muhammad is Allah's prophet." Sharif raised his head and looked over at the dreamer and the man who slapped him. Then he laid his head back down. He had the look of bewilderment in his eyes. Who was this foreigner that was to speak? It was still dark outside and everyone except the guards and Sharif was still asleep, and it would remain that way for another hour.

When Sharif and his fellow soldiers officially got out of their cots, they began to dress themselves and discuss what was to be done that day. They all agreed that they needed to police the area of the destroyed ark to see if they could gather any artifacts or intelligence. They noticed that Sharif was unusually quiet and disengaged, so one of them asked him, "What is wrong with you today? You are so quiet." Sharif answered, "I do not feel well. Leave me alone!"

More MREs were passed out for breakfast after the morning Muslim prayer. Dr. Sage quickly consumed his corned beef and hash, while his colleagues took their time. Christian was nervous as to what to say, where to say it, when to say it, and who to say it to. Outside of the tents was a large military formation. Commands were given in Arabic by a man whom the professors had not seen the day before. They could see Sharif lined up with the others in the front row. A bull horn was handed to their leader. He then shouted in English, "Americans! Come out here now!" Two armed men began walking toward the professors' tent. All five of them exited the tent, with their rucksacks on their backs, before the two men could get halfway there. The professors were shocked that the Muslims allowed them to keep their belongings without them even being searched. It was obvious that the American professors were not the main concern of these men.

When the five professors lined up behind the rest of the formation, the leader explained that they were to go and gather any valuables from the debris of the destroyed ark. Before they marched off, the leader asked the professors, "Do any of you have any information to share with us before we go?" Dr. Christian Sage meekly raised his hand and said to them all, "I do have something very important to tell all of you." He looked around for something to stand on to elevate himself so that he could be seen. An empty crate was on the ground a few paces from him. He put his finger up as to say, "Give me just a second." He grabbed the crate, set it upside down, and stood upon it, giving himself an additional 18 inches of height. Then he began to give his speech.

42

WHAT'S BEN MISSING?

Alicia Sage woke up the next morning and turned on the TV. She was looking at video footage of the firefight in the Ararat Mountains of Turkey that blew up the excavation site that held Noah's Ark. Alicia's eyes were filled with tears. The news reported that Jihadist Terrorists blew up the excavation site with grenade launchers and IEDs, and that the U.S. Military aircraft came just moments too late. There was an ensuing firefight with which the U.S. and their allies fought off the terrorists and scattered them throughout the mountains. The report said that Special Forces ground units were currently undergoing missions in the mountains trying to capture any terrorists who may have escaped. At that moment, she tried to call her father's cell phone again. The call went directly to voice mail. Alicia began sobbing. Next, she called Alex, but he too was unavailable.

Not long after, Alicia's cell phone rang—it was Ben. Alicia tried her best to stop crying and cleared her throat before answering. "Hello? Ben?" she asked, as she took his call.

"Good morning, Alicia. How are you holding up?" asked Ben.

"Not too good. Did you see on the news what happened in Turkey?"

"Yes I did. I'm sure your dad is okay, Alicia. Try not to worry."

"I know, Ben, but I'm scared. My world keeps getting turned upside down, and I can't seem to catch a break!"

"Yeah, you've been through a lot lately, but I'm here for you—I'm trying to help."

Alicia wept silently.

Ben continued, "Listen, Alicia: I've been keeping an eye out for you and I'm calling to let you know that the F.B.I. will probably come give you a visit within the next 48 hours."

"The F.B.I.? Why?" asked Alicia.

"It has to do with your brother. You haven't been calling him from your house phone or your cell phone, have you?"

"Well, yes. How else can I talk to him? There aren't many pay phones around here, you know."

"Yes, I know. But as you know, your brother is a wanted international fugitive, so the Feds are monitoring your calls. I'm sure they've listened to every conversation, but they are going to pay you a visit and question you about his whereabouts."

"But I don't know where he is. *He* doesn't even know where he is. All I know is that he is in Italy somewhere. Wait a minute—you're not trying to get info from me are you?"

"No, Alicia, of course not. I'm calling to warn you."

"Well, can't the Feds track this call too?"

"They *could*. But my number is listed as government, and the first 30 seconds of our conversation did not include any key words that would have cued them, so I highly doubt this call is being listened in on."

"Oh. So what do you suggest I do, Ben?"

"I think you should come with me for now."

"Are you close to here?"

"Yes, I am, as a matter of fact. I'm in Portland right now."

"Oh—so you planned this all along, did you?"

"Kind of," said Ben, smiling.

"Well, if you think it's best. But I'm warning you—no funny business. We are strictly just friends right now."

"You got it," replied Ben. "I know a hotel with separate bedrooms—we can stay there for the meantime."

"So when will we meet?"

"I will come and pick you up in two hours. Have your bags packed."

"Fine," said Alicia. "See you then."

Alicia Sage began to pack her bags. She had been feeling very alone for the last two days, and she would be happy to spend some more time with Ben—even as 'just friends.' With her brother somewhere in Italy, and her father—hopefully still alive—in Turkey, and all of her friends either in college or working full time, there was nobody for Alicia to talk to. She trusted Ben and he had the ability to keep her safe—which was something that seemed more elusive than ever at the moment.

Ben pulled into the driveway in a black Jeep Cherokee and honked his horn. Alicia grabbed all of her bags and joined him. A couple of hours later, Cheryl Brown would call Alicia's house phone to tell her that their interview would be aired the following evening. Cheryl had come to find out that Alex was indeed her brother. She even knew that her father was a missing person in the Ararat Mountain explosion. She had wished to get a little more information from Alicia, if possible, but she just missed her. Alicia did have Cheryl's cell number though. Cheryl knew that she would receive a call from her in the next couple of days anyway. Once you are a star in the media—which Cheryl knew she now was—your life will never be the same again. Most importantly, Cheryl believed Alicia's story. She believed that Alex was innocent of the charges. Cheryl also believed in Jesus Christ.

43

MIRACLE AT ARARAT

Dr. Christian Sage looked down upon his largely Muslim audience, with his colleagues standing to his left and slightly in front of him. Some of his captors scowled at him in disgust. Others had the look of shock on their faces, as if thinking, "How dare this man have something to say to *us*?" Christian's colleagues also had a similar look on their faces. What Dr. Sage didn't see was the pale face of Sharif who had figured out that the foreigner he was to listen to was none other than Christian Sage.

As Christian was about to speak, a sudden sound of wind came from over the mountain peak behind Dr. Sage. He looked back as the others also glanced in the same direction. An unusually warm wind blew into their faces like a hair dryer, and then ceased immediately. When Christian turned around, his face was slightly glowing with a bronze-olive complexion. He then began to speak: "Greetings brothers and friends!"

The Muslims all gasped out loud and looked at each other in confusion. The other professors looked at each other as if to say, "Why are these guys so surprised that Dr. Sage greeted them as brothers and friends?" The reason why the professors did not understand was because the Muslims all heard Christian speaking in their native Arabic tongue, while Dr.

Sage's colleagues heard him in his normal English. Christian continued his speech:

"It is not by accident that we are all here on this holy mountain together—a mountain that had contained the vessel that was built by the great prophet of God named Noah. I understand that you are all Muslims. I have something in common with you—I too willingly submit to the one true God! Last night, three of my friends and I were inside of Noah's Ark and an angel appeared to us. He spoke to us about many things, including God's original perfect creation. He told us of how the angels rejoiced while watching God finish the creation, which climaxed with the creation of humans who were especially created in the image of God. They were morally pure and without sin and in perfect fellowship with the Almighty. One of the most powerful angels created named Lucifer, however, was not happy that humans were given such a high status. He was filled with jealous rage and he devised a plan to destroy the humans and corrupt the goodness of God's perfect creation. He did this by persuading many of his fellow angelic beings to rebel against the holy throne of God.

"Of course, they were unsuccessful and the Most High could have destroyed Lucifer and his angels, but instead he made a wager with them. He allowed them to have a limited dominion over the earth and to try and get the humans to join them in their rebellion. If successful, God would allow Lucifer to rule in his place. But if unsuccessful, he would be cast down into a fiery lake. Lucifer had some initial success. He was able to deceive the first humans—Adam and Eve—to directly disobey God by eating from a tree that he commanded them not to eat from. However, Adam and Eve did not choose to join Lucifer, but they allowed God to cover their sin and wait for a future redemption. Even so, Adam and Eve were cast out of paradise and the earth would be cursed because of them. Furthermore, all humans who came after them would be born separated from God and with a natural inclination to sin against the Most High.

"God sent several prophets over time to call people to repentance and to follow the Almighty. Some of them were successful, but many were not, which resulted in being persecuted and even killed. The prophet we call Noah might have been one of the most unsuccessful prophets of all time. Only his wife, his three sons, and their wives believed his message that God would send a worldwide flood to destroy humanity, which by that time had become exceedingly wicked. When the flood waters came, every human and land animal that was not aboard the ark perished, and God started over with only the eight people on the ark. It is a crying shame that the discovery of this vessel was destroyed—and I believe you that it was the United States of America who destroyed it! Many great things could have come from the world's acknowledgement that such a vessel really did—and does—exist. Unfortunately, all they have now is our testimony. If nothing else, this could be the very reason why God even allowed it to begin to be discovered—our meeting that we are having here.

"But let me tell you—God sent many prophets after Noah, including our father of the faith, Abraham. God especially blessed his first two sons—Ishmael and Isaac. They both were to be founders of kingdoms. But it was through Isaac that the coming redeemer would eventually come through. His son Jacob would have twelve sons who were the heads of the twelve tribes of Israel. God would allow the Israelites to be enslaved in Egypt for hundreds of years before God called Moses to bring them out of slavery with powerful signs and wonders that the Most High would perform through Moses. Because the Israelites were so stubborn and sinful, they could not enter into the land of promise—Palestine—for another 40 years.

"Eventually, God permitted the stubborn Israelites to have a king, even though it was the Almighty who desired to be their king. Israel's second king, David, would capture God's heart because of his faith and devotion to the Most High. God promised David that one day the savior of the world would be born from his lineage. Many thought his immediate son, Solomon, might be that redeeming king. He built a lavish temple in Jerusalem for God and brought peace and prosperity to Israel for the first time. But Solomon allowed his heart to go astray by marrying foreign women who worshiped idols, and King Solomon allowed idol worship to take place in Israel. After Solomon died, a civil war broke out and Israel was divided into Northern and Southern kingdoms. The Northern kingdom continued the widespread practice of idolatry so the Almighty sent the Assyrians to destroy them and take them out of the promise land. Less than 150 years later, the Southern kingdom fell to the Babylonians for the same reason.

"After being in exile for over 100 years, the Jews were permitted to return to build their temple in Jerusalem. The Jewish people were ruled by Babylonians, Persians, then Greeks, and then finally the Romans. It was while the powerful Roman Empire ruled the world that the prophet Jesus was sent to his people. But Jesus was more than a prophet—he was the Lord himself. Yes—the only way that God could redeem sinful humanity was to become a man himself—in the person of Jesus! As you know, and as the Qur'an testifies, Jesus never committed any sin throughout his entire life. He was the only person to ever live a sinless life. Even your prophet Muhammad did not accomplish this. Jesus also performed many miracles, but Muhammad never did. Jesus was born of a virgin, Muhammad had a human father and mother. Check your own scriptures and you will see that Jesus was far mightier in deeds and holiness than Muhammad. The reason this is true is because Jesus was God in human flesh. He was truly a man, but he was fully divine as well."

A great stirring from the crowd began, as many began to murmur and grumble, but Christian did not allow them to interrupt, as he said:

"Please, please, let me finish, I beg of you—in the name of the Most High God! The prophet Jesus lived the sinless life that none of us could live. God did not need to be merciful to Jesus, because he was not in need of mercy—he was sinless. It was because God loved sinners like us that he became a man and sent Jesus into the world to save sinners and bring them back into fellowship with him—just as he had created Adam and Eve to do. God accomplished this by allowing Jesus to die on a cross as a substitute for sinful humanity. He was willing to sacrifice himself and offer his own blood as atonement for our sins. Jesus died on the cross so that we would not have to face the wrath of God, because it is written, 'The soul that sins shall die.' And more than this—Jesus not only suffered the penalty for sin, which is death, but he conquered death by raising himself from the dead three days later. By doing this he promises eternal life to anyone who would believe in him, his death and resurrection from the dead. And when Jesus returns to the earth at the end of time, he will also raise the dead bodies of his followers and unite them in their spirits, and we will live with the Lord forever!"

Some of the men could hear no more and began shouting at Christian Sage. "He is a false prophet!" one man shouted. "He is a jinh—the devil is inside of him!" shouted another. Some men began to reach down and throw dust into the air, and even others began to throw small stones at Dr. Sage. After being hit in the face with a rock, Christian got down from his crate and began to walk quickly back to his tent. The other professors followed him. They could hear some people yelling, "Allah is the only God," "Allah has no sons," "Muhammad is Allah's prophet!" among other sayings.

However, Sharif and a few other men were fighting to keep the disgruntled Muslims from attacking the professors, but they were outnumbered by the dissenters. Some of the men began to say, "Why did we let him speak!" "He is a blasphemer!" "He must die!" Finally, Sharif fired three shots in the air to get the angry mob to quiet down. "Silence!" shouted Sharif. "Are we so barbaric that we cannot even allow a man to speak his mind without killing him because we disagree? I had a dream about this man last night, so maybe we should consider some of the things he has to say."

"He's an American infidel!" one man shouted. "You cannot betray Islam!" another screamed. Sharif responded, "Let me go in and talk to him, and I will be right back." He followed the professors into their tent. Five of Sharif's faithful friends stood outside of the tent, facing the crowd to prevent any others from going in. Once inside the tent, Sharif sat down next to Christian, who was attending to some of the scrapes on his face from the rocks. Sharif said to him in Arabic, "Sir, I do not know what to think of what you just told me." Dr. Sage looked at him puzzled, and then said to him, "Why are you speaking Arabic to me—I do not speak your language."

Sharif replied in English, "What do you mean? We all just heard you speak in Arabic for several minutes."

"No I didn't," answered Christian. "I spoke English."

Sharif said to him, "Trust me, sir, only a few of us speak English and not enough of us speak it to have such an angry response to your speech. You spoke perfect Arabic and we all heard it!"

A few seconds of silence followed Sharif's statement. Then Cliff broke the silence, saying, "That warm wind—it must have been the Holy Spirit giving you the gift of Arabic speech—just like at Pentecost!"

With that, Christian Sage dropped to his knees and praised God. Sharif put his hand on Christian's shoulders and said to him, "Last night an angel visited me in my dream and told me to listen to you and to do what you say. Your speech was very troubling to me and especially to some of those people outside, but I have faith that Allah could be leading us into a special and different way of worshiping him because of the dream and its fulfillment."

Christian responded, "Gee, I don't know what to say to that. What is your name?"

"Sharif."

"Well, Sharif, are there any others who feel the same way that you do?"

"There are a few, but not many."

"Can we make peace with those who are not with us?"

"That would be difficult, but it is possible."

Sharif led the other professors outside of the tent to face the disgruntled crowd. Sharif told the people in his native tongue, "I believe that Allah has sent this man to us. He did not learn how to speak Arabic but God spoke through him like a prophet and enabled him to give us his message in our own language. We should be grateful. Allah is merciful."

One man interrupted him by saying, "What about what the Qur'an says? It is the word of Allah, and it says that Muhammad is Allah's prophet. It says that Jesus was not crucified, but that Allah put Judas on the cross instead. Allah would not allow his prophet to suffer shame."

Sharif responded, "I am fully aware of what the Qur'an teaches. I am also fully aware of my dream last night, the angel that appeared to me, and that this man fulfilled what the angel spoke to me. I am not ready to call him a blasphemer or to kill him. We should at least allow him to work with us and we can see if Allah will use him to speak any more words for us. If he is not from Allah, then it will be revealed to us in time. If the devil is in him, then this man will prove to be an imposter. But we should at least allow him to prove himself."

With those last words, a shot rang out from the crowd, striking Sharif on the neck. He fell to the ground, dying instantly. The only professors not to run back into the tent were Christian Sage and Cliff Cooper. They stood over the body of Sharif. A still small voice in Christian's ear told him to bend down, place his hands over Sharif's wound, and pray for him. Dr. Sage complied, and the Islamic crowd watched him silently. Christian prayed out loud, "Lord Jesus, I thank you for dying on the cross for my sins—not only my sins, but the sins of the entire world. Please forgive the man who shot Sharif. I am asking you a great favor: if it is your will, please heal your servant Sharif and be glorified. Let your precious gift of Jesus Christ be known to all standing here so that many would be saved this very day. I pray this in your holy name—the name that is above every name, and at which every knee shall one day bow—Jesus Christ, Amen."

The Muslim crowd again heard Dr. Sage's prayer in Arabic, unbeknownst to him. Immediately after the closing of the prayer, Sharif's wound was closed up by the flesh of his neck in sight of all who could see. Two seconds later, Sharif opened his eyes, and all who could see gasped loudly. A few seconds later, he sat up. Eventually, he stood up and looked at the amazed crowd. The crowd began to cheer now. The man who had shot Sharif was lying face down on the ground, begging Allah not to strike him dead. Sharif walked over to him and said, "The great God and Savior, Jesus, forgives you. Stand up and praise him with me."

The assassin looked up at Sharif's kind face, grabbed a hold of his hand, and stood up. They embraced one another and kissed each other on the cheek and cried. Soon after, the entire crowd looked toward Christian and fell prostrate to him. Dr. Sage nervously said to them, "Please, please, stand up! I am a man just as you are. Worship the one true God—the Father of our Lord Jesus Christ. He alone should we bow to and worship."

Slowly, each man got up and dusted himself off. Christian told them, "We should do what your commander set out to do originally—let us see if we can gather any valuables from the debris of Noah's Ark." Everyone agreed. By this time, the other professors returned to the crowd, and everyone began walking toward the desecrated dig site to search for valuable debris. They moved as one unit, one family. Their conversations were pleasant, and even the inter-communication between the Turks and Americans were calm and friendly. A few of them had empty duffle bags in case anything could be found. The front of the formation suddenly stopped and drew their weapons, as they approached an opening in the pass. What they saw must have been alarming.

44

FLIGHT FROM TURKEY

Dr. Christian Sage was summoned to the front of the formation to allow him to analyze the situation and get his opinion on what should be done. As Christian peeked around the bend of the trail he saw in the distance a brigade size military operation taking place around a new chasm—a chasm evidently created by bombs and missiles and other means. Much of the ground was badly burned, and debris was everywhere. Hummers, jeeps, armored vehicles, and dirt bikes drove around the chasm to police the area and to gather any evidence from the scene. The U.S. military was definitely present, but several other countries—including Turkey—were also involved in this operation. Choppers and occasional fighter jets governed the skies. The Ark had been totally demolished and little evidence remained of its former formidable presence.

The Turks looked to Dr. Sage to see what he would say. Christian looked over to Sharif, who held his hands up and shrugged his shoulders as if to say, "Don't ask me." Christian told them in English, "Time to go back and break camp. We must return to our homes at once." Another one of the men translated to those who did not understand, and they all understood and began walking back to camp, disappointed.

After the camp was brought down and everyone had gathered their things, Sharif invited Dr. Sage to his home, and Christian accepted the invitation. The other professors decided to return to their hotel and get on the first plane back to the United States. Christian stayed with Sharif for another three weeks to help him start a Church of Christ's Disciples in Igdir, Turkey. After much fellowship and instruction, Pastor Sharif was more than ready to lead his new church, full of the power of the Holy Spirit, and love for his people. He counted the cost with the growing Islamic culture and policies in Turkey, and he was more than willing to endure the inevitable persecution that would come. He would count it all joy to suffer for his new Lord and Savior. A few of the other local, underground churches collaborated with Pastor Sharif for support and networking purposes. They would all build each other up for the proclamation of the gospel of Jesus Christ.

In the short time that Dr. Sage helped Pastor Sharif build his church, the membership grew from 45 people initially to almost 100 people in less than four weeks! The Spirit of God was moving mightily in Igdir, Turkey. Sharif's church was sad to see Dr. Sage leave them, but they knew that he must. Many of them escorted him to the airport to give one final goodbye. Christian told them that he would try to return and visit them, but they all knew that would be a difficult task, although they were all hopeful. Dr. Sage's flight home was peaceful and uneventful. It had seemed like an eternity since he experienced an uneventful day. Christian also had time to talk to his children while he helped Sharif found his church.

45

THE SAGE SAGA CONTINUES

The next evening Ben Torres and Alicia Sage ate their Chinese takeout on the hotel room table in front of the television. The news was on. The top news story was that Muslim Jihadists had not only destroyed the large wooden vessel in the Ararat Mountains, but they had attacked and killed several of the archaeologists and taken a few of them as hostages as well. No names of the deceased or the hostages were mentioned. Alicia tried hard to hold the tears back, hoping that her father was not one of the deceased. She had tried calling his cell phone on several occasions, but the voice mail always picks up before any rings. The news story also said that the U.S. Army was leading a United Nations peacekeeping team to surround the mountainous region and to try and rescue any hostages as well as apprehend and/or kill any terrorists.

Surprisingly, the second top news story was the media's reaction to Alicia's interview with Cheryl Brown! The interview in its entirety had originally released on YouTube and it quickly became the most visited release of that day. Soon after, bits and pieces of the interview was aired on virtually every news station in the nation—and in more depth on news talk shows and opinion shows. The news even showed the Sage house from an aerial view with news vans surrounding the block attempting to find the elusive Alicia Sage, to no avail. Ben and Alicia's eyes did not leave the TV screen for hours, with each successive news show analyzing more of Alicia's story—especially the part about giant native Peruvian occult tribes. News pundits were asking how the American government would or should investigate these claims, and what—if any—action should be taken. Moreover, Alicia's story was taken seriously at every turn. Not one news channel blew her story off as if it were sensational fantasy. Even more surprising, not one channel had yet to make the connection between Alicia and Alex Sage.

Over time, Alicia appeared on several television talk shows, radio talk shows, and interviewed by several newspapers and popular magazines. She became a media sensation and a worldwide celebrity. At the same time, she and Ben Torres began courting. Ben had attended church with Alicia several times before their courtship began and Ben had also given his life over to Jesus Christ. They served in youth ministry together at the Lakewood Free Methodist Church. Of course, with Alicia's celebrity, church attendance grew so rapidly that an additional tent-section was added while a larger building was under construction. Alicia had spoken to the congregation as a whole a few times about her experience and how her faith in God brought her through it, with her witnessing several miracles in the process.

With all of the royalties that Alicia had gained, she ended up buying a home in the hills of Lakewood, Oregon. Her home had a large, protective security gate that kept the paparazzi at a safe distance, which gave her the much needed privacy. She had kept in touch with her brother, Alex, as well. Gio had given Alex a cell phone that had not been tracked by the international law enforcement, who were still searching for the international terrorist. Additionally, she also was able to finally speak with her father in Turkey. He would be arriving back in Lakewood soon to prepare for the next semester at the university.

Alicia's popularity had grown so rapidly that she was offered her own TV talk show on KABC, where contemporary topics were discussed with special guests. The station even allowed Alicia to openly express her Christian faith as long as she did not speak antagonistically against other religions. Her show steadily ranked high in the ratings—always in the top three for shows at 2:00. As a result, many people who might not otherwise consider faith in Jesus Christ became open to it because of Alicia Sage, her story, and her show. Nationwide church attendance increased by 8%, after years of decline. Her courting relationship with Ben grew into an official engagement after her father Christian Sage had returned from Turkey. Ben was often out of town for weeks at a time due his work assignments, but this actually worked well with Alicia's tumultuous schedule. Ben had been renting a studio apartment in Lakewood during their courtship and remained unknown in the media. Of course, that would change somewhat once they were married.

Alex Sage continued his intense theological training under the tutelage of Father Giovanni. Once Alex became accustomed to the theological terminology, he learned and faired well in the world of biblical studies and theology. Once Alex became exceptionally proficient, Gio even went into town and invited several other interested youths into his home on a weekly basis for Bible study and lessons of the Christian faith. After several weeks, Alex began to lead those studies all by himself, with Gio only occasionally intervening when the conversations became too difficult to be resolved by Alex or the group. Of course, Alex kept his identity as an international terrorist to himself, using his middle name, Luther, as his last name. Alexander Luther also kept in touch with his sister and father. All three of them were completely at peace with each of their respective situations, and all of them understood that the finger of God was behind this grand, divine plan. It was a joy and a blessing for the Sage family.

Christian Sage and his Lakewood University colleagues returned to Oregon just in time to make out their syllabi for the upcoming Fall Semester for each of their classes. They each received a hero's welcome. Professor Cooper's shiny black box and Professor Mockens' ancient hammer and pliers were donated to the University's Department of Archaeology, of which Richard Mockens was a member. Dr. Sage decided not to donate his angelic hologram jar until he knew what it was. Dr. Goldberg and Dr. Norton came back empty-handed, but had their experiences to share. All of the men were interviewed for the school newspaper and web site. Dr. Jabari Saal was officially declared a missing person—his body was never found. In addition to the classes that Dr. Christian Sage, Professor Cliff Cooper, and Professor Richard Mockens were to teach, each of them began writing their respective books according to the ancient scrolls that each consumed: The Book of Adam, the Book of Shem, and the Book of Mahalalel respectively.

When he returned to his home, Christian Sage had to fight his way through a media circus of news vans and reporters just to get to his front door. Alicia had forewarned him of this phenomenon, but words could not describe the frenzy that had awaited the next person to be seen at that home. The previous few weeks only had the mailman, the gas man, and the Edison man visit the Sage household—so the stakeout of reporters were starving for information. Dr. Sage solemnly swore that he did not know where his daughter was staying, so he politely asked them to let him sleep off his jet lag. Luckily for him, the media was unaware that he had just returned from Mount Ararat. Christian was excited to begin his new book project, as well as teaching his upcoming classes. He had never been prouder of his son, Alex, and his daughter, Alicia for their experiences and their total commitments to the Lord Jesus Christ. They now each had their own distinct mission for God, and he felt that God was about to move in a powerful way in the upcoming months—a way that he hadn't moved in a long time. His prognosis was correct.

46

NOT FOR SAAL

When all of the shooting began in the camp, Dr. Jabari Saal quickly took his rucksack and hurried back toward Noah's Ark. Whenever the Muslim insurgents were getting too close to him, Jabari hid himself off of the trail behind rocks, trees, or brush. Ever since he had consumed the additional scrolls he hadn't been feeling like himself. He swore that he heard whispering in his ears at times when he was alone. Flashes of images came and went before his eyes between blinks. Additionally, he had no desire to return to his privileged job back in Lakewood, Oregon. His desire to return to the ark went beyond an obsession or an addictive itch. Dr. Saal yearned to return to the ark like a lost child yearned to return to its mother.

Gun shots, shouting, and chaos rang through the air as Jabari marched toward the abandoned ark dig site. As he drew near the point of ascent to the actual digging spaces, he saw a bright flash above him. Before he had the chance to hear the explosion from the aerial assault from the U.S. military, his unconscious body flew several yards away from the ark and into a deep underground cave. His body landed at its bottom, which was about 60 feet below the surface. Jabari remained unconscious with a concussion, among other injuries, for three days. The reconnaissance mission by the

United Nations and the United States peacekeeping forces came and went before Dr. Saal regained consciousness.

When Jabari woke up his head ached as it never had before. He was in a dark place that looked like an abandoned well to him. The sunlight from the ground level vaguely illuminated the underground cave. Jabari knew that he could not survive for much longer in this cave. His head ached, his body was scraped up and severely bruised, and his throat was tormented from dehydration. Fortunately for Jabari, the cave had several rocks that stuck out from the rest to enable him to climb out of the dark place. As much as Jabari's body ached, he began his ascent to the surface. The cave was steep at the bottom, but leveled out as it got closer to the surface, where which the entrance to the cave was at the bottom of a large rock formation.

While Dr. Saal was climbing out of his deep cave, many curious Turkish citizens had arrived at the decimated dig site to take pictures and talk about these events amongst themselves. A few of them had ventured over to the cave that Jabari had fallen into and was now getting closer to the surface. One young man, who was a son of a local Imam, heard scuffling noises coming from the cave. He called his father and his uncle over to the cave as he peered inside. The boy's father, whose name was Ali, called into the cave, "Is anyone there?" When his echoing voice reached Jabari, he responded, "Yes, I'm coming out to you soon. Be patient."

When Dr. Saal was near the surface, Ali reached his hand down to grab Jabari's and pulled him out into the sunlight. Jabari stood up and began to dust himself off when he noticed that the clothes that he was wearing were not the clothes that he had on when he was blown into the cave three days earlier. He was now wearing an all white robe. Even more mysterious was the fact that his robe did not have one speck of dirt on it—the robe was brilliantly white without smudge or defect. The bystanders were equally amazed at this. Jabari also noticed that he had a full beard now, which was interesting because he was completely clean shaven the morning that he and his colleagues stepped out of their hotel in Igdir. Dr. Saal nor any of the bystanders could make any sense of this. Everyone was looking at Jabari waiting for him to say something, so he spoke: "Allah has spared me from death and given me new life." Everyone cheered.

Ali approached Jabari privately, putting his hand on his shoulder and whispered into his ear, "Are you the Twelfth Imam?" Before Jabari himself could answer, he felt an electric shock race up through his throat which spoke through him, saying loudly, "I am he." When he said this, all of the people who had gathered around Jabari immediately fell to the ground. When they got back to their feet, they saw Jabari Saal standing with his face to the sky, in which it appeared that his face was a glowing orange color. The sky thundered despite the fact that there were only a few white clouds scattered about. When Jabari's eyes met those of his onlookers, they too were a glowing orange color.

Dr. Jabari Saal went on to Igdir and then later defected to Tehran, Iran to start a new cult of followers called the Chosen of the 12th. He began to preach a radical view of Islam and called for war against the United States, Israel, and Western Civilization in general. He called for the restoration of a united Islamic republic in the Middle Eastern nations and to infiltrate and convert those of the infidel nations. He spoke with great authority and performed healings on occasion. The Muslims who peacefully disagreed with Jabari's ideas began to either disappear or become very ill until they ceased in their criticism of Imam Jabari Saal. In addition, Jabari began teaching about how to contact the angelic hosts of Allah and even the jihn by communicating through the stars and other sacred objects. He also began to teach about how these practices were originally a part of true Islam, which began with the descendants of Cain before the great flood, and then carried on by Noah, Ham, Canaan, Nimrod, and eventually Abraham and his firstborn son Ishmael. Jabari taught that Isaac and his Israelite descendants distorted the truth about Allah and Islam and brought forth a lesser, watered-down form of Islam that became more apostate as time went on.

His teachings were believed wholeheartedly and followed fervently by his disciples, who were absolutely convinced that Imam Jabari Saal would be the next world leader who would re-establish Islam as the only true religion. The powerful signs and wonders that he performed were definitely supernatural and undeniable by any who witnessed them.

47

POLITICS AS UNUSUAL

Solomon Greenfeld just finished dressing in his hotel room when he placed his magician's Lamen breastplate over his white, silk shirt which was concealed by his black tuxedo jacket. In about twenty minutes his limousine would arrive to take him to the lodge meeting in Istanbul, Turkey. Solomon got down into the lotus position and began to ohm as he meditated. Incense burned intensely from his censer. His tarot cards were placed before him. His favorite three—The Hermit, The Fool, and The Devil—were placed in triangular fashion above the rest. He began to summon his spirit guide:

> I invoke thee, O Shammael, Prince of Rome. Thy presence—for thou art everywhere, O lord Shammael! I confess humbly before thee my neglect and scorn of thee. How shall I humble myself enough before thee? Thou art a mighty hidden light in our universe. I am but a spark of thine unutterable radiance. But thou hast graciously designed to call me unto thee, to this exorcism of art, that I may be thy servant, thine adept, O bright one, O Sun of glory! Thou hast called me—should I not then hasten to thy presence? With unwashen hands therefore I come unto thee, and I lament my wandering from thee—but thou knowest! I bow my

neck before thee; and as once thy sword was upon it, so am I in thy hands. My trust is in thee. This ritual of art; this invocation, this sacrifice of blood—is unto thee. Behold, I stand in thy midst, O flaming star! Enlighten me so that I may lead the nations in this Age of Horus, this dispensation of Aquarius. Let all be subject unto thee. Amen.

Solomon then opened his eyes and all of the electricity in the room ceased to function, making the place dark. He got up from the floor and went into the bathroom and retrieved a turtledove out of a cage and a bronze laver. He returned to the floor and knelt before his tarot cards. He took out a knife from his breast pocket and decapitated the turtledove over the laver. He placed his hands in the bloody laver to cover his palms in blood, and then raised his palms to the ceiling. Just then, a dim light appeared before Solomon and he responded by placing his forehead on the floor with his bloody hands remaining before the light. Solomon felt the sting of electricity on his palms, followed by a faint voice saying, "Arise." He complied and stood before the light. His hands were now clean. Solomon then opened his mouth wide and the light forced itself inside of his open mouth, causing Solomon to shake violently and his eyes to roll back into his head. After fifteen seconds of convulsing, Solomon fell backward onto the bed where he remained for another two minutes, levitating six inches above the bed sheets.

When Solomon Greenfeld got out of bed, he felt energized, focused, and regenerated. The electricity was back on, as if nothing happened. He cleaned up the bloody laver, the pigeon, and carefully placed his tarot cards back into their folder. As soon as he finished cleaning up, there was a knock at the door. "Limo's here, sir," a voice said.

"Be right out," Solomon replied.

The United States Secret Service was in formation and waiting for President Solomon Greenfeld, when he stepped outside of his hotel room. His Rolex watch glistened and nicely complemented his tuxedo, along with his Masonic sash that decorated his abdomen and covered his Lamen breastplate. He walked toward the elevator within the Secret Service formation. The night was quiet and still. The President was *officially* in Turkey to visit the destroyed archaeological site of where the U.S. led peacekeeping forces destroyed Noah's Ark. There was also a special United Nations meeting that would take place on the following day, but he was now headed to a secret meeting with nine other high ranking Freemasons that were the heads of nine other nations that included: Russia, Saudi Arabia, Egypt, Great Britain, France, India, China, Venezuela, and Germany (these are in accordance with their respective ranks). This meeting at the Masonic Lodge in Istanbul was to discuss some of the current events.

President Greenfeld's limousine was the middle vehicle in a seven-car caravan on the way to the lodge. It was almost midnight, so there was little traffic on the road. Solomon began to day-dream about his being elected to president the previous year. He was the first ever Independent to be elected. The static and gridlock between Democrats and Republicans had become so frustrating to the American people, a clever negotiator and spokesperson such as Solomon Greenfeld was the obvious choice. He took the path of a populist who implemented pragmatic policies from each party that tickled the ears of the people, but yet spoke with the sincerity that no other politician had ever been able to do. He was a former psychologist who became a U.S. Ambassador to Egypt due to his understanding of culture and his ability to bring forth agreement between people and parties who did not seem to agree on anything. He negotiated a cease-fire between Israel, Palestine, and the neighboring nations without decreasing Israel's political borders. Concerning America, he was able to bring compromise on every hot-button issue that seemed to satisfy even the most extreme ideologues.

Solomon Greenfeld was also the first Jewish person to be elected President in the United States—well, he was half-Jewish anyway. His mother was a Cuban refugee who was officially Roman Catholic, although she practiced Santeria. She was also a musician and a Yoga instructor. His Jewish father was born in Egypt and practiced and taught Kabbalah, aside from being a medical doctor. He was also a prominent Freemason. So Solomon was raised in a mystical household that was filled with spirituality, herbal remedies, angelic intermediaries, and music. He had always been a keen communicator and was able to persuade and manipulate almost anybody to any opinion or position about anything—even if Solomon himself did not hold to such ideas. Solomon accredited this gift to his personal spirit-guide, Shammael, whom he encountered at a séance when he was fifteen. Shammael had told him that he was chosen to be a great world leader that would restore the ancient mystical rites and mysteries of the Egyptians and Sumerians. This would bring peace and safety to a violent world that was desperately in need of it. Additionally, when he was baptized into the Roman Catholic Church, his father prayed to the Supreme Architect of the Universe that he would be the next World-Teacher who would come and bring enlightenment and peace to the nations. Now as the President of the United States, he had the opportunity to fulfill that prophecy.

The other nine heads of state were already seated and mingling when Solomon arrived at the Lodge. Some of them even believed already that President Greenfeld was indeed the coming World-Teacher, often spoken of among the Masonic elites. Other World-Teachers had come—Thoth in Egypt, Zoroaster in Persia, Orpheus in Greece, Gautama the Lord Buddha in India, and the Lord Christ in Palestine. Since the Christ 2,000 years earlier there had been a void of any World-Teachers. This was partly because of the dominion of the Holy Roman Christian Empire that the Masons accredited with distorting the teachings of Christ and crushing the true forms of spirituality that the authorities of Rome deemed to be in conflict of their religion. The true world-religion had been suppressed for well over 1,800 years now. Since the Age of Horus in the 1960s, however, a revival of that ancient, true world-religion had taken place and its full world-wide acceptance was dawning and was ripe for harvest.

President Solomon Greenfeld stepped into the Lodge with his Secret Service agents remaining outside, securing the perimeter. The other nine members arose to their feet as he entered the round table in the meeting room. When he sat, the other sat as well. He looked to the others and said, "Brother Aleister of Great Britain—why don't you lead us in prayer tonight." They all bowed their heads as Prime Minister Aleister Clinton proceeded in prayer:

> *Dear Supreme Architect, Great Sovereign Lord of Love and Wise Prince and Master of the Universe, we beseech thy wisdom in our meeting tonight. Please guide us in our thoughts and speech. Send your angelic hosts to comfort and enlighten us. Reveal thy hidden light unto our souls, and your secret wisdom unto our minds. Restore what has been forgotten and lead us as we lead the nations of thy world. Let what has been destined be, and let your Order be restored and reign over all humanity—on earth as it is in the Grand Lodge above. O blazing Star, enlighten our brotherhood. In the name of the Mighty King. Amen.*

Solomon Greenfeld began the proceedings by banging his gavel on the table. He began, "Brothers, we are gathered this evening to discuss a few of the recent events that have taken place and a few of the events that will soon take place. First, the destruction of the Ark of Noah: does anyone here object to the decision to destroy the ark?"

Brother Rashari of Egypt answered, "Why was it necessary to destroy the vessel? Great profits could have been gained and an international interest in spirituality regain through this discovery. Is not that something we would all like here?"

Brother Xing Cheng of China answered, "Profits can be gained from anything. And regaining spirituality—yes, but not of biblical proportions."

A few of the others laughed. Brother Solomon replied, "It is not that some of the stories of the Bible can be verified that concerns us—many of them can already be verified, but most people are too busy to investigate or research the data. Archaeological discoveries do not produce sufficient faith to bother our agenda, and that is not why it was destroyed. Rather, it was the perfect opportunity to rekindle the animosity between the Islamic community in the Middle East and the rationalist Westerners that was the prime reason for the decision. Ever since the Israeli-Palestinian Peace-Pact, the friction between those two demographics have died down, which has lessened the influence of public and foreign policy-makers. The time of peace is merely temporary to pacify the fears of the populace. Once they are used to this peace and then war breaks out again, they will be begging for a mediator to bring back the former order of peace. The time of the Seventh Ray of Light is quickly approaching as the Sixth dwindles down. We must prepare for the transition."

Brother Jacques of France interjected, "But the coming World-Teacher has not yet been revealed. He must first come before the Seventh Ray begins."

Solomon answered, "Oh, he is in the world already and he will soon emerge."

"Who is it?" asked Brother Salih of Saudi Arabia.

"It must remain hidden until the appropriate time," replied Solomon. "Next on the agenda is what to do with the emergence of the Sage siblings—both in Italy and in the United States."

Brother Alfonso of Venezuela chimed in, "Yes! They must be arrested immediately. They are revealing too many of the ancient mysteries to the public—the people might actually believe what they are saying and doubt our leadership and agenda."

Solomon answered, "You are correct, Brother Alfonso, that they are revealing way too much and they must be silenced. I must admit, no one saw any of this coming. It must be that Prince of Deception, that bigoted god Yahweh who is behind this. There are a couple of problems with detaining these individuals, and yes, we have tried to do so already. One, the girl is becoming way too popular right now to destroy. We must be patient and let her popularity die down or try to set her up for a moral failure like so many of those other Christian leaders fall for. Two, we do not know the exact location of the boy, other than he might be somewhere in Italy right now. Has anyone here been able to divinize any information regarding him?"

They all shook their heads, 'no'. Brother Stanlislav of Russia then asked, "What if the girl's popularity does *not* decrease? And what if the boy is *not* found? What if those two become more powerful and popular? Can two young people thwart our plans all by themselves?"

Brother Vincent of Germany added, "Right, Brother Stanlislav. We all know what happened to our brother Jorge in Peru—his whole compound was blown up by *your* CIA agents, Brother Solomon!"

Solomon raised his hands to press down the air upon the table to motion them to silence. He then said, "Jorge Espinoza was becoming too arrogant and power-hungry. That is why he met his demise. Furthermore, I did not order his assassination. The CIA acted independently of my counsel. I was busy dealing with the freak hurricane on the East Coast and my Secretary of State okay'd that mission. I was trying to delay the girl's rescue until she was dead, but Jorge was trying to blackmail the U.S. for favors to be named later."

Brother Aleister boldly interrupted, "You mean you cannot even control your own cabinet?"

"Please, Brother Aleister," responded Solomon. "I can assure you that our plans will not be thwarted by those two juveniles. The girl will have her fifteen minutes of fame and the boy is an international terrorist fugitive. Neither of them will be of any lasting influence. Besides, most rationalists will regain their skepticism once the hoopla and sensationalism dies down. It will be another Area 51 conspiracy theory that will occasionally appear on the History Channel or National Geographic. Besides, the things that are about to take place between the nations and on a world-wide basis will overwhelm the majority of people and make them forget all about giant tribes, magical tunnels, and secret rituals of human sacrifice. The things that will soon take place will redirect and capture the hearts and minds of all people everywhere. Trust me."

The ten Masonic brothers spoke about these matters for another half-hour, and then adjourned their meeting. The night was very dark, and a new dawn was on the horizon.

48

THE WAR FOR SOULS
AND INFLUENCE

In the dimension of the spiritual realm, Satan was holding his own meeting with his chief princes in a region that corresponded and paralleled with Washington D.C. Satan and his demons were hovering over a river in the spiritual realm that corresponded with the Potomac River, as he addressed them, "Good to have you all here, my fellow hosts. The time is near when our full power shall be unleashed upon the earth as it was during the days of Methuselah, Lamech, and Noah."

A demon named Belial, replied, "How can this be, Master, since we can only go through those doors if we are summoned by humans?"

Another demon named Dubbiel, who was a Prince of Persia, answered, "Belial, those doors will soon be opened. There is a new powerful enchanter who has risen up in the ancient land of the Hittites who goes by the name of Jabari-Saal. He has consumed the scrolls of Cain, and of Ham, and of Summoning the Stars. His people believe that he is the 12th Imam prophesied by the early Muslims. He will learn how to open those doors so that we may fully engage the humans as we did in ancient times!"

Satan also added, "Yes Dubbiel, you speak well of it. There is also the American President who is possessed by our brother Shammael, the Prince of Rome. He will work together with Jabari-Saal to bring these things to pass."

Avatarael asked, "Will all of the people embrace our presence?"

Satan answered, "Of course they will. We have learned from our earlier failures before the great flood, at the Tower of Babel, and with the early human civilizations of the world. Now the human population is at an all-time high. Their technology and medical sorcery is at an unprecedented level, based on the collaboration and sharing of information resources. The invention of the internet has enabled our ideas and our presence at a rate unrivaled in human history. The humans are closer to becoming god-like than ever before. The only problem is that they are individual centered and not community centered."

Mohammael then said, "How can we remedy that, Master?"

Satan replied, "Well, it will not be easy. I mean, it is beneficial in some ways that the humans are involved with self-worship—doing their own thing and glorifying themselves. This is much preferred to worshiping Yahweh and his Son. But we must cause the citizens of the world to unite for a common cause. We have gotten them addicted to personal comfort, leisure, and pleasure—at least to the advanced nations. The downside is that they have not genuinely considered spirituality and its powers. They are into the physical pleasures and have neglected our domain. I mean their damnation is surely secured, but we must get them to call upon us so that they may gain a common power to fight against those who would dare to tell them that this power is immoral. That will be no easy task."

Indu interrupted, "You are correct, Master, but it can be done. I mean look at all of the progress that we have made as far as influencing human thought."

Satan answered, "True indeed, Indu. Yours and Avatarael's invention of the Hindu religion was almost totally forsaken. But you brought forth a revival in the human 1960's with the Sexual Revolution, and the Hippie Movement. Your inspiration of Rock n' Roll music and the sorcery of drugs is a big part of the so-called Age of Horus and the Dawn of Aquarius—our era to shine! And you, brother Butah—your raising up of that Gautama fellow—confounding his young mind with the suffering of the world, causing him to conjure up that Buddhist philosophy in which each individual can become spiritually enlightened as a means to escaping suffering. That idea was brilliant! It caught on in the West as an idea of self-empowerment and creating a self-religion. It takes an entire human lifespan for someone to realize that Sadartha Gautama was a pawn in my kingdom—and by then, their souls are mine! Zenshinto, your ideas for religion are equally noteworthy in the Eastern world.

"Brothers Ahuramahz and Dubbiel—I commend you for inspiring Zoroaster and that religion that dominated Persia for so long. The people were worshiping you as the good god and actually referring to Yahweh as the evil god—I loved every moment of it! Then, my brothers Hallah and Mohammael—your creation of Islam might be the greatest of all religious ingenuity. Hallah—I never thought that you would actually have sent Mohammael posing as the messenger Gabriel to that poor Mohammad character! You sure deceived him, ha! Talk about converting people by intimidation, force, and coercion—I must admit that I was skeptical that your methods would have worked—but look at your influence on the world today: your religion has more devout followers than any other. I mean there are many who profess to follow the Son of Yahweh, but in the West much of their professed faith is shallow and insincere. Good work, comrades!

"And Moroni—I always knew of your sense of humor, but did you actually believe that the Joseph Smith fellow and his disciple Brigham Young would have that much success?"

"No, I did not," answered Moroni. "It was supposed to be a big joke—a juvenile prank. I was bored and had nothing else to do. I appeared to that charlatan diviner Joseph Smith and told him that all of the churches were wrong and totally invented a new Jesus to follow after. I knew that those human-monkeys were naive, but I never thought that they would actually follow such doctrines: that you and Jesus were spirit brothers and that dark-skinned people were cursed because they sided with you in the war in heaven, and light-skinned people were on Jesus' side, ha! And that the Holy Spirit actually had sex with the virgin Mary and conceived the human Jesus. Or better yet, that humans could actually become gods and have their own universe—imagine that! Or that a woman's main role in this life is to bear children so that pre-existent spirit-beings can have bodies. And my personal favorite—that people lived on the earth's moon and dressed like Quakers! People actually believed Joseph Smith when he wrote that. Brigham Young even wrote that people lived on the earth's sun too—people believed that absurd lie too! And even after all of the false prophecies that Joseph Smith uttered—the people still follow his doctrines! The so-called Reformed Egyptian language translated into King James English—hilarious! The people gobbled it right up!"

Jinhael interrupted, "Yes, Moroni, you are quite the comedian! Master Lucifer was much more subtle with his religious inventions, though, and quite the genius. He merely manipulated the doctrines of the Godhead—mixing the truth with deception about who Jesus is. He began the Arian heresy that taught that Jesus was a created being and that Yahweh created everything *through* the Son..."

Satan interjected, "Well, I actually *do* believe that, somewhat—I just cannot prove it. But I do take pride in influencing people to doubt the justice of Yahweh and that he is all-loving. I have taught the people to deny the reality of the fires of the afterlife for those who reject the atoning death of Jesus on the cross. I myself doubted this, but we have all witnessed the perpetual torment of those who refuse to accept how Yahweh has decided to try and save them. And what a miserable failure he is! How can a loving god send people to hell? I mean, more humans today end up there than with him—how can there be righteousness with that method of so-called salvation? I just tell the people what they want to hear—that god is love and that all humans are his children. A loving god would of course bring all of his children to heaven with them—except for a few exceptions: the Hitlers and Stalins of the world. But the rest of humanity is basically good—that's what they want to hear. So I just create a different Jesus that is not judgmental, but only loving and accepting of all people—just the way that they already are!"

Anael added, "Yes, Master. And you also influence them to deny *your* existence—as well as ours!"

"Good point!" exclaimed Maijan. "If the humans doubt our existence, then they cannot possibly fight against what they do not believe exists—nor even seek Yahweh's provisional protection against us."

"Yes," agreed Mastema. "Only believing what they can sense is pragmatic, which is especially effective when their own inventions cause their lives to be so busy to even think of any possible spiritual realm. Denial leads to doubt, which leads to perpetual rebellion against Yahweh, which leads to damnation. Even if they do not directly follow us and worship us, we deny their access to Yahweh's kingdom!"

Satan then said, "Yes, causing the humans to rebel and create their own truth is beneficial to our agenda. But we must begin to gain their worship and following. That is what we are meeting here for at this moment. The doors will soon be opened and we will unite with the humans in common rebellion against Yahweh and his angelic hosts. It will be the Battle of Spiritual Hosts. With the humans on our side, our numbers will be almost equivalent to Yahweh's hosts. We must also free our brothers who are still locked up in the abyss of the earth and the dungeons of the cosmos. We must actively engage Yahweh's hosts to free our brothers. The time will soon be upon us. I myself will enter a human body—something I rarely do—and I will appoint one of you to possess another human of my choosing. At that moment we will engage in warfare, destroy the image of Elohim within humanity, and thus win the wager that Yahweh has placed with us—and the cosmos will be ours and Yahweh will be *my* personal slave!"

The other demons laughed and the sky thundered. Just then, an army of the spiritual hosts of Yahweh descended upon the demonic meeting, led by Michael the Archangel. Michael's sword was drawn along with the other hosts, but they did not strike at Satan and his demons. Michael only spoke to Satan, saying, "Lucifer, Yahweh has heard of your plan and he rebukes you. Nevertheless, he has granted you permission to attempt to carry out your plan, according to your ancient agreement. This will be your last attempted coup of the Kingdom of Heaven before it descends upon the earth with the return of the King Jesus Christ. After you fail this time, you yourself will be chained up for 1,000 human years in the abyss of the earth. Then you will be released one final time to again attempt to deceive the nations. After that, you will be cast into the Lake of Fire that was especially created for you and your demons, and you will be tormented day and night. Yahweh has been gracious to you and has granted you this many attempts to overthrow him, but you have not learned, you have not repented, but your heart has been hardened so that Yahweh and his Christ may be glorified. Hear the word of Yahweh."

Satan rebuffed, "Ha! Michael, you are a weak puppet of Yahweh—narrow minded simpleton! You just believe whatever he says without questioning any of it! I spit in your face and defy you and him! We will defeat you in what I will call, 'The War of Souls', and your race, along with Yahweh himself, will serve me and my army of Enlightened Hosts!"

Michael shook his head and replied, "We will see you then, in the Battle of Pneumatika! Until then, may you be accursed and Yahweh glorified!" With that final saying, Michael and the hosts of Yahweh the Most

High returned to the throne of God, with the Lord Jesus Christ physically sitting at the right hand of Yahweh. The Godhead had already foreseen all of this—along with every other contingent possibility. God also had a redemptive plan—not only to defeat the Satanic Majesties, but to save humanity and to redeem the image of God and restore humans to their initial condition of goodness in a new paradise. There will be a new heaven and a new earth at that time. Until then, God would work all things for good for those who love him and are called according to his purpose. The plan of God would soon cause a massive revival to counter the great deception that would soon take place. All who believe would be saved. All who reject the gospel of Jesus Christ are already condemned and susceptible to the great deception. God is not willing that any should perish, though, but that all should come to repentance and obtain the knowledge of truth, which is in Christ Jesus. God will raise up his own human prophets in those final days and perform mighty acts through them. His heavenly hosts would also be working fervently behind the scenes against the forces of darkness. All of these things must first take place before the end, when Jesus Christ returns to the earth. But before then, we must engage in The Battle of Pneumatika.

We hope you enjoyed reading *The Battle of Pneumatika*
by Brian Newberry.
For further reading including novels and non-fiction titles by
this author and others, please go to our online catalog at
http://www.signalmanpublishing.com